THE COMPLETE CASES
OF THE JONES BROTHERS

THE COMPLETE CASES OF THE JONES BROTHERS™

MAXWELL HAWKINS

ILLUSTRATIONS BY

JOHN FLEMING GOULD
JOHN NEWTON HOWITT

POPULAR PUBLICATIONS • 2021

TABLE OF CONTENTS

ALIAS THE CORPSE

THEY WERE MEEK AND MILD
LOOKING LITTLE MEN, THOSE
BROTHERS JONES. THE LAST TWO
IN THE WORLD YOU'D EXPECT TO
FIND MIXED UP WITH MURDER.
BUT TRACKING DOWN KILLERS
WAS THEIR SPECIALTY—AND A
SIMPLE JOB LIKE DOUBLING FOR
A CORPSE ON A COFFIN-RIDE WAS
JUST ANOTHER NIGHT'S WORK
FOR EITHER OF THEM.

CHAPTER ONE
JONES—JUST JONES

ONE NIGHT in Chicago, a lovely girl, clothed only in her night gown, crawled out the window of her room on the seventeenth floor and started along a narrow ledge. A few seconds later, she crashed into the courtyard below.

There was an account of it in the papers the next day. They called it suicide.

A few days after that, a sugar planter in Cuba found a letter minus its envelope on his warehouse floor. It smelled faintly of an exotic perfume and hinted at a murder to be committed in Chicago. It mentioned no names—merely the letter "S."

A New York paper carried a five-line cable dispatch about it.

Only one man in the world would have tied those two events together. He was Leander Jones, senior member of Jones and Jones. And because Leander Jones specialized in knotting slender threads together into the solution of a crime, where no crime was apparent, an Argentine gigolo went to the electric chair for the murder of that girl in Chicago, whose name was Stella.

AND THAT explains why Leander Jones listened so attentively to the young and attractive woman who was sitting on the opposite side of his desk.

She paused a moment in her recital. Leander removed his mild blue eyes from her face and let his glance drop to the oblong of green paper in his hand.

"Fifty thousand dollars," he murmured. "A check for fifty thousand dollars."

"It came in the mail yesterday," the young woman said.

"And this, Mrs. Minton, is the money on your late husband's insurance policy?"

Marvella Minton nodded. "I had no idea he carried all that insurance. We lived very modestly. But then, of course, Gerald was close-mouthed about his affairs. He never took me into his confidence at all," she added with something like a sigh.

"Had you been married long?" Leander asked absently, his eyes still intent upon the check.

"Only three months."

He looked up at that. He noted her large brown eyes, set wide apart and filled with a wistful trusting expression. Her plain black dress was becoming but inexpensive, he saw.

"A woman," Leander told himself, "of little worldly experience. Gullible even. My, my! An attractive widow— and fifty thousand dollars. The devil's own combination for trouble!"

Mrs. Minton seemed eager to confide in someone and Leander's kindly, almost benign, appearance was an invitation for her to speak freely. "You see, Mr. Jones," she continued. "I'm an orphan. And—" she hesitated. "Well, I met Gerald through a matrimonial agency. They called it The Lonely Hearts Bureau."

"Hey!" he shouted. "You can't do that!"

She looked to see if he were smiling, but Leander nodded grave encouragement for her to go on.

"I grew up in an orphanage, where I received a good education," she explained. "But afterwards I went to live with some people on a farm in Ohio. I was really only a hired girl—and lonesome.

"I saw the advertisement in a paper and wrote an answer just for a lark. But Gerald sent me a reply and we began to correspond. Finally, he sent me the money to go to Clarinda. And—well, we were married."

"Hmn!" Leander murmured. "Quite romantic. What was the cause of your husband's death?" he asked.

"Doctor Barnabas—he was our doctor—said it was heart trouble. Gerald complained of feeling ill, so I called in the doctor. An hour later, he came to me and broke the news that Gerald was dead."

Leander put his fingertips together and said nothing for a moment. Finally he asked in a kindly tone: "Just exactly why did you come to Jones and Jones? What is it that you are afraid of?"

She made a little gesture of hopelessness. "I can't say definitely," she replied in a low tone. "But I have a feeling that something terrible is going to happen. Has happened, perhaps. Don't laugh at me, please," she added, her voice an appeal for sympathetic understanding.

Leander's face was serious. "I am not going to laugh, Mrs. Minton. A woman's intuition frequently has been of great importance in my work. But there must have been something—" He looked at her reassuringly.

MRS. MINTON nodded. After a moment's fumbling in her handbag, she produced a worn newspaper clipping. It was an account of the capture of the Argentine gigolo for the murder of the girl in Chicago named Stella. It set forth in glowing terms the part Jones and Jones had played in unraveling that seemingly insoluble crime.

Leander glanced at it with a grimace and handed it back. "Ah, yes," he murmured. "It was unfortunate that this leaked out. As a rule, we manage to keep out of the public prints."

"It was wonderful!" she replied earnestly. "I cut the piece out and saved it. That's why I came to you, when—" She hesitated and bit her lip, then plunged on breathlessly.

"Last night, for some reason I had difficulty falling asleep. I lay in bed for a long time thinking over all that had happened to me in the last few months. My marriage—my husband's death.

"I must have dozed off at last. But, suddenly, I found myself sitting upright in bed. I was trembling all over, although I had no idea of the reason. Some impulse caused me to go to the window and look out.

"And in the moonlight on the lawn I saw—my husband!"

She paused, wide-eyed. Leander looked at her sharply.

"Are you certain?"

"Yes," she replied firmly. "I recognized the brown coat Gerald always wore so much—and the soft gray hat. He went swiftly toward the hedge and just before he reached it, he turned and looked back toward the house—toward my window. Then he was gone. I saw his face in that fleeting second—" She buried her eyes in her hands for a moment. "It was ghastly—white—just as it was when he lay in his coffin," she concluded softly.

She looked at him half sadly. "You may think that I was dreaming," she said. "But I know that I wasn't. It was all too vivid—too real. And so I came to you."

He rose from his chair and began to pace back and forth the length of his office with his hands behind his back, his head bowed in thought. She watched him anxiously, hopefully. At last, he stopped before her and held out the check.

"Here is your check," he said. "You can return home with the assurance that we are working in your behalf. But do not mention your visit here to anyone. Do you live alone?" he added suddenly.

She nodded in the affirmative, then quickly corrected herself. "At the moment, my husband's brother, Clarence Minton, is staying at the house. He's been there since the funeral, but he's leaving in a day or two."

"He knows about this insurance?"

"Yes."

Leander frowned. "Know you've got the money?"

"No. I didn't tell anyone it had been paid."

"Don't!" he said briefly. Again he held out the check. She pushed it away from her, as if afraid to touch it.

"Please," she said softly, "keep it here. And whatever the cost for your helping me, I'll be only too glad to—"

He interrupted her with a fatherly pat on the arm. "We'll keep the check in our office safe, if you wish. But as for the cost—there is no fee attached to the services of Jones and Jones."

She looked surprised. "But I want to pay," she protested.

"There is no fee, Mrs. Minton," Leander repeated with quiet dignity.

THERE WAS nothing about Leander Jones to attract more than a passing glance. His appearance was nondescript, his manner self-effacing. Only a certain nervous quickness of movement and a disarming twinkle in his pale blue eyes distinguished him from thousands of other middle-aged citizens.

As he climbed down the steps of the day coach on the two o'clock train, which had brought him to the little city of Clarinda, he was carrying a scuffed black grip. His bald head beneath his brown hat was faintly moist. His gray suit was wrinkled from several hours sitting on the cushions of the train.

Leander Jones, indeed, looked as if he might be a none too successful traveling man. And as the elder partner of Jones and Jones, that was more or less the impression he wished to create.

The decrepit taxicab which met all trains conveyed him to the Clarinda House. Having obtained a room, he refreshed himself with a cold bath and clean linen. Then he pulled a small red memorandum book from his pocket and turned the pages slowly. At last, he found what he was looking for and held his finger on the place while he read a name and address several times to fix it in his mind.

Ten minutes later, Leander arrived in front of a white frame house which was set back some distance from the street. On one side of the door was a small brass plate, and as he turned in through the gate in the picket fence and drew nearer, he saw that it bore the name of Doctor Barnabas.

His ring brought an almost immediate response. The door was opened by a maid, young and buxom, with red hair and close-set eyes.

"Doctor Barnabas—is he in?" Leander inquired.

She nodded and stepped aside to let him enter. "First door on your left," she said. "I'll tell Doctor Barnabas you're here."

"Thank you."

Leander had a feeling that she had given him a thorough, though veiled, appraisal.

He walked into the room she had indicated. It was obviously the waiting room for the doctor's patients. An ugly golden-oak table in the center contained a number of magazines and newspapers. A couple of red-plush chairs and a horsehair sofa with sagging springs completed the furniture. Several colored prints and a large photograph in a black frame adorned the walls.

Leander's attention was caught momentarily by the photograph. It was a picture of a tall man in full evening dress. Across the bosom of his shirt a ribbon had been drawn diagonally, and he was standing in a dramatic pose with one hand extended in front of him and his eyes staring straight ahead. Before he dropped into one of the red-plush chairs, Leander noticed that the photograph bore the inscription written in ink: "Barnabas the Great."

"You wish to see me?"

Leander turned at the words, which were uttered in a deep resonant voice. He found himself looking at a considerably older version of the tall man in the photograph.

LEANDER ROSE to his feet and made a quick jerky bow. "You are Doctor Barnabas?"

"Yes."

"My name is Jones, Doctor." Then he repeated with an apologetic smile: "Just Jones."

Doctor Barnabas' dark eyes, crowned by straight bushy brows which were sprinkled with gray, studied the small figure standing so meekly before him. Then he rubbed his hands together with professional unction.

"I'm glad to meet you, Mr. Jones," he said. "What can I do for you?"

Leander hesitated. "It's—it's about Mr. Gerald Minton," he finally murmured. "The late Mr. Gerald Minton."

"Mr. Gerald Minton?" Doctor Barnabas' grizzled eyebrows arched upward. "What about him?"

"You attended him in his last illness, I believe."

"Yes."

"If you don't mind, Doctor, I would like to have you tell me the circumstances attending Mr. Minton's death," Leander said.

Doctor Barnabas frowned and cleared his throat "My dear Mr. Jones," he said ponderously, "I should be very glad to. But first, perhaps, you will explain who you are—and the reason for your request."

"I beg your pardon, Doctor," Leander replied, apparently overcome with confusion. "I should have mentioned it. I'm employed by the Wide World Life Insurance Company. Mr. Minton carried a large policy with our company. Quite large, indeed. So we're merely verifying the circumstances of his passing. Merely routine, I assure you, but customary with us," he added.

The doctor's manner warmed up immediately. "Sit down, Mr. Jones," he urged. "I'm only too glad to give you the information you wish. I'm sure Mrs. Minton, the widow, is in need of whatever insurance her late husband may have carried."

Leander sat down again on the red-plush chair.

"The cause of Mr. Minton's death," Doctor Barnabas continued, "was a heart attack. That's how I described it on the death certificate. That was a general diagnosis. Specifically, he died from an embolism, which passed through his circulatory system and stopped his heart action." He paused and looked at Leander, who nodded in understanding.

"Ah, yes. An embolism—a blood clot. And what, in your opinion, caused this blood clot to form?" Leander asked.

"It resulted from a severe bruise on Mr. Minton's leg," Doctor Barnabas said after a second's thought. "He fell from a step-ladder."

Leander turned this information over in his mind, then rose to his feet. "Thank you very much, Doctor," he murmured. "That was exactly what I wished to know. Obviously, Mr. Minton's death was due to unfortunate, but perfectly natural, causes.

Doctor Barnabas made a pompous gesture. "Beyond question, Mr. Jones!"

At the door Leander shook hands with the doctor. "Thanks, Doctor. I'm sorry I had to trouble you," he apologized.

AS A result of consulting again his little red memorandum book, Leander's next stop was on a side street just around the corner from the hotel where he was registered.

He stood for a few seconds before a one-story brick building. The wide plate-glass window, behind which he could see two drooping potted palms, bore in black lettering—"B. Gerkin—Undertaker." Leander's pale eyes twinkled as he opened the door and stepped inside.

At his entrance, a young man with a yellowish complexion and a thin line of a mustache looked up from a desk.

"Are you Mr. Gerkin?" Leander asked.

The young man rose slowly from his seat. "No, I'm Mr. Viles, Mr. Gerkin's assistant. What can I do for you?"

"Well," Leander suggested, "you might tell me where I can find Mr. Gerkin."

Viles darted a quick suspicious glance at him, but Leander's face was bland and smiling. "I'll get Mr. Gerkin," Viles muttered and moved down a short hallway at the rear. He opened a door at the end of it, and Leander caught the unpleasantly suggestive odor of embalming fluid before the catch clicked shut.

Presently the door popped open and a short stout man wearing a Prince Albert coat with shiny elbows came bobbing down the hallway toward Leander. His mouth was drawn down sadly at the corners in a fixed expression of sympathy. He cocked his head on one side, looked at Leander and said: "I'm Mr. Gerkin. I'm certain that at a time like this, you'll find my services most satisfactory, Mr.—ah—" He broke off with a little cough.

"Jones. Just Jones," Leander murmured.

"Ah, yes, Jones," Gerkin intoned. "Where is the deceased, Mr. Jones?"

Leander's pale eyes blinked rapidly. "I—I'm afraid you've mistaken the purpose of my visit."

"Oh—it's not to arrange a funeral?" Mr. Gerkin looked disappointed.

"I wanted to ask you about a funeral you conducted recently. Mr. Gerald Minton."

"Ah, yes! Mr. Minton," Gerkin said, his eyes resting thoughtfully on Leander. "A most impressive funeral. A lovely corpse. Everyone remarked how lifelike it looked, if you'll excuse my professional pride. But a touch of rouge always—"

Leander interrupted Mr. Gerkin's flow of words. "Maybe I'd better explain," he said. "I'm verifying the details of Mr. Minton's demise for the Wide World Life Insurance Company. He was one of our policy holders."

"Life insurance. Ah, yes," Mr. Gerkin nodded. His tone was that of a man whose business gives him a profound respect for life insurance. "What do you want to know?"

"Where is Mr. Minton buried?"

For a moment, Mr. Gerkin hesitated. But finally, he said: "Well, I can't say he's exactly buried."

"What?"

Mr. Gerkin hurriedly explained. "I mean to say that Mr. Minton isn't underground yet. There's some question in the widow's mind where to have him interred."

"Then you are keeping the body here?" Leander asked.

"Oh, no!" Mr. Gerkin exclaimed with a shake of his head. "The casket containing the remains is in the receiving vault at the Poplar Hills Cemetery."

Leander was silent for a little while. He looked almost dreamily up at the ceiling, then down at the floor, as if debating with himself whether to ask the next question.

At last, he smiled blandly at the plump undertaker and said: "Mr. Gerkin, did you notice anything unusual about Mr. Minton's death?"

Mr. Gerkin looked at Leander sharply and then bristled. " 'Unusual?' I'm afraid you'll have to explain."

"I mean, have you any reason to suspect that his death might not have been due to natural causes?"

"My dear sir!" The undertaker's tone was horrified. "If you are insinuating that Mr. Minton was—er—done away with, let me assure you that you're barking up the wrong tree. Why, Mr.—Mr.—"

"Jones. Just Jones."

"Mr. Jones, his death was due to a heart attack. I could tell that from the appearance of the body."

Leander scraped his feet apologetically. "Please excuse me. Of course, you realize that I'm only doing my duty. I'm glad to hear that Mr. Minton's death was natural. I am, indeed." He seized Mr. Gerkin's pudgy hand and shook it vigorously. "Thank you for reassuring me," he said gratefully.

Taking his leave of the plump undertaker, Leander returned hurriedly to the main street of Clarinda. He glanced up and down until he caught sight of the blue sign of a telegraph office.

A few minutes later the wires were carrying a brief message in the secret code of Jones and Jones. It was addressed to Mr. Horatio Jones, Flatiron Building, New York City.

> Need you here meet me at Clarinda House before midnight drive and bring big screwdriver—Leander.

CHAPTER TWO
WHEN GRAVEYARDS YAWN

THE CLOCK on the front of the First National Bank Building stood at eleven-thirty when the Ford coupé containing Mr. Horatio Jones, younger member of Jones and Jones, pulled up before the Clarinda House. Removing a scuffed black grip from the seat, Horatio climbed from the car. He was wearing a brown hat and a gray suit, which was badly wrinkled from his drive.

As he appeared before the desk, the night clerk looked up from the paper he was reading. He noticed the grip in Horatio's hand and rubbed his eyes.

"Not leaving us so soon, are you, Mr. Jones?" he asked.

Horatio smiled, a self-effacing and disarming smile. "Oh, no. Just arriving." There was a twinkle in his pale blue eyes. He removed his brown hat and rubbed a handkerchief gently over his bald head. Then he swung the register around and ran his eye up the list of guests till he came to Leander Jones, Room 404.

The clerk watched him in bewilderment. "Just—just arriving?" he stammered.

"Yes. That's right," Horatio nodded. "I want a room. On the fourth floor, if possible."

"Why—why—" The clerk hesitated. He looked at Horatio keenly and then sniffed, trying to decide whether he might not be drunk.

"I believe," Horatio said, "that you have mistaken me for my brother, Mr. Leander Jones. He arrived this afternoon and is, I observe, assigned to a room on the fourth floor."

The clerk broke out in a grin. "I—I beg your pardon," he said. "But you look exactly alike."

"So we've often been told," Horatio murmured.

Still grinning, the clerk pushed a key across the desk and tapped a handbell. From somewhere behind the elevator shaft, a sleepy-eyed colored boy appeared, picked up Horatio's grip and led the way to the elevator.

When he had dismissed the bell-hop with a tip, Horatio opened his grip and removed a large parcel wrapped in brown paper. He slipped quietly out of his room and made his way down the hall to the door of 404, where he gave a light tap. Without waiting for a response, he turned the knob and walked in.

Leander was sitting in a rocking chair with his shoeless feet propped up on the dresser. The room was blue with cigar smoke. He looked at Horatio and waved his hand, in which he held a glowing stogy.

"Hello, Horatio."

"Hello, Leander."

"I see you brought it," Leander said, pointing his stogy at the parcel in his brother's hand.

"The largest screwdriver I could find."

"Good. I didn't like to buy one here in Clarinda—for reasons."

"What do you want it for?"

"Nothing much," Leander replied dryly. "Just to screw the lid off a coffin."

WHEN THE night clerk of the Clarinda House had declared that Horatio and Leander Jones looked exactly alike, he was not exaggerating. They were as alike in appearance as the two proverbial peas. And having found in carrying on the work of Jones and Jones that it was often an advantage to be mistaken for each other, they were accustomed to emphasizing their similarity by wearing the same kind of clothes.

Leander, however, had entered the world ten minutes ahead of his identical twin brother, and that fact caused him to refer to himself as the senior partner of Jones and Jones.

Horatio made himself comfortable on the edge of the bed and regarded Leander thoughtfully. "Well," he said, "why do you want to screw the lid off a coffin?"

"A hunch—based on what I learned this afternoon," Leander replied coolly.

"And you intend to open it without a permit?"

"In about an hour."

Horatio puckered his nose. "Do we have to dig it up?"

Leander shook his head. "Fortunately, no. It's in the receiving vault of the local cemetery. Late this afternoon, I visited the place and made a wax impression of the lock. I finished making the key only a little while ago."

He pointed to the dresser on which his feet were resting. A large key, the square bit of which showed indications of having been recently filed, was lying on the dresser cloth.

"Well, what have you found out?" Horatio asked.

"I've talked with a number of residents of this pretty little city," Leander said. He told about his calls on Doctor Barnabas and Gerkin, the undertaker.

"I also spoke to several people who attended Minton's funeral. Also, I called on the editor of the local paper to find out what he knew about Minton."

Horatio fished out a black stogy, a duplicate of the one Leander was smoking, and lit it. "What about him?" he demanded.

"He'd lived here about four years. Was formerly in the show business. But apparently he didn't do anything after he arrived here in Clarinda. He wasn't young. Fifty-three the obituary account in the paper said. Guess he'd just retired," Leander said.

Horatio got up from his place on the edge of the bed. "Well, suppose we get this coffin open—and find nothing?"

Leander chuckled. He began to pull on his shoes, stamping his stocking feet firmly into them. "My dear brother, if we find nothing, we will certainly have to start finding a lot!"

He walked to his black grip which was resting on a low bench and began to fumble around in it. When his hand finally emerged, it was holding a stubby revolver. He slipped the weapon into one pocket of his gray coat. Next he produced a flashlight, which he tested and put in the other pocket.

"You'd better bring your gun along, too, Horatio," he said.

HORATIO AT the wheel, the Ford coupé slid from the curb, moved smoothly down the main street of Clarinda. As the red tail-light grew dimmer and dimmer, a figure slipped out of the shadows beside the hotel and disappeared around the corner. But neither Horatio nor Leander noticed it.

"Which way?" Horatio asked.

"Straight out this street," Leander replied. "It's about two miles from town. Poplar Hills Cemetery."

For a while, the only sound was the smooth purr of the engine, the occasional rattle as the coupé struck an irregularity in the pavement. Overhead the sky was starless, mantled with heavy clouds, although the lack of humidity in the air made rain seem unlikely. They passed beyond the last street light and hit the open country. It was rolling terrain; fields divided by patches of woods and underbrush.

Presently Leander touched Horatio on the arm. "Turn right at the next crossroad."

"That take us to the cemetery?"

"Passes about a quarter of a mile this side of the cemetery wall. But there's a foot path across the fields that will take us to the cemetery. I looked the ground over this afternoon."

They reached the turn and Horatio swung off the main highway. The side road climbed a gentle slope, dipped down into a heavily wooded ravine and then rose again to an even higher level. Leander pressed his face close to the coupé window.

"Stop here!" he exclaimed suddenly.

The coupé came to a halt. Leander opened the door and stepped down to the road. His flashlight made a white circle on the ground for a few minutes, then went out as he returned to the car.

"You can drive over to the side safely," he said. "Pull up behind that group of bushes ahead."

THE PATH across the fields toward the cemetery was fairly level and smooth. With Leander leading and flashing his electric torch from time to time, they had little trouble in following it, although the clouds shut off even the starlight and submerged the countryside in utter blackness. Instinctively, they spoke in subdued tones.

"Anybody apt to see us?" Horatio asked.

"No. The few houses anywhere near are on the other side. It's late, anyway," Leander reminded him.

"What time?"

"A bit after midnight."

"When graveyards yawn," Horatio murmured.

Leander's answer was dry. "It's all right for them to yawn, but not for us."

In silence then, they continued forward till Leander finally called a halt. Horatio moved up to his shoulder. Snapping the flash on for a few seconds, Leander swung its beam back and forth in front of them. It played upon a low stone wall, crumbling in spots and blotched in many places with tangled vines.

Beyond in irregular rows, the tombstones stood like white sentinels of death.

Horatio spoke, his voice low and tense, a little breathless. "Where's the receiving vault?" Somehow, this standing on the edge of a city of dead men at midnight, with the prospect of soon gazing upon the still face of one of them, seemed to have disturbed his usual calm.

"About a hundred yards in," Leander replied softly. "Come on!"

They climbed the wall and found themselves standing on yielding turf. Again the light, its ghostly beam setting up dancing shadows as it moved past the headstones and the trunks of the giant poplars that gave the burial ground its name.

Above, a dense canopy of leaves seemed to press down upon them. It made the air heavy, motionless. There was an oppressive odor of damp loam, mold, mingled with the sickening scent of wilted flowers left too long upon some new-made grave.

"This way," Leander whispered, and moved ahead again.

A moment later, they were treading upon cinders, which crunched beneath their feet in spite of all effort to move silently. Leander slowed down and touched Horatio on the arm.

"This path leads directly to the vault. I've found my landmark—that marble angel on the left."

His flashlight went out and they advanced more surely now. No sound broke the ghastly stillness except the crunch-crunch of their feet upon the cinders. They seemed to be the only moving things in the world. Beneath lay the dead, around them the air was stilled, and above even the birds in the trees were silent in sleep.

At last Leander halted again. The flashlight's rays cut through the blackness. In its column of white light, a squat stone building took shape. It looked like some hideous crouching animal with the two slits of windows for eyes and the black oblong of the door in the middle, a gaping toothless mouth.

"That's it," Leander whispered.

They approached closer, moved forward step by step until they were standing in front of the iron door. The light glided over it, revealing each bolt-head, the square window with the cross-bars, the massive knob and keyhole.

"The screwdriver?" Leander breathed.

"I've got it."

"Good. Take the light, Horatio."

The flashlight passed from hand to hand.

"Fix it on the keyhole," Leander said softly.

Horatio obeyed. There was a moment of intense quiet, while Leander felt in his pocket for the key he had made that evening. From the distance came the faint sound of an automobile, some midnight motorist scurrying for the shelter of home. But the very remoteness of the sound made the stillness of the graveyard even more acute, more ghastly and disturbing.

Then Leander's hand, grasping the key, appeared in the light beam. It threw a weird distorted shadow upon the door. A grating noise, the scrape of metal upon metal, as Leander fumbled to insert the key. A moment later, he succeeded. His hand turned slowly.

With a dull clank, the heavy bolt of the receiving vault slid clear.

CHAPTER THREE
TWICE DEAD

LEANDER WITHDREW the key from the vault door and replaced it in his pocket. He turned the knob, at the same time putting his shoulder against the heavy iron portal. Slowly, it swung inward, the rusty hinges giving forth a low creak of protest. A sudden breeze, chill and damp, swept out from the vault, fanned their faces and then dissolved into the graveyard air.

"The light, Horatio." Leander's voice was husky.

Horatio handed him the flashlight and he stepped into the pitch darkness before him. Horatio was close behind. For a moment, they stood just inside the door, while the flashlight swung around the interior of the dank stone vault.

On the walls to the right and left of the entrance were open niches, like shelves, each designed to hold a single coffin. They were empty, the slabs with which they could be sealed standing on end against them. But what gripped the attention of the two men, caused them to breathe faster, was the object on which Leander finally brought the light to rest.

It was a plain black coffin, placed on two low wooden horses, its silver handles and name-plate glittering in the light rays. In the very center of the vault, it stood, with the head toward the door.

Leander walked silently to it, bent over and read the inscription on the silver name-plate.

GERALD LEROY MINTON
Born May 7, 1880
Died June 19, 1933
"He strutted and fretted his brief hour
upon the stage and then was heard no more."

At once, Leander's manner became brisk, the uncanny spell of the surroundings conquered by the urgent need for quick action. "The screwdriver," he said. "Hold the light for me."

He began to twist the first of the dozen black-headed screws that held the coffin lid in place. Little by little it began to loosen. The job of removing the screws was not easy, and by the time he was halfway through, Leander's breathing was growing heavy. But he refused Horatio's offer to relieve him and stuck doggedly at it.

The last screw—Leander was working now with feverish haste. Drops of sweat fell from his face, splattered upon the coffin top. A few more turns and the dead man would lie exposed.

"Wait!"

Horatio's whispered warning was accompanied by utter darkness as he snapped off the flashlight. There in that awful blackness, they stood as motionless as the dead men around them. But their ears were straining, their eyes fixed on the open door of the ghostly place.

Leander reached out and found his brother's arm. With that to guide him, he placed his lips close to Horatio's ear.

"What is it?" he breathed.

"Crunching—on the cinders."

Leander's hand glided into his pocket and came out with his stubby revolver. Once more they waited in tense silence. A minute. Five. Finally, Leander whispered softly: "You must have been mistaken."

"Probably," Horatio agreed, but his voice lacked conviction.

Leander returned his pistol to his pocket. "Let's get this over with," he muttered. "The light!" He laid the screwdriver on the floor and twisted the last screw clear with his fingers. He put it carefully on the floor beside the others he had removed.

"Step back a little," he ordered softly.

"I'll open it up."

Bending over the coffin, he hooked his fingers beneath the lid and tugged. With but a slight scraping sound, the lid came loose. He placed it carefully down against the wooden horses. Then he straightened up. Horatio, returning to his side with the flashlight, raised it so that the beams revealed almost the full length of the coffin.

"My God!" Leander gasped out hoarsely, and repeated: "My God!"

Before them lay the body of a man, a man with gray hair and a close-cropped gray mustache. The eyes were closed, and about the corners of the purple lips was a trace of a smile. It was a calm face, like a that of a sleeper who is having pleasant dreams.

The dead man was dressed in evening clothes. But the white bosom of his stiff shirt was marred by a hideous dark brown smear—coagulated blood that had gushed from the left breast.

And rising from that spot, directly over the heart, was the short wooden handle of a knife.

FOR A long breathless moment, Leander and Horatio stared with horror-filled eyes at the ghastly thing. A corpse that had been stabbed in its coffin!

Finally, Leander took his handkerchief from his pocket and wrapped it about the hilt of the weapon. He was obligated to use both hands and exert all his strength before the blade came out.

"Give me your handkerchief, Horatio," he whispered.

He bound the knife, an ordinary kitchen knife with an eight-inch blade, carefully with the two handkerchiefs and placed it in his pocket.

"One thing's certain," he mused. "This man was alive when he was put in this coffin. Or at least, he had just been stabbed. See—the stain is on the gray lining, too."

"Good lord!" Horatio muttered. "It looks as if they'd held a funeral for a man who was alive."

Leander shrugged. "There was no dagger in Minton's heart when he was lying in his coffin at the funeral. I talked with several people who were there and viewed the body." Leander placed his finger just above the ugly brown smear and added significantly: "A dead man wouldn't bleed."

"Are you certain this is Minton?"

Before answering, Leander studied the face of the corpse long and closely. "Yes," he said, "I believe so. He looks like the picture in the paper, and fits the description I got, too."

"What'd we better do about it?"

"What can we do, Horatio?" Leander murmured. "We're not exactly within the law in this enterprise, so we've got to find our own answers without outside help. Do you know, there's something familiar about this fellow," he added suddenly.

"You mean—"

"I mean he resembles someone I've seen before," Leander said. "But I can't place him." He made a little gesture and said with sudden grimness: "Give me your pocket knife!"

Horatio produced a knife and handed it over. "You're going to look for a bruise?"

"Exactly. The bruise that caused the blood clot that brought about Minton's death. His *first* death," he added dryly. He began to slide the knife swiftly up the material of the trouser legs.

"Perhaps Minton's death was a case of catalepsy— suspended animation. I've heard of such cases," Horatio suggested.

"Perhaps," Leander murmured noncommittally.

He snapped the knife shut and handed it back to Horatio. "But if he was buried by mistake while in a state of catalepsy, why should we find him now with a dagger in his heart? Bring the light closer," he said.

Horatio lowered the flashlight nearer to the corpse.

Spreading the slit trousers back from the dead man's legs, Leander started to examine them carefully for signs of a bruise. Horatio watched him closely. Suddenly Leander looked up with a start, and immediately froze into rigidity. Horatio drew in his breath with a quick gasp.

From far off, yet clear on the still night air, came a woman's scream. Once—twice—three times, her shrill cry of terror quivered on their eardrums. It was followed by a shot. A second shot—then another scream that choked, and ended in a gibbering wail.

LEANDER SPRANG toward the door of the receiving vault. Before the final agonized sound had ceased, he was outside.

"Put out the light!" he whispered over his shoulder.

Horatio joined him. Guns in hand, they stood listening.

"It seemed to come from the left—from the road where we left the car," Horatio finally whispered.

As if to confirm his words, again that ghastly scream broke out. This time it was farther away. But as Horatio had said, it came from the direction of the road. And once more, it ended in a bloodchilling mournful wail.

Leander seized Horatio fiercely by the arm. "Wait here!" he whispered tensely. "Keep out of sight!"

"Right!"

Horatio glided around the corner of the vault and then halted, pressing himself close to the stone side. Leander disappeared into the darkness. He followed the cinder path, his feet guided by the crunching beneath them.

It was difficult to make haste without a light, and for a second he considered returning and getting the flash from Horatio. Then he realized that it would be wiser not to herald his movements, even if he couldn't make such good speed.

He scrambled over the low stone wall bordering the cemetery and headed out across the open field that lay between him and the road. Out from under the cemetery foliage, the darkness seemed less dense and against the far-off glow from the street lights of Clarinda, he could discern the trees and shrubbery that lined the road.

Without trying to locate the path, he started cutting over in a beeline. From time to time, he stubbed his feet against outcropping stones, and low bushes scraped his ankles, but he pressed on. His right hand gripped his revolver.

A hundred feet from the far side of the field, Leander stopped to listen. Everything was deathly still. He moved forward again, his eyes straining to pierce the gloom. A moment later, he was stooping to escape low-hanging branches; then he was on the edge of the road.

He waited, every sense alert, nerves taut. Presently from up the road came a dull thud. Someone closed the door of an automobile. Cautiously, he started toward the spot from which the sound had come. He had advanced only a few steps, when the twin headlights of a car cut through the night, and he found himself directly in their glare.

As he leaped for the shadows, the engine started up, gears clattered and the car lurched forward. It roared by the spot where he was hiding; a streak of orange flame stabbed toward him! But the shot was wild. And in that second, Leander caught a flash of the occupants of the machine. A man and a woman, both in the front seat. But he was unable to distinguish their faces.

He jumped into the middle of the road and his pistol came up. Four times he fired. But the car kept on, and in a few seconds the tail-light vanished over the crest of the hill. He could hear the exhaust growing fainter and fainter. And presently, he could hear it no more.

"Now what the devil?" he muttered. Then he suddenly snapped his fingers and burst out fiercely: "Damn! A ruse to get us away from the vault!"

He swung around quickly and plunged into the underbrush along the road. And as he panted back across the fields toward the graveyard, the clouds parted and a silver crescent of a moon shed its cold eery light over the ground.

SLOWLY AND cautiously, Leander approached the receiving vault. He avoided the cinder path, creeping, instead, over the turf of the burial plots, slipping ghostlike from headstone to headstone. Now and then he paused to listen. But only the faint pounding of his own heart fell upon his ears.

Finally, he reached a point from which, in the shelter of a huge granite marker, he could distinguish faintly the outline of the vault. A break in the foliage of the trees allowed the pale moonlight to seep through. It bathed the squat stone building in a weird unearthly glow.

He waited. But there was no sign of life about the vault; no sign of Horatio.

A sudden feeling of disaster assailed him. He began to circle the vault, keeping well back in the deep shadows. Before taking a step, he made sure of his footing, guarded against making the slightest noise. At last, he stopped, crouching behind the trunk of a huge poplar. He was in front of the vault.

He leaned forward, eyes intent upon its grisly facade. With a tightening in his throat, he saw that the massive iron door had been swung shut. And he remembered distinctly that he and Horatio had left it open when they came out.

With his lips set grimly, he moved across the open space to the vault door. In one hand he held his gun; with the other he turned the heavy knob. He pushed and the door moved in a few inches. Another push and it swung wide. His finger caressed the trigger as he stepped into the black interior and slid to one side of the door, where he waited.

But there was no sound, nothing to indicate that anyone was concealed in that macabre gloom.

He regretted that he didn't have the flashlight. After a moment's fumbling in his pocket, he found a paper folder of matches. Putting his revolver away, he struck one of them. It flickered and almost went out, but by cupping his hands about the feeble flame he nursed it into brilliance.

Then, lifting the match high, he peered about the vault. A low cry of amazement and alarm burst from his lips.

"Gone—gone!"

The match spluttered out. He took a short step forward, and struck another. In its gruesome light, which filled the place with wavering shadows, he verified his previous discovery. The two wooden horses were still in the middle of the vault, but there was no sign of the black coffin which had held the corpse of Gerald Minton. The lid, too, was gone.

And then on the floor of the tomb just beneath the coffin niches, he saw something that sent his pulse leaping, made his throat muscles constrict. A dark figure sprawled face downward. He moved toward it quickly, too quickly, for the suddenness of his movement extinguished the match.

But he was beside the figure and he dropped to his knees before lighting another. In those few seconds, Leander passed through a torment of fear and horror. Then he had a light. He reached out and rolled the figure over.

It was the corpse of Minton. As Leander gazed at it with mingled relief and revulsion, the dead face seemed to smile up at him mockingly.

CHAPTER FOUR
MURDER

THE FIRM of Jones and Jones, consisting of the twin brothers Leander and Horatio, was unique—the only one of its kind in the world.

It could hardly be called a detective agency, strictly speaking, yet much of the business they carried on was of that nature. They were, to be exact, specialists in criminology. The distinguishing feature of their work was that they undertook to discover crimes which probably would never have come to light had it not been for their shrewd and persistent probing.

And once having unearthed a crime, they took it upon themselves to bring the guilty parties to justice.

In the course of twenty years experience, they had reached an amazing efficiency, had won an almost legendary reputation among those whose business had to do with crime. Their leads were many and varied. An innocent-appearing item in a newspaper, a suspicion transmitted to them by an acquaintance, a bit of overheard conversation—any one of a number of things—might serve to start them on a hunt that sometimes came to nothing, but more often revealed a startling crime.

Having inherited a more than adequate fortune, they weren't interested in profit. They regarded their work as their contribution to the public welfare. And so they accepted no fees except such voluntary offerings as grateful clients, who could afford it, might hand over to them. These, they promptly turned over to one of a number of pet charities.

Because the two brothers had always been so close together in their work, their play, and even their thoughts, it was with a heavy heart that Leander drove Horatio's coupé back toward Clarinda from the Poplar Hills Cemetery.

A careful search of the receiving vault and surrounding area had produced no hint of what had befallen Horatio. Or what had become of the silver-handled coffin which had held the stabbed body of Gerald Minton. Both had vanished completely while Leander was being led on a wild goose chase by the screams and pistol shots.

For half an hour, Leander had hunted for a possible clue to the drama—tragedy—that had been played in his absence. It had been fruitless. The only thing of possible significance was that whoever had removed the coffin and lid also had taken the screwdriver and long black-headed screws he had so laboriously removed only a short time before.

Instinctive caution prompted Leander not to drive the car up in front of the hotel. Instead, he left it at an open-air parking space a block from the main street, where a half dozen other machines were scattered about. He noted from a sign that it was Fred Stacey's Open Air Garage.

He looked at his watch. Almost three o'clock. The business district of Clarinda was completely deserted as he walked to the hotel. He crossed the lobby without disturbing the clerk, dozing in a chair behind the desk. And rather than let the colored elevator operator know the time of his return, he climbed the three flights of stairs to his room.

When he had shut and bolted the door, he selected one of the thin black stogies to which the brothers Jones were addicted, and dropped wearily into a chair. His pale blue eyes had taken on a deeper hue; his rather high forehead was drawn down in a series of furrows; his lips were pressed in a tight thoughtful line.

Leander dropped the self-effacing and embarrassed manner both he and Horatio affected in public. Now he was himself—a grimly determined man whose small wiry figure was in such perfect physical trim it gave the lie to his forty-two years of age. A man with a shrewd analytical mind and the tenacity and courage of a terrier.

Leander began to turn the situation over in his mind.

His main concern was the fate of Horatio. It was possible, he knew, that even at this moment Horatio was trailing the ghouls who had stolen the coffin. Possible but not probable, he decided with a slow shake of his head.

ON PREVIOUS occasions when Horatio had seen fit to leave an agreed meeting place, he had always left some message, some clue as to what had happened to him. There had been nothing like that at the cemetery.

He was in a tough spot, Leander admitted to himself. He couldn't go to the authorities because that would call for an explanation of what he and Horatio were doing at Poplar Hills Cemetery in the dead of night. Besides, it wasn't the practice of Jones and Jones to call on the police except for routine arrests.

But why, he asked himself again and again, had the mysterious invaders stolen the coffin and left behind the corpse? He could have understood in a way the theft of the body and coffin—or body alone. But why leave behind the cadaver with the gaping hole in its heart, a smear of blood that pointed to a murder while the victim was supposedly lying ready for interment anyway?

Leander squinted. Could it be, he wondered, that there was something hidden in the coffin. Something that was of such great value that it was a temptation to take a reckless chance to get the coffin out of the vault.

He concluded that the grave robbers had probably watched Horatio and himself enter the vault, had figured that they, too, were after whatever the coffin concealed. And so the strategy of screams and shots to draw them away while the coffin was being removed.

What was in Minton's casket? Money, jewels, important or incriminating documents? Leander's mind ran the gamut of possibilities. But in the end, he found himself more puzzled than ever as to the motive for the theft, and growing more and more alarmed over what had happened to Horatio.

It was after nine o'clock when Leander left his room and descended to the lobby. He had taken a cold shower, and except for a slight puffiness under the eyes, showed no marks of the harrowing night he had been through. Nor was there any outward evidence of the deep anxiety that stirred within him.

In the hotel dining room, he ordered a breakfast of orange juice, dry toast and coffee. But when it came, he found he had little appetite for it.

"Isn't it terrible, sir?" the waitress, who was hovering near, suddenly said in an awed voice.

Leander looked up in surprise, then smiled faintly. "No, I assure you, the food is quite all right," he murmured. "It's just that I'm not hungry."

"Oh, I don't mean the breakfast," she said solemnly.

"I beg your pardon," Leander muttered. "I seem to have misunderstood you."

"Maybe you haven't heard?" she continued.

A resigned expression appeared in Leander's blue eyes. "Heard? Heard what?"

The waitress moved closer to him and lowered her voice in the manner of one who is imparting bad news. "About poor Mr. Gerkin!"

Leander set down his coffee cup with a slow and deliberate movement. He wiped his lips with one corner of his napkin. Then he asked: "Gerkin? Mr. Gerkin?"

"Yes, sir," she nodded. "Mr. Gerkin the undertaker, whose parlors are just around the corner from here."

"What about Mr. Gerkin?" Leander asked with an air of casual curiosity.

"He's been murdered!"

"Murdered! My word!" Leander to all appearance was politely horrified. Actually, this unexpected bit of news had set his thoughts buzzing like an industrious beehive.

The waitress, having found what she believed to be an appreciative ear, grew more voluble. "It's getting so a person ain't safe anywheres nowadays. That's what I told Joe. To think of poor Mr. Gerkin! Such a nice man. He always ate here Tuesdays with the Rotary, and lots of other times. He was a bachelor and ate out mostly."

"My, my!" Leander clucked softly. "And how did you hear about this terrible crime?" he asked.

"From Joe Cluskey, my—my boy friend. He's a cop—a policeman," she explained. "He always eats breakfast here. He left just before you came in."

"When did this happen?"

"Joe says some time this morning early. Mr. Gerkin had been dead only a few hours when they found him. His skull was mashed in. Just like an eggshell, Joe said."

"Dear me!" Leander murmured, shaking his head. "Where did they find the body?"

"In a Ford car—a coupé with a New York license."

LEANDER RAISED his glass of orange juice and drained it in a gulp. "Oh! A Ford car—a coupé with a New York license," he repeated.

She nodded. "It was in Stacey's parking lot. Fred Stacey noticed it when he opened up this morning. It'd been left there during the night when no one was working. Fred looked in and saw poor Mr. Gerkin with his head mashed. So he called the police."

"Did they find out who owns the car?" Leander asked slowly.

"They don't know yet. But Joe says they're checking up on the license number. And when they find the owner, Joe says, they'll pinch him like that. I hope they do," she added indignantly.

Leander pushed back from the table. He placed a coin beside his plate and picked up the check. The waitress transferred the tip from the table to the pocket of her apron.

"Thank you very much, sir," she said.

Leander gave her an odd little smile. "Not at all. Thank you!"

As Leander, avoiding the appearance of haste yet moving rapidly, walked out through the revolving door of the hotel, he told himself that this was a pretty kettle of fish. He had no doubt that the Ford coupé in which Gerkin's body had been found was Horatio's. The car in which he, Leander, had driven back from the Poplar Hills Cemetery and left at Stacey's Open Air Garage.

He crossed the street and turned a corner, anxious to get off the main street of Clarinda as fast as possible. Thanks to the talkative waitress, he was forewarned. But it wouldn't be long before the local police learned the ownership of the coupé, and that would be followed quickly by the discovery that the brothers Jones were registered at the Clarinda House.

A worried look lurked in his pale eyes as he made his way along a shaded avenue deep into the residence section of the town. He couldn't afford to be picked up, held perhaps for hours while they were investigating the crime or he was establishing his identity and innocence.

He was satisfied that Gerkin's murder and the theft of the coffin were tied together some way. But try as he would, he couldn't figure out the exact connection or even a likely theory. Why had the coffin been stolen, anyway? Why had the corpse been left behind? Why had Gerkin been killed? And last, and most important, where was Horatio? Alive or dead?

Of one thing, Leander was certain. He's have to keep out of sight, since there were eight or ten persons to whom he'd talked on the previous day, who could identify him. And at the same time, it was up to him to work faster than he'd ever worked in his life.

It was a tough assignment, he admitted to himself. Keeping out of sight, and yet tracking down his foes. And with virtually no clues to go on.

He continued along the shaded avenue for a considerable distance. A small self-effacing figure in a wrinkled gray suit and a brown hat. To the few passersby, he appeared merely an inconspicuous and rather absent-minded man.

But Leander was far from absent-minded at the moment; he was well aware of everything going on around him; he made certain that those whom he passed didn't know him.

Gradually the houses became farther and farther apart. He was nearing the outskirts of Clarinda. At a street intersection, he paused, drew forth his little red memorandum book and consulted it. Then he looked at the street signs and nodded slowly. He was almost there.

Five minutes later, he turned in from the sidewalk of the street through an opening in a hedge. The shrubbery was unkempt and overgrown, and surrounded a large and weed-filled lawn. Set well back and approached by a winding gravel path was a large, weather-stained house. This drab structure was surmounted by two cupolas at the forecorners; the front and smaller side porches were ornamented with scrollwork and turned wooden posts, popular fifty years ago.

Leander twisted the flat bronze key of a mechanical doorbell and heard it ring just inside. He didn't have long to wait. The door was opened a crack and a face appeared, a face of ghastly pallor with a close-cropped gray mustache and crowned by a disordered thatch of gray hair.

"I wish to see Mrs. Minton," Leander announced.

CHAPTER FIVE
JAIL FOR JONES

FOR A few seconds, the man inside made no reply. His burning, deep-set eyes, in vivid contrast to his pasty complexion, surveyed Leander from head to foot.

Leander didn't believe he had ever seen the fellow before, yet a puzzling sense of resemblance disturbed him.

"Mrs. Minton isn't home." The words were uttered gruffly, slowly.

"Not home? How unfortunate. I'm very anxious to see her. It's important—to her," he murmured.

"She won't be home for a long time. She's gone away," the man in the doorway said.

His thin lips twitched into a faintly mocking smile as he spoke. And in a flash, Leander realized why this man seemed familiar to him. His thin face, close-cropped gray mustache and that peculiar taunting smile bore a striking similarity to the dead man he had gazed down upon the night before.

This, then, was Clarence Minton—the brother of whom Mrs. Minton had spoken.

"Maybe you can tell me where I can reach her," Leander suggested. He was still smiling that retiring apologetic smile of his. But there was a new note in his voice, a sharp authoritative note. It caused the man with the ghastly white face to look at him narrowly, suspiciously.

"Who are you?" The question came abruptly, almost shot out from the blue lips.

"I'm from the insurance company. The Wide World Life Insurance Company."

"Oh!"

There was a moment of tense silence. Gradually the feverish light in the deep-set eyes seemed to fade, and in its place came an ingratiating, conciliatory expression.

"Why didn't you say so at first. Come in!" The voice was still gruff, but not unfriendly.

The door opened wide and Leander, inwardly alert, entered the house. The hallway in which he found himself was close and stuffy; it was in semi-darkness, the only light filtering in through squares of colored glass which formed a transom above the door. Coming from the glare of outdoors, he was at first unable to see the figure of the man who had admitted him, although the pale face was visible.

"We'll go into the parlor."

Leander followed him through a set of double doors, only one of which was opened, into a big room with a high ceiling. It was shielded from outside observation by old-fashioned wooden blinds, tightly closed, which covered all the windows. Only enough sunshine penetrated to fill the place with a bilious yellowish glow.

Now Leander saw that the man he had decided was Clarence Minton was of medium height, his shoulders slightly stooped. As he walked across the parlor, he moved with a distinct limp.

"Have a seat," he said, pointing to a wicker chair.

Leander sat down. An air of embarrassment masked his face, but his sharp eyes were taking in every detail of the white-faced man. Minton remained standing, supporting himself with one hand on the marble top of an ancient walnut table with bulging legs.

"Mrs. Minton isn't here, as I told you," he said slowly. "But I am her brother-in-law. Clarence Minton."

"Ah, yes," Leander nodded. "I'm pleased to meet you."

Clarence Minton studied Leander for a moment, cleared his throat and then continued: "Marvella—that is, Mrs. Minton—has been in a very nervous condition ever since my brother's death. I've been urging her to take a trip, go away for a rest. A change of scenery, I believed, would benefit her health. Make her forget her great loss."

He stopped and, lifting his hand from the marble-topped table, stroked his chin thoughtfully. Then he went on speaking.

"She finally accepted my advice and left last evening in her car. She planned to be away ten days at least."

"A very sensible idea," Leander murmured.

MINTON NODDED. His face was inscrutable, that faintly mocking smile playing about his lips. "However," he said, "I'm looking after my brother's affairs. That's why I've remained here since the funeral. And in going over his papers, I discovered that he was carrying a large amount of insurance with your company."

"Fifty thousand dollars," Leander replied with a touch of awe.

"Fifty thousand dollars," Minton repeated, his tongue seeming to caress each word. He leaned forward a little, cocking his head on one side as if to focus his eyes better on Leander. "I regret to say, Mr.— Mr.—"

"Jones. Just Jones," Leander supplied.

"Mr. Jones, I'm sorry to say that's all the estate my poor dead brother left. So, naturally we're anxious to have it paid as soon as possible. When will that be done?" he added abruptly.

Leander coughed impressively and appeared to be considering the question. His thoughts turned back to his meeting with Mrs. Minton in the office of Jones and Jones. She had told the truth. Apparently, no one in Clarinda except herself knew that her fifty-thousand-dollar check had been received.

"You must remember that there was a deep bond of affection between my brother and myself," Minton said earnestly. "And that is why I am so determined to look after his widow, whom he loved dearly. She is my only living relative now. And I hers."

"About the payment," Leander said. "Our company takes pride in its prompt handling of all business. This matter will be attended to as soon as Mrs. Minton signs a couple of papers. That's why I'm here," he explained. "To get her signature."

A strange look flitted over Minton's face as he drummed nervously on the marble top of the table. "I don't understand. The policy was in good standing, wasn't it? All premiums paid?"

"Oh, yes."

"You received proof of death?"

"Certainly."

"Then what are these papers?"

"A couple of affidavits. Customary in the case of large policies, although really just formalities," Leander lied blandly. "But the beneficiary must sign them."

He smiled apologetically at Minton, but he was watching the other's reaction shrewdly. He was making a play to insure the safety of Mrs. Minton for a while, anyway, he believed. Whether she was still unharmed would be revealed by Minton's answer.

Clarence Minton stood leaning against the table in deep thought for a long time. His brows were lowered till they all but hid his burning eyes. At last he shrugged with an air of resignation and said: "I'll try to get in touch with Marvella—Mrs. Minton. By long-distance telephone. She mentioned some friends where she might stop for a brief visit today." He smiled, but this time the effect was more crafty than mocking.

Leander rose from his chair. "Splendid," he murmured. "You can find me at the Clarinda House."

They started toward the door to the hallway. When they reached it, Minton bowed courteously and moved aside to let his visitor pass through first. Leander had no sooner set foot in the dim and stuffy hall than he heard a low, maniacal chortle behind him. At the same instant, something round and hard was jabbed into his back between his shoulder blades.

"Put up your hands! And stand still!" Minton snarled in his ear.

EXCEPT FOR a faint flicker of his eyelids, Leander displayed no emotion at this sudden turn of events. He raised his hands high. Minton, keeping his gun against Leander's back, rapidly went through his pockets.

"Insurance company—hell!" he sneered. "Carrying a gun!"

He transferred Leander's pistol to his own pocket.

"As soon as you got to talking about that insurance policy, I had you spotted," Minton said. "But I thought I'd let you play your string out. See what your game was."

"Spotted?" Leander asked mildly.

"Don't play dumb! You know what I mean. What's your racket? You ain't a cop—they wouldn't put a sappy little guy like you on the cops," Minton said.

"Oh, no, I'm not a cop. I'm in the insurance business," Leander murmured.

"You're a liar!"

"No—no!" Leander insisted. "I came here to speed up the payment of the fifty thousand dollars to Mrs. Minton."

Minton laughed savagely and dug the muzzle of his gun hard against Leander's spine. He stuck his head forward so that when he spoke his hot breath was on the back of Leander's neck.

"Listen, you sap! Mrs. Minton got that check for the dough day before yesterday. She thought I didn't know." Again he uttered a low vicious laugh. "Now you're going to get what's coming to you. Move along!"

Propelled forward by the gun in his back, Leander was forced to walk down the hall. With Minton giving orders, he climbed a flight of stairs. Down another hall and they entered a bedroom. Like the parlor below, its windows were covered with old-fashioned wooden blinds, tightly closed.

Minton removed several neckties from a rack beside the dresser. A few minutes later, he had bound Leander hand and foot, gagged him and stretched him out on the bed. Before going out of the room, Minton paused in the doorway.

"Now, wise guy, you can start getting ready for trouble. I'll show you what happens to people who don't stay on their own side of the street!"

The door slammed shut behind him.

Leander strained at his bonds. It took only a minute for him to decide that he stood no chance of slipping out of them. Whatever this man with the half-mad eyes planned to do to him, he would find his victim still on the bed when he returned.

Things were breaking badly—very badly, for Jones and Jones, Leander decided with a sinking sensation in the pit of his stomach. Horatio mysteriously missing, perhaps dead! He, Leander, a prisoner in this lonely house at the mercy of a man whose mind was clouded.

And yet, even in his despair, Leander had one satisfaction. He knew now why both Gerald and Clarence Minton had looked vaguely familiar. He had identified Clarence Minton—and the identification did nothing to help his peace of mind.

How long he had been lying there, when he finally heard footsteps on the uncarpeted boards of the upper hallway, Leander wasn't sure. Perhaps ten minutes. Perhaps twenty. He recognized the uneven tread of the lame Minton. But someone was with him.

Muffled voices drifted in from the hall and immediately afterward the door was opened. The neckties were removed from Leander's wrists and ankles, the gag was unfastened, and he was jerked roughly from the bed to his feet. He found himself facing Minton and a burly six-foot policeman.

"Take him to the station, officer," Minton said. "He's a crook. Came here just as I told you, and tried to pass himself off as from the insurance company."

Leander, concealing his surprise behind a meek smile, stared at Clarence Minton. The fellow's pasty face appeared whiter than ever, his deep eyes were bright and about his mouth that mocking smile clung once more. But his voice was steady, marked by the sort of indignation a righteous householder would display upon having caught a burglar red-handed.

"Come on!" the policeman said, thumbing toward the door. "You and me're going down to the lock-up."

A swift picture of the Ford coupé and Gerkin's body lying in it went through Leander's mind. The police station was one place he didn't care much about going to right now.

"Perhaps I can explain, officer," he murmured.

"You can explain to the chief," the policeman growled. He took Leander by the arm. "Don't try to make a break."

Leander gave a resigned shrug. "Oh, no, I won't try that," he said. "I seem to have made one break already." He looked steadily at Minton. "I'll see you again soon, Mr. Minton," he said.

Minton gave him a sharp glance. "Only when I come down to sign a complaint against you," he snapped back.

CHIEF OF POLICE Delos Atwell, head of the Clarinda forces of law and order, was sitting in his office following with a frowning stare the meanderings of a blue-bottle fly on the grimy ceiling. But Chief Atwell was not really thinking much about the erratic movements of the fly. His thoughts were on quite different matters.

It had been a day unique in Clarinda police history for two atrocious occurrences. In the first place, one of the city's leading citizens—Mr. B. Gerkin—had been discovered brutally murdered in an automobile in a public parking lot. The fact that an arrest had been made in this connection, mitigated only in a slight degree the enormity of the murder.

In the second place, Atwell had received a startling piece of information from the sexton of Poplar Hills Cemetery.

Some time during the night, the receiving vault at the cemetery had been entered. Not only had the coffin been stolen from a recently deceased and highly respected citizen, but the cadaver of that citizen which had been lying therein, had been dumped out on the floor and left behind. And in the dead man's heart was a deep wound, evidently the result of a knife thrust.

The chief of police had just returned from the scene of this atrocity. His visit had served no other purpose than to confirm the facts as the sexton had phoned them. There were no clues. He could figure out no possible motive.

With one hand, Atwell brushed back a damp lock of hair; with the other he mopped a handkerchief over his florid and perspiring face. His coat hung upon a hook on the wall, and he was reclining in his chair in his shirt sleeves, a state of dress which displayed his brilliant green galluses.

A sudden knock upon his office door caused him to turn slightly. "Come in!" he commanded with a touch of annoyance.

The door swung open and a hulking six-foot policeman entered. Before him, he was pushing the unresisting Leander Jones. Leander's face wore its habitual apologetic smile, which served as an effective mask. His pale blue eyes took in the details of the office and its robust occupant with a meek, but thorough glance.

"Here he is!" the policeman announced with an air of triumph.

Atwell let his glance linger a moment on Leander. Then he looked at the policeman. "Well, what about him?" he demanded.

"This is the guy I brought in from the Minton place."

"The what—from where?" Atwell wrinkled his forehead.

"The guy from Minton's," the policeman persisted. "Mr. Clarence Minton caught him out there about half an hour ago. He's some kind of a crook. Minton'll be down as soon as he gets dressed up to sign a complaint."

For a long moment Atwell stared at the policeman, after which he transferred his puzzled glance to Leander for an equal length of time. Suddenly his face took on an apoplectic hue and he frowned at the policeman.

"Minton's! Half an hour ago!" he exploded. "Listen, Rafferty, you're nuts!"

Policeman Rafferty's mouth dropped open.

"I was talking to this man right here net more than five minutes ago!" Atwell bellowed, glaring at the luckless Rafferty. "We picked him up in the lobby of the Clarinda House."

Rafferty set his heavy jaw stubbornly. "I don't know nothing about that, Chief," he said. "But I do know I been gone from here almost half an hour—and I found this guy all tied up in a bedroom at the Minton house. And that was more than fifteen minutes ago!"

Atwell jumped to his feet. "Listen, you big palooka!" he roared. "Are you trying to make a liar out of me? I'll show you! By God, I'll show you. You stay right here for a minute!"

With that, he jerked open the office door and disappeared into the other room, slamming the door angrily behind him.

CHAPTER SIX
ALIAS THE CORPSE

RAFFERTY, THE picture of bewilderment, gazed blankly at the closed door. He raised a big hand and scratched his head long and thoughtfully. Then, suddenly remembering Leander, he glowered at him.

"Say, you—" he began.

Leander raised both hand palms outward. "I—I'm afraid I'm not saying anything, officer," he protested. "You understand. Say nothing without advice of counsel, and all that sort of thing."

Rafferty spluttered. "Wait a minute! You know damn well—"

"No, indeed!" Leander cut in promptly. "I don't know anything. I'm quite confused. I am, indeed." A suspicious grin swept across his face and was gone, but his mild eyes continued to hold a hint of a twinkle.

Before Rafferty could say anything more, the door burst open and Atwell came in. His brow was corrugated into ridges of bewilderment and most of his blustering assurance seemed to have vanished into air. One huge hand was closed firmly about the small muscular arm of Mr. Horatio

Jones, whom he conducted to the center of the room. Then he walked back and shut the door.

"Hello, Horatio," said Leander.

"Hello, Leander."

"I'm glad to see you."

"I'm glad to see you, too, Leander."

Atwell stomped over to Horatio and waved a finger under his nose. "You!" he thundered. "Didn't you and I talk here just about five minutes ago? Before you were locked up?"

Horatio nodded calmly. "You talked. And I listened," he said with dignity.

"Well, anyway, you admitted the car they found Gerkin in was yours. Even if that's all you'd say," Atwell muttered.

"Yes," Horatio replied. He glanced at Leander and his eyelids flickered faintly.

Atwell rubbed the back of his neck. He stared back and forth from Horatio to Leander. Then he glared at Rafferty; then he stared again at Horatio and again at Leander. He passed his hand over his eyes, mumbled under his breath.

"Listen!" he suddenly exclaimed. "Am I going crazy? Do you two look alike—or am I seeing double?"

Leander answered. "We look alike."

The chief of police exhaled with a heavy sigh of relief. "Didn't you tell me your name was Jones?" he asked Horatio.

"Yes. Jones—just Jones."

"What's your name?" he demanded, looking at Leander.

"Jones. Just—Jones."

"Jones and Jones, huh?"

"Exactly," Leander murmured. "Just Jones and Jones. You may have heard the name before," he added dryly.

Atwell started and fixed his gaze on Leander's pale blue eyes. Slowly and deliberately, Leander closed one eyelid in a movement that could be interpreted only as a wink.

Atwell let out a gasp; then his face broadened into a wide grin. "By God!" he exclaimed, striking his tends together. And as he dropped heavily into his chair, he repeated: "By God! Jones and Jones!"

"Rafferty!" he bellowed. "Get out! And keep your mouth shut!"

Rafferty got out.

When the door had closed, Atwell pulled open the drawer of his desk and drew forth a box of cigars. "Smoke?"

"No thanks. Only this kind," Leander said, producing a couple of the thin black stogies he and Horatio used. "Have one, Horatio?"

"I ought've recognized you sooner," Atwell said, "but I was a little upset the way things have been going here today."

"We weren't sure you'd ever heard of us," Leander murmured.

"What! Never heard of Jones and Jones? Come now, Mr. Jones, Clarinda is a small city but we're up-to-date. And every police chief that's on his toes has heard of you," he replied, shaking his head. "What brings you here?" he added curiously.

Leander made a deprecatory gesture with his stogy. "Nothing much. Merely an attempted fraud, a confidence game, a grave robbery and a couple of murders."

ATWELL LOOKED at Leander incredulously. Then slowly an expression of relief, almost happiness, suffused his ruddy countenance. "You mean—you mean the robbing of the vault at the cemetery? And the killing of Gerkin?" he stammered.

"Those are two of the crimes I mentioned."

"Think you can catch the guilty parties?" Atwell asked.

Leander took a thoughtful puff on his stogy. "Yes," he said with quiet confidence.

"Well, count on me to help you!" Atwell exclaimed heartily. "I'll pinch the mayor, if you say so."

"Good!" Leander said and moved over to the door of the office. He placed his ear close to the panel, meanwhile gesturing with his finger to his lips for silence. Presently, he walked back to Atwell and said softly: "Might as well start now."

"Huh?"

"Mr. Clarence Minton has just arrived—to sign a complaint against me. He hasn't lost his old time nerve, it seems," he added.

"You mean—Gerald Minton's brother?" Atwell gasped.

"Right!" He looked at Horatio. "Don't you recall him? Clarence Minton—alias Louis Miller—alias Louis the Limp?" He turned back to Atwell. "Louis the Limp was one of the trickiest confidence men that ever lived. But he ended in Matteawan Hospital for the Criminal Insane. He must have escaped. Anyway, that's Louis the Limp outside. You'd better grab him, Chief!"

Atwell leaped to his feet and headed for the door. "You bet I will!" he exclaimed excitedly.

When they were alone, Leander chuckled softly. "Remember, Horatio," he said, "I thought the face of Gerald Minton looked familiar last night?"

Horatio nodded.

"That was because he and Louis the Limp are brothers. And it's funny, but when I first saw Louis this afternoon at the Minton house, I thought he looked familiar because he looked like Gerald Minton. And all the time, it was a picture of Louis the Limp, confidence man, that was in the back of my mind. I didn't place him, till it was too late. He already had me tied up," Leander said.

"You think he stabbed his own brother—in the coffin?" Horatio asked.

Leander shook his head dubiously. "I don't know," he said, and then added, "What happened to you?"

"Well, Leander," Horatio said, making a wry face, "I was careless. I apologize."

"Careless?"

"Very careless. After you left me at the vault, I let myself be caught off guard," Horatio explained. "I was overpowered and tied up by two men I couldn't even see. They left me lying on the ground for a little while. But a little later they returned, carried me for some distance and—placed me in a coffin!"

"My word!" Leander exclaimed. "Are you sure it was a coffin you were in?"

"I could tell that. By the feel of the material with which it was lined. And once when I tried to sit up, I bumped my head on the lid. I was pretty worried, Leander. I expected to be smothered."

Leander was looking at him intently. "Go on!" he urged.

"I wasn't smothered, as you can see, although I must have been in the thing at least half an hour," Horatio murmured. "My captors finally must have decided they didn't need me in their plans. They dumped me out behind a hedge near the road. Luckily a farmer found me this morning and brought me into town.

"I went to the hotel looking for you. But no sooner had I put my foot inside the lobby than I was arrested. It seems a dead man had been found in my coupé. Naturally, I wouldn't talk any till I'd seen you and knew what had been taking place."

"You must have been in Minton's coffin," Leander said.

"No doubt about it."

Leander half closed one eye and stared dreamily at one corner of the ceiling. Suddenly his face broke into a smile. He slapped Horatio on the back and exclaimed: "By Gad! I've got it. I've got it, Horatio!"

"What?"

"The reason the coffin was stolen!"

"Why?" Horatio asked eagerly.

"Because," Leander said exuberantly, "it was the only thing that would expose the whole dastardly plot! It was the one flaw—the one damning bit of evidence that could be traced!" He started for the door. "Come on! We haven't a minute to lose!"

As they crossed the outer room, Atwell appeared from the hall that led to the cells. "I got him locked up," he said.

"Hold him till we get back!" Leander called over his shoulder, as he and Horatio hurried to the street.

Back in his hotel room five minutes later, Leander picked up the telephone. "Operator," he said crisply. "I want to put in a long-distance call to New York." He gave her the name of a weekly publication famous for many years as the "bible" of the theatrical profession.

ON THE front of the undertaking establishment of B. Gerkin was pasted a small typewritten notice. Leander read it aloud, while Horatio looked over his shoulder.

Due to the death of Mr. B. Gerkin,
this funeral parlor will be closed for several days.

"Well," Horatio murmured, "that is that."

Leander nodded slowly. "Perhaps," he said, "there might be someone in the back part of the place. If not we'll just have to—"

A voice behind him broke in. "How about this fellow Louis the Limp, Mr. Jones? Can we put a murder charge against him?"

The brothers Jones turned to behold the robust form and florid face of Police Chief Atwell.

"I was up at the corner and noticed you reading this sign down here," Atwell explained. "If you want to take a look at Gerkin's body, it's here all right. But I don't know exactly how we can get in until tonight."

"Why not until tonight?" Leander asked quickly.

"'Cause young Viles has gone away. He had to take care of a funeral over at Valley City. That's sixty miles away so he won't get back till tonight."

Leander clutched Atwell's arm. "How do you know that?"

"He got a permit to take the body on the one o'clock train," Atwell replied, looking at Leander in surprise. "Things like that can't wait, even if Gerkin is dead. When a person's ready to be buried, he's got to be buried."

"By Gad! By Gad!" Leander muttered. He jerked his watch from his pocket. The hands pointed to three minutes of one. Leander sprang into action. "Hurry up! We've got to make that train!" he called out over his shoulder, as he started running down the street.

Horatio, accustomed to such startling moves, took after him at once. But Atwell, a look of blank amazement covering his face, merely stared after them for a few seconds. Then, coming to life, he, too, broke into a run in the direction of the railroad station.

The train was already moving when, breathless and red, he grabbed the handrail and stumbled up the steps. Both Leander and Horatio had disappeared inside. But as soon as he opened the door and stepped inside himself, Atwell caught sight of them in the aisles of the coach ahead. He rushed forward. The passengers, sensing that something out of the way was happening, followed him with curious stares.

Leander had a firm grip on Viles' shoulder, when Atwell panted up. The yellow-skinned undertaker's assistant was cringing back against the cushion, clutching with one hand at his cheek and holding with the other to the arm of a woman beside him. She was the red-headed maid from Doctor Barnabas' house.

The conductor bustled up. "Here! Here! What's this?" he demanded. He saw Atwell. "What's the meaning of this, Chief?"

"These people are under arrest!" Leander snapped.

"Why—that's Mr. and Mrs. Viles," Atwell stammered.

"Well, bring 'em along!" Leander ordered.

"Bring 'em along? Where we going?"

"Up to the baggage car!!"

WHILE THE conductor remained behind to reassure the passengers, Atwell and Horatio herded Viles and his wife up the aisle of the coach, then through the smoking car ahead. Leander already had made his way forward. He pushed open the door of the baggage car and held it while the others filed through.

"What the hell! Get out of here!" the baggageman exclaimed. "Passengers ain't allowed here!"

"We're not passengers," Leander said dryly. "We're police."

"What?"

"There's the chief," Leander said, jerking a thumb in Atwell's direction.

The baggageman's mouth and eyes opened simultaneously. "Cops? What's happened?"

Nobody took the trouble to answer him. Leander was striding toward the forward end of the car, toward a big oblong box of new pine. It was the rough box for a coffin. Near the bottom on either side, rows of round holes had been cut in it. On the top rested a funeral wreath.

Leander picked up the wreath and tossed it into a corner. Then he glanced about the car. He seemed about to speak to the baggageman, when his eye lit on a red glass-covered case fastened to the wall. It contained a saw and fire ax—emergency equipment.

Horatio had moved up to Leander's side. Atwell, holding Viles and his wife firmly by the arm, was in the middle of the baggage car. Behind them, the baggageman was watching with an uneasy expression, unable to decide where his duty lay in this strange situation. All eyes were on Leander, but he appeared unconscious of the fact.

He smashed the glass that covered the lock of the emergency tool box, turned the key and took down the fire ax. Then he stepped to the rough box again. The baggageman, suddenly galvanized into a decision, jumped forward.

"Hey!" he shouted. "My God—you can't do that!"

"Stand back!" Leander ordered. "You'll get hurt!" His usually mild eyes were blazing now, and the commanding note in his voice brought the baggageman up short.

With a rending crash the fire ax came down upon the soft pine. Again Leander swung, and again, the blade biting deep into the wood with each stroke. A couple of minutes later, he tossed the ax on the floor and began yanking the broken boards from the top of the box. Horatio helped him, and presently they had exposed the entire length of a black coffin.

"My word, Leander! Look!" Horatio exclaimed. He pointed to a silver plate on the coffin lid.

GERALD LEROY MINTON

Born May 7, 1880

Died June 19, 1933

"He strutted and fretted his brief hour

upon the stage and then was heard no more."

Leander gave it only a hurried glance. He picked up the ax once more and, forcing the blade under the coffin lid, pressed down with all his weight on the handle. The lid, held only by two screws, snapped loose and toppled to the floor.

Stretched out in the coffin, hands clutching and his face contorted into an expression of wild terror and agony, lay Doctor Barnabas!

With a low exclamation, Leander dropped to his knees. He laid his hand upon the face, pressed his ear close to the breast. After a moment, he rose slowly to his feet and solemnly faced the little group in the baggage car.

"Dead!" Leander announced. "Dead! Smothered in the coffin of his first victim!"

Mrs. Viles covered her face with her hands and began to sob. Viles, who was staring as if fascinated at the body in the box, suddenly began to tremble. His knees seemed to turn to wax, he began to sag. Then he uttered a terrified scream and would have collapsed, had not Atwell yanked him erect.

Leander strode over to Viles. He seized him fiercely by the shoulder.

"By God!" he burst out. "I knew you didn't have any sense, or you never would have committed those two murders. But I didn't think you were this stupid!"

He turned to Horatio. "Horatio, it proves our point again. No criminal has any brains—or he wouldn't be a criminal! This man was helping Barnabas get away—at the same time making his own escape. But his stupidity killed the man he was trying to aid."

Leander pointed to the coffin. "That's a trick coffin," he said. "It has ventilators, so that anyone confined in it can breath. The air comes in through vents in the bottom, passes up through the hollow sides and into the coffin near the top. But—" Leander paused and looked at the whimpering Viles with a shake of his head. Then he went on.

"This murdering idiot, after carefully cutting holes in the sides of the rough box to admit air, didn't stop to think that if he let the bottom of the coffin rest on the solid bottom of the rough box, he'd plug the air vents. So Doctor Barnabas smothered," he added.

"Why did Barnabas pick this way to try and get out of town?" he suddenly demanded of Viles.

Viles shrank back, gulped, but finally found his voice. "Because—because he thought you were on to him and he was being watched. He knew all about the coffin. Used it hundreds of times, so he figured it was a safe and smart way to—"

Leander cut him short with a gesture. "Never mind the rest now," he said. "I know all the answers." He reached up and, seizing the signal rope that ran through the car, yanked it down.

Almost immediately the scream of the locomotive whistle broke out and the train began to grind to a stop.

LATE IN the afternoon, Leander and Horatio paused before a door on the second floor of the Minton home.

"This must be the room Louis the Limp meant," Horatio said.

"I'll try the key be gave us," Leander replied. He drew a key from his pocket and inserted it in the lock. "Yes, it's the right one."

Leander threw the door open and walked into the room with Horatio close behind him.

"You're all right now, Mrs. Minton!" Leander exclaimed. "You've nothing to fear!"

Marvella Minton was seated in a high-backed chair. Her ankles were bound to the chair legs; her wrists to the chair arms. Around her mouth a handkerchief had been wound to prevent her making any outcry.

At the entrance of Leander and Horatio her eyes widened with terror, then, as she recognized Leander, an expression of relief and joy flooded them. They freed her quickly. She slumped down in the chair and began to weep. Leander hesitated, then put his arm comfortingly about her shoulders.

"Now, now, don't cry," he begged her. "Everything's all right. My word, Horatio, do something! Get a glass of water!"

"He—he threatened to kill me," she sobbed brokenly. "If—if I didn't turn the money over to him."

"Yes, we know all about that," Leander said soothingly. "He told us all. He came here to your husband's funeral and would have left right afterward, but you unfortunately let him know that Mr. Minton had left a lot of insurance money. So he decided to stay, to swindle you if possible, and if that didn't work he planned to use force. But you don't have to worry any more. He's going back—well, he's going back to a place he won't get out of again soon."

Her sobbing gradually ceased and she looked up at Leander with a look of such gratitude in her large brown eyes that he began to fidget. "I'll never be able to thank you—for saving me."

"Don't try! Please, don't try!" Leander said hurriedly. "We've had a splendid time doing it. Splendid!"

CHIEF OF Police Atwell ate dinner that night with Leander and Horatio at the Clarinda House. When they had given their orders, Atwell leaned forward eagerly.

"Now," he said, "I'd like to have you straighten this whole thing out in my mind. I've got to confess, I'm a little bit balled up, what with things happening so fast."

"Louis the Limp," Leander said, "thought his brother had died a natural death. He was playing his own game, trying to pick up fifty thousand dollars." Leander gave a dry chuckle. "He was the cause of Jones and Jones entering this most interesting case. He appropriated Gerald's clothing supply without Mrs. Minton's knowing it. She saw him prowling around one night, while in one of his spells, and thought it was Gerald. So she came to us."

Atwell nodded. "How about the others?"

"A simple plot to start with," Leander replied. "For the last ten years, Barnabas had been a practicing physician in Clarinda. Above reproach. But in his earlier life, he'd strayed from the fold of ethical medicine and was known as Barnabas the Great."

"Barnabas the Great?"

"A stage name," Leander explained. "He was a hypnotist—had his own show. I saw it once myself years ago. The big ballyhoo for it was to put a man in an hypnotic trance and seal him in a coffin. That's where Minton first came in. He was the man who was hypnotized.

"Barnabas eventually gave up his show," Leander continued, "and came to Clarinda. Four years ago, Minton showed up. One or the other of them conceived the notion of a juicy insurance swindle—using the old coffin trick.

"But they had to have a beneficiary who'd be above suspicion and dumb enough to get the money away from afterwards. Minton solved that by marrying an orphan from out of town. They'd waited four years, Barnabas footing the bills, to quiet all suspicion with the insurance company. The stakes were big—they could afford to play slow and safe.

"I'm beginning to get it," Atwell muttered. "And they needed an undertaker, too. That's where Gerkin got mixed up."

"Exactly," Leander said. "Gerkin—and Viles—and Viles' wife. Barnabas soon developed an almost fiendish control over Viles, who's weak-willed, anyway. Then, when Doctor Barnabas found out what a charming wife Minton had chosen, he had an idea. Briefly, it was to make a real widow and then marry her. Thus getting the money and simplifying the whole thing.

"So when the time came to bring Minton out of his trance and let him slip away, Barnabas influenced Viles to bury a dagger in his heart. By the way, those were Viles' prints on the knife, weren't they?"

"Yes," Atwell said.

"I expected so," Leander murmured. "Viles didn't bother about gloves, since the coffin was due to go underground pretty soon, anyway. Well, when I came to town and began to ask questions, it threw a scare into the doctor.

"He knew the trick coffin was a giveaway—could be traced to him by any first-class detective. It was part of the stuff he had left from his show. So he told Gerkin and Viles it had to be retrieved at any cost. While he and Mrs. Viles drew me away from the vault, Gerkin and Viles got the coffin—and Horatio," Leander added with a grin.

"Why'd Viles kill Gerkin?" Atwell wanted to know.

"He told me Gerkin was going to squeal. Gerkin didn't know Minton had been stabbed. When he saw him there, it scared him stiff. And he figured he could worm out with only a mild sentence as an aid to the fraud."

Horatio spoke up. "And Viles, already steeped in murder, beat his brains out and threw him in my coupé."

"Exactly. But it was an accident that your car was chosen. I'd parked it near the outside of the lot."

Atwell shook his head. "By George! By George!" he said. He suddenly looked at Leander. "What put you on to this?"

Leander considered for a minute. "A picture of Barnabas which I saw in his house," he said finally. "It was inscribed 'Barnabas the Great.' I didn't think anything about it, until Horatio told me he'd been sealed in Minton's coffin and hadn't smothered. Then it all came back to me. To make sure, I phoned New York and got all the data on Barnabas the Great and his show."

Atwell looked at Horatio and gave a chuckle. "How did it feel to ride in a coffin, Mr. Jones?"

Horatio shuddered slightly. "The only time to ride in a coffin is when you can't feel."

There was a twinkle in Leander's eyes. "You see, Chief," he said, "our name is Jones—just Jones. Everybody's heard that name. So occasionally, we travel under an alias of some kind." He turned to Horatio with a dry smile and said: "I believe, Horatio, this was the first time you were ever alias the corpse."

THE DEVIL'S DOZEN

THE ONLY LEAD LEANDER HAD WAS THE HORROR-LOOK HE SAW MIRRORED IN A PAIR OF HAZEL EYES. BUT THAT WAS ENOUGH TO SET THE BROTHERS JONES OFF ON A BLOOD TRAIL THAT DIDN'T END UNTIL A MADMAN SHRIEKED, "THE DEVIL DIES TONIGHT!" IN THE SECRET MEETING PLACE OF A CULT OF FIENDS.

CHAPTER ONE
THE GIRL IN BROWN

TO THE other passengers in the subway car who noticed her, and they were more than a few, the girl across the aisle from Mr. Leander Jones was just another unusually pretty girl.

She was simply dressed. But her suit, of some soft brown material, was of modish cut. All her clothes had an air of costly smartness.

That she was unusually pretty, one sensed rather than saw, for she kept her face demurely lowered.

At a casual glance, she might have been one of the well-groomed business girls who journey daily by the thousands to their offices in the skyscrapers of Manhattan. Considering the hour—nine o'clock in the morning—this would have been a natural assumption.

But Leander Jones, lifting his mild blue eyes over the top of his newspaper, suffered no such delusion. Although forty-two years old, bald headed and a bachelor, Leander possessed a surprising fund of knowledge about feminine apparel, as, indeed, he did about a great many things.

He knew, for example, that the fur which adorned the collar and cuffs of her plainly styled suit was real sable. The suit itself, he decided instantly, had been designed and tailored on upper Fifth Avenue, if not on the *Rue de la Paix*.

"My, my!" Leander murmured to himself. "Must've cost eight or nine hundred at least to turn her out in that simple little costume. And riding in the subway!"

As if his thought wave had crossed the aisle, the girl suddenly raised her head. For a single moment, her large hazel-brown eyes stared straight into his pale blue ones. Then, abruptly, she bowed her face again.

Leander lowered his own glance to the paper before him. His manner was apologetic, half-embarrassed, as if he had been caught in some heinous act, instead of the

"We'll change that name to Jones—
just dead," Delfax remarked casually.

common pastime of the New York male—filling the eye with anything pretty in skirts that happened to be sitting nearby.

But whatever Leander's manner may have been, his reaction to that one fleeting glance from her eye was quite different. His hands imperceptibly tightened on the edge of his newspaper, he sat up just a little straighter, and although he seemed to be reading, he was totally unconscious of the words.

He had noted the rich perfection of her attire, before she had looked at him. And when she had lifted her face, he had seen that her eyes were large and hazel colored. But whether her face was beautiful or not, he couldn't have told you. For the expression in those eyes had driven everything else from his mind for the moment.

They were filled with stark, wild terror.

LEANDER CONSIDERED. He knew he was not mistaken as to the significance of that look in the girl's eyes. In his twenty years as a specialist in criminology, as the senior partner of Jones and Jones, he had often seen similar expressions in the eyes of many persons, men and women.

It was not an expression such as any ordinary worry or fright would cause. It was unreasoning, an elemental terror, a panicky thing, stirred up by some ghastly experience.

He stole another glance over the top of his paper.

The girl was sitting motionless, hands still clasped on her lap, her eyes cast down.

Leander felt a surge of admiration for her calmness and self-control. It was something he could appreciate, even more than the girl's obvious attractiveness.

The business of Jones and Jones was not merely tracking down criminals, solving mysterious crimes, but also discovering crimes that probably would never have been known had it not been for their shrewd and searching investigations.

From apparently trivial things, this unique firm of criminologists was accustomed to work.

And so there was nothing strange in Leander's professional interest in this expensively dressed girl. Even if he had not had that momentary glimpse of the haunting terror in her eyes, her presence in a subway in the midst of this workbound throng would have been sufficient to set his mind speculating as to why she was there.

As it was—well, this might be another blind lead. But again it might—

"Twenty-thoid! Twenty-thoid Street!"

The guard's husky voice bellowed through the car. A large number of the passengers elbowed, pushed, squeezed their way to the platform.

The girl in brown remained rigid in her seat. She didn't so much as raise her eyes.

Normally, Leander left the subway at this station. His office was in the Flatiron Building, almost directly overhead. But now he, too, kept his place, and gave a first-rate impersonation of a meek little business man engrossed in reading about the latest counter-revolution in Cuba.

AS THE train pulled into City Hall Station, the girl lifted her head, flicked a glance up and down the car. Then she rose to her feet with an abruptness that bespoke the tension within her.

Leander waited until the car door had opened and she was stepping to the platform. Dropping his newspaper on the seat, he followed—on up to the street.

She spoke a few words to the policeman on the corner, then started west. She walked north on Broadway to Chambers Street. Once or twice she glanced quickly over her shoulder. But if she recognized Leander as the man who had been sitting across from her in the subway car, she made no sign.

Indeed, there was nothing about Leander Jones to attract even the most casual notice. His appearance was nondescript, his manner self-effacing.

Clad in a slightly rumpled gray suit and brown hat, Leander was completely inconspicuous, a condition entirely to his liking.

The girl in brown continued west for two blocks, walking with long athletic strides. At the Chambers Street Station of the Seventh Avenue subway she disappeared into the kiosk. Leander, close behind, lingered a moment to buy a newspaper and then followed, edging down through the crowd that was jostling its way up the steps.

He caught a glimpse of her brown hat as she slipped through the turnstile and headed for the uptown platform. A moment later, an uptown express roared into the station. The car was crowded, but the girl obtained a seat near the front platform.

Leander worked his way up the aisle until he was standing only half a dozen feet from her. Half hidden behind his paper, he stole a cautious glance.

Again she was sitting with downcast eyes, although now she seemed to be less concerned with keeping her face hidden. Several times she looked up and gave her fellow passengers a brief survey. And Leander, missing no move that she made, saw that her wide hazel eyes were still clouded with that look of mortal dread.

"Strange," he said to himself. "She rides downtown on one subway line, and walks a few blocks and goes right back uptown on another."

Fourteenth Street, Penn Station, Forty-second, Seventy-second—but at none of these express stops did the girl in brown rise from her place. The crush of passengers had ceased. Now the aisles were cleared, half the seats unoccupied. Leander had dropped onto the rattan cushion near the middle of the car, where he could watch the girl from behind the shield of his newspaper.

As they pulled out of the Seventy-second Street station, he suddenly became aware that he was not the only passenger who was covertly keeping an eye on her.

At the far end, a glint-eyed man with a complexion the color of satin-wood, repeatedly glanced from beneath tilted black brows in her direction. But there was a stealthiness, an obvious attempt not to have his scrutiny noticed, that convinced Leander it was not mere admiration for the girl's good looks that prompted the glances.

Then, with an inward start, he realized he had seen the man with the yellow-tan skin before. He had ridden downtown on the other subway train, the one on which Leander had first noticed the light of terror in the eyes of the girl in brown.

He was of medium size, but there were indications of a lithe, muscular body beneath his neat, dark blue suit. Something oriental in his face, Leander thought, although he couldn't identify the nationality.

THE TRAIN came to a stop at Ninety-sixth Street. For a moment, the girl seemed to hesitate. She peered through the windows trying to catch a glimpse of the signs which would tell her where she was. Then, abruptly, she got to her feet and made her way to the platform.

The man with the tilted eyebrows also rose hastily. He slipped out the middle door of the car.

They emerged from the subway kiosk onto upper Broadway, an odd procession for the heart of New York at ten o'clock in the morning. First, the expensively clad and pretty girl with the frightened eyes; next, the man with the satin-wood complexion, following at a discreet distance; and lastly, Leander, inconspicuous and harmless-looking, keeping a sharp eye on both the others.

A block up Broadway, the girl turned into a drugstore. The man with the tilted eyebrows paused uncertainly, stepped to the curb where a taxi was parked. He spoke to the driver, who nodded, and the man walked into the store.

Leander strolled past and looked in the open door. He couldn't see the girl, but the man was standing at the cigar counter at the front and from the direction of his gaze, Leander surmised that she was in one of the phone booths. He retraced his steps slowly, finally halting before a shop window a few doors down the street, where he waited.

Presently, the man with the tilted eyebrows came out of the drugstore. He walked to a point near the taxi. Soon, the girl appeared. She started to swing up the street, but the man with the tilted eyebrows took two swift strides and touched her on the elbow.

She stopped, drew herself up, took a backward step. But the man's hand closed on her arm, and almost before Leander realized what was happening, he had flung open the door of the taxi and pushed her inside. The smoothness and dispatch of his maneuver bespoke a thorough familiarity with the procedure.

A short scream, quickly choked off, came from within the cab.

Even as Leander sprang forward, the man with the tilted eyebrows leaned through the window and pressed a pistol against the side of the driver's head. The cab lurched from the curb.

Pursuit on foot was hopeless. But a second later, Leander had jumped to the running board of a second cab, cruising up Broadway. He jerked the door open, and clambered inside.

"Follow the blue cab!" Leander emphasized his command by shoving a banknote over the driver's shoulder. "Another ten for you, if you don't lose it!"

The driver grabbed the money and stepped on the gas simultaneously. The car leaped ahead. Leander, tense on the edge of the cushion, could see the other taxi about two blocks in front. While he watched, it swung off Broadway, east toward Central Park West.

Although there were a number of pedestrians on the sidewalks and a considerable flow of traffic on the street, the abduction of the girl in brown had been executed with such swiftness and efficiency that it had gone unnoticed.

As they slued into Ninety-fourth Street, the blue cab was still in sight. But almost at once it disappeared around the corner, heading south.

They were only a block behind as they crossed Ninetieth against the lights, racing south on Central Park West.

And then from one of the side streets, a small coupé sped out into the main thoroughfare, directly in the path of the blue car. The taxi driver swerved violently. Too late. There was a terrific crash. The coupé spun around several times, slid along the pavement, and turned completely over.

The blue cab caromed crazily off. For a moment the driver seemed about to get it under control, but suddenly it slithered across the street, leaped the curb and brought up with a rending of metal against the stone retaining wall of the park.

CHAPTER TWO
RESCUE

WHEN **LEANDER** reached the smashed cab beside the park, the driver was slumped over the wheel. He raised his head and stared dazedly about. Blood was trickling down his face from a gash over one eye.

Looking through the open window of the rear door, Leander saw the man with the tilted eyebrows lying in a crumpled heap on the floor. One hand still clutched his revolver.

The girl in brown was bolt upright on the cushion. Her eyes were wide with panic. Her hands were pressed to the sides of her ashen face. At the sight of Leander, peering through the window, she opened her mouth as if to give voice to a scream of hysteria.

Then, with a quick deep breath, she gained control of herself. "Please!" she leaned forward. "Please—get me away from here!"

Leander yanked the cab door open. She got out, and he took her arm. A crowd was beginning to collect, but the coupé, lying upside down in the middle of the street, was attracting most of the attention.

The driver of his cab was standing only a few feet away, and Leander beckoned to him. "Hurry! We're going!"

Driving swiftly away from the scene of the crash, the girl partially recovered her composure. But Leander, observing her closely saw that look of terror still in her hazel eyes. "I know you probably are wondering what—what—" She hesitated.

Leander smiled reassuringly. "No, no!" he murmured. "I understand. Don't try to talk now. You're perfectly safe."

Her eyes suddenly grew wider. "Why—why, you were sitting in the subway car that I rode downtown in," she said.

"Yes."

"You—you've been following me?"

He nodded. "I hope you'll excuse it. But you see—well, your expression—that is, you awakened my interest. I knew you were in trouble. That's our business—helping people in trouble."

She didn't say anything for some time. Then, she asked with an air of bewilderment: "Who are you?"

"My name is Jones," he said, and added almost apologetically, "just Jones."

"Just Jones," she repeated wonderingly.

"We—my brother and I—comprise the firm of Jones and Jones," Leander explained. "Specialists in criminal investigation. Perhaps, we might even be called detectives."

"Detectives!"

She looked at him steadily, and little by little the frightened look in her eyes seemed to fade. Somehow, this mild-mannered little man had awakened a feeling of confidence in her. "If you are a detective, then you can—help me."

"Quite likely," he agreed. "But we'll wait until we get to my office and then you can explain why you need help. Meantime, you'd better just relax."

HORATIO JONES, junior member of the firm, was in the office when they arrived. If he was surprised to see his brother appear, accompanied by a beautiful and smartly dressed girl, he gave no evidence of it. It was difficult to make either of the brothers Jones display any emotion other than their habitual meekness and air of embarrassment.

"Good morning, Horatio."

"Good morning, Leander."

Leander turned to his lovely companion with a smile. "This is my brother, Horatio, Miss—" He lifted a questioning eyebrow.

The girl in brown smiled for the first time. She looked from Horatio to Leander and then back to Horatio. A tiny puzzled frown appeared on her forehead, and Leander, observing it, said quickly: "Yes—we're twins. However, I'm ten minutes older, so I'm generally considered the senior member of Jones and Jones."

She gave a low musical laugh. "Please forgive me for staring," she said. "I am Miss Chauvenet. Eloise Chauvenet."

Horatio made a stiff jerky bow. Leander spoke to a girl who was sitting at a desk at one side of the office. She was a tall girl, wearing a simple black dress with stiffly starched collars and cuffs.

"Miss Millard," he said. "This is Miss Chauvenet."

"I think, Horatio," Leander said, "we'd better conduct Miss Chauvenet into the private office."

Horatio opened a door with an upper panel of opaque glass, and followed Miss Chauvenet into the inner sanctum he shared with Leander.

When they had been seated, Leander at his old-fashioned roll-top desk and Horatio at the duplicate of it on the other side of the room, with Miss Chauvenet occupying a comfortable armchair between them, Leander said: "Perhaps it would be best, if I explained for Horatio's benefit, just what has happened."

With a keen instinct for essential facts, he rapidly sketched the events which led up to his bringing Miss Chauvenet to the office of Jones and Jones.

"This man who forced you into the taxicab," Horatio said. "Did you know him?"

Miss Chauvenet shuddered. "I'd never seen him before in my life. But—" She stopped suddenly, and that look of deadly terror, which Leander had noticed in the subway, began to creep back into her eyes.

"You have nothing to fear now," Leander said. "But you mentioned needing help. If you'll explain, you can rest assured that Jones and Jones will help you."

"I—I'm certain you will!" she exclaimed gratefully. For a little bit, she was silent, as if trying to determine how to begin. "I suppose," she said at last, "I should tell you my whole story."

"By all means," Leander agreed.

OUTWARDLY CALM, yet speaking with a breathless earnestness, Miss Chauvenet began. "As you can tell from my name, I'm of French descent, although I was born in this country. Here in New York. My father was one of the two partners of Chauvenet Brothers. The name may be familiar to you."

"Yes," Leander said, with an almost wistful smile. "*Chauvenet Frères*—importers of fine vintage wines."

She nodded. "My uncle, Henri Chauvenet, was the other partner. But when prohibition came in the States, they retired from business.

"In nineteen twenty when I was ten years old, we moved to France, and I was placed in a convent school. A year later, my father died, but my mother and I continued to reside in France. The land of her birth.

"Three years ago, shortly after I had finished at the Convent of the Sacré Coeur, my mother also died. I was alone in the world, except for my Uncle Henri, here in New York. But all my friends were in France, so I had no reason for returning here.

"My uncle, who had never married, apparently wasn't much upset by the law which had put an end to his business. He remained here, taking over the house in which we had lived and where I was born, on Murray Hill. From what I remember my mother telling me, Uncle Henri welcomed the opportunity to pursue without restraint what had been a lifelong hobby."

She paused and wet her lips with the tip of her tongue. Leander noticed that her eyes were clouded.

"What was this hobby?" he asked.

"Religions. The study of strange and obscure religions. He was quite an authority, I believe, on odd rites and ceremonies, both ancient and modern."

"Your uncle, Henri Chauvenet, is possessed of ample means to indulge in this unusual hobby of his, I assume."

"My father left an estate of more than a million dollars. And I've always understood that Uncle Henri was even wealthier. He was the older, and also more conservative in his way of living."

"You control your inheritance, Miss Chauvenet?"

"No. It's in trust until I am twenty-four. My uncle is my guardian, and looks after my affairs. All the investments are in this country."

"Until you are twenty-four? When will that be?"

"Why—tomorrow."

Leander nodded slowly. "Ah, yes. Please continue, Miss Chauvenet."

"Two weeks ago, a cable came signed by my uncle. In it he said that it was imperative for business reasons that I make a trip to the States at once. I crossed on the *Ile de France*. Because of the fog, we didn't dock until rather late yesterday afternoon. I took a taxi directly from the pier to his house on East Thirty-eighth Street.

"I had expected my uncle to be waiting for me. I'd cabled him when I would arrive. But there was no one at the house except the servants. However, the butler, who admitted me, said they were expecting me and that my rooms had been prepared. My uncle, he said, had been obliged to go out of the city for the day, but would return sometime during the evening."

Eloise Chauvenet paused, as if dreading to go on with her story. Her hands were tightly clasped, and most of the color had drained from her face.

Leander looked at his twin brother. "Smelling salts, Horatio!"

When Horatio had disappeared into the outer office, Leander gave the girl a reassuring smile. "You say you have no friends here in New York?"

She shook her head. "I was only a child when I left. Of course, some of my childhood friends must still be here, but I had no way of locating them. There was only one person I could go to—when I fled from that ghastly house."

"Who was that?"

"My old nurse. When you first saw me in the subway, I was almost out of my mind. I had only one idea. To get away. I had gone into the first subway entrance, because I imagined that I would be safe where there was a crowd. I wanted time to think, to decide what to do.

"Then I thought of Madame—Madame Renoir, who was my nurse. All I remembered was that she had lived somewhere on the upper west side of the city. That's why I rode directly back uptown on the other subway. I went into the drugstore to try to find her name in the telephone directory. I found a Renoir, but it was not the right one.

"When I came out— But you know what happened after that," she said.

Horatio returned with smelling salts. She put them to her nose.

"After you arrived at your uncle's house—" Leander prompted her.

She set the bottle down. "I went immediately to the rooms that had been set aside for me. They were the rooms I had had as a little girl. The bedroom and nursery on the third floor.

"I asked the butler to have a maid come up and help me unpack. He informed me that my uncle employed no women servants. I decided to let the unpacking go for a while, and lay down to rest. I fell asleep and when I awoke it was dark—almost nine o'clock.

"It seemed strange that no one had awakened me for dinner. I hurriedly dressed and started downstairs. On the second floor, I met the butler. He told me that my uncle had left instructions that I was to have my dinner served in my room.

"That seemed strange to me. But I returned to my rooms and a little later, the butler brought dinner on a tray. I was beginning to have a feeling of uneasiness, and it was a great relief when, just as I finished eating, he came up and informed me that my uncle had returned and wished to see me in the library."

ELOISE CHAUVENET took a deep breath, and plunged on with her story. "It had been thirteen years since

I'd last seen my uncle, so my memory of him was naturally vague. But I was overjoyed at the prospect of a reunion with my only living relative.

"He was sitting at the big desk in the library. I noticed, as I entered the room, that it had changed very little from the way I recalled it. There were the same old-fashioned book cases, with the books behind glass doors. The same heavy drapes over the windows, the same heavy Empire furniture.

"He greeted me cordially. As he rose from his chair, it seemed to me that he was taller than I had pictured him in my mind. But he still had the pointed beard and the peculiar droop to his right shoulder, which I remembered.

"We talked for some time. Chiefly about family matters. My father and my mother, my life in France. He asked me numerous questions and said he was sorry to put me to the inconvenience of a trip to this country. It was necessary to have me sign certain papers in connection with receiving my inheritance next month.

"After about half an hour, he said that I was probably weary from my voyage, and suggested that I retire. The discussion of the business matters could wait until morning.

"As I climbed the stairs to the third floor, I was deeply puzzled by one thing. Although my uncle had seemed glad to see me and had been unusually gracious, there had been no instinctive response on my part.

"I sat in my room thinking it over for a long time. Gradually I realized that not only did I have no feeling of affection toward him, but that the man down there in the library actually repelled me. And almost in that instant the explanation came to me. It left me filled with terror, panic-stricken.

"The man with whom I had just been discussing family matters, who seemed so familiar with the affairs of the Chauvenets was not Henri Chauvenet at all!"

"My word," Leander murmured. "How Miss Chauvenet, did you know this man was not your uncle. You hadn't seen Henri Chauvenet for thirteen years."

"Because of his ears."

"Ears? My word—ears?"

By way of answer, Miss Chauvenet pushed back the soft waves of her brown hair until one of her ears was exposed. She turned her head slightly so Leander could see it better.

"You'll notice that my ears are small and set close to my head. But they have unusually large lobes. Do you see?"

He nodded.

"My father had the same kind of ears, and so had my Uncle Henri. Chauvenet ears—a family characteristic."

"And this interloper who was posing as your uncle?"

"Had large ears." She closed her eyes, as if to refresh her memory. "They came to a point at the top and grew right out from the side of his head—without any lobes at all."

Horatio moved his head slowly up and down. "I believe they are sometimes called satyr ears, Leander."

"Quite right, Horatio. Or devil's ears."

"I must have observed them subconsciously," Miss Chauvenet said. "When I was talking to him, I don't remember thinking about his ears. Not till I was back in my room, trying to analyze my strange feeling of abhorrence, did I suddenly realize he couldn't be my uncle. In making up to resemble Henri Chauvenet, he'd overlooked one of the most distinguishing physical points."

"When you'd made this discovery, what did you do?" Horatio asked.

"I didn't know what to do at first. I was frantic—terrified. My only impulse was to get out of that awful house as fast as possible. I packed a small bag and started downstairs. It was after eleven o'clock.

"When I reached the lower hallway, I heard voices in the library. I recognized one as that of the man who was impersonating Uncle Henri. I listened. I can't repeat the exact words of the conversation, but it concerned me. This man was saying that he was certain I believed he was Henri Chauvenet. The other man seemed unconvinced.

"The man who was posing as my uncle said—and I do recall this part distinctly, because the words were burned into my brain— 'If she discovers the truth, it doesn't matter. She's in our power. I'll put her in an asylum, or put her out of the way forever.'

"I waited to hear no more. I rushed toward the front door and pulled it open. But as I stepped into the vestibule, a man was standing there. He seized me and dragged me back into the house.

"At the sound of the commotion, the two men came out of the library. I have never seen such a look of insane fury on anybody's face as appeared on the face of the man who pretended to be Uncle Henri, when he discovered I had attempted to leave the house. At his order, I was dragged back to my rooms. The door was locked. I was a prisoner."

MISS CHAUVENET paused, looked from Leander to Horatio. "I know this must sound fantastic to you."

"No," Leander said solemnly. "It doesn't sound fantastic. Please go on, Miss Chauvenet."

"It was a night of horror," she said. "For when I thought of what I heard—'I'll put her in an asylum or put her out of the way forever—' it seemed to me I really was going mad.

"Somehow I fell asleep. Probably from sheer exhaustion. And when daylight came, I was more calm, able to think more clearly and plan how to escape.

"The rooms that had been set aside for me were, as I mentioned, my childhood bedroom and nursery. I remembered that there was a door opening from the nursery into the upstairs servants' hall. It was put there so the nurse and maids could reach me without passing through the front part of the house.

"If these men were not thoroughly familiar with the house, they might have overlooked that door. I hurried to it. It was locked—but from the inside. As cautiously as I could, I managed to get down the rear yard, and finally through a nearby apartment to the street.

"I rushed away from that horrible neighborhood as fast as possible, entered the first subway I came to—and then you saw me," she said, looking at Leander.

Leander nodded slowly and thoughtfully. "And somebody also saw you leave the house. The man who tried to abduct you on upper Broadway must have followed you. Probably your escape was discovered only a few moments after you had left your rooms. That was the first chance he had to recapture you—and he almost succeeded."

Leander stood up. The shrewd and alert air with which he had listened to Miss Chauvenet's story had vanished. In its place was his customary mask of self-effacement and mildness. Horatio, also, had an apologetic air about him similar to that of Leander.

"What am I going to do?" Miss Chauvenet asked anxiously.

"Nothing," Leander replied. "We'll arrange for you to stay with Miss Millard. You're safe there. Leave everything to Jones and Jones."

She looked at him eagerly. "I don't know how I can ever thank you. And whatever the cost is, I'll be only too glad to pay it."

"There is no fee," Leander said.

"You mean you—you don't charge for your services?"

"Exactly."

THE FIRM of Jones and Jones, consisting of the identical twin brothers, was probably the only one of its kind in the world. In the usual sense it was not a detective agency. Having inherited a considerable fortune, the brothers were not concerned with profits. They usually worked for nothing; now and then if their client was very wealthy, they charged a fee. But at once it was turned over anonymously to one of a number of pet charities in which they were interested.

When Miss Millard and Miss Eloise Chauvenet had left the office of Jones and Jones to go to the former's apartment on the upper east side, Leander picked up the telephone. He gave the number of police headquarters, and a moment later he was talking to Captain Colby in the detective bureau.

"This is Jones, Captain," he murmured, "Leander Jones. There was an automobile smash-up this morning on Central Park West near Eighty-sixth Street. I'd like to find out—if it isn't too much trouble for you," he added apologetically, "what happened to the man who was riding in the blue taxicab."

Leander listened then for a short time, while a funny little smile appeared on his face. Horatio watched him curiously.

"It's just one of those things, Captain," Leander continued. "We don't know yet what it means. What's that? No—

no, we don't need any help yet. But if we do, I'll call on you. Thank you, Captain, thank you." He hung up.

"It strikes me, Leander," Horatio said, "that Mr. Henri Chauvenet has been the victim of a diabolic plot."

"Victim? You believe he is dead?"

"Assuredly. Don't you?"

"No," Leander murmured, shaking his head. "I don't believe he is dead—yet. But unless we do something very quickly, I feel certain he will be, Horatio."

"Evidently a scheme to gain control of Henri Chauvenet's money," Horatio said.

"And also the fortune of his niece, Eloise Chauvenet," Leander added. "However, I believe they are blocked there, so long as we keep her out of their clutches."

"They'll probably make an attempt to capture her again."

Leander smiled. "They'll first have to find her."

There was a moment of silence, then Horatio asked: "Any idea who this impostor might be?"

The tinkling of the telephone interrupted. Leander lifted the receiver and pressed it against his ear.

"Jones speaking. Leander Jones." He waited a few seconds. "Oh, yes, Captain. What is the news?"

As he listened, Leander's face became grave. He made a little clucking sound, and finally said: "My word! Most unfortunate. But thank you very much, Captain, thank you." He turned from the telephone to Horatio. "Colby says the police report several witnesses say a girl got out and drove away in another cab with an unidentified man in a gray suit. Also a man was seen to climb out and disappear into the park. The driver is in Bellevue. They found a pistol on the floor of the cab. The police are puzzled," he added with a low chuckle.

Slowly and thoughtfully, Leander rose from his chair. He walked to the hat tree by the door and took down two identical brown soft hats, one of which he handed to Horatio and the other he clamped on his own bald head.

"Come, Horatio," he said, "I feel that we should call at the Murray Hill residence of Mr. Henri Chauvenet."

CHAPTER THREE
DEATH PLAYS HOST

DISMISSING THEIR taxi at the corner of Fifth Avenue, Leander and Horatio walked east on Thirty-eighth Street. A short walk and they came to an old-fashioned brown stone-front house, which differed from its neighbors chiefly in the fact that it occupied a slightly larger plot of ground.

Leander glanced at the number. "This is it," he said softly.

It was a four-story structure, the facade perfectly flat and unadorned with any bay windows or other protuberances. All the window shades were drawn, but the brass knob and lock on the double, plate-glass doors were brightly polished. So also was the brass railing that ran along the edge of the stoop.

They climbed the dozen steps that led up to the entrance. Leander pressed his finger against the bell button. They waited, but the ring brought no response. Again Leander pushed the button.

"No one here," Horatio murmured.

"At least, they refuse to answer," Leander said. "We'll try the basement door."

They returned to the sidewalk, then down a flight of steps that led beneath the stoop.

Here, Leander found another bell button. But once more all his efforts to obtain a response proved fruitless. He lifted his brown felt hat and rubbed his head meditatively over the shining baldness of his head. "Dear me," he said.

"Gone," said Horatio.

"I hope so."

"Why?"

"Since they won't answer the bell, I intend to enter uninvited. It might prove embarrassing, if they haven't gone."

Horatio shook his head dubiously. "That's house-breaking, Leander."

"Quite right, Horatio," Leander agreed blandly.

From the inner pocket of his coat, he produced a flat leather case. Selecting one of the dozen oddly shaped tools which were fastened to the inside of it, he went to work.

It was little more than a matter of seconds, before the lock yielded to his expert manipulations.

Followed closely by Horatio, he stepped inside, closed the door behind them.

The air in the place was stale and dank. For a little while, the two brothers stood in tense silence, peering about them.

From his vest, Leander drew a fountain-pen flashlight. A slender, brilliant beam of light cut through the gloom.

"Come, Horatio," he whispered.

SILENTLY, THEY moved along the passageway, which led toward the rear of the house. They came to a door. Leander opened it and flashed the rays of his light about. It was a storage room of some sort. Dust lay thick upon everything.

Shutting the door, Leander continued on down the passage. At the end was a second door. It opened into a furnace room with an ancient hot-air heating plant, and beyond was visible the black opening of the coal bins.

With only a cursory glance around, they continued on their way. The next room of the basement was a laundry. But it had long been unused. The enameled tubs were dusty, the small gas range for heating the sadirons covered with rust. Leander brought the light to rest on a door at one side of the room.

"That must lead upstairs," he murmured. Horatio nodded.

Step by step, careful to prevent any loose board from creaking, they mounted the stairs into the kitchen. Here Leander spent a longer time, peering into the cupboards and even swinging open the doors of the big ice chest and gazing within. He placed his lips close to Horatio's ear.

"No sign of any food in the place. Nobody's been living here for a long time. That's why they served Miss Chauvenet in her room, instead of the dining room. Brought that tray in from outside."

The butler's pantry was of good size. High on the wall along both sides were china closets, filled with stacks of china and glassware. Everything was in perfect order, arranged in neat and precise piles and rows.

At the far end of the pantry was a swinging door, and in the middle of the upper panel a small glass window, not more than three inches square. Once upon a time, it had enabled the servants to observe the progress of the meal they were serving.

Leander tip-toed forward, placed his face against the glass.

An instant later he drew back; then he reached out and seized Horatio's arm in a fierce clutch. Snapping off his flashlight, he drew Horatio to his side.

"Look!" he breathed.

Horatio peered through the little window. He found himself looking into the dining room. It was almost in darkness, except for a ghostlike glow of many colors that entered through a stained glass window above a huge mahogany sideboard.

In the center of the room was a large oval dining table. Three chairs were drawn up to it, a fourth was pushed back a little way. The chairs at the table were occupied by three men.

For a long moment Leander and Horatio stood there, undecided just what to do next. Then Leander again placed his face close to the little window and stared into the dining room. A beam of bluish light from the stained glass was falling directly on the man who was facing the entry door.

"Gracious!"

Leander pushed the door open swiftly, stepped into the room. Horatio was hard on his heels, and as he released the door, it swung closed with a noisy swish. But none of the figures at the table moved. Leander took a step forward, stopped. For a moment he seemed stunned. But at last he turned to Horatio, and when he spoke there was stark horror in his tone.

"Dead! They're all dead, Horatio!"

IN AWED silence, Leander and Horatio stared at the grisly scene before them. The uncanny colored glow from the great stained glass window added to the macabre picture of the three corpses, sitting as if alive at a festive board.

"A banquet of death," Horatio said softly.

"Not a banquet," Leander amended. "Merely a drinking bout." He pointed to the table.

Before each of the dead men was an amber wine goblet. At the unoccupied place, where the chair was pushed back, was a fourth one. And beside it stood a bottle.

Leander stepped close to the table, peered into the glass. It was empty. He flashed his light on and turned it toward the floor. As it came to a rest on a broad dark stain on the thick rug, he smiled grimly.

"The murderer sat here," Leander murmured. "He didn't touch his drink. He poured it on the floor."

"Poison?"

"Quick poison." Leander picked up the bottle gingerly, squinted at the label. "Peach brandy! A strange beverage to—" He stopped, lifted the empty goblet and sniffed it lightly.

Horatio was watching him curiously.

"Clever! My word—a clever fiend," Leander muttered.

"Why clever, Leander?"

"What, Horatio, is the most deadly poison you can name off-hand?"

Horatio thought a few seconds. "Hydrocyanic acid."

"Right. Sometimes called prussic acid. And one of its most distinguished characteristics is its odor. The odor of peaches. Do you see, Horatio?"

"By gad! In peach brandy, the odor of the poison would never be noticed."

"Certainly, Horatio. The perfect way to administer it to the victims."

He replaced the bottle on the table. Then with his handkerchief, he carefully wiped the spot on the neck where he had grasped it, and also the stem of the goblet he had lifted.

For a moment then, Horatio and Leander stood looking at the three gruesome forms in the chairs.

The man who had been facing the pantry door was sitting almost bolt upright, one hand outstretched with the lifeless fingers closed about the stem of his goblet. His glazed eyes were wide-open, staring. A batwing collar with a bow tie encircled his neck, and where his coat was open was visible a waistcoat with black and red horizontal stripes.

"The butler," Horatio said.

The man next to him was clutching the edge of the table with both hands. Apparently, he had suffered a brief agony before the swift poison stilled his heart. His head was dropped forward. A burly man with coarse black hair and a fat nose with flaring nostrils. From the position of the body, he might have been deep in his cups and sleeping off the ill effects of drinking too heavily.

The third was sitting up. His hands were in his lap and beneath tilting eyebrows his eyes were closed. Even in the dim light his peculiar yellowish-tan complexion was noticeable.

"Good God, Horatio!"

"What is it?"

"That's the man who tried to abduct Miss Chauvenet!"

UNCERTAIN WHAT they might come upon next, but prepared for anything, the brothers Jones began a room-by-room search of the big and gloomy mansion. From the first floor to the fourth, where the servants' quarters were situated, they made a noiseless cautious way. They peered into closets, looked everywhere for a trace of the mysterious poisoner or a clue to his identity.

They found nothing, not even Eloise Chauvenet's luggage. So far as they could determine, the premises were deserted, except for the three dead men.

At last, Horatio and Leander returned to the first floor, to the library, the room in which Eloise Chauvenet had conversed with the bearded man, who had posed as her Uncle Henri. It was as she had described it, austere, filled with heavy pieces of furniture and lined with glass-doored bookcases.

Leander ran his flashlight over some of the titles. There were sets of standard and classic authors in morocco bindings. But one entire group of cases was filled with volumes devoted to religious subjects, ancient and modern. Some of them, Leander noted, bore titles that showed they were concerned with Dionysian and Eleusinian mysteries.

He shrugged faintly, dropped into a chair at the big library table. "A trap, Horatio. Just a trap."

Horatio looked puzzled. Leander explained.

"You must have noticed that the house shows every sign of not having been occupied for some time. Perhaps several months."

"Yes."

"The hardware on the front door, however, has been recently polished. The hallways, this room, and the rooms which Miss Chauvenet occupied have been cleaned, the dust covers removed from the furniture. Also the dining room, That was done so that Miss Chauvenet might get a first impression that her uncle was still living here.

"But this—let us call it a gang for convenience—moved here temporarily and for only one purpose. So Miss Chauvenet would walk right into their clutches."

"And where are they now?"

Leander made a little gesture. "Who knows? But we must find out, if we hope to save the life of Henri Chauvenet. I'm satisfied of that."

"It may be too late already."

Leander said nothing for a long time. He sat slumped down a little in the big chair, his eyes half shut in thought. It was Horatio who finally broke the silence.

"The killer may come back."

Leander shook his head. "No. I thought of that, too, but it's not likely. The killer made no effort to remove the bodies. That means he expected the house to remain closed, maybe for months, and this was as good a place as any to hide them."

"But, Leander, you forget that the poisoner may have been the man who posed as Henri Chauvenet. If he knew Miss Chauvenet had escaped wouldn't he expect her to go to the police and bring them here?"

"By gad, Horatio, that sounds reasonable." A sudden look of alarm spread across his face. He snapped to his feet. "Unless he felt certain he'd soon have her in his power again."

Leander walked swiftly across the room to a small table, on which rested a telephone. He lifted the receiver. A faint buzzing informed him that the phone was still connected. He put his finger in the dial holes and started to call a number. But he never moved the dial. A slow knowing smile touched his mouth and he placed the receiver on the hook.

"No," he said, almost to himself. "We won't need the police." He turned briskly to Horatio. "Come! We'll search the bodies, and then leave this awful place."

From the library, they made their way back along the hall to the dining room. Leander opened the door and entered. The next second he gave a gasp of surprise.

The man with the tilted eyebrows was gone!

LEANDER AND Horatio stood in stunned silence for a brief moment. Then down in the basement a door slammed. The sound was faint, but unmistakable. Instantly Leander turned and ran through the hall toward the front door of the house. Horatio followed.

Boldly, they dashed out the main entrance, and looked up and down the street. In the Fifth Avenue direction were several pedestrians; from the east, a taxicab was approaching. But nothing that might be taken for a man bearing a corpse, or a vehicle in which he might take it.

"Damn!" Leander exploded.

"We'd better go back in. Perhaps the door slam was a ruse."

"No matter. We've got to get Miss Millard and Miss Chauvenet first. You get the big car. I'll meet you at the office in an hour. Go to Miss Millard's apartment and pick them up as soon as possible." He turned, without waiting for Horatio to speak, and swung down the street.

Horatio hailed the cab that had reached him by now.

A little later, he drove a large black sedan from a garage on the upper East Side.

His first stop was in front of a modest apartment building on Eighty-second Street. He took the elevator to the eighth floor, walked down the hall and rang the bell of an apartment at the rear. A white-haired woman with a pleasant face answered.

"How do you do, Mr. Jones," she said cordially at sight of Horatio.

"How are you, Mrs. Millard?"

A sudden look of anxiety appeared. "What—what's wrong?" she asked.

He smiled reassuringly. "Nothing. Nothing at all. I only want to speak to Janet."

"Janet?"

He nodded. "Just for a minute."

"Why, Janet isn't here. Isn't she at the office?"

Horatio's heart sank. He could feel a cold sweat breaking out on his forehead, which he hoped Mrs. Millard wouldn't notice. He forced a smile. "Oh, yes she was at the office," he said, keeping his voice calm with an effort. "But we had to send her on a short trip out of town. A little matter of business. We had more instructions to give her. I hoped she might have stopped here on the way to the station."

With a feeling of relief, he saw that his explanation seemed to have quieted Mrs. Millard's apprehension.

"No, she didn't stop here. But if she does, I'll say you want to see her."

"Thank you."

"Will she be gone long?"

"She should be back tonight," Horatio lied smoothly. "If not, she'll probably wire you. She's in a—a—Asbury Park."

But as Horatio hurried back to his car, he told himself that unless he was mistaken, there was a slim chance only that Janet Millard would return to her mother's side tonight. Or ever—unless he and Leander could do something, fast. For Horatio was sure of one thing. The sinister gang who had taken possession of Henri Chauvenet's house, in order to capture his niece, and who, in all probability, had killed three men, had struck once more. Somewhere between the Flatiron Building and East Eighty-second Street, the two girls had been seized. Where were they now?

He drove quickly back to his office. When he put his key in the door and opened it, a folded sheet of paper caught his eye. It was lying on the floor, as if it might have been pushed over the jamb.

Horatio picked it up, unfolded it, read its brief message in pencil.

> Death is the only reward of those who interfere with the Devil's Dozen.

CHAPTER FOUR
THE DEVIL DIES TONIGHT

IT WAS well along in the afternoon, when Horatio and Leander, in their big sedan, headed out of the city on the Albany Post Road. Their destination was the hamlet of Fox's Glen, in the Catskill Mountains of western Greene County.

As they drove up the shore of the Hudson River the sky began to cloud up. By the time they reached Bear Mountain Bridge, night was beginning to come on, and a fine drizzle had set in.

At the town of Catskill, where they left the river and pointed back into the hills, the rain stopped. But in its place came fog, a thick yellow blanket that obscured the sides of the road.

The tiny particles of moisture reflected back the rays of the headlights and made driving difficult. Their progress was slow. It was only a little before midnight when they crept into the small cluster of houses and stores that was Fox's Glen.

Horatio stopped the sedan in front of the general store, and Leander got out.

Three men looked up with curiosity as he entered. One, a tall man with scraggly gray hair and steel-rimmed glasses was behind the counter, and obviously the proprietor. The other two appeared to be farmers. One sat on a cracker box; his companion leaned against the store counter.

Leander smiled apologetically. "How do we get to the Chauvenet estate?"

The two rustics exchanged glances. The man with the glasses jerked up his head and peered down his long nose at Leander.

"The Chauveny place?"

"If you please."

The proprietor squinted. "Well," he finally said, "I can tell you just exactly how to get there." He gave his head a doleful shake. "But, mister, if I was you, I'd not go messing around that neck of the woods at night."

Leander stared at the long proprietor with an air of surprise. "Is it—dangerous?"

"For a fellow your size, I'd say it might be right dangerous."

Leander gave a nervous cough. "My word! I—I'm afraid I don't quite understand. Why should it be dangerous to go to the Chauvenet estate?"

The man sitting on the cracker box answered. "What Zeb means is that they don't have no welcome mat out up there."

There was a moment of impressive silence. Finally, Zeb leaned over the counter and waggled a bony finger in front of Leander's face. "Mister," he said solemnly, "I don't know what your business is. But if it makes it necessary for you to go up there to Chauveny's, you'd better change your business. There's strange goings-on there, since you happened to ask me."

"Perhaps you'd tell me—that is—I suppose I don't understand," Leander faltered.

Zeb appeared to hesitate, but finally he said: "This here Chauveny place—I remember when it was built about thirty year ago—ain't been open for a long time. But a while back, it was opened up again. Chauveny, himself, opened it, they tell me. There's a lot of other men up there, too. In the old days, Chauveny used to come down here to the village right often and was real friendly. But now he's made it plain as the nose on your face he don't want anybody bothering him or his friends. They got men guarding the place," he added.

"Guards?"

"Yes, sir! About a week ago, Bud Peeler's boy and some of his pals decided to take a peek in. They skinned over the fence and was going for the house, when up pops three men. Bud's boy and the rest started to run. These men begun shooting at 'em. They got away, but Bud got hit in the arm. He can't do nothing about it, because he was trespassing, wasn't he?"

"Yes," Leander conceded. "How do we get to the Chauvenet estate?"

Zeb and the two loafers looked at the meek Leander aghast. "Well, I declare!" Zeb burst out. He shook his head ominously. "If you insist on going up there, all right. But don't say I didn't warn you. Keep right on this road in front till you come to the fork. Then, take the right-hand road. About a mile down you cross a bridge over Beaver Creek and almost right off there's a road off to the right again. You go up that—it's every foot uphill—and you'll come smack up against the main gate. 'Bout three miles from here, all told."

AS THE big sedan crawled forward through the dense fog which enfolded them like a ghastly yellow pall, Leander repeated to Horatio the substance of his conversation in the general store at Fox's Glen.

"Means we can't drive all the way," Horatio said.

"Exactly, We'll have to walk."

Leander put his hand into the pocket of his coat and pulled out his gun. He spun the cylinder, reassured himself that it was ready for use, then slipped it back into his pocket.

They came to the fork, and Horatio eased the car into the right-hand road. It was slow going. Only by constant vigilance did Horatio keep from getting off the course and into one of the ditches that lined it. Beyond the bridge, he stopped.

"Hadn't we better leave the car here?"

"Yes, Horatio."

Leander got out, groped around in the fog till he found a place where they could run the car to one side and park it.

As they toiled slowly up the winding road that led to the Chauvenet estate, the fog thinned somewhat.

Suddenly, a vagrant gust of wind rolled apart the bank of mist. For a few seconds, they had a clear glimpse ahead, before the fog again closed in about them. Leander, who was in the lead, glided to the side of the road, drawing Horatio after him with a quick gesture.

The tall wrought-iron gates, flanked by lofty stone columns, were barely fifteen feet away. And in that swift moment, when the fog was swept aside, Leander made out the blurred figure of a man.

He was standing with his back to the gates and facing down the road toward them. A tall man, his hat pulled low over his face, his body protected from the wetness by a coat that came almost to his ankles.

Breathless, Leander waited with a warning hand on Horatio's arm. Had they been noticed? It seemed impossible that he could have failed to see them. Yet no sound came from in front, no menacing form emerged from the mist.

Leander began inching forward with his pistol leveled. Horatio was on his heels. The soaked grass of the roadside made their movements noiseless. Five feet—ten, they advanced, their eyes straining to pierce the yellow-murk. With a few quick strides, Leander covered the remaining distance to the gates.

"Don't move!"

Leander jammed the muzzle of his revolver hard on the tall figure before him. There was no answer, no move. With his free hand, he reached out and touched the man, then pushed up his hat. He gave a quick, low gasp.

"The light, Horatio! Hurry!"

A tiny beam shot from Horatio's pencil flash. It fell full on the man's face, a horrible face, in which the eyes seemed to be popping from their sockets. The mouth was half open, and out from between the parted lips protruded a black and swollen tongue.

"Strangled to death!" Leander breathed.

A HASTY examination explained why the corpse was standing upright. The strangler evidently had come upon his victim from behind, reaching through the iron bars of the gate at which he was standing guard. Around the dead man's neck was a stout cord, and this was drawn through the grillwork and securely tied. The instrument of death was supporting the body.

Horatio laid a probing hand upon the purple cheek. "Hasn't been dead long. Still warm."

Once more in the clammy fog, Leander felt his way along till he came to where the gates joined together. He found a massive knob, tried it, and to his relief discovered that the gates were unlocked.

Inside was a gravel driveway. Moving to one side until they reached the yielding turf, they started forward in the direction where Leander had surmised the house was. They advanced with greatest caution, pausing from time to time to listen.

Above lay a thick canopy of foliage from the trees which lined the drive. Beneath it, the fog was exceptionally dense. But presently they came to a point where the trees ended, and through the ghostly gloom ahead, they saw a dozen or so yellow blurs.

"Lighted windows," Leander breathed.

"Do we go into the house?"

"We do, Horatio."

They resumed their advance, guided now by those furred gobs of light, like great gold eyes watching them through the mist. And as they drew nearer to the house, the fog itself seemed to take on a different character, to be less opaque.

Leander stopped abruptly. Horatio, following just behind, almost bumped into him. He caught a low warning hiss from his brother, as Leander placed his lips close to his ear.

"There's someone right ahead."

They waited with straining eyes. Leander, who had sensed rather than seen a crouching form alongside a clump of shrubbery, began to think that his taut nerves might have deceived him. And then, like a gray specter, something floated between them and the lighted windows. A second afterwards, the phantom appeared in front of another window and was gone.

"What was it?" Horatio's whisper was barely audible.

"A man—I think."

At that instant, from somewhere off to the left, came a brief shrill scream of agony. It ended, as suddenly as it had broken out, in a ghastly choking gurgle.

Leander paused in indecision. The fog had echoed and reechoed the horrible cry, and it was impossible to tell exactly where it had come from. But there could be no mistaking the nature of the sound. It was the wild outburst of someone already in the paroxysm of violent death.

Leander cursed, sprang forward blindly. Almost without thinking, he chose the direction the mysterious gray form had taken. Fighting for a foothold on the slippery grass, he plunged ahead. Horatio was right in his tracks.

His foot struck an object on the ground, and he tumbled headlong. As he scrambled to his feet, shaken but uninjured, Horatio was beside him.

"Look—look, Leander!" he gasped.

"Where?"

"By the bushes! You tripped over it!" Leander peered intently. They were standing near the house. From one of the windows poured forth a prism of yellow light; it appeared almost to have substance, to be solid, as it cut through the fog. And where it ended on the lawn, the feet and ankles of a man were plainly discernible, sticking out from beneath a mass of shrubbery.

Before Leander and Horatio could start to investigate, the awful quiet was broken again. But this time the sound was not so loud. It was a low maniacal laugh. In the fog its direction was elusive, and immediately it was followed by a voice, hoarse and grating.

Like the voice of doom, came to their ears the words: "The devil dies tonight!"

CHAPTER FIVE
MURDER MANSION

ON HANDS and knees, Leander crawled beneath the shrubbery. For a few seconds Horatio caught the tiny glow of his flashlight. Then, Leander reappeared. He jumped to his feet, seized Horatio by the arm.

"We'd better get away from here!" he panted.

Not until they had retreated a considerable distance from the house, where the ominous yellow eyes formed by the windows were barely visible, did Leander offer any explanation. When he decided they had reached a point of temporary safety, he stopped and whispered: "Didn't want to talk while we were so close to that light from the window."

"What about the man?" Horatio asked.

"Dead! Blood was pouring from his throat."

"Good Lord!"

"Had a knife clear through it," Leander continued. "That's what choked off his cry."

They were silent then for a bit, appalled by the phantom horror that was roaming the grounds of this lonely mountain estate and striking in the fog. At length, Horatio said in an undertone: "The devil dies tonight! Good God! What does that mean?"

"My word, Horatio, I wish I knew," Leander murmured. "I expect that scream and crazy laugh may bring somebody from the house to investigate. It must have been audible indoors."

They remained watchfully waiting for a long time. But no indications that the death shriek and the mad cry of the phantom voice had been heard came from the house. No doors opened, no sounds of commotion within those lighted precincts fell upon their listening ears.

As Leander stared speculatively at the glowing windows that marked the country house of Henri Chauvenet, he wondered if those walls hid Eloise Chauvenet and Janet Millard? Or their dead and mutilated bodies? And what of Henri Chauvenet? Was he dead or alive? Had he been following a blind trail in coming up here to this mountain retreat in the Catskills on this dismal night?

Leander doubted it. The strangled guard at the gate, the man beneath the bushes with the dagger in his throat—both were signposts on a warm and bloodstained trail.

And yet, Leander asked himself, were not these dead men here on the grounds members of the murderous band which had abducted Eloise and Janet? If so, who was so brutally killing them, and for what reason?

Finally he touched Horatio lightly on the shoulder. His voice was hard, determined, far different from its usual apologetic softness. "Come—we're going in!"

Slowly, under Leander's guidance, they circled the building till they had reached a point in the rear. It was a brick house, of three stories, a square solid-looking house, with an air of stolid respectability about it.

There were no lights at the back. But after a little time, they managed to locate a door which opened onto a small porch, hardly more than a glorified stoop.

While Horatio stood watch, Leander tip-toed up the short flight of steps. He tried the door. It was securely fastened. For the second time that day, he drew forth the little black case with its assortment of oddly shaped tools and began to pick the lock. It took him but a minute or two. He opened the door a crack, then soundlessly shut it again and returned to Horatio's side.

"Wait here, Horatio," he said softly.

"You're going in?"

"Yes."

"Hadn't we better stay together?"

"No. If anything happens to one of us, the other will still be able to carry on. Keep your eyes open."

INSIDE THE house, Leander risked a brief flash of his light. He was in the kitchen, a big room, with two windows in the far wall and two on the left. All were closed. In the center was a large table, and on it were half a dozen bottles.

Leander picked one up, examined it swiftly. "Pol Roget 1906," he murmured to himself. "One of the best vintage years."

And in the second before he snapped off the light, he noted two things. The labels were old and stained, as if from moisture, and about the necks of the bottles clung a few shreds of cobweb.

Replacing the bottle, carefully, he crossed to one of the doors in the far wall and cautiously opened it. Beyond all was dark, but another quick flash of light revealed a small hallway, at the other end of which was a closed door. At the bottom was a thin line of yellow. Whatever lay beyond was illuminated.

Little by little, he eased the second door open and peered through the crack. He was looking into the main entrance hall, leading to the front of the house. He could make out the balustrade of the stairway, and near the stairs a couple of arched doorways, one on the right and one on the left. Both were hung with heavy portieres.

Leander's hand darted into his pocket and came out with his pistol. He opened the door wide, stepped through and closed it noiselessly behind him. He waited then, listening, alert. Only one sound broke the tomblike silence of the house. It was the regular tick-tick of a pendulum clock somewhere ahead. Probably on the stair landing, he decided.

He started forward and had taken only a few steps, when a voice, low, threatening, came from the stairs just above him.

"Drop that gun! And stick 'em up!"

The fingers of Leander's right hand relaxed; the gun dropped to the floor. It made only a soft thud, as it struck the heavy carpeting of the hallway. Hands held high, Leander waited for the next move of his unseen foe. He heard footsteps, and then a man appeared around the foot of the stairway. He was holding an automatic before him.

"Who are you?" he demanded, coming to a stop before one of the archways.

He was a short man, with glittering dark eyes and a bristling black mustache.

"The name is—Jones," Leander said.

The man with the gun frowned blackly.

"Jones, huh?"

"Yes. Jones—just Jones," Leander repeated evenly.

"Well, Jones," the other man snarled, "come here! And if you can't explain what you're doing in this house, you'd better start saying your prayers!"

There was no mistaking the deadliness in the tone, as well as the words. Leander started forward slowly, and on his face was a funny little smile, disarming and apologetic. His customary mask of meekness, however, was hiding a deep chagrin that he had walked into this fix, more than any feeling of fear.

He had taken only a couple of steps, when his alert glance caught a gentle movement of the portieres. A faint swaying. And almost immediately, the heavy drapes were forced out roughly. There was a loud crack, sickening in its violence.

The man with the gun gave a spasmodic grunt, collapsed heavily to the floor. His pistol rolled from his hand.

Instantly, Leander wheeled, took two swift steps and picked up his own weapon. He sprinted down the hallway in the direction his rescuer had gone. Somewhere a door slammed, a second before he burst through the portieres.

He was in a long, comfortably furnished room, obviously the living room. It was brilliantly lighted. But there was no one in it.

He stood still for a moment, looking around. He could see no place where anyone might conceal himself. But at the rear of the room was a door, and recalling the slam he had just heard, he knew that his mysterious rescuer had made his escape in that direction.

His rescuer? This time, yes, Leander told himself. But remembering the strangled guard at the gate, the corpse beneath the bushes, he was far from certain that he had not been saved only temporarily from the mysterious killer who had struck through the portieres. The next attack might be on him.

He walked back to the man in the hallway, bent over. The blow that had felled him had been delivered with terrific force. The back of the fellow's skull was dashed in; blood was welling out upon the floor in an ugly crimson pool.

And then Leander saw the murder instrument. It was lying beneath the drapes, where the murderer had dropped it. A heavy iron poker with an ornate brass handle. A quick survey of the living room disclosed that it was part of the fire-place set there.

WALKING TO the wall, Leander snapped an electric switch. The living-room lights went out. Apparently the phantom slayer was familiar with the layout of the house. But in the darkness this advantage would be more or less neutralized; there would be less chance that he could make one of his deadly and unexpected assaults.

Stealthily, feeling his way, Leander started toward the door at the back of the living room. He was not hoping to find the killer beyond it. He was bent on quite a different mission, for he had suddenly interpreted the meaning of the cobwebs on the empty champagne bottles.

Ready in every nerve and muscle to meet an attack, Leander groped his way through the darkness. He made slow headway. But eventually he had progressed through a dining room, pantry, and back once more into the big kitchen. He located one of the two doors on the left of the rear entrance.

Unwilling to chance even a momentary flash of his light, he opened it in the dark. He put his foot out and felt around cautiously.

"Stairs," he murmured to himself. "But leading up."

He shut the door and moved to the one beside it. This time he found what he wanted. A flight of steps going down into the basement, and as he shut the door and started to descend, he caught a feeble glow beneath.

At the bottom, he located the source of the glow. It came through an open doorway from a room beyond. Step by step, he moved forward.

In the second room, a single light bulb hung from the ceiling. As he entered, a faint breeze fanned his face. It was cool, damp, and bearing a sweet odor of decay, which brought an odd smile to his pressed lips. He crossed quickly to a half-open door, passed through and found himself in another lighted room. It was a vegetable cellar, with huge bins lining the walls, and above them shelves for holding preserves.

But what caused him to breath a trifle more rapidly, take a firmer hold on his pistol, was a massive door of oak. It had wrought-iron hinges and a ponderous lock. On either side were heavy cleats, into which an oaken cross-bar could be dropped.

Before this stout portal, Leander came to a halt. He brought his light into play for a moment, directing its beam at the hinges. Both of them had been recently oiled.

He gave the oak door a tentative tug. It yielded easily and he gradually pulled it open. Before him stretched a long tunnel-like passage with an arched ceiling. It was barely high enough for a man of average height to walk erect, and extended straight ahead for about a hundred feet. At intervals, dim electric lights were suspended from the top.

He paused. Faintly there came to his ears the sound of voices.

With the tread of a panther, Leander moved down the tunnel. It was built of large stones, roughly hewn, and covered with green mold and fungus growths. The air was dank and redolent with that sweetish decaying odor, which had caused him to smile when he had first smelled it.

The voices grew louder. He could catch an occasional word now and then. His progress became slower and slower, till he was scarcely creeping.

He came finally to a point where the tunnel made a right-angle turn. For a long while, he waited there, his ears tuned to hear the conversation which was coming from around the bend. The speaker's voice was vibrant, deep, and he spoke with a cultivated accent. But beneath was an undercurrent of vicious intensity, a thinly coated hatred and threat.

"Tonight you sign! The time for compromise is over!"

Leander pressed against the slimy wall of the tunnel and wormed forward till he could see around the turn. He stiffened, and instinctively his right hand with the gun in it came up. Almost immediately, however, he changed his mind and slid back out of sight.

The glimpse he had had around the bend revealed that the tunnel ended in an arched doorway. Beyond lay a vast stone chamber with a vaulted ceiling—an old-world wine cellar such as one would never expect to find on this side of the Atlantic. Great wooden casks and butts were ranged along the sides. In the dim shadows at the back were tiers of racks, filled with bottles tilted neck down to keep them from "corking."

In the middle of this huge wine vault was a long refectory table. Chairs were arranged around it. The ones at the near end were occupied by six men, but Leander had given them only momentary notice for his stunned gaze had been fascinated by three figures at the far end of the table.

The middle one was an elderly man with a gray beard. On his left sat Eloise Chauvenet. On his right, Janet Millard. All three were tightly bound to the chairs they were occupying.

CHAPTER SIX
SATAN'S CELLAR

H ARDLY DARING to breath, Leander listened as the speaker with the deep voice continued. "You will sign the necessary papers which will enable me to convert all your security holdings into cash. Also the securities of your niece."

"So that you may steal them." The voice was bitter, with a faint French accent, and Leander knew it belonged to Henri Chauvenet.

"Not steal. Merely a contribution to the Cult of the Devil's Dozen."

"And if I refuse?"

"I have told you before—you die. And with you, your niece and this young lady who has had the misfortune to meddle in our affairs."

This time Henri Chauvenet's tone was defiant. "Well, Delfax—or whatever your right name is—I do refuse!"

"Think carefully. It is not a pleasant death I plan. You shall die in the winepress. All three of you."

Leander's eyes grew dark, his hand tightened on his pistol. In all his years of dealing with murder, he had never heard anyone promise it with such casual ruthlessness.

The man whom Chauvenet had referred to as Delfax continued. "Your fate will never become known. We shall close this wine vault—which you so conveniently provided when you built this lovely estate—with masonry. You will rest in a tomb that will never be discovered."

"By God! You are a devil!" Henri Chauvenet burst out.

Delfax chuckled. "Exactly. The Devil of the Devil's Dozen. And I have planned well. I knew of your interest in strange cults—and so I schemed long and carefully to awaken your interest in a cult that I devised for no other purpose than the one I have just mentioned. Do you think it was only by chance that we encountered each other in the Public Library, where you were pursuing your researches?"

"How do we know that you won't kill us anyway?" Eloise Chauvenet asked.

"My dear young lady—you don't! Indeed, it might be a better idea to dispose of you all. I bear a strong resemblance to your uncle. In some quarters I am taken for him. A bit of carefully executed forgery—and we have accomplished our purpose!

"In that way, we would get the real estate, too. As it is, we are leaving you the real estate investments."

Abruptly Delfax dropped his casualness and became brisk and efficient. "I will give you," he said, "just five minutes to agree to sign!"

LEANDER CONSIDERED. Something had to be done at once. He was armed, but there were six men in the other room. He could steal in, take them by surprise, cover them with his pistol and release Chauvenet and the girls. And yet he knew that as one against six, even though armed, he would be taking a chance.

He decided too much was at stake for needless risks, determined to get Horatio. Five minutes allowed ample time for him to leave this house of violence and return with his brother. Together they could well handle the six members of the Devil's Dozen there in the wine vault.

He turned on noiseless feet and glided back toward the entrance to the tunnel. With a sudden hollowness in the pit of his stomach, he saw that the great oaken door which guarded the entrance was shut. He distinctly remembered that he had left it ajar.

He reached it, pushed gently, then more firmly. But it refused to yield, and Leander knew that his worst fears were realized. He was trapped in this dank underground passageway. And if Henri Chauvenet, Eloise and Janet were to be saved from a horrible death, he must accomplish their rescue alone.

Before he could turn from the door, a snarling voice came from behind. "Up with your hands!"

Leander's pistol clattered to the stone floor of the tunnel. His hands moved slowly above his head, and a funny little twisted grin flickered for a second on his face. Then his customary mask of apology and self-effacement returned.

Something hard was pressed against his back, and the snarling voice spoke again. "Turn around!" A prod from the gun in his back emphasized the order.

Leander turned, but he was unable to see his captor, who moved round behind him. Propelled by repeated and painful jabs, Leander was forced to walk down the tunnel, around the bend and into the wine vault.

At his entrance, Eloise Chauvenet gave a little cry. Janet Millard stared with eyes that were wide with surprise and alarm. Five men jumped to their feet. And one of them had a pointed gray beard, glowing dark eyes, and large and tapering ears that had no lobes. Leander knew instinctively he was Delfax, the Devil of the Devil's Dozen.

"What's this, Prontius?" Delfax demanded. He fixed his cruel eyes on Leander.

"I caught him. At the tunnel door. He was just sneaking out," the man behind Leander said.

"Good. Very good!" Delfax spoke suavely, but there was no mistaking the threat that lay beneath his words. "And how did you get in here?" he demanded.

"I'm afraid I walked in," Leander said with a wry grimace.

Delfax stiffened. "Who are you?"

"Jones—just Jones," Leander murmured.

"Jones—just Jones," Delfax repeated mockingly. "Well, Jones—just Jones, in a minute we're going to change that to Jones—just dead! Take him!"

The men about the table moved forward to obey, but before they could so much as lay a hand on Leander they were suddenly halted. From out of nowhere, yet seemingly from all directions, came that weird maniacal laugh that Leander and Horatio had heard in the fog. The laugh that was connected with the murder at the gate, the murder on the lawn, the murder in the hall.

And instantly floated into the wine cellar that harsh, grating voice.

"The devil dies tonight!"

THE EFFECT on the members of the Devil's Dozen was startling. They stared from one to another, some with their mouths open, the rest with gaping eyes.

But it was Delfax who exhibited the greatest amazement. He took a step forward, then drew back against the wall. Wildly he swept his gaze in all directions. And again it came, that ghastly warning of death.

"The devil dies—"

The rest was lost in a report, a report that resounded in the vaulted room with hideous significance. Delfax gave a cry, pitched forward and his skull cracked on the edge of the great refectory table. But he didn't feel the blow.

Between his eyes was a round hole, from which the blood was welling.

A wisp of smoke drifted from the back of the vault. A second roar filled the wine cellar, and a second member dropped to the floor with a scream of agony.

Then mad panic seized the others. They forgot Leander, they forgot the man and girls bound to the chairs, they forgot everything but this deadly unseen avenger, striking apparently from nowhere. They fled, three fighting, clawing men in a wild scramble to escape through the tunnel.

Leander stooping low, ran after them. And as he left the vault, he swept up from the floor the gun which the man who had captured him had dropped in his terrified flight. Around the corner of the tunnel he dashed, his weapon ready.

The three members of the Devil's Dozen were at the oaken door. They were pounding upon it, screaming and cursing in their effort to get it open. Leander's pistol came up.

"Throw up your hands!"

One of the men let out an insane growl and lunged toward Leander. Leander's pistol poured forth an orange streak, and the fellow staggered back from the impact of the slug. The others raised their hands high.

At the back of the wine cellar was a sudden commotion. Two figures locked together came rolling, writhing down over the wine butts. They struck the floor with a violent crash. One of them groaned, then lay still. The other rose slowly and painfully to his feet.

It was Horatio Jones.

His hat was gone. His gray suit was covered with dirt and cobwebs. But his face was flaming exultantly. The light of battle was in his eyes. He dragged the unconscious figure of his foe into the light of the vault and turned him over.

The evil face of the man with the tilted eyebrows stared up.

IN THE living room upstairs a little later, Horatio and Leander, with Henri Chauvenet, Eloise and Janet, awaited the arrival of the sheriff and his deputies. The members of the Devil's Dozen who were not dead lay tightly bound on the floor nearby.

"… after you went into the house, Leander, I concealed myself nearby," Horatio was explaining. "In a little while, a man came sneaking out the back door. I knew it wasn't you. Too tall. And so I followed.

"He made his way toward one side of the house. Finally, he stopped and I waited. Pretty soon I heard a grating sound, and right after that he vanished before my eyes. I crept forward in the fog and when I came to the place where he was last seen, I found an iron grill, which had been moved from a small round opening on the side of a little hill."

Henri Chauvenet nodded understandingly. "That was the ventilating shaft to the wine cellar. Naturally it was necessary to have some fresh air get into it."

"So I found out," Horatio murmured. "And, my word, what a dirty air shaft. I could hear this fellow moving along ahead of me, and I thought I'd better find out what he was up to.

"A short distance in and there was a faint light ahead. I could make out his figure. As soon as I heard the shooting, I knew it was time to take a hand and went on after him. We tumbled out of the opening at the other end. Luckily I landed on top," Horatio added dryly.

"Dear me, Horatio, you might have been killed," Leander said. He got up and walked over to the recumbent figure of the man with the tilted eyebrows.

"What," he said, "was the idea of trying to kill everybody around the place?"

The man with the tilted eyebrows looked up with sullen eyes. "If you want to know, it was because he tried to poison me with Bayles and Munter. He wanted to get us out of the way, so he'd get all the money. He'd have killed the rest later. But I was onto his scheme and didn't take the poison.

"I played dead dog, till he left, cause I was planning to let him carry out his plan to get the money. You almost caught me at the house, but I heard you coming and slipped back to the table, figuring you'd think I was dead as the others."

"My word," Leander murmured.

"After that, I changed my plan and decided to kill the whole dirty doublecrossing gang. But I wanted to scare hell out of them first. That's why I went around throwing out wild laughs and threats. I thought at first I'd find Delfax in the house. When he wasn't there, I knew he was in the wine cellar. I saw you in the tunnel and shut you in."

"And you'd already found out about the air shaft," Leander suggested.

"Yeah. But I was the only one who knew about it."

"My, my, let's see. Two men died in town. Two on the lawn and one in the house. Delfax and two others in the cellar. We've got three prisoners." He looked at Chauvenet. "That's only eleven. A Devil's Dozen should have twelve, it seems to me."

Chauvenet made a wry face. "I was Number Twelve. But I joined only out of curiosity to see what sort of an organization this Delfax had," he put in hastily.

Leander smiled faintly. "And you found out."

"Only when it was too late—and I've you to thank for my life." He looked up with sudden puzzlement. "How did you happen to decide to come out here?"

"I hope you'll excuse me," Leander replied with a touch of embarrassment.

"Excuse you? For what?"

"Posing as your secretary. When I discovered the phone in your town house was connected, I went to the company and obtained a duplicate bill. There were a number of long-distance calls to Fox's Glen."

"LEANDER," HORATIO asked the next day, when they were back in his office, "how do you suppose Delfax knew Miss Chauvenet had been brought here?"

"The curiosity of the driver who drove us down," Leander replied. "He cruised back to the scene of the crash. Delfax, after he pulled his poisoning, hurried over there and was lucky. He met him and learned what had happened. The driver was most voluble. Then Delfax watched this building and when the girls left, trailed them with some of his gang.

"It was no job for him to snatch them, as I believe it's called, as they were entering Miss Millard's apartment building. Then he tried to frighten us with that note."

Horatio picked up a green slip of paper from his desk. It was a check for ten thousand dollars, signed by Henri Chauvenet.

"What do you think we should do with this?" he asked.

Leander thought a moment. Suddenly he grinned widely. "I believe, Horatio," he murmured, "we should give it to some deserving church organization."

"Any special reason for giving it to a church organization, Leander?"

"My word, yes, Horatio!" Leander exclaimed. "We've chased down one devil. But somebody else will have to keep after the other."

DEATH FROM DOWN UNDER

THEY NEEDED A VACATION
BADLY WHEN THEY STARTED
OUT—THOSE TWO DETECTIVES
EXTRAORDINARY—THE BROTHERS
JONES. BUT THEIR JAUNT WAS
TURNED INTO A HORROR HOLIDAY.
FOR DEATH FROM THE OTHER
SIDE OF THE WORLD STRUCK
BY NIGHT, AND LEFT A GHASTLY
CHAIN OF HEADLESS CORPSES IN
ITS WAKE.

CHAPTER ONE
WEIRD WARNING

MR. LEANDER JONES, senior partner of Jones and Jones, turned his head slightly and let his glance wander out the open window of his private office. It came to rest upon the broad expanse of greenery that was Madison Square in early summer. The vista of trees and shrubbery brought a faraway, mellow expression into his pale blue eyes.

Reluctantly, he removed his gaze from this pleasant prospect and swung around in his chair until he faced his twin brother, seated at a desk across the room.

"A beautiful day, Horatio," he murmured.

Horatio Jones looked up from a sheaf of clippings he was poring over with an air of quiet surprise.

"Why yes, so it is, Leander," he replied.

"Summer is here."

"Why—ah, so it is," Horatio agreed.

"And about this time of year, one is apt to be aware of certain stirrings, certain restless desires," Leander continued dreamily.

A look of alarm flashed over Horatio's smooth ruddy face. He dropped the clippings to the desk and stared at his older brother—older by ten minutes. But Leander appeared to be oblivious to the effect he was creating.

Fascinated with horror Horatio stared.

"Lately, I haven't felt my usual zest in my work," he said softly. "Somehow, the pursuing of the criminal element in our population has lost its fascination. In short, I—"

"Leander!" Horatio interrupted. "Are you sick?"

"Sick? Why no, Horatio."

Horatio's look of alarm suddenly turned to one of horror. "Leander," he faltered, "you—you aren't—in love?"

It was Leander's turn to be startled. For a moment, he was speechless. Then gradually, an odd little smile touched the ends of his lips. He chuckled. And at last he bent back his head and burst into a hearty laugh.

"No, Horatio," he said, when he had regained his composure. "It is not illness. It is emphatically not love. It is only that I have decided you and I both need a vacation."

"A vacation?"

"Exactly! Far from this sordid sphere of crime. Some quiet spot, where there is peace and rest, where we can forget there are such things as violence and death."

Horatio shook his head slowly, dubiously. "It all sounds very pretty, I'll admit. But Leander, you forget—Murder takes no holidays!"

Again Leander chuckled. "No, Horatio, but Jones and Jones do. And they start this afternoon!"

It was characteristic of the brothers Jones that once having determined upon a course of action, they allowed no grass to sprout beneath their feet.

Leander's announcement was made at exactly eleven twenty in the morning. At eleven twenty-one, Miss Millard had been apprised of, but not surprised by, their plans. Nothing that happened in the office of Jones and Jones ever surprised their personable and efficient secretary. At eleven twenty-six, Leander and Horatio were rolling north on Fifth Avenue in a taxicab. Their destination was the bachelor apartment on Central Park South, which they shared.

"Horatio," Leander said, lighting one of the thin black stogies to which both of the brothers were addicted, "I have just been thinking over our impending holiday."

"Yes?" Horatio replied expectantly.

"I have been thinking that we should go to different localities for our vacations."

"You mean—we should separate?"

"Exactly!" Leander nodded between puffs. "We have been together constantly for forty-two years, except such times as the exigencies of our work have drawn us apart. I propose that we now take our vacation in different places. It will be a new experience for both of us. Do you agree?"

Horatio gave the question a brief moment of thought. Then he said, "I am inclined to believe that you are right."

"It will insure that we forget temporarily our work," Leander continued with a dry smile. "Together, we would be sure to be on the alert for some evidence of a hidden crime. Divided, both of us may be able to relax and enjoy ourselves."

"Quite true," Horatio nodded.

"I will not tell you my destination—indeed, I don't know it myself yet. And you keep your vacation spot a secret. That will insure that neither of us will be tempted to get in touch with the other, if some suspicious circumstance should be observed."

"Agreed, Leander!" Horatio exclaimed.

SOME THREE or four hours after the Jones brothers had conceived the plan of going on their holiday without either revealing his whereabouts to the other, Leander approached the ticket window in the Pennsylvania Station. He was wearing a slightly rumpled gray suit and his inevitable brown hat. He set the scuffed black grip he was carrying down on the floor to wait his turn at the window.

There was only one person ahead of him, a man of less than average height, with an Oriental cast of features, yet of a light brown rather than yellow complexion. As the ticket seller pushed a small pile of change through the grill, he raised his eyes and shot a quick appraising glance at Leander. Then he stepped aside and back.

Leander moved forward. From long habit, he, too, unconsciously sized up the brown-skinned man. He noted the dark eyes, faintly slanting, the short and somewhat pugged nose, the thick lips, the coarse black hair, and the small strong hands.

"My word," Leander thought, "a Malay!"

He realized that the ticket seller was looking at him expectantly, waiting for him to make his wants known, and he smiled apologetically.

"I wish to buy a ticket," Leander said.

"Yes, sir. Where to?"

For a moment, Leander seemed to be thinking it over. Then a sparkle appeared in his mild blue eyes. "I believe I'll take one to the same place as your last customer."

"Cornwall, New Jersey?"

"Quite so," Leander nodded. "Cornwall, New Jersey." And he added to himself, "That should be as good a place as any to get a good rest."

The agent raised his hand, extracted an oblong pasteboard from the rack beside him and deftly slipped it under the dating machine. "Two fifty-four," he said, sliding the ticket out to Leander. His manner was crisply impersonal.

Ticket in hand, Leander backed away from the window and looked down for his grip, which he had placed on the floor only a couple of feet from the window. It was gone. And then he noticed, close to the spot where it had been, another grip. It, too, was black and scuffed, and of the same general style as his own.

"My, my!" he murmured. "There seems to have been a mistake made."

He picked up the black grip and looked around. He felt sure that it belonged to the brown-skinned man who had preceded him at the ticket window.

There were scores of people in sight, most of them hurrying to or from trains, but he saw no sign of the Malay. From the concourse, Leander made his way through the waiting rooms, the washroom and restaurants. Nowhere did he catch a glimpse of the man whose traveling bag he was seeking to return in exchange for his own.

With a little shrug, he walked up to the information desk. "At least," he told himself, "I know where he's going. Probably can find him on the train." He addressed the information clerk. "When is the next train to Cornwall, New Jersey?"

The clerk cast a fleeting glance at the big station clock. "You've just missed one. But there'll be another train for Cornwall in half an hour."

"That's splendid. Thank you," Leander murmured diffidently. Outwardly he showed only a mild and self-effacing manner, a manner both the Jones brothers were accustomed to assume. But inwardly he was suffering a decided sense of chagrin. While he had been searching futilely through the big railroad station, the brown-skinned stranger he sought undoubtedly was on board the train for Cornwall. Too late, Leander realized that it would have been more astute if he had inquired about the departing trains first.

He decided there was only one thing left to do. That was to open the grip and see if it didn't contain some clue to the owner's identity. Walking into the men's waiting-room, Leander sat down and placed the grip between his feet.

He snapped up the catches at the ends and tried the lock. It yielded to pressure, and he pulled the grip open. Instantly, a gasp of horror and surprise broke from his lips. In one convulsive movement of his hands, he slammed the grip closed again.

It was seldom that Leander Jones was caught off guard. Under the most perilous circumstances, his air of meekness and self-effacement was generally unshaken. But now he pulled a handkerchief from his pocket with a hand that trembled ever so faintly. He mopped his forehead, caught his breath.

"Good heavens!" he breathed. "What a narrow escape!"

Within the black grip belonging to the Malay, he had beheld a snake, coiled and ready to strike. And in that brief flash he had of this repulsive and terrifying sight, he had recognized it as a deadly spitting cobra.

LEANDER HAD come to the Pennsylvania Station with no definite destination in mind. He was headed for a vacation alone, and he had decided to let the whimsy of the moment dictate his future plans. Now fate, in the form of a native of Malay, had stepped in and already was pointing out the way to this retiring but highly effective man-hunter who was Leander Jones.

Sitting in the crowded waiting room, with the black bag containing the venomous reptile at his feet, Leander gave thought to the situation.

He had asked for a ticket to Cornwall on a sudden impulse, prompted perhaps by a certain curiosity concerning the brown-skinned man. Had the exchange of bags been purely accidental? Or had the Malay heard him ask for his ticket and made the exchange for some sinister purpose? Perhaps with the idea that Leander would open the grip carelessly and suffer a fatal bite, which would prevent him from ever reaching Cornwall.

Why, he asked himself over and over, was the Malay carrying around this poisonous snake? He might be a snake-charmer, a member of some sideshow or carnival troupe. But that explanation somehow failed to satisfy Leander.

Finding no adequate answers to the countless questions that were darting through his mind, he turned his thoughts to what he would best do with the cobra.

"Certainly," he murmured to himself, "it should be killed as soon as possible. And yet—" He half closed his pale eyes. "There's no place here in the station to accomplish that without danger."

He could, he realized, return to his apartment and dispatch the hideous thing. He could even turn it over to the police. The latter course was what anyone else would do under the circumstances. But Leander Jones was in the habit of attending to his own problems without the aid of the authorities.

Suddenly a funny little smile glided across his face.

"Poor Horatio," he thought. "It's too bad he'll not be in on this. But he really needs a rest and vacation."

Leander looked at his watch. Still smiling, he reached down and picked up the black bag and its slimy occupant. As he walked from the waiting room toward the train gates, a close observer would have noticed a certain eagerness in his stride. He was no longer the carefree vacationist, but the shrewd criminologist, the discoverer of hidden murders, convinced in his own mind that he had stumbled onto a menacing mystery.

When the train paused for a few seconds at the tiny station at Cornwall, it was well along in the afternoon. Besides Leander, no other passengers alighted.

Cornwall was town of about a thousand inhabitants, and well beyond the commuting limits from New York. Leander looked about, spotted a dilapidated Ford sedan with a taxi sign affixed to the windshield.

"The best hotel," Leander said, as the driver pulled the door open for him.

The driver grinned. "Ain't but one, Mister. That's the Central House."

"My, my," Leander said. "Then the Central House it must be." He climbed into the taxi, placed the black grip gingerly on the floor, and settled back against the seat with a semblance of a sigh.

CORNWALL'S ONLY hostelry proved to be a large frame structure, its clapboards covered with scabrous gray paint. The clerk, who greeted Leander with a nod and a "howdy," was an elderly man in a collarless shirt. His stubble of beard was the same shade as the hotel. At each corner of his mouth was a brown spot from the chew of tobacco that bulged his cheek.

"A room and bath," Leander said, placing his grip on the floor.

The clerk shifted his tobacco. "We ain't got rooms with no private baths. But there's a bathroom on each floor."

Leander looked apologetic. "That'll do very well for my purposes."

The clerk swung around a dog-eared register. While dipping the pen into the ink, Leander ran his eyes up and down the page before him. He saw that he was the first guest to register in two days. At least, the Malay hadn't come here, unless he happened to be a permanent resident of the place.

When Leander had signed his name, the clerk emerged from behind the desk and picked up his grip. With a funny, amused expression, Leander followed him up a flight of stairs.

"If he knew what he's carrying," Leander thought, "he'd probably swallow that chew of tobacco."

As soon as he was alone, Leander placed the bag on the table. Taking a pocket knife, he carefully cut a series of small holes along the bottom. Then he made his way to the bathroom a short distance down the hall. He locked the door securely behind him, filled the tub with water, and deposited the bag in it.

Not until fully fifteen minutes had passed did he lift the dripping bag from the tub. When all the water had drained out the holes, he wiped it off and returned to his room. Carefully he unfastened the catches and lock. Turning the bag upside down, he eased it open and gave it a quick shake.

Out upon the floor tumbled a forbidding black reptile, still coiled as if to strike. Leander waited. There was no movement on the part of the snake and, still on the alert, Leander bent over to examine it. An instant later, he gave a surprised gasp and picked the repulsive thing up from the floor.

"My word!" Leander said, and then repeated: "My word!"

The careful measures he had just taken had been entirely unnecessary. The spitting cobra had been dead for some time. It had been dead long enough to have been stuffed and modeled into its present menacing attitude.

In the coil of the dead reptile, he noticed a piece of water-soaked paper. Taking pains not to tear it, Leander drew the paper free. He carried it to the window to look it over better. Blurred from the immersion, yet still legible, he saw printed in rough letters the words:

THIS IS YOUR FINAL WARNING!
Death Comes from Down Under

CHAPTER TWO
SIGN OF THE SERPENT

LEANDER PLACED the cryptic threat gently between the leaves of his pocket memorandum book. The stuffed cobra he lifted from the floor and with a faint grimace of repugnance, dropped it back into the black bag, which he shoved beneath the bed. Then he pulled forth one of his thin stogies and contemplatively touched a match to it.

"Death comes from down under," he said softly. "Down under. That's the way Australia and the Malay Archipelago are often described."

This would tie in perfectly with the brown-skinned man who had switched the grips, either accidentally or on purpose. But for whom was the death warning intended? For himself? Leander pulled gently on the stogy. It was possible. He had many enemies, who would delight in having one or both of the Jones brothers scratched from the lists of the living.

Leander clamped his soft brown hat firmly on his head, and, locking the room behind him, started down the tattered carpet of the stairs. The unkempt clerk looked up at him as he entered the lobby.

"Be with us long, Mr. Jones?"

Leander turned his mild blue eyes on the speaker. "Well, that all depends," he said.

"Traveling man, ain't you?"

"Yes," Leander smiled. "You might call me a traveling man." It wasn't the first time by any means that either he or Horatio had been mistaken for knights of the grip. It was the impression they wished to convey—the impression that they were none too successful traveling salesmen, or perhaps underpaid clerks. It furnished an excellent screen behind which they could hide the real nature of their occupation, an occupation that was also their hobby.

From the clerk's desk, Leander strolled across to the door of the dining room. But a hasty glance inside showed him that it echoed the general uncleanliness of the rest of the hotel. He walked out of the lobby and onto the main street of Cornwall.

For a short time, he stood there looking around him. The business part of the town extended along both sides of a concrete motor highway. The dwellings scattered out behind. A lunchroom sign at the next corner attracted his eye, and he headed for it.

It was a small place, a counter with stools, and three tables. But it looked clean, so he pushed open the screen door and entered. Only one other customer was in the place, a man in a chauffeur's uniform, who was sitting at the counter.

LEANDER PERCHED himself on one of the stools and gave his order to the waiter. When the order had been duly shouted through a small window at the rear of the establishment, the waiter sauntered to where the chauffeur was sipping his coffee and leaned his elbows on the counter.

"Kind of tough, Mark, losing a job nowadays," he said.

The chauffeur shrugged, made a little gesture with his opened palm. "I been expecting it for some time."

"That so?"

"Sure," Mark nodded. "Old man Carter's been losing his dough lately."

"He had a lot to lose, eh boy?"

"Plenty—up to about six months ago."

The waiter clucked his tongue against his teeth. "How'd he make it all in the first place? He's never done anything around here. Seemed to be retired."

"Lumber," the chauffeur grunted, shoving his empty cup away and rising to his feet. "Mahogany and teakwood, whatever that is. He used to be down in Australia or Siam, or one of them places. Then he was out around Seattle."

Leander turned his head slightly, his blue eyes seemingly gazing off into space.

"I'll be seeing you!" the chauffeur said, banging the screen door.

The waiter brought Leander's food from the little window. He set it down on the counter, and Leander looked up at him with a faintly puzzled expression.

"Excuse me—that is, I couldn't help hearing what you gentlemen were saying. Seems to me I've heard about this Mr. Carter."

"If you haven't, you must be a stranger around here."

"What's his first name?" Leander asked thoughtfully.

"Dan. Daniel Carter."

"That must be the one. In the lumber business. But I didn't know he lived here in Cornwall." Leander applied himself to his food, as if he had about lost interest in the subject.

"He lives in that big house west of town," the waiter said. "They say it set him back half a million."

"My, my," Leander murmured in a tone of awe.

"Now he's pretty near busted," the waiter added.

Leander merely nodded, and continued with his food. He had learned all he needed for the moment. Daniel Carter, who had made a fortune in mahogany and teakwood in the land of down under, lived in a house that cost half a million dollars on the west edge of town. And now he was virtually broke.

It was almost dark when Leander paid his check and left the restaurant. His first stop after that was at a cigar store a few doors away. As he purchased half a dozen of his favorite stogies, he asked the clerk casually:

"Can you tell me how to get to the residence of Mr. Daniel Carter?"

"Yes, sir," the clerk replied, pointing with his thumb. "Take the first turn to your right down that way, and keep going west. You can't miss it. A big place about half a mile out."

"Thank you. Thank you," Leander said effusively.

AS HE followed the route indicated, he moved with a springy and athletic step. Beneath Leander Jones' rumpled gray suit was a lithe, muscular body in the pink of condition. Often it had fooled unwary antagonists, who imagined he was little to be feared physically.

At the end of a ten-minute walk, he came to a well-trimmed hedge of boxwood. Beyond it and well back from the road, the shadow of a low rambling house was still visible in the fast-fading light. Several windows on the first and second floors were aglow.

He continued along the hedge until he came to an opening, through which passed a driveway with a sidewalk adjoining. He paused for a moment, regarding the place before him. He noted the extensive lawn, sloping gradually up to the house, and the dark patches that marked the trees and shrubs of the landscaping.

He slipped inside the hedge and began a cautious circuit of the grounds, keeping close to the outer limits and sticking to the shadows of the trees as much as possible. Behind the main house, he made out a group of smaller buildings, which he judged were the stables and garage. They were all dark.

When he had almost completed the journey around the estate, seizing every opportunity for concealment, Leander suddenly stopped, tense and motionless. He was on the opposite side of the drive from which he had started, and only some fifty feet from the house.

Up to this time, he had seen no signs of anyone about the grounds. But now he fancied he had caught a movement ahead of him. He remained frozen to the spot, his eyes striving to pierce the gloom that had settled down. For at least five minutes, he stood there.

"Must've been my imagination," he thought. "My word, am I getting jumpy?"

He moved over to the sidewalk which paralleled the drive. When he reached it, without any attempt at concealment, he advanced boldly up to the house, climbed the short flight of steps that led to a broad veranda. The front entrance was brightly lighted. Leander rang the bell.

Almost at once, a porch light overhead was switched on, and the wide front door swung back. In the opening stood a maid, young and buxomly pretty, with a crisp, starched white apron and cap.

"I beg your pardon," Leander said, "but I would like to see Mr. Carter."

The maid looked him over quickly. "Yes, sir. Will you step in, please?"

She held the door open, while he entered a wide hall-way, from which stairs curved in a majestic sweep up to the second story. He observed that the stairs, as well as the floors, were of gleaming dark mahogany. About the hall were scattered Oriental rugs, the colors mellow and rich.

Opening a door on one side of the hall, the maid switched on a light and said:

"Will you wait in here, please. What name shall I give Mr. Carter?"

Leander looked embarrassed. "Jones," he murmured. "Just Jones."

"Mr. Just Jones," she repeated. "Yes, sir."

LEANDER CHUCKLED to himself and sat down on a chair near the door. The maid disappeared into the hallway.

The room into which he had been conducted was of small size, evidently used as a sort of reception room.

Again he was struck by the gleaming mahogany flooring, on which were other luxurious Oriental rugs. But what caught his eye even more was the paneling of the walls, which ran almost to the ceiling. It was of teak, a wood but seldom put to such a purpose in the Occident, he knew.

"Mahogany and teakwood," Leander murmured. He closed his eyes for a few seconds, and an introspective, pensive expression rested on his face. And again he said softly, "Mahogany and teakwood. Cobras—and death from down under."

For a long time, he waited patiently. The house was oddly quiet, and a strange feeling of uneasiness began to steal over him. Leander had an uncanny ability for sensing the presence of danger, and more and more he was beginning to think that this second-sight was warning him now.

A grim set to his lips, he rose at last from the chair. At the same moment, he heard the purr of an automobile turning into the driveway. Stepping silently to the window, he looked out.

Leander watched the headlights glide up to the house entrance. From the front seat of the car, a limousine, a man in chauffeur's uniform sprang out. He was the chauffeur Leander had heard called Mark by the waiter in the restaurant.

He flipped the door of the car open smartly. From the black depths, a girl emerged and moved swiftly up the steps of the veranda. She was cut off from Leander's view too quickly for him to get a good look at her.

As he hurried back to his chair, he heard the front door of the house open, and simultaneously the motor pick-up of the limousine pulling away. Leander fastened his glance on the doorway to the hall. He had only another brief glimpse of the girl as she passed. But it was enough to reveal to him that she was young, of unusual beauty, and wearing some sort of a hat that was cocked at an angle on her red hair.

Her footsteps on the stairs faded away. He sat on the edge of the chair for a while, his hand slowly stroking his chin. Once more that ominous stillness settled on the house.

With sudden grim decision, Leander got to his feet.

Gliding to the hallway, he looked out. Directly across was a wide doorway, and beyond it blackness, except for a prism of light that entered from the hall. At the top of the curving staircase was a light. And beyond the foot of the stairs, at the rear of the hall, he caught the glow from an open door.

A dozen noiseless strides and Leander was within a few feet of it. He placed his back against the wall and, edging forward, looked in. For a second, he was like a man who has turned to ice—motionless, cold. Then he took a quick breath, darted into the room. He moved swiftly to the far side, to a still and ghastly figure, lying on the rich rug.

"My God!" he panted. He dropped to his knees beside the body.

It was the body of a man well beyond middle age. His hair was silver gray, matching a closely clipped mustache. The face was heavy, deep-lined, an imperious and dominating face, even in death. And that he was dead, there could be not the slightest doubt.

Driven deep into the bosom of his dress shirt was a dagger of unusually large size. The shirt, which had once been starchily white, was now red—a ghastly red, a red that had welled up and spread out onto the rug and had crimsoned the dead man's collar and throat.

Some three or four inches of the death blade still protruded. The edges of it were not straight. They were waving, flamelike, serpentine. And Leander saw with a shock of horror that the black handle of the weapon was fantastically carved in the form of a cobra—coiled and ready to strike!

Before he could note anything more, he was startled to his feet. From above had come a cry. A shrill cry of terror, a woman's voice screaming wildly for help.

Leander sprang toward the door!

CHAPTER THREE
COPS AND CORPSES

ALTHOUGH LEANDER and Horatio Jones were identical twins, affecting the same dress to accentuate their physical likeness, and even assuming the same self-effacing, half-embarrassed manner, there were certain underlying differences in their natures.

Leander was a shade more given to introspection and deductive reasoning whereas Horatio was more apt to consider things at their face value, to choose direct action. This was exemplified in the fact that Leander, even though a skillful driver, seldom cared to take the wheel of their automobile when they were together. Horatio, on the other hand, took delight in piloting either their nondescript Ford or their big sedan.

It helped to explain, too, why Leander elected to spend his vacation going where the mood moved him by public conveyance, while Horatio chose to pass his holidays in an entirely different fashion.

And so, at about the time Leander was buying a ticket to Cornwall, which pitched him headlong into the mystery of the stuffed cobra and the murder of Daniel Carter, Horatio was sitting in their apartment carefully scanning the advertisements of vacation resorts in the morning paper.

At last, he tossed the paper aside, got out of his chair and stretched leisurely. His face bore a reminiscent smile.

"I believe," he said half-aloud, "that it will be Atlantic City. Let me see—I haven't been there in seven years, at least. Not since we captured what the press so flamboyantly referred to as the Beast of the Boardwalk. Dear me!"

Walking into his bedroom, he removed a well-worn black traveling bag from the closet. Into it, he packed a number of essentials. And quite from force of habit, at the last moment he took a small automatic out of the dresser drawer and placed it in one of the pockets of the bag.

Leaving the tall apartment building overlooking Central Park, Horatio walked around the corner onto Fifty-eighth Street. A few minutes afterwards, a large black sedan rolled out of one of the numerous garages on that thoroughfare, with Horatio at the wheel.

At a moderate pace, as befitting a man starting on a vacation, he headed south through the traffic of Fifth Avenue.

"Leander was right," he thought. "We both needed a rest. I have a suspicion that I'm going to enjoy Atlantic City."

At Fourteenth Street, he cut over to Seventh Avenue and a short time later was entering the Holland Tunnel. Through Jersey City and on toward Newark, the big car glided smoothly along. Horatio's pale blue eyes were bright with anticipation, his bland face was wreathed in a happy smile.

He was well into Newark, when he became aware of a shrill siren behind him, which was rapidly growing louder. Discreetly he pulled to one side. A police car whizzed past. Horatio subconsciously speeded up as soon as the green roadster was in front of him, and he was only a little distance behind, when he heard a report like a pistol shot come from it. Then it swerved over to the curb and halted.

One of the uniformed occupants sprang out, ran around to the front of the car. He made a sweeping gesture with his arm, and the second policeman joined him. Immediately, the first man stepped out into the street and, after a quick glance back, held up his hand. Horatio put on the brakes and stopped a few feet from him. He jerked open the door of Horatio's sedan and climbed into the seat, while his companion jumped on the running board.

"Had a blowout!" the first man said. "We'll have to use you!"

"Certainly!" Horatio exclaimed, with a quick bob of his head. "Where to?"

"Straight ahead! I'll tell you when to turn! And step on it!"

HORATIO STEPPED on it with an alacrity that snapped his sudden passenger's head back on his neck and all but dislodged the officer who was riding the running board. In a matter of seconds, they were weaving through the streams of vehicles at hair-raising speed.

The uniform on the side of the car was sufficient explanation of their haste. The sedan roared through red lights, past the uplifted hands of traffic police and amid the angrily squealing brakes of crossbound trucks and cars.

"What's happened?" Horatio asked.

"Guess it's a killing."

"Dear me," Horatio murmured. "Murder." His eyes sparkled.

"Radio call," the policeman beside him said laconically. "Turn left at the next."

Horatio took the turn at a speed which caused his companion to catch a quick breath and then gulp violently. They flashed along a narrow street lined with two and three-story buildings, most of them dingy and soot-stained. On the windows were names in Chinese—laundries, chop-suey joints, shops, importing firms, rooming houses.

It was Newark's Chinatown.

Horatio recalled the exodus of Celestials from the Chatham Square district of Manhattan, which had been going on for the last ten years. It had left New York's Chinatown with only a shell of its former glory, or ignominy, to serve as a tourist catcher. It had made Newark the most important and populous Chinese center east of San Francisco.

"Next corner—pull up!" the policeman ordered.

Horatio obeyed. He slid the sedan to a stop that skill-fully nestled it against the curb. The officer on the running board jumped off, dashed around the corner.

"Thanks!"

The door of the sedan burst open and the second police-man took after his partner. Horatio was only a split second behind him. Vacations, Atlantic City—everything, except that a killing, perhaps a murder, had just taken place around the corner had dissolved from Horatio's mind.

The street into which they turned was even dirtier and more squalid, if possible, than the one on which they had parked the car. Halfway down the block, a large crowd was gathered. As he drew near, Horatio saw that it was composed of a medley of Chinese, whites, and negroes.

The two policemen elbowed their way roughly through the motley gathering. Horatio, a guileless smile on his face, was behind them step for step. He passed through the jabbering, drawling, buzzing mob in the wake of his big companions like a skiff being towed by a tugboat.

In front of a vacant two-story building, a couple of blue-coats were keeping a cleared semi-circle with their night-sticks.

"Where is it?" the man who had ridden on the running board of Horatio's car demanded.

"Upstairs, Joe!"

All four of the policemen seemed to be too much occu-pied to notice the small man in the rumpled gray suit and brown soft hat who tagged along into the building.

An abrupt change took place in Horatio's manner. He was no longer mild and self-effacing, but brisk, jaunty, with an air of complete self-assurance. Although he had no more than an inkling of what was on the second floor of this wretched structure, already he was planning his line of action. This new pose was part of it.

Behind his recent passengers, Horatio climbed the creaking steps to the upper story. It was one big room, dusty, festooned with cobwebs, and littered generously with odds and ends of refuse. In front were three windows, at the rear two more. But so dirty were the panes that even in daylight the place had a dim, gloomy atmosphere.

In a corner near the street side were two policemen and two men in civilian clothes. As Horatio and the two additional bluecoats entered, they raised their eyes from the floor and looked at the newcomers. One of the men in civilian clothes, who had been stooping over, straightened up.

"What is it? A killing?" the policeman who had sat beside Horatio asked, as they approached the little group.

One of the men gave a funny sort of laugh. "Take a look, and figure it out for yourself."

"God!" the policeman exclaimed, and then repeated it.

Horatio edged into the circle, looked down at the floor. For a fleeting instant, he felt an acute nausea. But he had seen too many gruesome sights for that sensation to last. And he moved closer to get a better look.

Lying side by side on the grimy floor were two bodies. One was obviously, from his dress, a Chinese. The other was clad in a dark suit of good quality and in good condition, except for the dirt on it. His white hands were neatly manicured.

But both of the dead men were headless!

THE POLICEMAN who had ridden with Horatio spoke up again.

"Where's their heads?"

"You tell us," one of the men in plain clothes, whom Horatio had spotted as detectives, replied.

"My God! Who found 'em?"

"Mulvaney. One of the cops downstairs. He noticed some blood spots on the sidewalk near the front door. Then he looked in and saw some more on the floor. The door was unlocked. He just crashed on in—and found these two stiffs lying up here."

"Know who they are?"

The detective shook his head. "Not yet. I was just starting to frisk the white guy, when you got here." He squatted down on his heels and put a hand in a pocket of the headless cadaver.

The rest of them stood around in silence, while he went through the clothing. The amputation of the heads had been accomplished with a sure stroke; the cut was clean. A guillotine could not have done the job better, Horatio mused.

He glanced down and back toward the stairs. In the dust of the floor, he saw a trail of brown spots. Whoever had brought those grisly relics into this empty building had butchered his victims outside, and a considerable time before the bodies were lugged in. Horatio's speculations were suddenly interrupted by a none too gentle tap on the arm.

"What the hell are you doing here?"

He looked at the speaker, the cop who had stood on the running board of the sedan. At the question, all eyes except those of the detective searching the corpse, were turned on Horatio. He gave a faintly derisive laugh.

"Who me?" he said breezily. "Listen, I'm a reporter. *Daily Mirror.* This is my dish!"

"Oh, yeah? A reporter?" the policeman replied sarcastically. "Where's your police card?"

Horatio shrugged. "Think I'm kidding you? Just a minute!" He walked close to the window. From the inner pocket of his coat, he brought forth a leather billfold. For a few moments, he fumbled around with a bunch of cards it contained, then returned to the policeman.

"Take a look!" he said.

Between his thumb and forefinger he was holding a small blue card. In large letters at the top was printed: PRESS. He gave the policeman a flash at it, then tucked it back again with a grin.

"That suit you?" Horatio asked.

"Okay," the policeman nodded. "Just wanted to be sure. My name's Gossard. *Sergeant* Frank Gossard."

"It'll be in the story," Horatio said dryly.

The detective who had been searching the headless body of the white man rose to his feet. He was holding a miscellaneous collection of articles—a handkerchief, a half a dozen coins, watch, pocket knife, memorandum book and a pocket book. He opened the pocket book, then whistled softly.

"Had a bunch of dough!"

After that, he opened the memorandum book and almost immediately exclaimed: "Guess this's his name! Henry Bisco. Real estate and—"

"Hold on!" the other detective interrupted. He flipped out his notebook, consulted it hurriedly. "That's the guy!"

"Who?"

"Henry Bisco. Reported missing by wife this afternoon. Hadn't been home since he left for his office yesterday morning," the detective read. "Well, we don't have to look for him any more," he added with a note of finality. "How about the chink?"

The other detective laughed briefly. "Doesn't make much difference. But I'll see what I can find."

While the rest stood about watching him search the mutilated body of the Chinaman, Horatio began to wander around the room. He gave only a casual glance out the rear windows. That direction seemed of little importance, since the cadavers had been brought in the front door, as shown by the trail of blood.

He started toward the front windows, his eyes ranging over the dirty floor. Suddenly, he stopped near the head of the stairs and squinted. A round object, a little smaller than an English walnut, had caught his attention. He picked it up, looked at it quizzically.

"Now what—" he started to ask himself, when the voice of Sergeant Gossard again broke into his thoughts.

"We might as well be going, Ed. Get our bus fixed up. How about you, *Mirror?*" he added to Horatio.

"Think I'll stick around a little while," Horatio replied. "What did you get off the chink?"

"Not a damn thing but thirty-six cents!"

HORATIO STAYED in that dismal, ghastly room with its two horrible objects for almost an hour. He stayed until the medical examiner had come and gone, until the police photographer had taken pictures, until the headless corpses had been hauled away in the morgue wagon. Then he left with the two policemen and the detectives.

He learned little that he hadn't already figured out for himself. The murdered men had been dead more than twelve hours, at least. Their heads had been severed with a large and extremely keen weapon, wielded with tremendous power. It had probably taken two men, or one very strong man, to have lugged them up there, for, according to the medical examiner's estimate, Bisco's body weighed around a hundred and eighty pounds.

The two detectives had found a few footprints in the dust that they had deemed important. They'd measured them, had them photographed. To Horatio they seemed feeble clues, although he admitted that such material might be useful evidence at times.

Of the small round object he had picked up, Horatio said nothing. He could turn that over to the police—after he was through with it himself.

When he returned to the sedan, it was just about sundown and still light. He drove to the business center of Newark, parked his car in a garage, and walked to the Robert Treat Hotel a few blocks away. He carried his bag with him.

Once in his room, Horatio suddenly recalled that he had started out only a few short hours ago for Atlantic City to spend a vacation and forget all about crime and criminals. The thought brought a twinkle to his pale eyes. He admitted to himself that he was like an old fire horse. When the alarm rang, he had to answer the call. It was a lifetime habit that couldn't be denied.

He stretched out on the bed for a few minutes and went over in his mind the astounding and horrible events of the afternoon. But suddenly in the midst of his grisly meditations, a broad smile spread across his face. He got to his feet.

From his pocket he pulled forth his billfold; from his billfold he pulled forth a blue card. Holding it between his thumb and forefinger, he looked at the large printing, which spelled: PRESS. He removed his thumb, looked again, and chuckled. The card now read:

PRESSING

For A-1 work call Minski

Fordham 8-1234

Horatio put the card back. His expression had grown serious, thoughtful. He took out of his pocket the small round object he had found on the floor of the building in Chinatown. He turned it over and over in the palm of his hand.

The surface was composed of some kind of leaf, dried and brown. Carefully, Horatio removed this covering. Then he lifted the ball inside to his nose and sniffed.

"Smells like tobacco," he murmured. "In fact, it is tobacco. But what else?"

He stood there deep in thought, his mind turning backward through the archives of his experiences.

"By George!" he suddenly exclaimed. "Of course that's it. I should have guessed at once."

Once more, he sniffed the round object, and, placing it between his teeth, bit off a small hunk and began to chew it.

He spat out the piece of the ball he had in his mouth. His blue eyes were shining; his manner was that of a man who is highly pleased about something.

"No doubt about it. *Sirih!*"

Horatio picked up his brown hat and yanked it down on his bald head. From his grip, he removed his automatic and stuck it carefully in his hip pocket. And as he headed toward the door of his room, he murmured half-sadly:

"Poor Leander. It's too bad he'll not be in on this. But he really needs a rest and vacation."

CHAPTER FOUR

HORATIO GOES SHOPPING

AFTER LEAVING the hotel, Horatio walked to a nearby drug store.

"I wish to buy ten cents' worth of powdered charcoal," he told the clerk.

The clerk disappeared behind the partition and a few minutes later came back with a small parcel, which he handed over to Horatio.

"Anything else?"

"A small jar of cold cream, please."

The clerk walked along the glass cases, slid one of the doors back. "Any particular kind?"

"No," Horatio murmured. "Just cold cream. But a very small jar."

Removing a jar from the case, the clerk held it aloft. "Here's one for eighteen cents."

"Perfect."

Horatio paid for his purchases, put the charcoal and the cold cream in his pocket, and went out to the street.

He gave the other stores in the vicinity a quick glance, then continued on his way. He had been walking only a little while, when he saw a sign which brought a smile to his lips. It was a flourishing scroll on a brightly lighted window, that read: "Palace of Sweets." Horatio entered.

A Greek with a round face and blue jowls came forward to wait on him.

"I wish to buy some peppermint drops," Horatio said with a hint of embarrassment. "Very small red peppermint drops. I believe children sometimes call them 'red hots'."

The Greek bobbed his head. "Redda hots? Sure, Mike!" He turned and took down from a shelf a glass jar half full of red candies about the size of a small split pea. "This him?" He dug a hand into the jar and gave Horatio several of the red pellets.

Horatio tasted one. "Yes. That's what I want."

"How much?"

"Fifteen cents' worth, please."

From the Palace of Sweets, Horatio returned to his room at the hotel as quickly as possible. Although it was dark and past his customary dinner time, the thought of food was far from his mind. He was occupied with a task that took the place of food and drink for him.

Removing two-thirds of the cold cream, he threw it in the waste-basket. Then he poured a quantity of the powdered charcoal into the jar and worked it around until he had obtained a thick black paste.

He screwed the top back on the jar of black paste and put it in his pocket with the candy. Then, having reassured himself that his automatic was ready for use, he once more left his room and descended to the street.

He walked along briskly until he reached the edge of the district where the Chinese had settled. Looking about for a moment, he located a dark doorway and slipped into it.

Taking out the charcoal and cold cream mixture he had made, Horatio dipped a forefinger into it. Then he began to rub the stuff over his teeth, working it up on the gums. But he took care not to get any on his lips. This operation completed, he replaced the little jar and stepped out from the doorway.

At the first opportunity, he glanced into a plate glass window as he walked by it and caught a faint reflection of himself. He made a grimace. The sight of his black teeth and gums gave him a feeling of satisfaction.

From time to time as he walked along, he placed several of the tiny red peppermint drops on his tongue. As soon as he had sucked the coating from them, he spat them out and put in others.

AS HORATIO walked along the street on which was situated the grimy vacant building, where the headless cadavers had been found, he noticed that a policeman was stationed at the front door. No doubt, he decided, to keep out curiosity seekers.

He consulted his watch. It was a little past nine o'clock.

There were many pedestrians abroad—white men, Chinese, some in Occidental clothes, others in their native coolie coats and flapping pants, and a sprinkling of negroes. Automobiles and trucks rattled over the pavements. Chinatown was far from asleep....

He turned a corner. As he moved along, he scanned each store building, and finally stopped before one of them.

"Looks likely," Horatio murmured. "I might as well start here."

He pushed open the creaking door and walked in. It was a small curio shop, filled with a hodgepodge of Oriental merchandise. Ebony stands, Chinese vases and figurines, embroidered mandarin coats, and innumerable knick-knacks. A Chinaman in a cheesebox hat and long silk robe presided over this exotic stock.

Horatio smiled broadly, displaying his blackened teeth and his tongue, made fiery red by the candies.

"*Sirih?*" he asked.

The saffron-faced shopkeeper looked at him blankly. "What you say you want?" he demanded in careful English.

"*Sirih,*" Horatio repeated.

The Chinaman shook his head. "What that?"

"Excuse me," Horatio apologized. "I must have the wrong address." He smiled again, without opening his lips, and retreated to the sidewalk.

He yanked his hat down over one eye, distorting the brim out of shape, and headed on down the street again. He kept putting red peppermints into his mouth and spitting them out as soon as he had sucked off the color.

His next stop was at a Chinese restaurant, but with a result almost the same as at the curio shop. A shrug and a shake of his head from the almond-eyed proprietor, and Horatio was on his way. For an hour, he continued to roam the streets of Newark's Chinatown. He went in and out of curio shops, laundries, chop-suey joints, Chinese rooming houses, and even groceries.

Sometimes he found Chinamen who spoke English; sometimes they evidently understood nothing except their native dialect; but he knew that if they had what he was looking for, his blackened teeth and red tongue would be sufficient explanation for them. Yet none of the inscrutable faces he studied, as he asked his question again and again, betrayed the slightest comprehension of what he was talking about. He was beginning to wonder if he were following a hopeless lead.

And then across the street from where he was standing, he saw a small shop. It was mostly below the sidewalk level. There was a sign over the window, but it was in Chinese ideographs, and undecipherable to Horatio. Nevertheless, he understood the significance of the bunches of roots and herbs that hung behind the grimy glass.

He cut across the street, descended the narrow steps and walked in. At first he imagined the place was deserted. A second later, he had the feeling that he was being scrutinized from somewhere. And immediately afterwards, from behind a partition at the rear, a Chinaman shuffled forth.

He was a little stooped man, with the traditional pigtail which so many of the Chinese in America have discarded, or else wear coiled beneath their hats. But his pigtail, scanty and gray, hung down from his pate like a piece of old clothesline. His face, the color of ancient parchment, was withered into dozens of wrinkles, from the middle of which peered two sunken, but beady-bright eyes.

Horatio opened his mouth in a momentary smile, opened it just long enough for the old fellow to catch a glimpse of his black teeth and flaming tongue. Before Horatio could speak, the Chinaman wiggled his head on its scrawny neck.

"Vellee good! Vellee good!" he squeaked. "How muchee?"

Horatio dug into his pocket and fished out a bill. "One dollar," he said.

The wizened Oriental closed a shriveled talon about the money and scraped his way back behind the partition.

Presently, the ancient reappeared. He handed a small package to Horatio and stood with his hands tucked up the sleeves of his jacket, while Horatio left the basement shop and mounted the steep steps to the sidewalk.

IN A doorway a short distance off on the other side of the street, Horatio took up his vigil. Whenever anyone passed, his attitude was that of a man who has drunk too much. Drunks lounging in doorways of Chinatown were sufficiently common to evoke little attention. Besides, he was partially hidden by the shadows and visible only to pedestrians who passed close by and chanced to look in his direction.

The minutes ran into hours. Several times customers walked down the steps into the old Chinaman's herb shop and soon climbed out again. But Horatio could see that they were Chinese, and he paid little attention to them.

Midnight came. He was slightly surprised at first that the light behind that basement window across the way wasn't extinguished. Then he realized that although the streets of Chinatown might become still and deserted, behind the closely shaded windows of many of the buildings, the yellow inhabitants were just beginning to come to life.

A figure rounded the corner a block away. Horatio's blue eyes narrowed. He could tell by the walk that this was no Chinese. It was a smooth pantherlike sort of glide that brought the figure of the man rapidly into view. Horatio stiffened, watched with held breath.

Without hesitation, the object of Horatio's attention descended into the basement shop.

Slipping out from his hiding place, Horatio walked swiftly to the corner, crossed the street and sauntered past the window. He glanced down. The customer was standing too far back for his face to be visible. But Horatio could see his hands and the lower part of his body.

The man was dressed in a dark suit; his feet, noticeably small, were encased in black shoes, which somehow didn't have the look of being American-made. But what caused Horatio to smile strangely, to make his way with all haste back to the doorway and stand motionless and alert in the shadows were the fellow's hands.

"A Malay," Horatio murmured softly.

At the same time, a puzzled wrinkle fanned out from the corners of his eyes. He was thinking of the two headless cadavers. It had taken a strong man to sever the heads and lug the bodies to the second floor. The Malay across the street, with his small golden-brown hands, would hardly have been capable of doing it.

Just then the Malay came out of the shop.

Waiting until the brown man retraced his steps around the corner, Horatio moved from the doorway. He made all possible speed after him. The Malay was about a hundred feet ahead. Boldly Horatio followed, quickening his pace just enough to lessen the distance between them gradually.

There was no object in stealthy tailing. If the Malay should happen to glimpse a figure skulking behind him, he would be immediately suspicious. As it was, he would take Horatio merely for a late pedestrian intent upon his own affairs.

When they had traversed a dozen blocks, Horatio suddenly realized that they were approaching the empty building where the murdered men had been found. The Malay walked by without so much as glancing at the gruesome place. The policeman was no longer in front.

In the middle of the next block, the Malay halted before a door at the top of a couple of stone steps. Without pausing, Horatio continued ahead. But when he came abreast of the door, the brown-skinned man he was following had disappeared. The door itself was tightly closed.

CHAPTER FIVE
THE FACE IN THE DOOR

FROM ACROSS the street, Horatio studied the
building. It was three stories high and clearly a dwelling. There were no signs on the front to indicate otherwise.

Like many of its neighbors in the section, it was of brick,
weather-stained and grimy. On one side of the entrance
were two windows and three others on each of the two
floors above. All were dark, although from where he stood,
Horatio was unable to determine whether that was because
they were tightly shaded or because there were no lights
behind them.

Horatio considered. He had been following a clue,
which had finally brought him to this house—almost, he
thought, he might say it had brought him to a blank brick
wall. But was the secret of the headless corpses behind
that closed door?

His clue had been a small ball of *sirih* picked up from
the dust of the floor, on which lay those two grisly relics.
He had suspected what it was, confirmed his suspicions
in the hotel room. *Sirih*—loosely referred to as betelnut—
which almost every Malay chewed. Actually, *sirih* was a
mixture of areca-nut, lime paste and tobacco, wrapped in
betelnut leaves.

But if almost every native of the East Indies chewed
sirih, by the same token virtually no Chinese used that
mild narcotic. Knowing this, Horatio had eliminated the
crime as the work of Chinamen. He had concentrated on
finding a Malay in this section of the city. In the islands of
Malay, a large percentage of the population was Chinese, so

it seemed natural that any Malays coming to this country would take up their abode in Chinatown.

Horatio's first step had been to simulate the outstanding characteristics of a *sirih* addict—blackened teeth and tongue reddened almost to disfigurement. As a white man, he knew, he might scour the districts for weeks without discovering the source of the stuff. As an obvious user, it was only a question of time till he located it.

Now he had found a house, where at least one Malay who was an addict of the betel, apparently lived. But Horatio sadly admitted that was quite a different thing from proving that the brown man he had trailed was involved in the double butchery.

There was only one answer to the problem, he decided with a trace of a grin, and that was to see for himself what lay behind those dark windows across the way.

Before he could take a step to put his decision into action, however, a pair of headlights appeared up the street. Horatio drew back against the wall. As they came near, he saw that they were on a taxicab. It stopped before the house into which the Malay had disappeared. There was only one passenger, who got out and walked up beside the driver to pay him.

In the faint radiance of the dash lamp, Horatio was able to get a partial view of the newcomer. He was a heavy-set man, almost stout, with a moon face and wearing glasses. A white man, beyond question. Before Horatio could observe him further, he wheeled from the cab, which pulled quickly away.

Standing on the steps, the man fumbled in his pocket. Then he drew forth a key and inserted it in the lock. For a fleeting moment, his bulky form was silhouetted against an oblong of dim light. Then the door shut behind him with a faint click.

Keeping as much in the shadows as possible, Horatio moved down the street and approached the building on the side where it stood. He glided up close to the door, a spot where he was hidden from anyone looking out the windows.

He examined the door thoroughly. It had a new lock, and the fact that the white man who had just entered had used a key showed it was fastened. Given time, and the flat leather case with its assortment of slender tools which he usually carried, and Horatio felt certain he could manipulate the tumblers.

But he had left New York to go on a vacation. The flat leather case, he realized with a feeling of regret, was reposing in the drawer of his dresser. And then, a round black spot on the cement of the sidewalk caught his attention.

HORATIO MOVED quickly to it and bent over. It was the iron cover of a coal hole, through which fuel for the building was dumped into the bins beneath the walk. He found a place to hook his fingers under it and gave a tug. The cover was heavy, stuck in place. He gave another tug, and it moved slightly. Encouraged, Horatio exerted all his strength. The iron disc came free.

As noiselessly as he could, he slid the cover to one side, leaving a few inches of it still extending over the black hole.

Horatio shot a hasty glance up and down the street. There was no one in sight. From his pocket, he took a small flashlight, shaped like a fountain pen, and pointed the slender beam downward. The bins were empty, the floor about eight or nine feet below. He squirmed through the opening, held for a moment by his hands and dropped.

Once more, he brought the flashlight into play. He swung it around him. He was in a long, narrow cellar that occupied a space the width of the sidewalk and extended along the entire frontage of the house. In the middle of the back wall was an opening, leading into the basement proper. And leaning against the door frame, he saw a coal shovel.

Horatio smiled with satisfaction. He grasped the shovel and holding it above his head began to slide the iron lid of the coal hole back into place. Little by little, he maneuvered it over the opening. It fell into its groove with a dull metallic clang.

Breathless, he waited in the inky darkness, darkness so intense that it almost seemed to have substance. Had the noise been heard by anyone in the house? If it had been, would the hearer identify what it was?

Caution held him motionless for a long time, while he listened with straining ears. But there was no sound, nothing but the creepy blackness that enfolded him. He flashed the light on and moved from the coal bin into the basement of the house.

The first room he entered was occupied by the heating plant. Behind the boiler, he could make out a wall of masonry, which he estimated just about bisected the basement. In the center was a wooden door, tightly closed. Horatio advanced slowly, carefully, the groping finger of light picking out the beams of the ceiling, covered with cobwebs, and the walls, dank and moist.

The air was close and fetid. It smelled of rot and decay, in the manner of old houses, and it seemed to Horatio that he could detect another and more repugnant odor intermingled.

His light came to rest on a flight of steps with a wooden handrail. It was against a side wall, and patently led to the upper part of the house. He started toward it. When he had taken only a few steps, he stopped in his tracks. Someone was moving about up above. In a flash, Horatio glided to the door in the stone wall behind the boiler.

The latch yielded readily, and he stepped through. Behind him, he left the door slightly ajar, in order to hear better. He waited. Once he thought he heard a step beyond the wall. But it was not repeated and finally, deciding to risk the flashlight again, he pressed the button.

The beam showed him that he was in another part of the cellar about the size of the room which contained the furnace. It appeared at first glance to be entirely empty. He raised the light, let the beams wander over the ceiling. Suddenly, he took a sharp breath, and the flashlight wavered uncertainly.

He steadied it, brought it to rest on one spot. And in the white circle of brightness, he saw two faces staring at him. They were faces with wide, sightless eyes—one was ghastly white, the other a sickening shade of greenish-yellow. They were on heads without bodies that hung suspended from a steam pipe by a cord fastened to the upstretched hair.

Fascinated with horror, Horatio stared at the macabre spectacle. He knew he had found the heads belonging to the two cadavers he had seen in the afternoon.

A faint click snapped him out of his lethargy. He turned his head sharply, put out his flash.

A light had been switched on in the cellar room beyond, the rays shining through the crack of the half-open door. And almost at once, a vicious chocolate-colored face, of unbelievable ugliness, appeared in the opening. It was followed by a huge hand, grasping two writhing objects. It tossed them on the floor, where they landed with a slap.

Some instinct restrained Horatio from moving toward the door. Instead, he backed away and his hand reached for his automatic. Before he could draw, the door slammed shut.

He whipped his light beam toward the floor. It disclosed four glittering eyes, eyes in upraised heads attached to long black bodies that were looped over each other. As he watched, they began to disentangle and glide apart.

Horatio was sharing his cellar prison with two deadly and enraged black cobras.

CHAPTER SIX
REMEMBER SOERABAYA!

BY THE time Leander Jones had burst from the room, where Daniel Carter lay dead with a serpentine blade through his heart, the terrified cries for help had ceased. But the wild panic of the sound rang in his ears as he raced toward the front of the great hallway. He took the steps of the curving stairway two at a time.

And then, in a square upper hall, he was forced to pause. On either side were two doors, and at the back a fifth one. All the doors were closed.

In the brief moment he stood there hesitating, trying to decide from behind which one that frantic call for help had come, one of the doors in front of him was pulled abruptly open. A girl, a young and strikingly beautiful girl, staggered across the sill.

She stopped, leaned back against the door frame for support and drew a slender white hand over her eyes. Her dark red hair was disarranged, falling down over her pale and frightened face. Her breath came in short, labored gasps.

Leander recognized her as the girl who had arrived in the limousine only a few minutes earlier. He took a step forward. For the first time, she seemed to be aware of his presence. Her deep gray eyes dilated; she opened her mouth as if to scream, and then thrust her clenched fist against her teeth.

Leander raised his hand, smiled reassuringly. "It's all right," he said in a quiet tone. "You have nothing to fear. I—I heard your call for help."

She made no reply, just leaned there and stared at him with wide eyes.

He moved nearer. "Why did you cry out?" he asked soothingly. "What has happened?" He knew that every second was precious, but he also knew that this girl was on the verge of collapse or hysteria. He had to act calmly, afford her a chance to regain her composure.

"Who—who are you?" she faltered.

"My name is Jones," he smiled. "Just Jones."

"W-what are you doing here?"

"I came to see Mr. Carter. I was waiting downstairs, when I heard you call," he said.

She peered at him long and earnestly. Something about this small man in the rumpled gray suit, his pale blue eyes smiling in a friendly way, seemed to win her confidence. The fear gradually faded from her face.

"Then you aren't—with him?" she said.

Leander was at her side. "With whom?" he asked quickly.

"The brown man. He tried to choke me—just now."

"Tell me about it."

She straightened up. She was more sure of herself; her breathing had become almost normal. "I came in about five or ten minutes ago and went directly up to my room. It seemed to me I had no more than gotten there, when I heard the door open. I turned around—" She shuddered, hid her face in her palms for a few seconds. Then she continued more calmly:

"He was small. He had a round face and black eyes. That is all I can remember about his appearance, except that his skin was brown—a light brown. I started to speak, to ask him what he was doing there, when he jumped toward me. I—I screamed. And then he was upon me. He seized my throat and began to choke me." She rubbed her hand across the white skin of her neck, where several red spots bore witness to her words.

"I struggled with him. Even though he was small, he seemed to have tremendous strength. I was just about to lose consciousness, when he suddenly released me. I saw him go out the window to the roof of the verandah. I—I opened the door—and found you here," she concluded.

"He must have heard me coming up the stairs," Leander murmured.

"Where is my uncle?" the girl asked.

"Your uncle?"

"Yes. Uncle Dan. Mr. Carter."

Leander didn't answer her question. Instead, he said, "Then you are—"

"Cynthia Carter," she supplied.

RELUCTANTLY, LEANDER spoke. His voice was kindly, in an effort to soften the effect of his words. "Miss Carter," he said, "you must prepare yourself for a sad blow. Your uncle is—dead."

"Dead?" She appeared unable to credit her ears.

"Yes," he nodded. "Daniel Carter has been killed."

"What!" She clutched his arm. "Where is he? Where—"

"You must keep calm," Leander said firmly. "We will go to him in just a little while. For the moment, your safety demands that you stay with me."

"But—"

He cut off her protests with a quick shake of his head. "You'll have to do as I say!" There was an air of quiet authority in the way he spoke that would not be denied.

"Very well," she agreed limply. "What do you want me to do?" She choked back a little sob.

"Have you a gun?" he asked briskly.

She nodded, and turned back into the room from which she had come. Leander followed. Walking to a low vanity dresser, she pulled out one of the drawers and removed a small pearl-handled revolver. Leander took it. He smiled to himself as he spun the cylinder and found it was fully loaded.

"Which window did he go out of?" he asked.

She pointed, and Leander walked across the room and pushed aside the curtains. In the lower half of the screen was a huge rent. The Malay in choosing this means of escape had evidently put his foot through it and then squeezed his way out.

"Wait here!" Leander said.

He climbed through the torn screen and found himself on the roof of the verandah, which extended the entire width of the main wing of the house. It was pitch dark. But off to the left, he could see the myriad of lights that marked the town of Cornwall. Below, the grounds of the Carter estate lay deep in shadow.

If the Malay were still lurking about the premises, he had plenty of good hiding places. If he had fled from the scene, he had had ample time to reach town.

He returned to the room.

Cynthia Carter had straightened her hair, powdered her face and appeared to be entirely composed. She looked at Leander with a brave attempt at a smile, as he climbed in through the broken screen.

"I don't understand, Miss Carter," Leander said thoughtfully, "why none of the servants answered your call for help."

"Servants?" she repeated. "We have no servants any more."

"A maid admitted me."

"That was Magda," she replied. "This is her last day. Only she and Mark are left, and this is his last day, too. We planned to move out of here very soon ourselves. You see—" she paused, thinking of what Leander had just told her about Daniel Carter— "my uncle had lost all his money."

"But Magda must have—" He broke off suddenly, a look of alarm in his eyes. "Quick!" he exclaimed. "How do we get to the back part of the house—the kitchen?"

The thought that had flashed into his mind appeared to have been transmitted to Cynthia Carter. She gasped. Then she turned and ran toward the door of the room, calling over her shoulder:

"This way! Follow me!"

THEIR WORST fears were confirmed. Magda, the pretty maid who had let Leander into the house, was dead. Her red and swollen face, her eyes protruding from their sockets, bore mute testimony to the ghastly fact. While

Leander dropped to his knees beside her still form, lying on the kitchen floor half under a table in the middle, Cynthia looked on, fascinated with horror.

Leander lifted one of the limp hands. He pressed on a fingernail. It was white, and no matter how much he pressed it and then released the pressure, no trace of pink appeared. He stood up.

"Dead," he said softly. "Strangled." He saw the marks of the killer on her throat, and knew she had been choked with bare hands.

A tremor passed over Cynthia. "If it hadn't been for you, I—I'd be dead now, too," she said.

"I'm afraid so," he agreed.

"We'd better phone the police."

He moved his head slowly up and down. "Yes. But not for a few minutes. I want to look around a bit myself first—before any local constable comes in to interfere."

"Who—what are you?" she asked, wonderingly. She was looking at him closely.

"As I told you, my name is Jones. Just Jones," he replied with a disarming smile. "I suppose you might call me a detective of a sort."

"A—a detective?"

"That's close enough."

"How did you happen to come here? What did you want with my uncle?"

"My dear young lady," Leander said solemnly, "I shall answer all your questions in due time. For the moment, you must trust me. Do you?" he asked.

Her voice was barely audible. "Yes."

"Good!" He patted her hand in a fatherly fashion. "And now, if you'll take a firm hold on yourself, we'll go in to your uncle."

Cynthia withstood the shock of seeing Daniel Carter lying on the floor with the knife in his heart even better than Leander had hoped. She gave a choking sob, but after that made no sound. She sat on the edge of a chair and watched dry-eyed, as he conducted a rapid but thorough examination of the murder chamber.

Carter had been slain in his study. It was a large square room, the walls on two sides lined with bookcases. The furniture was of choice mahogany, dark-stained and lustrous. Cutting off one corner of the room was an immense flat-top desk, its only adornment a blotter pad and desk set of bronze. In front of this desk lay the body.

Leander's delay in notifying the police had been with a purpose. He knew that it would be some time before the local authorities or the state troopers would arrive. There would be countless questions, explanations, and at least an hour would pass before any organized hunt for the Malay would be under way. Then the pack would be turned loose in full hue and cry for their brown-skinned quarry.

And this was not the way to catch him, Leander felt certain. If he were to be taken, it would only be by stalking him, like one of the wild beasts of his own native jungle.

The pockets of the dead man produced nothing that Leander deemed of importance. He walked to the two windows. Behind their heavy drapes, they were closed and locked, even though it was a warm evening. From the windows, he made his way to the big desk. As he came around the end of it, a sudden smile lighted his face.

On the rug behind the desk was a scuffed black bag.

Before he had opened it, Leander recognized it as his own. The contents were undisturbed. It appeared that the Malay to the very last had been unaware that he was carrying around a different bag from the one he started out with.

THE DRAWERS of the desk were locked. Getting the key case from the pocket of the dead man, Leander turned the master lock. The upper drawers were filled with various papers, canceled checks, bank statements and other items. He gave them only a hurried glance. He opened the big drawer on the lower right hand side of the desk.

"My word," he murmured.

In the drawer was a hideous black cobra, coiled as if to strike. This time, however, the discovery did not catch Leander unawares. He had expected to find something like this. He lifted the ugly object from its resting place and set it on top of the desk. Cynthia gave a little exclamation of alarm.

"Don't worry," Leander said. "It's dead—quite dead, and stuffed."

Nestling in the coils of the loathsome thing was a folded sheet of paper. He took it out, spread it open on the desk.

The single sheet bore a message in the same rough lettering as the note he had found in the other coiled cobra. He took that one from his memorandum book and also spread it on the desk. Then he studied both for several minutes through half-closed eyes.

The newest message read:

REMEMBER SOERABAYA!
BY THE SNAKE YOU WILL KNOW US

Your life or one hundred thousand dollars? Get the money in old bills with none larger than fifty dollars. On Thursday afternoon, you will drive along the Philadelphia highway alone.

We will do the rest. Don't fail!
DEATH COMES FROM DOWN UNDER

Leander put the two messages together between the leaves of his memorandum book and slipped it back into his pocket. Thursday afternoon. Yesterday had been Thursday. Daniel Carter, apparently, had disregarded the threat. And today the Malay had returned to deliver the final warning. Or more likely to sneak into the house and plant it where Carter would be sure to find it, Leander concluded.

But what had happened? Why had he killed Carter, instead? It ended any chance he might have had of getting the money. Even if Carter had wished to pay the extortion demand, however, he was not able to, if what Leander had heard about his finances were true.

Why hadn't Carter notified the authorities? Was he held back by fear? Did the coiled cobra represent some sinister power that he imagined was beyond the ability of the police to cope with?

He walked over and sat down in a chair beside Cynthia.

"Miss Carter," he said, "perhaps I'd better explain how I happen to be here."

She listened with parted lips, as Leander related his experiences, which had finally brought him to this great rambling house and the ghastly murders that had just been committed beneath its roof.

"Malay," she said softly, when he had finished. "That would mean that—that all this goes back to the time when Uncle Dan lived in Java." She glanced at the still figure on the floor, and for a moment pressed her hands against her grief-filled face.

"Undoubtedly," Leander nodded. "Did your uncle seem to be worried recently? Have anything on his mind?"

SHE REMOVED her gaze from the dead man and turned back to Leander. "He's been worried for six months," she said. "Ever since his business troubles began. But for the last couple of days it did seem to me that he was laboring under some tremendous strain. He was always very reticent about himself."

Leander leaned forward slightly. "Miss Carter," he said, "do you happen to know where your uncle was yesterday afternoon?"

"Yesterday afternoon?" She looked at him in puzzlement. "Why—no, I don't. But I remember now that he did something that was quite unusual for him."

"What?"

"He asked me if I was going to use my coupé. Said if I wasn't, that he would like to take it for the afternoon."

"What was unusual in that?"

"It was the first time he'd ever done it. He hated to drive, and always had Mark take him where he wanted to go."

"Did you see him leave?"

She nodded. "Yes. I walked to the car with him, after Mark brought it from the garage. I kissed him good-bye."

"Do you remember," Leander asked slowly, "whether he had anything with him? A package?" He watched a tiny wrinkle appear between Cynthia Carter's deep gray eyes, and then disappear.

"Yes," she said. "He was carrying a package. A rather large package, wrapped in brown paper."

Leander stood up abruptly. "Thank you, Miss Carter," he said. "Just one more question. Did your uncle have any enemies that you know of?"

"No. And I'm afraid he didn't have very many friends, either. He was a man who kept very much to himself," she said, and then added quickly, "But of course, I really knew almost nothing about his personal affairs."

Walking across the room, Leander lifted the phone from the big flat-top desk. While he waited for the operator to answer, he let his glance drop to the body, to the knife still sticking in the murdered man's breast in the middle of a great crimson smear. He recognized it—a *kris*, with a fantastically carved cobra handle and a long flamelike blade of razorsharp damascened steel.

It was a weapon used by the natives of the East Indies. Indeed, in certain parts of the islands, no Malay was ever seen without one, worn fastened to the waist near the middle of the back. And it seemed to eliminate all doubt that Daniel Carter had been killed by a Malay.

The voice of the operator came to him over the wire.

"Give me the nearest state police barracks," he said crisply.

When he had finished reporting the tragic happenings at the Carter home, he replaced the phone on the desk. He started to walk back to Cynthia, when the sound of an automobile outside halted him. He paused to listen. The car was being driven at high speed, as evidenced by the roaring of the motor. Then the noise faded rapidly away.

At that moment, the door of the house was opened. A second afterwards, it was slammed violently.

CHAPTER SEVEN
PURSUIT

WITH CYNTHIA close behind him, Leander rushed into the hallway. Mark, the chauffeur, was hurrying toward them. He was wearing neither hat nor coat. His face was crimson and he was panting heavily. At the sight of Cynthia, he exclaimed:

"Where's Mr. Carter?"

Cynthia stepped forward. "Why—Mark, what's wrong?"

"The big car's been stolen!"

"My word!" Leander exclaimed.

"When did this happen?"

"Just now. I was up in my room over the garage, when I thought I heard a noise down below. I started down the stairs. Before I could get there, he drove out the door and headed down the drive as fast as he could go."

"He?" Leander asked.

"Sure! I could see there was only one person in the car. A man. And he took my hat and coat. I left 'em on the seat." He suddenly scowled. "But he won't get far in that bus!"

"What do you mean, Mark?" Cynthia asked.

"It was almost out of gas when I brought it in, Miss," Mark replied. He started to move around them. "I'd better phone the cops right away."

Leander detained him with a touch on the arm. "Did you notice which way the thief turned from the drive?"

"Sure! Toward town. Probably heading for New York."

"Miss Carter, you mentioned a coupé—" Leander began.

She didn't wait for him to finish. "Hurry! He'll have to stop for gas!" She ran to the front door, threw it wide and ran along the verandah toward the garage at the back of the house.

Leander, his blue eyes sparkling, was only a step behind her. The chauffeur hesitated for a moment, confused by the suddenness of Cynthia's action. Then he, too, dashed out the front entrance and after them.

While Cynthia was starting the car, Mark pushed back the big double doors of the garage. Another set of doors, behind which the limousine was kept, was already open. Leander climbed into the seat beside Cynthia, opened the window of the coupé and addressed Mark. He had to shout to make his words audible above the sudden roar of the motor.

"Go in the house and wait for the state police!"

"What?"

"State police!" Leander repeated. "Mr. Carter's been killed."

He had a glimpse of the chauffeur's startled face, as Cynthia let in the clutch and the car seemed to catapult from the garage. They took the turn from the drive into the road at a speed that brought a squeal of protest from the tires. In a matter of seconds, they reached the main motor highway that ran through the center of Cornwall, and Cynthia, turning left toward New York, jammed the throttle to the floorboard.

Any doubt Leander might have had about this red-haired girl's ability as a driver was dispelled in the first few minutes. She handled the wheel like a veteran of the speedways, with a sure and instinctive skill. The numbers on the dial of the speedometer grew larger—seventy—seventy-five—eighty! It was only a little after ten o'clock, and there still was considerable traffic. But Cynthia threaded in and out at top speed.

Leander was convinced that the limousine had been stolen by the Malay killer. He had come to Cornwall on the train. But that means of escape was highly risky, if not impossible. And in making off with his victim's car, he had shown an audacity that was only equaled by the cleverness of the move. It also spelled a certain familiarity with the Carter estate and the habits of those who lived there.

There was a chance, of course, that the Malay had not taken the road to New York. But he had come from there, and to Leander it seemed logical that he would make every effort to get back to the city, where his chances of hiding would be much better.

He touched Cynthia lightly on the arm and, leaning over, said:

"Better slow down. We should be catching up with him soon—if he came this way."

She nodded, and the coupé's reckless speed slackened to a mere fifty miles an hour.

AS THEY came over the brow of a hill, the lights of a roadside filling station appeared on the right about half a mile ahead. A car was just pulling out into the highway from the line of pumps.

"Stop here, Miss Carter," Leander said.

She drew up before the small brick building. An attendant, his change-maker strapped about his waist, came up to the car.

"Pardon me," said Leander, putting his head out the window of the coupé, "but could you tell us if that car which just left here was a—a—"

"A Packard limousine! Last year's model!" Cynthia exclaimed quickly.

The station attendant looked from Leander to Cynthia and bobbed his head vigorously. "You said it! A coon chauffeur. He got ten gallons of gas."

Leander smiled. "Thank you. Thank you very much," he murmured.

As they swung back onto the highway, Cynthia said with a trace of triumph, "I can overtake him in five miles."

"No, don't do that, if you please."

She took her eyes from the road long enough to turn a surprised glance on the mild little man beside her. "Why—why, you have my pistol. Do you mean you don't want to capture him?"

"Oh yes, I intend to capture him," Leander replied. "But not just yet."

"I don't understand," she said, frowning. "You aren't afraid of him, are you?"

"No, I'm not afraid of him," he answered with an amused twinkle. "But you must realize that he's only one of a number—I've no idea how many—whom I intend to capture."

"Oh! You're going to trail him! Have him lead you to the others!"

"Exactly! Miss Carter, the man we are chasing is a Malay. He's obviously able to speak English. But it's very doubtful if he has enough control of the language to have written the note I found in your uncle's desk. It was the work of someone with a command of English, both written and spoken."

She nodded understanding. "You mean a white man."

"Yes. A white man," Leander said. "An educated white man. In that note, he even paraphrased the Gospel. 'By the snake you will know us—by their fruits ye shall know them',"he added.

Ahead of them about a half a mile, the twin red discs of the double tail-light on the limousine were like two malignant, flaming eyes. Cynthia was compelled to slow down, in order not to overtake the car they were trailing. The Malay was driving at a conservative speed… either because he was not any too capable a driver, or else he was taking no chances of being arrested for speeding, Leander surmised.

"Better keep about this distance," he suggested. "But don't lose him."

"I won't," she said grimly.

He glanced out of the corner of his eyes at the girl beside him. She couldn't be more than nineteen. Her features were delicately molded, yet there was a set to her chin that indicated a determined will.

"Have you lived in Cornwall long?" he asked abruptly.

She shook her head. "Only since a year ago. When I finished school, I came to live with Uncle Dan. My father and mother are both dead," she added.

They fell silent after that. Mile after mile rolled beneath the wheels. Always Cynthia kept the distance between the two cars. Other automobiles passed them in both directions, and Leander didn't think that the Malay suspected he was being followed, since they were careful not to overhaul the limousine, and he showed no indication of a desire to shake them off.

"How long ago was your uncle in Java?" Leander asked finally.

"I think it must have been twenty-five or thirty years ago," she said. "I know he was in the lumber business in Seattle for a long time. Until he retired. He went to Seattle after he left Java."

AT A leisurely rate of speed they continued for almost two hours. They passed through numerous villages and towns. But Cynthia kept those two red lights always in view. At length, the towns began to be nearer together, almost a continuous stretch of dwellings and low store buildings.

"We're getting close to Newark," she said.

Horatio didn't answer. He was watching the car ahead intently. Then suddenly he said: "He's stopping. Better pull over. Put out your lights."

She obeyed promptly, drawing the coupé close to the curb. They were in the outskirts of the city. The limousine had come to a halt about three blocks ahead of them, before a lighted store of some kind. They saw a figure get out of it and cross the walk.

It would be relatively simple to catch the Malay now, Leander surmised, and for a brief moment he was tempted to do so. The brown-skinned fiend was guilty of two murders. Of that he was convinced. But the belief that the native was only an instrument of some far more dangerous and vicious leader restrained Leander.

Presently, they saw the figure recross the sidewalk and get in the car. It pulled away, and once more they took up the trail. As they passed the place where the Malay had stopped off, Leander saw that it was an all-night lunch-room.

He had half expected the limousine to push on through Newark and take the skyway over the marshes to Jersey City. But instead, when they were well inside the city limits, the driver turned abruptly to the right into the residence section of the town.

Cynthia followed, speeding up a little so as not to let their quarry slip away around another turn. When they reached the corner, the two red discs were plainly visible, and she swung the wheel of the coupé.

The course now led through back streets, quiet and poorly lighted. A purled frown touched Leander's brow. It seemed to him that the car ahead was simply making a wide circuit.

The apartments and dwellings gradually gave way to factory buildings and warehouses, with tumbled down tenements sandwiched in between. The streets, too, became rougher, the pavement worn by the passage of heavy trucks and drays.

They were getting close to the waterfront along the Passaic River. Suddenly, the car ahead vanished around a corner. Cynthia speeded up, followed the route of the other car. As they came to the corner, the twin tail-lights were nowhere to be seen. Without hesitation, she turned down the street. It was pitch dark. On both sides loomed the gloomy outlines of warehouses, visible against the sky.

An instant later, their headlights picked up the limousine. It was parked alongside the curb with all the lights out. And at the same time, Leander saw that they had swung into a dead-end street. Cynthia applied brakes hurriedly.

Like jungle cats leaping upon their prey in the night, two small and active figures sprang out of the shadows. Before either Leander or Cynthia could move, they were on the running board and shoving the muzzles of menacing pistols through the open windows of the coupé. In the glow of the dash-light, Leander saw that they were brown-skinned, thick-lipped, with malevolent black and glittering eyes. Malays—but neither one was the native they had trailed from Cornwall.

Cynthia's face blanched; she gave a quick gasp, but said nothing.

Leander turned his mild blue eyes on the man nearest to him. "My word," he murmured. "My word, it seems to be a hold-up."

"Get out," the Malay commanded gruffly. "Keep quiet, or we kill!" He pulled the door open.

Leander slid from the seat. He was watching for an opportunity to seize his foe, wrest that ugly gun from his brown hand. But the Malay gave him no such chance. He kept out of arm's reach; and he continued to point the pistol directly at Leander's heart.

Although he was calm and deliberate to all appearances, Leander was giving himself a mental lashing. "A trap," he thought with chagrin. "He stopped at that lunchroom and phoned these two devils. Then he led us right into their hands!"

So far as he was concerned, the situation was bad enough. But when he glanced at Cynthia's white and frightened face, and visualized what fate might be in store for her at the hands of these savage and bloodthirsty brown men, his heart sank and his eyes grew dark with helpless rage and horror.

CHAPTER EIGHT
MURDER'S END

HORATIO JONES, for all his mild appearance, was a man of dauntless courage. The same thing was true of both the Jones Brothers. But like many people, brave or timid, he had a deep-rooted dislike and fear of snakes. They filled him with revulsion, sent little prickles chasing up and down his spine.

Facing those two deadly black cobras in the cellar room of the house of mystery in Newark's Chinatown, Horatio felt his knees begin to quiver. The hand that held the flashlight on their lidless, gleaming eyes shook slightly. He would far rather have been confronted by a maniacal killer in that dank vault than those two slimy and poisonous reptiles.

He moved slowly along the back wall, keeping the light full on the cobras. They had slid apart now and were lying in loose coils. As the light moved, they reared up their heads and about a foot of their bodies. They stared at the white circle of light with fixed intensity, swaying faintly and almost in unison.

With a fierce effort, Horatio steadied his jangling nerves, controlled that terrible feeling of repugnance, amounting almost to nausea. He leveled his automatic and took careful aim at the larger of the two snakes, which was a little in front of the other one.

But suddenly his finger froze on the trigger. He was not at all certain that the hideous brown man who had tossed these snakes in with him knew that he was there. It was possible that this was simply a convenient place to keep them until they were needed.

If, as he hoped, his presence was unknown, it was much better not to reveal it. Should the snakes attack him, he could always use his gun as a last resort and take the consequences. But, if possible, he wanted to learn more about what strange and sinister things were going on in this house of death, before coming to grips with his foes.

He swung the flash up and about. It glided across the two gruesome faces of the bodyless heads, hanging from above. And in that quick instant, he saw that the two-inch steam pipe from which they were suspended ran entirely across the ceiling at the bottom of the floor joists.

He brought the light back again to the cobras. They had changed their positions. They were nearer, and directly between him and the door. As the bright rays struck them, they immediately repeated their rearing movement of a moment before. And once more their unwinking eyes fixed on the face of the flashlight.

Horatio's eyebrows suddenly lowered, and a peculiar expression appeared on his face. He moved the light from side to side. The reptiles swayed gently, ominously, but their eyes remained glued to the light. Horatio smiled. He shot the light upward again, then instantly brought it down to the floor, where he left it. He slipped his gun into his pocket.

In the next instant, he raised his hands and jumped upward as high as he could. The steam pipe rapped the knuckles of one hand, but the other slid around the metal and his fingers closed in a desperate grip.

He pulled himself up, caught his feet around the pipe. Like a South American sloth clinging to the under side of a tree limb, he began to work his way along the pipe toward the door.

From time to time, he glanced down. The cobras, directly below him, were waving the upraised portions of their bodies from side to side in a slow, sinuous movement. But they kept their eyes on the light....

They were, Horatio knew, fascinated—hypnotized by the light. It had come to him only a moment before that all wild animals, including reptiles, were unable to resist the spell of a bright light in their eyes. And he had acted promptly on this knowledge to keep these two venomous serpents occupied.

PULLING HIMSELF along in his upside down position, Horatio finally reached the wall. He hooked his knees about the pipe and swung head downward. By stretching his arm as far as it would reach, he managed to grasp the doorknob. He tried it with a silent prayer. The door was unlocked, and he pushed it open a crack.

Horatio heaved a sigh of relief. He had guessed correctly. The man who had tossed those two cobras into the room hadn't known he was there.

A quick glance showed that the snakes were still weaving gently, entranced by the flashlight. He grasped the pipe with his hands, unhooked his knees, and dropped lightly to the floor. Instantly, he slipped through the door and shut it noiselessly behind him.

He was in utter darkness. But he had obtained a general idea of the layout of the furnace room, when he had passed through it before. He put a hand on the damp, clammy masonry and began to advance step by step toward the stairs. Cautiously, feeling his way in the blackness, he mounted to the floor above.

The head of the stairs was barred by a closed door. Horatio, crouching with his ear against the panel, listened. All was quiet. He turned the knob, inched the door open. A slit of feeble light appeared. Again he waited, and again only silence from beyond.

He eased through the doorway and found himself in a long narrow hall. At the front was a door and it terminated in another at the back. Two more doors were in the wall to his left. But all were shut. Above him, the illumination came from a single electric light globe in an old-fashioned gas fixture, which had been converted for electricity.

Horatio looked up. The stairway continued to the upper floors. He drew his automatic from his pocket and stood there, hesitating, for just a moment. Then he heard faintly the sound of voices, although he couldn't distinguish the words. It came from somewhere overhead.

Tensed and prepared for whatever might come, he began the ascent of the stairs.

The arrangement of the second floor was identical with that of the first. And again he was faced by four closed doors. But as he moved silently down the hall toward the next flight of steps, he could hear the voices more plainly. They were on the top story.

As he climbed, he was thankful for the carpeting that covered the treads. It was worn and spotted by mildew, but it deadened his footsteps. Pausing on the top step, he listened. The voices were in a room beyond a partially opened door at the front of the hallway. There seemed to be several different speakers taking part in the conversation. And it was in some strange, rather musical tongue, which he assumed must be Malay.

Silent as a ghost, Horatio advanced until he could peer through the opening of the door into the room beyond. It was a large room, occupying the entire front of the house, he decided, noting the three closely shaded windows in a line. In the middle of the room was a library table of ugly golden oak. Around the wall were several chairs and a battered sofa. Straw matting covered the floor. What caught and held Horatio's attention for a moment was a large square box against the wall. Behind a glass front, he could see the shiny scales of a number of snakes.

More cobras, he thought, with a reminiscent shudder.

He pressed back against the wall and surveyed the occupants of the room. There were five of them. At one end of the table, a gray-haired man with a moon face and wearing glasses, was sitting with his hands gripping the table edge. Horatio recognized him. He was the man who had arrived in the taxi and admitted himself to the house with a passkey.

He was talking excitedly, almost angrily, and he was addressing his words to a gigantic figure, standing with folded arms at the other end of the table. The object of his remarks was naked to the waist. His legs were covered with a cloth or body *kain* of reddish brown stripes, which was drawn up so that he seemed to be wearing gaudy cotton knickerbockers. His feet were bare.

The giant's thick lips were drawn back in a half snarl, revealing teeth blackened by betel and his fiery red tongue. His eyes were small and piglike, the whites shot with blood.

It was a face of unbelievable ugliness. It was the face of the man who had tossed the cobras into the cellar room with the two bodyless heads.

STANDING ON either side of the white man were two short brown individuals in European clothes. From their pug noses and dark eyes, as well as the smallness of their hands, it was plain that they were Malays. One of them, Horatio identified as the man he had trailed to this house from the herb shop of the old Chinaman.

A third Malay was sitting on the side of the table opposite the door. He was better dressed, more intelligent looking than his two fellows. When he opened his mouth to inject a few words into the conversation, he displayed white and even teeth, unstained by *sirih*.

What race the brown giant belonged to puzzled Horatio. He was sure he was not a Malay. And then in a flash, it came to him. The beastlike native was a Dyak, a race closely akin to the Malays, but historic enemies of theirs. The Dyaks were the tribesmen of the interior of Borneo and Celebes. They were the headhunters!

And with that realization, Horatio knew he had solved the mystery of the headless cadavers. He was gazing upon the butcher. A half-savage with an irresistible urge to collect the heads of his victims as trophies. And no doubt, Horatio thought, he had put the snakes in the cellar room to guard those gruesome mementos.

He looked at the Dyak closely. "Dear me," Horatio said to himself. "That fellow's half insane. I wouldn't try to arouse him any further. He might go berserk."

But the white man with the moon face didn't seem to be swayed by any such feeling. He continued to berate the huge man in that strange tongue. Finally, he stood up, shook his fist threateningly. At the same time, the well dressed Malay on the far side of the table rose to his feet. He, too, turned on the brown giant, his dark eyes snapping with every word he uttered.

What followed took place almost too fast for Horatio to follow.

The huge Dyak muttered a few guttural words. Then he seemed to crouch slightly, the muscles of his magnificent body corded. But in spite of his size, he moved with the suppleness of a black panther, the dazzling speed of a striking cobra.

His hand went behind him and came forward in a powerful overhand stroke. And in the hand was a shining blade with a waving, flamelike edge. It was a *kris*, which he had drawn from his waist near the middle of his back.

Too late, the Malay saw his peril. He tried to retreat. But the glittering knife whistled through the air. It caught him just where his neck joined his shoulders, crashed through the muscle and bone, and then was jerked clear.

With a screech of agony, the Malay went over backwards. He landed against the snake box in a welter of blood and a tinkling of broken glass. With a sweep of his left arm, the giant native sent the table tumbling to one side. Then growling like a cornered beast, saliva bubbling at the corners of his mouth, he advanced with his dripping blade uplifted.

The other Malays had whipped their long daggers from their backs. Like their foe's weapon, they were serpentine, although not so large. Steel rang on steel. While his companion engaged the Dyak from in front, one of the Malays tried to slip behind him. But the big fellow was not to be fooled. With a snarl, he half wheeled and his arm shot out. The Malay screamed. His *kris* clattered to the floor, his amputated hand still clutching the handle.

All hell seemed to be loose in that blood-spattered room.

Horatio pushed the door wide, stepped across the threshold with his automatic raised. At that moment, the moon-faced man, who had been cowering against the wall, dashed for the opening. Wild with terror at the raging fury which had been unleashed, he did not even notice Horatio. He stumbled blindly by him, his arms shielding his face. As he passed, Horatio swung his automatic in a swift arc. A dull thud, and the moon-faced man crumpled to the floor.

Another scream. The last of the Malays was hurled back against the wall, his skull split open like a peanut shell by the gory *kris* of the Dyak.

CHAPTER NINE
THE COBRA CULT

THE BROWN giant turned. His piggy eyes, flaming with blood lust, fell upon Horatio. He bared his hideous black teeth in a fiendish grin. He raised the deadly blade, sprang forward.

The roar of Horatio's gun was deafening. It completely drowned the thump of the slug against the Dyak's head. Squarely between those cruel eyes, the bullet struck. The impact checked his forward movement, and for a moment he teetered crazily. Then the huge figure toppled over sideways.

The place was a shambles. On the floor lay three dead men, and one Malay with his hand cut off at the wrist. Near the door, the moon-faced white man was still unconscious. Blood was everywhere. In all his experience, Horatio had never seen anything like it.

Suddenly, he recalled the snake box. He remembered having a vague glimpse of a black reptile gliding out the broken front, slithering over the floor. Cautiously, he approached the box. It was still occupied by a number of tangled forms. He turned a chair, which had a solid back, on its side and blocked the opening. Then he warily began a search of the room. But he found no trace of a snake and decided he must have been mistaken.

Then, from beyond a partially closed door, he heard a peculiar sound. It was like a person strangling, or trying to cry out while being slowly choked.

He swung the door wide and dashed through. Lying on the floor against the wall, he saw a man, bound hand and foot, his mouth covered with a dirty towel. It was from behind this impromptu gag that the strange sounds were issuing.

"Good lord!" Horatio exclaimed. "Leander!"

Leander looked at him, rolled his eyes, and at the same time moved his feet as much as his cords would permit. Horatio followed the direction of his brother's frantic glances. His lips parted in horror.

On the other side of the room, a girl was lying. She, too, was bound and gagged. And not more than a foot from her ashen face was a cobra in a figure eight coil. The deadly snake's head was lifted up, swaying lightly from side to side. Only the fact that Cynthia Carter had the presence of mind not to move a muscle had saved her from the venomous fangs so far. But at any second, they might be driven into her soft flesh.

Horatio's first impulse was to try to distract the cobra's attention. But instantly, he realized that might well be a fatal move. It might be just the thing to cause the cobra to strike.

Hardly daring to breathe, he crept softly around until the girl and the reptile were no longer in line. He raised his gun. For the second time its roar shook the house, as a streak of orange flame leaped toward the cobra. Simultaneously, the loathsome black body began to thresh about on the floor. But it was a body without a head.

Quickly, Horatio whipped out his pocket knife and cut Cynthia's bonds. He helped her to her feet and led her to a chair, where she sank down, limp and trembling. While he was freeing Leander, the sound of a heavy crash drifted up from below. Then footsteps pounded on the stairway.

Just as Leander was getting up from the floor, a uniformed policeman appeared in the doorway between the two rooms. He was holding his service revolver in one hand and his night-stick in the other.

"My God!" he shouted. "What's going on here?"

A second cop came up behind him. Horatio looked at them and smiled apologetically.

"Why nothing, gentlemen," he murmured. "Nothing's going on. It's all over."

IT WAS after eight o'clock in the morning when Horatio and Leander, accompanied by Cynthia Carter, left police headquarters. The intervening hours had been spent piecing together the story of the murders at Cornwall and the mystery of the headless cadavers.

Horatio had ordered his car brought from the garage. As they moved toward it, a young man, in need of a shave, rushed up to them.

"Mr. Jones!" he exclaimed. "How about giving me the low-down on this yarn. I'm a reporter. From the *Mirror.*"

Leander shook his head. "I'm sorry," he murmured, "but we never talk for publication. You understand our position, of course."

"Oh, sure, I know all that. But this's different. My God! I never ran into anything like it. A house filled with dead Malays and cobras and heads without bodies. And another couple of murders in a millionaire's home at Cornwall, which the Inspector says are mixed up in this other. Listen! It's one hell of a yarn!"

"What paper did you say you represent?" Horatio asked.

"Mirror!"

Horatio grinned faintly. He drew Leander to one side, and presently Leander was grinning, too. He walked up to the reporter. "My brother thinks we should make an exception to our rule in your case," he said. "He seems to feel that he's indebted to your paper."

"What's that?"

"Never mind," Leander murmured.

"Are you ready?"

The reporter pulled a few sheets of soiled copy paper and a stub of a pencil from his pocket. "Shoot!"

"You know something about the affair, of course," Leander said, as Horatio and Cynthia entered the sedan, leaving him alone with the newspaper man.

"Yeah. The Inspector gave me some of the dope. Names and stuff like that. But I want to know what all the killing was about, see?"

"I see," Leander nodded with a twinkle. "In the first place, you'd better say that this information came from Mr. Hendrik Van Zorg, of Soerabaya, Java. Under pressure, Mr. Van Zorg became quite loquacious."

"I got it! Van Zorg's the fat guy your brother conked with his gat."

Leander lifted an eyebrow, smiled softly. "Very descriptive," he murmured. He became serious, and continued: "About thirty years ago, Mr. Daniel Carter also lived in Soerabaya. He operated a teakwood concession from the Dutch government. He prospered, and as a result became the object of an extortion plot by an organization that was known locally as the Cobra Cult."

"Swell!" the reporter exclaimed, scribbling vigorously. "Cobra Cult! Boy, what a headline!"

"They were called that," Leander explained, "because they sent their demands for money in the coils of a dead cobra. When Daniel Carter received one of them, he laughed at it. Paid no attention. And a week later, he was bitten by one of the snakes. He almost died. Only the fact that he received immediate medical attention saved him.

"That was enough. He paid the extortion money, sold out his business and moved to Seattle, where he built up a considerable fortune."

"Where does this Van Zorg figure in?" the reporter asked.

"He was a friend of Carter in Soerabaya," Leander said. "Van Zorg remained there. In time, authorities wiped out the gang of native extortionists. Executed a number of them. But with the passage of the years, the evil reputation of the cult became almost a legend."

"And Van Zorg decides to revive it and try to make a few shakedowns himself. That it?" the reporter asked, squinting at Leander.

"Exactly! He was in desperate need of money. He'd heard Carter was wealthy. Carter had paid once and Van Zorg felt sure he would again—if he could be sufficiently terrified. So Van Zorg came to the United States and brought along three Malays and a Dyak."

"And a bunch of snakes," the reporter added.

"Quite right. To use in his campaign of terror. The Dyak, like most of his tribe, was an expert snake handler. He was brought here to look after the cobras."

"What'd this Van Zorg want the Malays for?"

"The original cult was composed of Malays. Besides, Van Zorg wished to keep in the background. That's why he rented a house here in Newark for his natives, while he himself lived in a hotel in New York."

LEANDER TOOK out a stogy and lit it. He took a few meditative puffs.

"One of the Malays—his name was Jarapa—was educated after a fashion," Leander resumed. "At least, he could speak English. He went to Cornwall and planted the extortion demand where Carter would find it. The plot might have succeeded, because Carter had never forgotten his experience in Java, except for one thing."

"What's that?"

"He was broke. He carried out the instructions, all but producing the money. In a bundle of newspaper, which he turned over on the highway, he enclosed a letter explaining his financial state. But Van Zorg didn't believe him.

"He started Jarapa out with another warning. But while trying to plant it, he was discovered by Carter. In the excitement of the moment, the Malay stabbed Carter to death. Then, in the kitchen, he came upon the maid and choked her.

"Having already committed a couple of murders, Jarapa decided to ransack the house. The first room he entered was Miss Carter's bedroom. Fortunately, I was in the house and she escaped with her life."

The reporter nodded. "That explains the killings out at Cornwall. But how about the two guys who had their heads chopped off here in Newark?"

"Accidental victims of a drug-crazed head-hunter."

"What? A—a head-hunter?" The reporter's eyes were popping.

"The Dyak! He used betelnut, as all the members of his race do. But when he came to this country, he was also introduced to more powerful narcotics. It unbalanced his none too strong mind. He ran amok. The ancient custom of his tribe to collect the heads of their victims, came to the surface."

"My God!" the reporter exclaimed. "A savage head-hunter doing his stuff in a big American city. What a yarn!"

"Yes," Leander agreed. "It's quite horrible to contemplate. When Van Zorg read about the finding of the headless bodies, he realized that his brown-skinned gang was getting out of control. They were like Frankenstein's monster.

"He lost no time getting over to Newark. And when Jarapa admitted bungling things out at Cornwall, he was badly frightened. He actually hadn't expected that murder was going to be part of his plot. He hauled the Dyak on the carpet, you might say, and laid down the law to him. No more head-hunting!" Leander added with an odd smile.

"That might have settled it, even though the Dyak was half-crazy from drugs, because he had a hearty fear of the white man. But Jarapa also took him to task. For centuries there's been bad blood between Malays and Dyaks. This Dyak went berserk—and I guess you know what happened."

"I'll say so! I saw the joint. It looked like a slaughter house. I'm much obliged to you, chief," he added with a breezy wave.

On the way back to New York, Leander and Cynthia sat in back. Horatio was behind the wheel. Leander turned to her.

"You can go home with Miss Millard, our secretary, and get some sleep," he said. "Then we'll get in touch with your uncle's lawyer."

Cynthia Carter looked at him with a grateful smile. "I'll never be able to thank you enough. But if there's any money in Uncle Dan's estate, I'll see that you are well rewarded."

Leander shook his head slowly and firmly. "There is no fee," he said.

"You mean—"

"I mean," he said, "there is no fee."

"I'm afraid I don't understand you."

He gave a pleased laugh. "Miss Carter, there are times when both Horatio and I feel we don't even understand ourselves." He glanced at the back of Horatio's head, covered with his disreputable looking hat. "Horatio," he said suddenly, "I'll bet you a new hat you enjoyed your vacation."

From the front seat a low chuckle drifted back to them. "Yes, indeed, Leander. And did you enjoy yours?"

"Very much. The rest did me good," Leander replied solemnly. Then he added: "But it's going to be hard to settle down to work again."

DUCHESS OF DEATH

A COOL HALF-MILLION! THAT
WAS THE FABULOUS STAKE, IN
CASH AND GEMS, THE SINISTER
DUCHESS OF DEATH WAS OUT TO
GET. BUT THE BROTHERS JONES—
THOSE MEEK AND MILD LITTLE
DETECTIVES EXTRAORDINARY—
WERE HARD WATCH-DOGS TO
EVADE. NO WOMAN HAD PUT
ANYTHING OVER ON THEM IN
FIFTY YEARS AND THEY WEREN'T
GOING TO LET THIS MISTRESS OF
MURDER BREAK THE RECORD.

CHAPTER ONE
MURDER IN THE PARK

IT HAD started to rain late in the afternoon. A chill, penetrating drizzle, harbinger of the winter soon to come. At the theatre hour, taxicabs and glistening limousines were slopping through Times Square, where the traffic policemen, their dripping raincoats reflecting the myriad lights, waved frantic arms to keep the flood of vehicles from becoming hopelessly ensnarled.

Some ten minutes after the curtain had gone up, a sleek town car of foreign manufacture halted before a theatre in West Forty-fourth Street. On the marquee above it, electric lights spelled out the words—

HONEY DEW

MUSICAL HIT OF THE YEAR

A footman in plumb-colored livery sprang from the front seat and, whisking open the door of the car, stood smartly at attention. A man in a high hat and opera cape, of the type so common on the boulevards of Paris, emerged from the dim interior. He assisted his companion, a woman in a chinchilla evening wrap, to the sidewalk, then turned to the footman.

"Ten minutes, Ivan," he said briskly.

The man in livery touched his cap, snapped the car door shut, and leaped back beside the driver. With a silken purr the ten thousand dollars' worth of automotive luxury glided from the curb.

THE FOYER of the theatre was deserted. As the two late arrivals moved swiftly across it to the entrance, the box-office treasurer glanced through the grill of his cubby-hole.

He caught a brief view of the man's long, sallow face, with its thin eyes and carefully pointed black mustache. Of the woman who accompanied him, the treasurer received only a fleeting, blurred impression. It was of blue-black hair, drawn back tightly on her head and disappearing into the large collar of the chinchilla wrap, which she was holding about her face with one hand.

The treasurer had been connected with the theatre for many years. He knew most of the wealthy patrons, the celebrities who visited the playhouses. But he was unable to place either the man or woman who had just arrived. Nevertheless, he could appreciate that chinchilla, worth a king's ransom. His mouth pursed into a silent whistle, his eyebrows lifted.

Inside, an usher glanced at the ticket stubs which the man held out.

Not until they were settled in their seats did the woman lower the collar of her wrap. In the semi-darkness, her face gleamed whitely. It was a small oval face, set with large eyes under faintly sloping eyebrows. The lips were full, making a dark gash against the pallid background of her skin. It would have been a strikingly beautiful face, except for the length and thinness of the nose and the pinched nostrils.

Their seats were in the last row on the aisle. Without removing their wraps they sat down, their arrival occasioning little attention, except from a woman in the third seat, who gave a quick envious glance at the chinchilla, then returned her attention to the stage.

A world-famous comedian had just made his entrance. At his first lines, a ripple of laughter swept the house. But neither the man nor the woman with the blue-black hair smiled. Their expressions were set, tense.

He leaned over, placing his lips close to her ear. "It will be only a few minutes now, Tanya. This is a short scene."

She nodded. "The glasses, please, Grigory."

From the pocket of his opera cape, he produced a small pair of opera glasses. They were of mother-of-pearl, the lenses encircled with a ring of gems.

She let them rest in her lap, covering them with her hands, while the comedian continued his antics, which brought repeated waves of laughter. The sound seemed to annoy her, to be alien to her own mood, for she bit her lip.

The soubrette began a song number. On the chorus a dozen girls danced onto the stage and took up the refrain. Again the man spoke, this time with suppressed excitement.

"There she is!" he said. "The second from the left."

His companion raised the opera glasses to her eyes. Almost at once, her hand closed about his wrist in a fierce grip. But she said nothing, merely leaned forward slightly and kept her gaze fixed upon the brightly lighted stage.

When the number was finished and the chorus had vanished into the wings, she turned to the man with the black mustache. Her eyes were glowing; the grip upon his wrist tightened.

"You are right, Grigory," she breathed. "You are right— as always. How did you happen to discover her?"

"Quite by accident. I came here last night with a theatre party. The minute I saw her, I knew she was the one. That's why I brought you tonight. To confirm my belief," he said softly.

She fled up the ratlines.

She made a little movement "Come! It is enough," she said. "Let us go."

WITHOUT ATTRACTING more than passing attention, they rose from their seats. As they were crossing from the head of the aisle to the front exit, a man stepped out of the shadows at the back of the house. He was a short man, a man with broad shoulders and a shaggy head of snow-white hair. He detained Grigory with a light touch upon the arm.

"Your Highness doesn't remember me, perhaps?"

Grigory stiffened. He peered down at the stumpy figure, into the round, deeply lined face with the sunken eyes that looked up from beneath the mane of white hair.

"No, I do not," he said brusquely. He started to move on to where the woman was waiting with signs of impatience at the exit door. But the short man tightened the hold on his arm.

"I am Ratvinov!" he said softly.

"Come, Grigory!" the woman whispered.

Grigory tried to shake the detaining hand free. But Ratvinov moved around in front of him and held on the more tightly. His eyes looked red in the darkness.

"I will refresh your memory," he said. "I was once assistant ballet director of the Imperial Theatre at Moscow. When you were a young man. A very elegant young man," he added with a trace of a sneer.

Grigory drew himself up to his full height. Ratvinov released his hold, but did not take his burning eyes from the other's face. With a little gesture, Grigory brushed the spot on his sleeve where Ratvinov's hand had rested.

"You have made a mistake, sir," he said.

"You are not then His Imperial Highness, the Grand Duke Leonid?"

"Certainly not. I am Grigory Vorlovitch."

Ratvinov laughed coldly. "In America, perhaps. But in Russia you were the Grand Duke Leonid." He stepped closer, an ugly smile parting his colorless lips. "Why are you here?" he asked.

The woman, whom Grigory had called Tanya, was standing silently beside the exit door, her eyes fixed on the short man with the mop of white hair. They held an expression of curiosity tinged with fear.

"That, my friend, is no concern of yours," Grigory said, and made a move to pass around Ratvinov.

Again Ratvinov blocked his way. "You do not have to tell me," he muttered. "I know. But you are wasting your time. This is not the Russia of the Czars—this is America. A free country," he added cynically.

For a brief moment they stood there, the woman in the regal fur wrap, the tall impressive Grigory, and the short, almost deformed ballet master. On the brightly lighted stage, the comedian was again bringing roars of laughter from the audience. No one was noticing the little drama taking place at the front of the house. Even the several ushers were standing at the head of the aisles, watching the performance behind the footlights.

Grigory's thin eyes were mere lines in his long sallow face. His right hand was beneath the fold of his opera cape. His fingers were toying with the handle of a slender dagger, which nestled in a leather scabbard concealed inside the lining of the cape. He broke the tension with a sudden shrug and grim smile.

"Perhaps," he said, and his voice was a low whisper, "we could discuss this better somewhere else. We might be able to help each other," he added.

Ratvinov's white mane bobbed up and down. "Spoken with good sense. I'll get my coat. Perhaps we can help each other."

He glided to the side aisle and down to one of the boxes, from which a door led backstage. Grigory stepped to Tanya's side.

"Who—who is he? What does he want?" she asked anxiously.

"Some idiot of a ballet master. He remembers me from Moscow."

She frowned. "Can he—will he cause us trouble?"

"On the contrary," Grigory said, "I believe he may be of great assistance—for a price. If not—" He broke off with an expressive lift of his shoulders.

"He is going with us?"

"Yes."

They waited then, without speaking, until the short figure again appeared in the side aisle. Ratvinov was bundled in a huge ulster that added to his grotesque appearance. In the foyer, he placed a black felt hat with a wide wilted brim on his head at an angle that shielded his deep-sunk eyes.

The glistening town car with the liveried chauffeur and footman was waiting beneath the marquee. It was still raining.

IN FRONT of a towering apartment on upper Fifth Avenue, the car drew up. Before the doorman could reach the curb, the footman had whisked the door open and was standing at attention. The woman in the chinchilla coat turned to Grigory.

"Will you be long?"

"No, my dear Tanya," he replied. "Mr. Ratvinov and I can transact our business in a very short time, I imagine."

She walked to the building beneath the canvas canopy without looking back. Her movements were graceful, and there was something unconsciously imperial in the way she held her head.

"Drive through the Park," Grigory directed the footman. He settled deep into the soft upholstery, his eyes straight ahead, seemingly gazing off into space.

"Well," Ratvinov finally broke the silence.

"You are connected with the production, of which we witnessed a part this evening?" Grigory asked.

"I directed some of the dances."

"Then you are acquainted with the members of the company."

"Yes."

Grigory considered a moment. At last he said: "There is one of the young ladies of the ensemble—" He hesitated.

"I know! I know!" Ratvinov exclaimed, a peculiar glint in his deep eyes. "You are speaking of Irina."

"She is dark-haired, and—"

"Yes, yes," Ratvinov interrupted. "She is the second one from the left in the second dance number. She is dark-haired—and beautiful."

Grigory nodded. "Her name is Irina, you say. Irina what?"

"Ratvinov!"

Grigory smiled sharply. "Ratvinov?"

"That is the name she goes by."

"Your—a—daughter?"

Ratvinov gave a brief mirthless laugh.

"You know very well that she is not. Does she look like me? No! She looks more like—" He didn't finish, but looked shrewdly at the tall man beside him.

"What do you mean?" Grigory asked slowly.

"You know what I mean. You know Irina Ratvinov looks like a Romanoff!" There was a note of hatred in the way he spat out the name of the last royal family of Russia. Then he added softly: "She is the living image of the Princess Anastasia at seventeen!"

Slowly Grigory nodded. "Now that you mention it, she does," he said blandly. "It hadn't occurred to me before."

"Bah!"

"I am interested in meeting the girl," he continued ignoring Ratvinov's interruption. "You can arrange it?"

"Perhaps."

"Of course," Grigory continued, clicking on the dome light in back of the car, "I would expect you to benefit by your kindness." He brought forth a brown wallet, and his slender fingers plucked at the sheaf of bills within it. When he had counted off ten of them, he drew them out. Clean, crinkly banknotes that had never been folded. He held them toward Ratvinov.

"Here is a thousand dollars. We will go to the theatre at the close of the performance." He switched off the dome light.

Ratvinov took the money without replying. His round deeply lined face was expressionless as he tucked it in the inside pocket of his ulster, but there was an odd sparkle in his sunken eyes.

"It will be quite conventional," Grigory continued with an easy laugh. "My wife, whom you have just met, will be with us."

"Why do you wish to meet Irina?" Ratvinov asked slowly.

Before Grigory could reply, the car ground to a stop with an abruptness that almost dislodged the two men on the back seat. They were in a desolate section of the park. The rain was slanting down past the windows in a steady downpour that obscured the sides of the roadway.

In front, where the footman and chauffeur were sitting, there was a sudden movement. A second later, the rear door of the car was flung open. The man in plum-colored livery, whom Grigory had called Ivan, appeared in the opening.

Without a word, he raised his right hand. There was a spurt of flame, a deafening blast. Ratvinov's mouth fell open, his face twisted in surprise and pain as he slammed back against the cushion from the impact of the slug. Then he tumbled forward.

"Don't move!" the man named Ivan commanded sharply. "And keep your hands in your lap!"

Grigory's face was pasty. But he obeyed the footman's order. As if by prearrangement, the opposite door of the car was opened. The chauffeur seized the bleeding corpse of the ballet master and yanked it out of the car. Across the soaking pavement, he dragged the grotesque form in the huge ulster. When he returned from the clump of bushes, behind which he had deposited the dead man, Ivan was sitting beside Grigory. His pistol was against Grigory's ribs.

The chauffeur slid behind the wheel. With a faint thump of gears, the car shot ahead into the darkness and the rain.

CHAPTER TWO
ENTER JONES & JONES

MR. LEANDER JONES, senior partner of Jones & Jones, was slumped deep in an easy chair beneath a reading lamp. His feet were encased in worn and comfortable slippers. His mild blue eyes were fixed intently on a newspaper which he held before him.

Across the living room of the apartment, which looked out upon Central Park, his twin brother—younger by some ten minutes—was likewise engaged in reading. Mr. Horatio Jones, the junior member of the firm of crime specialists, was engrossed in a magazine, *The Farmer's Weekly*.

It was not that Horatio had any deep-rooted interest in agriculture that he was so absorbed in this periodical. But he was seeking mental relaxation in a subject as far removed from his daily occupation of crime detection as possible.

Leander folded his paper carefully. "Dear me, Horatio," he murmured, "there seems to have been a murder last night. Right here in Central Park."

Horatio blinked over the top of his magazine. "My, my," he said. "How unfortunate."

"So far it has been unfortunate only for the victim," Leander replied with a dry little smile. "There have been no arrests. The police are baffled."

Horatio chuckled. "The police baffled? Most unusual. Who was the victim of the murder, Leander?"

"A dance director connected with a Broadway musical show. His name was Ratvinov. The body was discovered by park workmen behind a clump of bushes this morning. He had been shot through the heart at close range. His clothing had been burned by the powder."

"Had he been dead long?"

"The medical examiner stated, according to the account in the paper, that he must have been killed some eight or ten hours before the body was found?"

"Clues?"

Leander shook his head. "If there were any, the police didn't tell the press. The rain must have washed out any footprints or similar trivia of detection. He had a thousand dollars in new bills in the pocket of his overcoat."

An almost wistful look appeared in Horatio's pale blue eyes. "Leander," he said, "it has been almost three weeks since we have been engaged in any investigation. Don't you suppose we could—" He hesitated, and glanced at his twin brother.

Leander shook his head firmly. "By no means, Horatio," he said. "There is nothing in the case, so far as I can see from this newspaper story, that would interest us. Plainly, the fellow had some enemy who took him motoring, shot him to death and then placed the body behind the shrubbery, where it was found."

"That is true," Horatio agreed reluctantly.

"In time," Leander continued, "the police will dig into Mr. Ratvinov's past life. They will discover who might have killed him. They will make a couple of arrests on suspicion. Later, the suspects will be released. The case will be closed—unanswered. And again justice will have triumphed in this fair city of ours."

He gave a little laugh, in which was a hint of bitter irony. The sound of a telephone bell broke in. Horatio started to rise, but Leander was already on his way to the house phone. When he returned a minute later, he said: "We are having a visitor."

"Who?"

"Mr. James Jennison Reece, of the legal firm of Reece, Reece, Butler and Obolinsky."

ANSWERING THE buzzer at the apartment door, Leander was surprised to discover that Mr. James Jennison Reece was not alone. But he concealed his surprise beneath a disarming and half-embarrassed smile, as he made an almost instantaneous appraisal of the woman who was with the lawyer.

She was, Leander decided, about forty-five years old. She didn't look more than thirty-five, but he noted the little signs that even the most skillful beauty operators were unable to erase. The white contour of her throat, the thickening of the skin at the corners of her large eyes, and the red-nailed hand, which she held out at the introduction, especially, told a story to Leander. And he shrewdly guessed that were her blue-black hair untouched, there would be a few strands of gray in it.

"Madame Vorlovitch," Reece said with a touch of unction. "Mr. Leander Jones."

Leander bowed with a jerky, sparrowlike motion. "A pleasure, Madame Vorlovitch," he murmured.

"We are sorry to bother you at this time, Leander," Reece said. "But it is a matter of vital importance. On my advice, my client and I hurried right over here."

"The hours for Jones and Jones are not limited by the clock," Leander smiled.

As they entered the living room, Horatio stood up. For an instant, Madame Vorlovitch looked from one to the other of the brothers with an air of complete bewilderment. Reece, noticing, laughed lightly.

"No, you are not seeing double," he said. "This is Mr. Horatio Jones. They are twins—and I never knew two people who looked so exactly alike. They even dress alike to fool their friends. And their enemies," he added significantly.

"And—and these gentlemen are the famous detectives you were telling me about?" She appeared bewildered.

"Perhaps," Leander suggested mildly, "you should rather think of us as adventurers in crime detection. It is our avocation as well as our vocation. We are not detectives in the usually accepted sense of the word."

"Oh, I beg your pardon," Tanya Vorlovitch replied. She smiled from Leander to Horatio, a wan worried sort of smile.

When they had taken seats, Reece cleared his throat impressively. "Leander," he said, "Madame Vorlovitch is in great trouble. It seems to me that you and Horatio are the only persons in New York who can help her. That is, without publicity. There must be no publicity."

"We never care for publicity ourselves," Horatio put in.

"I remembered that," Reece nodded. He turned to the woman who was studying the brothers Jones with a doubtful expression. It was clear that she was far from convinced that these two little men, nondescript and unimpressive in appearance, could be of much assistance.

"Suppose you tell just what has happened, Madame Vorlovitch," Reece suggested. "Just as you told it to me a little while ago."

"Very well," she replied quietly.

Sitting with her hands folded in her lap, Tanya Vorlovitch related the story of her visit to the theatre with her husband, Grigory, the previous evening. She told about Ratvinov, and how her husband, after leaving her at the entrance to the apartment building where they lived, had driven away with the dance director.

"… and I haven't seen him since," she concluded, with a catch in her voice. "He did not return. I have been unable to locate the car, or the chauffeur or footman. So, this evening I telephoned Mr. Reece. He came out at once, and suggested that we come to see you. That is all."

"I am Mr. Vorlovitch's attorney," Reece explained.

"I understand," Horatio nodded. He was silent for a moment, then he said: "And the murdered body of this fellow Ratvinov was found this morning in Central Park. You knew that?"

"Yes." The woman's voice was a husky whisper. "It was when I read that, that I telephoned to Mr. Reece. Until then, I had been hoping that Grigory would return."

HORATIO HAD edged forward on his chair. He was looking at the woman, with the blue-black hair and long thin nose with an air of almost childish innocence.

"Why were you interested in this a—this young lady in the chorus of the musical show?" he asked.

Tanya Varlovitch pressed her white teeth against her lower lip. She glanced quickly at Horatio and then dropped her eyes toward her hands, still resting in her lap. Before she answered, she drew a deep breath, a breath that sounded like a heavy sigh.

"Because—" she began, and then stopped. Once more she inhaled deeply. "Because she reminded both my husband and myself of our own dear daughter," she said, her words barely audible.

"Your daughter?" Leander repeated.

"Yes. Our daughter—who died several years ago."

Leander apparently was staring at the rug. "Have you lived in this country long?" he asked.

"For almost ten years."

"Did your husband have any enemies that you were aware of?"

She considered the question for a moment. "No, I hardly believe he did. At one time, shortly after we fled from Russia, I would have said that he had many enemies— political enemies—everyone opposed to the old regime was his enemy. But since coming to America, we have lived very quietly. I can think of no one who would wish Grigory harm."

As Leander walked to the door with Madame Vorlovitch and Reece, the attorney asked: "Then you will start at once on the case—that is, to find Grigory Vorlovitch?"

"Dear me, yes," Leander said with a self-effacing smile. "That is exactly what we will do. At once." He addressed Madame Vorlovitch. "Let me suggest that you remain at home for the present. Until you hear from me."

Horatio was standing at the window, staring out toward the Park shrouded by a mantle of darkness, in which the boulevard lights sparkled like countless jewels. He turned as Leander reappeared in the living room.

"Well, Leander," he said. "It appears that we are involved in the murder in the Park, whether we wish to be or not."

"Exactly."

"A charming woman, Madame Vorlovitch," Horatio mused.

A twinkle lighted Leander's pale blue eyes. "At any rate, she is a charming liar."

"What?"

"Her explanation of the interest she and her husband had in the—a chorus girl, was decidedly fishy, it seemed to me," Leander said.

"But why should she prevaricate about such a matter?"

Leander shrugged. "I don't know. And it doesn't seem to me that it is of much importance at the moment." His manner became brisk. "We'd better get started."

"You are going to the theatre?"

"Yes. And you, my dear Horatio, are going down to Centre Street. Captain Colby, at headquarters, will undoubtedly be glad to inform you of what progress the police have made in solving the murder of Ratvinov."

They descended in the elevator together. No one would have given either of the Jones brothers more than a passing glance, so completely insignificant and inconspicuous did they appear. Both were wearing rumpled gray suits and identical dark gray topcoats. Their bald heads were covered with soft brown hats, slightly battered out of shape.

At the entrance of the building, Horatio said: "I'll take the car."

Leander nodded agreement. And as Horatio disappeared around the corner toward Fifty-eighth Street, where the garage in which they kept their big sedan was situated, he hailed a taxi. He directed the driver to take him to the theatre on West Forty-fourth Street that housed the musical hit *Honey Dew*.

THE STAGE manager was tall and gaunt, with a harried look in the slightly protruding eyes behind his nose glasses. He listened to Leander with an air of impatience.

"It is too bad! Terrible!" he said. "The police have been here half a dozen times already today. Why, they woke me up this morning to ask me about this dreadful affair. But I know nothing about it. Poor Ratvinov. He was a nice old fellow. I don't understand why anyone would want to murder him. But he must have had enemies—some crazy Bolshevik perhaps."

"When did he leave the theatre?" Leander asked.

"That's what I'd like to know. He was backstage before the curtain went up. I saw him myself. But nobody around here seems to know just when he left. Or whether he went alone or with someone else. His daughter was asking for him after the performance."

"His daughter?"

"Right. Irina Ratvinov. She's in the chorus."

"I'd like to speak to her," Leander said.

The stage manager shook his head. "She didn't come to the theatre today. But I didn't expect she would."

"You have her address?"

"Yes. I'll get it for you."

He returned a few minutes later with a slip of paper, which he handed to Leander. "Here it is, Mr.—Mr.—"

"Jones. Just Jones," Leander supplied.

"I—I hope you find the person who killed poor Ratvinov," the stage manager said. "And if there's anything else I can do, let me know. I want to help the police all I can."

"Thank you," Leander murmured. He was smiling to himself. The gaunt stage manager had accepted without question his explanation that he was a detective, and had assumed that he was attached to the city force.

Outside the theatre, Leander hesitated for a moment. The address of Irina Ratvinov was on the upper West Side. He wondered that it was not the same address as had been given for Ratvinov in the news story of the finding of his body. Looking at his watch, he saw that it was half past ten.

He walked to Broadway, and there got into a taxi. His visit to the theatre had disclosed, among other things, that no one there and probably not even the police knew that the murdered man had left the theatre in the company of Grigory and Tanya Vorlovitch. Leander had considered going at once to the address where Irina Ratvinov lived. But on second thought, he decided to return to his apartment and wait for Horatio to return. He might have obtained information of value at Centre Street.

He had scarcely closed the door behind him, when the ringing of the telephone bell sounded. He strode swiftly into the living room, flipped the receiver from the hook.

"Leander Jones," he murmured.

A woman's voice, breathless with alarm, answered. He recognized the husky contralto of Tanya Vorlovitch.

"Mr. Jones!" she gasped. "Can—can you come over here right away! Something has happened!"

"I'll be there in five minutes!" Leander whipped out. He snapped the receiver back on the hook and dashed toward the door of the apartment.

CHAPTER THREE
THE GIRL IN GREEN

A MAID in a trim black uniform with starched apron and cap admitted Leander to the penthouse apartment in a lofty building on Fifth Avenue near the Museum. She surveyed the meek little figure standing in the hall with a puzzled frown.

"Mr. Jones," he said. "Mr. Leander Jones."

The maid nodded quickly. Her face brightened with relief. "Madame is expecting you," she said, and stood aside while he entered.

Tanya Vorlovitch was waiting in a vast living room, through the wide windows of which one could look far over the rooftops of the city to where the lights in distant Jersey twinkled upon the bluffs above the Hudson. It was a magnificent room, high of ceiling and furnished with rich and massive Circassian walnut. Upon the walls were half a dozen oil portraits of men and women, the former for the most part dressed in brilliant uniforms. As Leander advanced, his feet sank deep into the soft nap of an immense rug that covered almost the entire floor.

When she saw him, Madame Vorlovitch rose abruptly from the chair in which she had been sitting. "Thank God, he's alive!" she exclaimed. "But—" Her voice broke. "But— we've got to do something quickly! Or he'll be killed— murdered in cold blood!"

Leander noticed that she was holding a couple of folded sheets of paper in her hand. "You've had a message?" he asked quickly.

She nodded and handed him the papers. He glanced at them and saw that one was written in Russian, the other in English.

"That one on top," she explained, "was left here while I was away calling on you with Mr. Reece. I didn't think you would be able to read it, so I made an English translation."

He took the second sheet, and his eyes moved swiftly over the vertical script.

Upon receiving this communication, you will do as I demand, or the life of your husband will be the price. If you inform the police, he will be killed immediately, and his death will be one of lingering torture. I know the source of the wealth you and your husband have been enjoying these last fifteen years. And so I am demanding what is as much mine as yours. The value I place upon your husband is five hundred thousand dollars. You will immediately make arrangements to get this sum. One half must be in bills of small denomination. The other half may be in gems with a minimum appraisal value of one quarter of a million dollars, exclusive of the settings. When you are ready to pay—and it must be within forty-eight hours—you will have the following message broadcast over Radio Station KVKD during the Town Gossip Hour—"Madam Vorlovitch is reported to have found the jewel she believed lost."

It was signed—

Duchess of Death.

And beneath it—

Darling Tanya: Please do as this note says. My safety and
yours depends upon it. Affectionately—
Grigory.

For a long time Leander studied the translation Tanya
Vorlovitch had made. He also devoted considerable attention to the Russian version, and he had sufficient knowledge of that language to see that she had stuck closely to
the original in putting it into English.

She watched him anxiously, rubbing the backs of her
white hands with a nervous gesture. Suddenly, he looked
up at her.

"Have you this money—this five hundred thousand
dollars in cash and gems?"

Slowly she nodded her head. "My jewels, which are in
the safety-deposit vault are worth much more than that I
am certain. As for the cash, I do not know. Mr. Reece, who
handles my husband's affairs, would be able to tell me. But
I feel sure that Grigory has that much at least. If not on
deposit, then in negotiable securities."

LEANDER FELL silent. He was thinking about the
ransom demand he was holding. Except for two things—
the murder of Ratvinov and the statement in the message
that the writer had as much right to the money as Grigory
and Tanya Vorlovitch—it had all the earmarks of a simple
abduction case. He asked Madame Vorlovitch if she understood what was meant by the second.

She frowned. "There is only one way I can account for it," she said. "I know that among certain Russian refugees, the story has long been circulating that my husband took with him, when he fled during the revolution, a large quantity of the Imperial jewels."

"And this Duchess of Death, as she styles herself, believes she has some claim to them."

"It is a lie!" Tanya Vorlovitch exclaimed vehemently. "Grigory did take a large collection of jewels with him from Petrograd. But they did not belong to the Romanoffs. They belonged to his own family, had been in their possession for generations. He was the Grand Duke Leonid," she added.

"The Grand Duke Leonid," Leander repeated thoughtfully. "Dear me!"

"We have never used our titles. Not since we came to democratic America more than ten years ago. We are not like certain of our fellow countrymen—trading on a vanished and stupid social order," she added proudly. "It is very bad taste to use titles that are meaningless, when one adopts as a homeland a country that does not have a titled aristocracy."

Leander nodded approvingly. "Quite right. And this—a—Duchess of Death. Have you ever heard of anyone with that melodramatic title?"

"No," Tanya Vorlovitch replied. "If—if I didn't feel positive that Grigory was in great peril, I would consider it ridiculous. But even though this creature who signs herself Duchess is theatrical, my instinct warns me she is in deadly earnest."

"I'm inclined to agree with you," Leander murmured.

"What shall I do?"

"Nothing."

"Nothing?" She was plainly taken back. "You mean I shouldn't get the—the money ready?"

Leander shook his head, smiled reassuringly. "Not yet. At least, we have forty-eight hours. So for the present, you'll do nothing. However, you must remain here in this apartment. It will be safer."

Her eyes widened. "Do you—do you think that I am in danger?" she faltered.

"Not especially," he said. "But there's no use taking any chances, you know." But to himself, he admitted that Tanya Vorlovitch might be in very grave peril. "You can leave everything to my brother and me," Leander added.

She looked at him long and steadily. The doubt in the ability of the Jones brothers to be of assistance to her, which she had experienced when first she met them, now seemed to have disappeared. There was an air of quiet efficiency about the meek-appearing Leander that inspired confidence.

"Very well," Tanya declared. "I will do just as you say."

"Excellent!" he exclaimed. "By the way, how was this message delivered?"

"It was lying half under the door when I arrived here. I'm certain it was left in my absence, because there was nothing on the floor when Mr. Reece and I left."

FROM A drugstore nearby, Leander telephoned the apartment which he shared with Horatio on Central Park South. He was gratified to hear his brother's voice answer.

"Pick me up at Fifth Avenue and Forty-eighth Street," Leander said. "As soon as possible!"

While he waited for Horatio, Leander thought about the ransom note, resting in his pocket.

Was it really the work of a woman, he wondered. In the same second he devoutly hoped that it wasn't. Experience had taught him that a clever woman criminal was more to be feared than a man. Women seemed, once they had given themselves over to crime, to be craftier, more inhuman and pitiless in achieving their objectives.

Why had Ratvinov been murdered? What connection was there between his slaying and the abduction of Vorlovitch, the one-time Grand Duke Leonid, with the subsequent demand for the stupendous ransom? What had become of the automobile, the chauffeur and footman who had manned it? And lastly, Leander wondered why Tanya Vorlovitch had lied to him about the girl Irina.

The arrival of Horatio at the wheel of the sedan put an end to Leander's speculations. He climbed into the seat beside his brother.

"Where to?" Horatio asked.

"Go through the Park to the West Side," Leander replied. "What did you find out from the master minds at Centre Street?"

Horatio chuckled, but immediately grew serious. "Well, Leander, our friend Colby wanted to know what our interest in the case was."

"What did you tell him?"

"That we only knew what we had read in the papers. Things weren't very busy with us, I explained, so we were merely keeping our hands in."

"The police know nothing then about the kidnaping of Vorlovitch?"

"Not a whisper."

Leander squinted. "Do they know about Irina Ratvinov?"

"Irina Ratvinov? Who is she?"

"The girl in the chorus of *Honey Dew* whom Vorlovitch and his wife were interested in. I learned at the theatre that she is, or is supposed to be, Ratvinov's daughter."

"Colby said nothing about her. The police must have missed that angle."

"How about Ratvinov? What do they know about him?"

"He's been in this country for a little more than three years. Lived alone at a midtown hotel. Naturally, they searched his room, and my dear Leander, they made a discovery from certain documents there that is probably of considerable significance."

"What?" Leander asked eagerly.

"Ratvinov was a member of the OGPU!"

"The Soviet Secret Police!"

"Quite right. And now what puzzles our Centre Street friends is what he was doing in this country."

Leander was silent for a long time. At last he murmured: "And that, Horatio, is something that puzzles me also."

They emerged from the Park onto Central Park West. Horatio glanced at his brother, who seemed wrapped in introspection.

"Where are we going?" Horatio asked.

"West Ninety-third Street. It's near Riverside Drive."

"What's there?"

Taking out his watch, Leander held it beneath the dash light so he could see the hands. "Almost midnight. Rather late for a call, Horatio. But, nevertheless, we are going to pay a visit to Irina Ratvinov!"

THE ADDRESS Leander had obtained from the stage manager of *Honey Dew* was a four-story gray stone house, with rounded bay windows protruding from the first two floors. He had Horatio drive past and stop a quarter of a block beyond.

"Wait here," Leander said softly, and Horatio nodded.

The house entrance was at the top of a flight of steps lined with low stone balustrades. There was a vestibule, the outer doors of which were opened inward. The vestibule was dim, only a few beams from a street light at the curb reaching into it.

Leander saw, as he climbed the steps, that the house was dark. But that was not unusual, considering the hour. Doubtless the occupants had all retired. He took out a small pen flashlight and swung it around the vestibule. A row of brass mail boxes with bell buttons beneath them confirmed a conjecture he had made. The house had been broken up into small apartments.

He found a bell labeled with two names—Ratvin-ov-Dana.

"She has a roommate," Leander thought.

He was about to press the bell button, when his attention was attracted by an automobile which pulled up at the curb directly in front of the house. It was long and low, a town car, a thing of gleaming enamel and chromium trimming. In front he could see two men in uniform.

Instinctively, Leander drew back in the shadows behind the opened door of the vestibule. He was virtually invisible. There was no movement in the car after it stopped. It simply remained at the curb, the men in front as motionless as statues. He couldn't tell whether there was anyone in the back.

Then he heard footsteps within the house, followed almost at once by the rattling of the doorknob. The door opened and a girl, a young girl, he could see as the rays of the street light fell on her face, stepped forth. Leander pressed against the wall. He could easily have reached out and touched her, but she didn't seem to be aware of his presence.

She glanced out toward the curb, toward the car waiting there. Then she fumbled for a moment in her purse and, taking out a key, opened one of the mail boxes. It was the one that bore the names Ratvinov and Dana. After a moment, she shut the front of the box with a metallic click. Then she turned and started quickly down the steps. And as she moved, the light coat she was wearing flew open and Leander saw that she had on an evening gown of bright green. He saw, too, that her hair was a golden blond and waved back from a pert little face.

"My word," he murmured to himself. "My word. Is that Miss Ratvinov?" He regretted that he had failed to get a description of her from the stage manager.

While he stood there in momentary indecision, the girl in green ran lightly across the sidewalk to the waiting car. One of the men in front had climbed from his seat and was holding the door open. As she disappeared in the dark interior, he slammed the door and jumped back to his place beside the driver. The car shot forward.

Leander darted from his hiding place in the vestibule and dashed down the steps to where Horatio was waiting for him in the sedan.

"Quick, Horatio!" he exclaimed as he leaped in. "Follow that automobile!"

THE RAKISH town car bearing the girl in green had already vanished, swinging north on Riverside Drive, when Horatio took up the pursuit. At the corner, it was impossible to tell which one of the score of red tail-lights ahead of them belonged to it. But Horatio pressed down on the throttle and they began to slip past the machines in the stream of traffic.

Leander explained to Horatio about the girl he had seen in the vestibule, the girl with the blond hair and the green dress.

"I watched her come out and get in the car," Horatio said. "Who is she? Irina Ratvinov?"

"Dear me, I wish I knew," Leander murmured. "I decided we should follow her after I saw her open that mail box with the name Ratvinov on it."

There was a moment of silence then, while Horatio deftly maneuvered the sedan around a lumbering motorbus and another automobile that was likewise trying to pass it.

"I observed that the car we are after had twin tail-lights," Horatio remarked.

Leander nodded. "I can't see it."

"They must be driving very rapidly. Though we should be creeping up on them." Suddenly, Horatio said: "Leander, why did the young lady open that mail box?"

"No doubt to see if any mail was in it."

"No, no," Horatio replied. "It has just occurred to me."

"What?"

"One doesn't look for mail at midnight."

"Quite true. At least, not as a rule."

"On the other hand," Horatio continued, "she was probably leaving a message of some sort."

"By George!" Leander exclaimed. "That's it!"

"And whatever the message is, it might be of interest to us."

"Exactly."

A couple of hundred yards ahead of them, the red tail-lights of the automobiles were bunching up, as if the flow of vehicles were stopping for a traffic signal. But Leander, leaning forward to obtain a better view, saw that the interruption had been caused by a smash-up of some sort. Two cars were at angles to the curbing, one with a single headlight pointing crazily toward the sky.

He placed a restraining hand on Horatio's arm. "An accident," he said. "Maybe we'd better stop and see what it is."

Horatio nodded and eased the sedan to a halt a short distance from the two smashed cars. Leander sprang out, hurried forward to where a small group of people were clustered on the parking. As he drew near, he could see a man in the uniform of a taxi driver waving his arms, and talking in excited tones.

Leander wormed his way through the ring of onlookers. The object of the taxi driver's eloquence was a tall policeman, holding an open notebook in one hand.

"You say he slammed right into you?" the policeman demanded.

"That's what I'm fellin' you. I swung over to make a turn. He could see me plain as day. But he just give her the gun and tried to cut by."

"Where's the driver of the other car?"

"Yeah, where is he? He scrammed out. Him and the flunkey beside him—both of 'em in purple uniforms. There was a dame in back. The last I see of 'em, each of them guys has got one of her arms and they're lamming up the street there toward Broadway. Hell, they've beat it in a hack by now."

"Well, they left the car," the policeman said calmly. "We'll get the number and the owner'll have to pay." He pushed through the crowd toward the car, from the radiator of which the water was spraying out behind a crumpled bumper. One of the front wheels was twisted sideways.

"I'll say they gotta pay," the driver muttered. With the back of his hand he wiped away the blood from a long gash on his forehead.

The policeman wrote down the license number in his notebook; Leander made a mental memo of it. The car was the long, powerful town car in which the girl in green had driven from the West Ninety-third Street address. Of that much, Leander was certain.

He walked slowly around it, peered inside through the open door. Nothing was there except a laprobe, neatly folded and hanging on its rail. Then a monogram of silver embossed on the door caught his attention. He bent over and examined it, and a thoughtful wrinkle fanned out from the corners of his mild blue eyes.

The initials on the door were G. V.

"Grigory Vorlovitch," he murmured to himself, as he hurried back to rejoin Horatio.

CHAPTER FOUR
DANCE LADY

WHEN THE brothers Jones returned to the gray stone house on Ninety-third Street, they were surprised to discover that it was brightly lighted. Before the door a green police car was drawn up. And even as Horatio put the brakes on and stopped the sedan on the other side of the street, an ambulance gong sounded. An instant later, the ambulance itself whirled around the corner from West End Avenue and pulled up behind the police car.

"Dear me," Leander murmured. "Something has happened in the short time we've been away from here." He opened the door of the sedan and stepped out. "You'd better come along, Horatio."

They paused a moment on the sidewalk at the foot of the steps which led up to the entrance. A young interne with a wisp of a mustache and wearing a white uniform sprang from the door at the back of the ambulance. At the same moment, a uniformed policeman appeared in the doorway of the house.

"Hurry up, Doc!" he called out.

Leander and Horatio trailed the interne up the steps. The policeman held out his hand and barred their way as they reached the level space before the outer doors of the vestibule.

"Where you think you're going?" he asked gruffly.

Leander smiled and gave a little embarrassed cough. "Why, inside, officer."

"Like hell!"

"And what's the reason we can't go in?" Leander asked with an air of mild surprise. "What's the ambulance doing here? Indeed, what are you doing here?"

"None of your business! On your way! You can read all about it in the papers tomorrow." He motioned to Horatio and Leander to descend the steps and started to turn back into the house.

"Just a minute!" Leander's tone was sharp, with a ring of authority that caused the policeman to wheel quickly with an amazed look on his ruddy face. Leander's pale eyes sparkled through half-closed lids. He held out his hand; in it was a small white card. "Better read that—and then decide whether you want to keep us out."

Things were happening a little too rapidly for the officer's mental speed. He took the card with a dazed look and raised it close to his eyes, so that he could make it out. Almost instantly, his manner underwent a complete change. His hard-boiled attitude melted away and he became almost deferential.

"You—you are Mr. Jones? Of Jones and Jones?" he said slowly, looking first at Leander and then at Horatio, who was just behind him.

"Yes," Leander murmured. "Jones."

"Just Jones," Horatio echoed softly.

"Well, I'm glad to meet you," the policeman said, holding out a massive hand, which Leander gave a vigorous shake. "There's a dead one here," the policeman continued, lowering his voice. "At least, she'll be that any minute, because I don't think that young sawbones can save her."

"Her."

"Yeah. And a swell looker, too. On the top floor front."

"Perhaps we'd better go up," Leander suggested. "And I'll have that card back, if you don't mind."

The policeman nodded, handed the card back. He held the door open while Leander and Horatio stepped into a hallway, poorly lighted and close. They followed him up the stairs. On every floor at least one of the doors was open, and figures of men and women in dressing gowns, bathrobes or hastily donned overcoats peered out. As they saw the policemen, there were questions— "What's happened? What is it? What's wrong?"

His answer was invariably the same to every query. "It's nothing. You'd better go on back and go to sleep."

A door at the front of the highest hallway was ajar several inches. From beyond came a low murmur of voices. The policeman, with Leander and Horatio at his heels, pushed it open and stepped in.

THE ROOM was large and comfortably furnished, with three windows looking out into Ninety-third Street. A door beside the entrance opened into a bathroom, and another one farther along gave access to a small kitchenette. The place was ablaze with light.

The interne was bending over one of two day beds, on which was stretched the still figure of a girl. A second uniformed policeman was standing beside him, and in one corner of the room an elderly man and woman were huddled close together, staring anxiously toward the bed. The man was wearing a bathrobe and the woman's buxom form was covered by a worn dressing gown of blue corduroy.

As Leander and Horatio appeared, the interne straightened up. He gave them only a quick disinterested glance, then looked at the policeman standing beside him and shook his head.

"She's gone," he said. He wasn't old enough to be entirely calloused and his voice sounded a little strained. "You don't need me any more, you need the medical examiner."

The elderly woman in the blue dressing gown gave a low moan. The man she was with patted her reassuringly on the shoulder. "Now, now, Mama," he said. "We couldn't help it. We did all we could. Called the police and the ambulance."

"She was always so cheerful. Such a sweet girl," the woman sobbed.

Horatio moved over to the bed, but Leander made his way to the couple in the corner. He had spotted them as the superintendent of the building and his wife. His guess was quickly confirmed.

"Who is the young lady?" Leander murmured.

The elderly man in the bathrobe stared at him dumbly for a moment and then replied: "Miss Ratvinov."

"Miss Irina Ratvinov," the woman amended.

"Ah, yes. The dancer," Leander said.

"Oh, you know her?"

Leander shook his head. "I've merely heard of her. What happened?"

"You tell him, Mama," the man said.

The woman ceased her sobbing. "I'd just got out of bed to take a look at the hall lights. Make sure they wasn't all left burning, the way they are sometimes. You see, my husband and I have charge of this building," she explained.

"When I stuck my head out the door, I heard someone give a little scream. Kind of choking like. I thought it came from this apartment here, so I woke Henry. The door was locked, but Henry got his passkey and we come in. Miss Ratvinov was lying on the floor all doubled up and groaning. We put her on the bed there and Henry called the police and ambulance."

Across the room the interne and one of the policemen were talking in low tones. Horatio was close to the bed and looking down at the body of the dead girl. She was beautiful, with dark brown hair, long and drawn back from her high white forehead into a tight knot at the nape of her neck. Her features were regular, almost classic, in their perfection. She was dressed in a dark tailored suit, the coat of which lay on a chair.

Not more than seventeen or eighteen, Horatio thought, and even the agonized death she had suffered had failed to dim her youthful loveliness.

"Well, another suicide. Probably out of dough," the policeman muttered. "It's a damn shame the way these kids come here and then when the breaks go against them, bump themselves off."

"I said she died from poison," the ambulance surgeon replied. "Everything points to it, but of course, it'll take an autopsy to find out what it was. She was dead when I examined her." He hesitated a minute. "I don't know that it's suicide."

"What do you mean?"

"That's for you to decide," the ambulance surgeon shrugged. "All I'm supposed to do is pronounce them dead. Well, I'm on my way," he added.

WHEN LEANDER and Horatio departed from the house some fifteen minutes later they were in possession of a considerable store of information.

They had learned that Miss Ratvinov had lived there for the last four months with a Miss Phyllis Dana, also of the *Honey Dew* company. Occasionally, she received visits from her father, a short man with a mop of white hair, a round deeply lined face, and sunken eyes.

A thorough search of the apartment had been made by the policeman, who had failed to uncover the source of the poison, which the interne had declared was the cause of Irina Ratvinov's death. No empty bottles, no box that might have contained deadly powder or capsules.

The brothers Jones didn't wait for the medical examiner to arrive. As Leander pointed out to Horatio, he wouldn't have much of an idea of the nature of the poison until an autopsy was performed.

The elderly couple had volunteered the information that Miss Ratvinov was a very quiet and retiring girl. She never had any "gentleman callers." Miss Dana, on the other hand, was continually going out with men friends, and, according to Henry, coming in at what seemed to him to be very late hours, indeed.

"Why, just tonight," Henry had said, "I heard her leave not more than five minutes before Miss Ratvinov came up the stairs."

In the vestibule, Horatio paused to flash his light into the mail box with the names Ratvinov-Dana on it. But through the holes in the front, he saw that it was empty. Leander watched him with a funny little smile, but said nothing.

They returned to their apartment at Leander's suggestion.

"It looks as if we were temporarily balked, Leander," Horatio remarked, as he divested himself of his dark gray topcoat. "It strikes me that the young lady may well have committed suicide. It wouldn't be strange, considering that her father was murdered last night."

"And her father was a member of the Soviet Secret Police, the OGPU," Leander reminded him. "But there's nothing to show that she was connected with it, or knew that he was. Possibly his desire to keep that knowledge from her may have been the underlying reason for their not living together."

"True," Horatio agreed. "It's puzzling," he added, half to himself. "How do you suppose the poison was taken?"

Leander put his hand in his coat pocket. "I can tell you that, Horatio," he murmured. "And it proves to my complete satisfaction that the death of Miss Ratvinov was not suicide but—murder!"

"What?"

"Look at this." Upon the table Leander placed a tooth-brush and beside it a small can of tooth powder, such as is sold in five- and ten-cent stores. The bristles of the brush had a faintly bluish tinge.

"Where did you get that?" Horatio asked.

"I found the toothbrush lying in the wash basin in the bathroom. The coloration of the bristles is unusual." Horatio bent over and examined the two objects, with-out, however, picking them up. Leander left the room. A minute later he returned bearing a glass half full of water. Into it, he sifted a small amount of powder from the can. At once the water turned a pale blue.

"As I expected," Leander murmured. "One of the cyanides. Which one it'll take a chemist to determine, although I don't believe it makes much difference. There's only a small amount mixed with the tooth powder, but then it requires only a small amount to cause death."

He studied the glass of water for a moment. Then he carried it to the kitchen and dumped it down the waste pipe. After that, he broke the glass and threw the pieces into the rubbish basket.

Back again in the living room, Leander said: "I guessed that the poison which killed her was probably a cyanide compound by the rapidity with which it worked. And when I saw the bluish stain on that tooth brush, I knew she didn't take it intentionally. A person wishing to commit suicide doesn't go to all that trouble," he added.

"Do you think—" Horatio paused uncertainly.

"That it was the girl in green?" Leander supplied. He shrugged faintly. "I don't know, of course. But whoever it was, the poisoner knew that Miss Ratvinov used powder to clean her teeth. There was a tube of paste in the cabinet, which undoubtedly belonged to Miss Dana."

HORATIO DROPPED into a low easy chair. He let his breath exhale between pressed lips in a prolonged sigh.

"And now—we do what?" he asked.

Leander grinned faintly. "We sleep. After I enjoy the solace of a little tobacco." He, too, sat down and touched a match to one of the thin black stogies, which both the brothers Jones were addicted to. When he had sent several spirals of heavy smoke toward the ceiling, Leander continued.

"Did it strike you as odd, Horatio, that this Duchess of Death should direct Madame Vorlovitch to make use of radio in replying to the ransom message?"

"Odd? In what way, Leander?"

"It's a common custom—and much more convenient— to have the answer placed in a newspaper. As a classified advertisement."

"So it is," Horatio assented.

"But there must have been a reason why Madame Vorlovitch was told to have The Town Gossip put the reply on the air in this case."

"Exactly."

"And I believe I know the reason. This Duchess of Death has established a headquarters, where, no doubt, Grigory Vorlovitch is at this moment a prisoner, in some remote spot where the New York papers are not available. But, on the other hand, a radio message would be easily and instantly received."

"By George! That's it, Leander! It dovetails perfectly!"

"We are not dealing with doves, Horatio—but with vultures. But there is really nothing we can do until daytime, since it is now almost two o'clock in the morning."

Before he dropped off to sleep, Horatio spoke to Leander, lying in bed across the room from him.

"Leander—that was an excellent idea of yours to have cards engraved with the name of the police commissioner."

"Well—yes," Leander murmured. "I knew they'd be bound to come in handy some time or another. Especially with that message I wrote on them."

Horatio chuckled softly. "A message introducing you—and ordering all members of the department to assist you in any way possible." He was silent a moment. When he spoke again there was a note of concern in his voice. "But, Leander, I'm afraid there will be a—er—hell to pay, if the commissioner ever finds out about it."

"The men I use them on, aren't apt to be talking with the commissioner," Leander said, with a little laugh. "Besides, my dear Horatio, you'll notice I always get them back. And it's what you get back that counts in this world."

CHAPTER FIVE
TOWN GOSSIP

THE STUDIOS and offices of Radio Station KVKD were situated in the upper reaches of the Bronx. It was a broadcasting unit of small power, depending largely upon the merchants of the borough for its supporting advertising. Nevertheless, with a high-grade receiving set the signals could be picked up at a considerable distance, a fact of which Leander was well aware as he rode upward in the elevator.

He remained at the KVKD offices only a short time; just long enough to obtain the name and address of the man who, every evening at six o'clock, put the program known as The Town Gossip on the air.

A short taxi ride took him to the place where this individual lived. It was only a little after ten o'clock, when Leander rang the bell of an apartment on the third floor of a six-story walk-up. A short, rotund man, his eyes squinting through thick lenses and his buttonlike mouth puckered up, answered almost at once.

"Mr. Martingale?" Leander asked, half apologetically.

The rotund man in the doorway gave the cord of his silk bathrobe a jerk and bobbed his head vigorously up and down. "Yes," he said. "Yes, I am Homer Martingale."

"My name is Jones," Leander murmured. "Just Jones."

"How're you?" Homer Martingale replied, again bobbing his head as though it were hinged to his neck. "Glad to meet you, Mr. Jones. What can I do for you?"

"You're the gentleman who broadcasts under the name of The Town Gossip?"

"Yep. I'm him."

"Well, Leander said with an air of embarrassment, "it's about radio—about your radio program, that I've come to see you."

Homer Martingale frowned ponderously. "If you're serving me with papers in any kind of a slander suit, you're wasting time. There's fifteen suits ahead of you. And anyway, I'm judgment proof!" he added with a snap of his button mouth.

"Oh, no!" Leander assured him hurriedly. "Nothing like that. It's just that—well, I wanted to see if you couldn't include a little item in your most excellent and entertaining hour this evening."

"Come in, come in," Martingale said. He was beaming, but behind his glasses there was a crafty glint. "Excuse my appearance. Life-long habit, sleeping late. All actors do—and I was on the stage for twenty years."

"I believe I've heard of you."

"No doubt," the round little man agreed complacently. "Now about this message. Sit down."

Leander took a seat. From his pocket he brought forth a slip of paper. "This is it. I thought that you might be able to broadcast it for me. It's quite important that it be expressed just as written."

"*Hmnn!* Let me see—" Martingale dropped his eyes to the slip of paper and read—

> Madame Vorlovitch is trying to find the jewel she believed lost and by tomorrow evening expects to report to The Town Gossip that she has it in her hands.

Until Homer Martingale spoke, Leander imagined that the length of time he was taking over the message was devoted to understanding the possible meaning. But, finally, The Town Gossip's eyes filmed over dreamily and he said: "Twenty-nine words. Twenty-nine words." He looked at Leander expectantly.

"Yes—at, let us say, a dollar a word," Leander murmured. He produced a billfold and extracted three ten-dollar bills.

As Homer Martingale tucked the money in his bathrobe pocket, he said: "I really hate to take this, Mr. Jones. But when one has a family—and that damned KVKD pays a mere pittance for the services of a man of my ability."

"You're quite right," Leander replied heartily, but he thought, "My word, what a splendid little graft!"

"It's only since the repeal of prohibition that I've taken to accepting commissions from the general public," Martingale murmured. "Before that I limited myself to one or two clients. Confidentially," he added, lowering his voice, "they were bits of gossip which had a deep significance for certain ships at sea. Loaded with excellent whiskies." He smacked his lips, sighed faintly. "Ah, those were great days. It was most lucrative. By the way," Martingale said suddenly. "I don't seem to be very hospitable. Wouldn't you like a little smile? An eye-opener?"

"Eye-opener?" Leander half closed one of his mild blue eyes. "Why, yes," he said with a friendly chuckle, "I seem to need an eye-opener."

IT WAS more than an hour later when Leander left Martingale's apartment. He had partaken of several drinks of his host's excellent Scotch; the host himself had partaken of several times several. And with each libation, under the adroit and flattering prodding of Leander, he had grown more and more expansive and confidential.

Something like a tear glistened in his watery eyes as he escorted the senior member of Jones and Jones to the front door.

"We part—but we shall meet again," Homer Martingale declaimed dramatically.

"Dear me, yes," Leander nodded. "It's been a great pleasure." And then he added to himself: "You haven't any idea how much help you've been to me."

HORATIO WAS pacing back and forth in the living room, when Leander arrived home. He breathed a deep sigh of relief at sight of his brother.

"I'm glad you're back," he said. "Madame Vorlovitch has phoned at least five times. She wouldn't tell me what she wanted. Said she had to speak to you. She doesn't seem to understand that I'm a member of the firm and actively engaged in this case."

"I'll call her right away," Leander said.

He thumbed rapidly through the phone book till he found the number, then lifted the receiver. "Mr. Leander Jones calling Madame Vorlovitch," he said presently. Another wait. Leander stared at the ceiling; Horatio took out a thin black stogy and set it going.

"Hello," Leander said. "What has happened?"

Horatio, watching him, saw a look of exasperation gradually appear on Leander's face. "But my dear lady, you shouldn't have done that until I told you to… No, it's all right now." His tone was the sort one might use to a fractious child.

"Leave everything to us. And remember what I told you about remaining at home…. Yes, I know you had to go out to do that. But the point is that you shouldn't have done it. Well, never mind. You'll hear from me before long—with good news," he added, and hung up.

"My God, Horatio! Women!" He made a helpless gesture with both hands.

"What's the matter?" Horatio asked, hiding a grin.

"Madame Vorlovitch informs me that she went to the safety-deposit vault as soon as it was open this morning and removed her jewels. Half a million dollars' worth, or more. And she's got them in her apartment with her—at a time like this—when she knows that a gang of extortionists have kidnaped her husband."

"Why did she do that?"

"Said she wanted to have them ready to pay the ransom," Leander all but spluttered. "If she wants to pay the ransom—why should she bother with us? If it weren't for the two murders and the disappearance of Miss Dana, I'd be tempted to let her pay."

Horatio gave a short laugh. "No, you wouldn't, Leander."

"Well—" A slow smile broke out on Leander's countenance. "No, I wouldn't. You're right, Horatio."

"Did you fix it up to broadcast that message this evening?"

"Yes. It will postpone any crisis another twenty-four hours. In fact, I am quite the bosom companion of The Town Gossip by now. We imbibed together." He suddenly grew serious. "And while Mr. Homer Martingale poured liquor into me, I managed to pump a very important bit of information out of him."

Horatio had started to raise his stogy to his lips, but his hand stopped in midair. "What?"

"In the first place, The Town Gossip, before the repeal of prohibition, was accustomed to broadcast code messages for a certain notorious bootlegger and rum-runner.

"You may recall, I decided that the reason for using radio to answer the ransom message was because the daily papers were not readily available?"

"Yes, Leander. And a very astute conclusion, too," Horatio murmured.

"Well, what could be more inaccessible than a ship at sea?"

Horatio's eyes sparkled.

"And whoever sent the ransom note knew that The Town Gossip could be persuaded to broadcast the reply—for a consideration. Who would know that better than the man who had used him before—a man who owned ships—liquor-running ships?"

"Who is it?" Horatio asked eagerly.

"Fox Fogarty!"

Horatio whistled long and softly. "Fox Fogarty! Then Fox Fogarty is behind the abduction of Vorlovitch. And probably the murders."

"At least he's mixed up in it. But don't forget the Duchess of Death," Leander said solemnly.

"You believe there is such a person?"

"Absolutely!"

Horatio was thoughtful for a moment. "Then, Leander, it seems to me that the Duchess of Death and Fox Fogarty must be working together."

"Exactly!" Leander's lips tightened grimly. "And I think I know how to find out what boat or boats the Fox still owns."

"So we're going to sea," Horatio murmured.

"No. You're going to New London, Connecticut."

LEANDER WENT to the Grand Central terminal with Horatio. As they waited for the gate to the train to open, Leander said: "You won't have any difficulty up there, I'm certain."

"I shouldn't."

"You'll hear from me just as soon as I have any news."

"I'll be waiting for it," Horatio nodded. The guard slid the gates aside and the crowd began to file through. "Remember," Horatio said softly, "that there's a reason why Fogarty is called the Fox."

Leander's blue eyes twinkled. "He'll have plenty of sour grapes before we finish with him," he said.

At the cab stand in the station, Leander climbed into a taxi. "Floyd Bennett Airport," he ordered crisply, as the driver pulled down the flag.

The driver beamed. It was a long and profitable haul to the municipal flying field on the far outskirts of Brooklyn.

Leander settled back in the seat, his eyes divided by a tiny thought wrinkle. Almost unconsciously, he put one hand behind him and felt his hip. A hard bump that marked the place where his pistol reposed met his touch and he smiled.

It was the middle of the afternoon when they arrived at the airport. Leander paid the driver and made his way to the office. A tall man, wearing laced boots and a leather windbreaker glanced up at his entrance.

"I wish," Leander said meekly, "to hire an airplane."

The tall man's bronzed face broke into a grin. "You've come to the right place."

"A flying boat—and a pilot," Leander continued. "I don't fly myself."

"Where do you want to go?"

"Well, I don't know the exact spot."

"Just want to take a little hop, huh? See what it's like to be up in the air?"

"It may be quite an extensive hop, as you call it," Leander murmured. "You see, I want to join a party of—of friends who are on a boat. Somewhere in Long Island Sound, I believe."

The tall man nodded. "I get you. Want to cruise around and if you can locate it, have the pilot put you on board."

"That's almost it," Leander beamed. "Except that I may not want to go on board. I'll have to decide later. Do you think you can find this boat? It's quite large—with three masts. I believe they call it an auxiliary schooner."

"What's the name of it?"

"The *Gretchen B.*"

"Well, Mr.—"

"Jones. Just Jones," Leander supplied.

"Well, Mr. Jones, we'll see if we can't find *Gretchen B.* for you," the tall man said with an amused twitch of his lips. He got up from the desk at which he had been sitting.

"There's just one other thing," Leander said apologetically. "I'm a little timid about flying. Could I take a plane that has a radio—a two-way radio in it?"

The tall man whistled thoughtfully. "That makes it a little more difficult," he said. Then he suddenly held up the palm of his hand and gave it a nonchalant wave. "Wait a minute!" He strode out the door and disappeared around the corner of the building.

In a few minutes he returned, accompanied by a sandy-haired man, about Leander's stature, and with a two days' growth of beard adorning his chin.

"Meet Gus," the tall man said. "He'll fly you. You'll have to take a big ship. A Boeing amphibian. The only one we've got here now with the radio you want." He looked doubtfully as Leander's wrinkled suit, his battered brown hat and the meek blue-eyed face beneath it. "It'll be pretty expensive."

Leander had anticipated him. His billfold was already out of his pocket and he drew forth a number of banknotes.

"Here's a couple of hundred dollars," he murmured. "When we get back, you can give me the change, according to how long I have to use the plane."

As Leander was about to climb through the hatch into the cabin of the airplane, the tall man, who had accompanied him to the runway, handed him a pair of binoculars.

"Better take these," he said, smiling. "You may need them to find *Gretchen.*"

CHAPTER SIX
DERELICT

IT WAS a clear, crisp day. The visibility was unusually high, and as the airport slid away beneath them,
and Gus pulled the big plane up and up, New York began
to spread out. A toy city, shadowed by a billowing haze of
smoke. Far to the west the hills of northern Jersey were a
pale lavender. Toward the east and north stretched Long
Island; beyond, the waters of the sound, a deep blue, and
beyond them the line of the Connecticut shore. Gus
banked sharply and headed northeast. From time to time,
in the distance, they caught sight of other planes. And even
after they passed the north shore of the Island and were out
over the Sound, they saw still others flying above the water.

"Excellent," Leander thought. "With a lot of planes up,
we won't attract any special attention."

Within the cabin it was warm and comfortable. The
steady drone of the motors pounded on their ears, yet the
noise was sufficiently muffled to permit conversation. Gus
shifted the chew of tobacco that was bulging one of his
cheeks.

"Where you think this windjammer is?" he asked.

"Well—" Leander hesitated thoughtfully. "That's the
trouble. It may be almost anywhere. But the most likely
place, it seems to me, is out around Montauk. Perhaps
Gardiners Bay."

"Lotta places around Shelter Island for 'em to anchor, if
they wanted to," Gus suggested.

"Yes."

"We'll give every schooner we spot the once-over."

"That's a splendid plan," Leander agreed.

FOR SEVERAL hours they continued to cruise above the Sound. The sea was calm, only a gentle ground-swell rolling. Occasionally Gus dipped the plane down to look over a ship, but none was a three-master. And then at last, far beyond Montauk Point in the wide stretch of the Atlantic, Leander spied a sailing vessel.

"We'd better come down," he said.

"Sure."

"Up wind."

"O.K.!"

The giant amphibian settled gracefully on the sea in a shower of white spray a half mile from the schooner.

"We'll let the wind drift us up to it," Leander murmured.

"O.K.," Gus agreed.

The afternoon was drawing to a close, and in the west the sun looked like a red-hot stove lid, blood red. The plane floated closer and closer. But they could see nobody on the deck; the sails were flapping idly.

"Doesn't seem to be anybody home," Gus grunted.

"Dear me," Leander murmured. He raised the binoculars the tall man at the airport had given him. On the stern he made out the name—*Gretchen B.—Halifax.*

"What we gonna do now?" asked Gus.

"I believe—that is, I suppose I'd better go aboard. Can you maneuver the plane under the stern? Without using the motors?"

"Yeah."

Slowly but surely the ship of the sky and the ship of the sea came together. Leander climbed out on the wing and as they passed beneath the taffrail, he caught it with both hands and scrambled to the deck. The plane drifted away, with Gus standing in the hatch watching.

Leander moved forward cautiously. A pat on his hip, where his pistol reposed, gave him reassurance. Beyond the mainmast, he came to a companion way and then from below the sound of voices fell upon his ears. Leander peered down and his pale blue eyes widened.

Seated on a huge scarlet chair, the back of which was in the form of a hideous demon, was a woman in a black satin gown. A low-cut gown that revealed every sinuous curve of her figure. Her hair, blue-black, was drawn away from her forehead; her eyes slanted sharply under tilted eyebrows.

"She looks," Leander thought, "like a younger and more beautiful version of Madame Vorlovitch."

Apparently all the partitions below decks on the schooner had been removed to store liquor in the days of its rum-running. The room in which this exotic-looking woman sat on her ghastly throne was more like the saloon of a liner than the cabin of a sailing ship. And at first glance Leander was startled by the number of persons gathered in it.

There were six men—six men with black masks and monkish brown cowls. They were ranged before the demon throne, three on each side, and in the hand of one was a leather knout. It was bloodstained from the bared back of a man who was on his knees.

And standing beside him was the girl in green—Phyllis Dana! Her wrists were firmly bound.

"Dear me," Leander murmured to himself. "Applying the lash."

At the opposite end of this nautical torture chamber were three more men, two of them apparently seamen, and the other Leander recognized as the notorious Fox Fogarty. A grim smile touched the corners of Leander's lips. His guess had been right, and when he had discovered at the Barge Office the name of the boat which Fox Fogarty still owned, he was on the trail of the missing Grigory Vorlovitch.

The woman on the demon throne spoke. Her voice was icy; her accent Russian. "My dear friend Fogarty, if I choose to have this man whipped, it is not for you to protest in his behalf."

Fogarty glowered. "All I'm saying is there ain't any use in it. We snatched him and there's going to be a pay-off. But that doesn't mean I'm gonna stand here and let you have him licked like a dog. What the hell's the idea anyway?"

The woman laughed. "Only my pleasure. He's Grigory Vorlovitch to you, but to me he is the Grand Duke Leonid—once of Moscow." Her eyes flashed venomously. "This cringing creature here is a member of the aristocracy I loath—have always loathed—because as a child in Russia they made me suffer."

LEANDER HESITATED, and instinctively he reached toward his pistol. Then almost instantly, he realized that it would be foolhardy to try to rescue Grigory Vorlovitch and the girl in green. There were nine men down in that cabin, and undoubtedly all armed.

Leander had discovered what he wanted to know, the whereabouts of Vorlovitch, and Vorlovitch was in no immediate peril.

Noiselessly Leander drew back from the companionway and moved to the rail of the schooner. The plane had drifted a hundred yards away, but the helmeted head of Gus was visible in the hatch. He was watching Leander curiously. Leander raised his hand and beckoned to him to bring the plane closer.

In a few minutes the senior member of the firm of Jones and Jones would be using the two-way radio he had been so insistent on at the airport. And in another few minutes Horatio Jones would be leaving the Coast Guard Station at New London, heading for the open sea beyond Montauk in a cutter, a cutter equipped with rifles and machine guns and manned by a crew whose business it was to handle just such situations as this.

But Gus was unaware of what was going on aboard the *Gretchen B.* At Leander's signal he opened both of the powerful motors on the Boeing wide and started to taxi toward the schooner.

Leander gasped. "Dear me," he murmured to himself. "Dear me. That is sure to start trouble. I suppose I should have taken him into my confidence—he would have been more careful."

The trouble Leander Jones had expected was not long in coming. There was a scuffling of feet on the companionway, and Leander had just time to duck behind a deckhouse when the two seamen and Fogarty dashed into sight. Under the Fox's arm was a sub-machine gun and the other men were brandishing automatics.

"What the hell!" Fogarty burst out. He looked at the plane roaring toward him. The weapon came up. There was a streak of flame and a splatter of bullets on the fuselage. As Leander watched, the plane swung in a wide arc, grazed the stern of the schooner. And he saw then that some of the slugs had found their mark. Gus was slumped over the stick.

Like a crazy thing, the big amphibian went roaring out to sea in an erratic course. And with it went Leander's hopes of getting through a radio message to Horatio.

"You got him, Fox," one of the seamen said.

"Yeah, I got him. What was he doing out here anyway?"

"Looked like he was trying to come right up to us," the second sailor said.

"I don't like it," Fogarty growled.

The other men both laughed. "You don't have to worry none about that guy," one of them said. "He'll just be another lost ocean flyer."

"Well, he had it coming to him." Fogarty suddenly lowered his voice, and Leander had to strain his ears to catch the words. "Listen, you birds. I'm beginning to get a notion this Duchess dame is getting ready to pull a fast one on us."

"What do you mean, Fox? I thought you was sweet on her?"

"Yeah—I've been nuts about her for a long time. But I don't stay nuts on any dame who double-crosses me."

"That gang of hers gives me a pain. All them robes and hoods and masks. And that damned red chair she sits in gives me the willies," the sailor said. "What's the idea?"

Fogarty hooked the tommy gun in the bend of his arm and shrugged. "It's a lotta baloney. But she's half-cracked, I think. I'm just tipping you off. Keep your eyes open and when that Town Gossip message comes through, and we find out the dough is ready, we're gonna be sure we get ours. Two hundred and fifty grand. After that, she can take her red chair and her six mugs and get off the *Gretchen B*. I don't like those birds who can't speak good English."

"What are they? Russians?"

"Three of 'em are and the others are Frogs. She picked 'em up somewhere in Europe and organized this gang. When things got too hot, they all came over here."

"Where'd you meet her?" one of the seamen asked.

"She used to come in that joint I had on Fifty-second Street. I fell for her, and then she cooked up this Vorlovitch snatch. She knew he had heavy jack, although I don't understand how she found it out."

"She's a swell looker," the first sailor said.

Fogarty nodded. "She's the best looker I ever saw. But she's got a bad eye, and mister, she's got the meanest streak in her of anybody I ever knew. She's just naturally cruel."

Leander, crouching in the shelter of the deckhouse, puckered his lips into a soundless whistle. "Dear me," he thought. "I'm afraid that when thieves fall out an honest man may have a chance to prosper."

Fogarty was speaking again. "I'm just warning you to be on your toes. Keep your mouths shut and your eyes open. Come on! We'll go back down. I'm gonna see if I can't get her to lay off having that guy whipped. First thing you know, she'll probably be wanting to give the blonde some of it."

Their footsteps sounded on the companionway. Leander emerged stealthily from behind the deckhouse and again went forward to where he could peer down into the cabin and hear what was being said. He was in a ticklish spot, he acknowledged to himself. Marooned on this drifted vessel with a band of heartless cutthroats. Now it was not merely a matter of rescuing Vorlovitch; he would have to think fast even to save himself.

As he squinted down at the Duchess of Death, he asked himself the question over and over: "Who is she?" There was something vaguely familiar about her appearance, yet Leander couldn't quite place her.

THIS SELF-STYLED Duchess of Death was looking at Fogarty with a scornful sneer, an expression of cold viciousness. "My friend," she purred, "you must realize that I allow nobody to interfere in what I wish to do. I had Ratvinov killed. I had Alphonse here very adroitly put poison on Irina Ratvinov's toothbrush."

From one of the hooded and masked figures nearest to the hideous demon throne came a low chuckle. "Highness, it was quite simple. After Joseph's phone call had lured this little lady from the apartment."

"Joseph did well. He also did well to help Ivan eliminate Ratvinov. It was excellent work, the obtaining of positions for the two of them to drive, the beautiful automobile of Monsieur Vorlovitch." She looked at Fogarty again and her lips curled. "You American gunmen use crude methods. They lack subtlety."

The Fox's face crimsoned, but he only muttered: "Why'd you want to bump off the old guy for, anyway?"

"Because he belonged to the OGPU. He was what you so naively refer to as a shoofly."

"And that's the only reason?"

"Yes," the Duchess of Death said with a feline smile.

"My God! And the kid?"

She lifted a graceful red-nailed hand to her glossy hair and patted it with a nonchalant gesture. "Because Irina Ratvinov resembled the late Grand Duchess Anastasia of Russia."

Fox Fogarty looked bewildered. "Huh?"

"Exactly. And you may have heard that some people believe that the Grand Duchess Anastasia survived the execution of the Romanoffs." Again that careless gesture. "Perhaps—perhaps not. And some people also"—with a glance at the bloody figure of Vorlovitch "—believed that Irina Ratvinov was the daughter of Anastasia and a renegade soldier who helped her to escape.

"That, however, my friend Fogarty, is not true. Irina Ratvinov was—my half-sister," she concluded blandly.

A look of utter amazement distorted The Fox's face. "You—you had your own sister bumped off?"

"My half-sister," she corrected him. "We had the same father."

"Well, I'll be—" Fogarty let the sentence go unfinished.

The Duchess's eyes moved to Vorlovitch. They glittered with an intense hatred. "And you, Monsieur Vorlovitch—as you choose to call yourself—believed no one knew your plans, plans to take advantage of the Soviet State, in the event that it should become involved in a war with Japan."

The man on the floor groaned. "You hell cat!"

His words seemed to amuse the Duchess of Death intensely. She threw back her head and a taunting laugh rang from her scarlet lips, which appeared to be bloody, so vivid was the rouge upon them.

"I believe it is sometimes known as a *coup d'etat,* this scheme of yours. You were going to place on the throne once occupied by Catherine the Great, my half-sister, Irina Ratvinov—whom you accidentally discovered in the chorus of a musical show. You noticed the resemblance to Anastasia as a young girl. And you imagined that monarchists would rally around her. What folly!"

Fogarty moved close to the Duchess and stuck out his lower jaw. "Listen," he snarled, "how did you find out all this cackle you're giving us?"

"Very simple. Every bit of conversation which took place in that beautiful Hispano was perfectly audible to Joseph and Ivan sitting in front. Ivan is quite clever at fixing up such usual devices."

Leander at the top of the companionway smiled softly to himself. The words of this beautiful, dangerous and boastful vixen were fast clearing up numerous questions in his mind. He was startled to hear of the scheming by Grigory Vorlovitch; but it explained why Tanya Vorlovitch had lied to him about the reason behind her interest in the girl Irina.

The girl in green, whom Leander had identified as Phyllis Dana, had been standing silent and motionless. Leander was unable to get a glimpse of her face, since her back was toward the companionway, but he noticed that her fingers below the cords binding her wrists twitched spasmodically.

And now she spoke, with a choking voice, a voice in which terror and wild horror were mingled.

"Why—why did you bring me to—this awful ship? What have I done to you?"

The Duchess turned on her with an animal snarl. "You little fool, it was an accident. We only wanted to get you out of your apartment, because we knew you were in the habit of leaving the key in the mailbox. Ever since Irina Ratvinov lost hers."

"But—but what do you intend to do with me?" the girl in green faltered.

One of the cowled men replied. "If Madame Vorlovitch fails to answer our ransom demand, you won't be long for this world. Nor will this cringing thing on the floor." He gave a disagreeable and mirthless laugh, then stepped forward and swung the knout upon the helpless form.

Leander's usually mild eyes blazed. Only with an effort was he able to control himself, to keep from springing down the companionway into the cabin, and, gun in hand, attack these vicious murderers in their grotesque costumes. But he instantly reminded himself that it was worse than useless. They would kill him before he could dispatch more than one or two of them.

And yet he knew that something had to be done very presently. In only a short time, The Town Gossip would be broadcasting his reply to the extortion letter. The probable effect of that upon this inhuman woman below made a tingle travel down Leander's spine.

With a sinking heart he wished that Gus had used more discretion in handling the plane. It would have saved his life; and it would have enabled Leander to radio to Horatio for help.

With cautious steps Leander backed from the companionway and aft along the rail. It had seemed to him risky to remain where at any instant either one of the brown-cowled killers or Fox Fogarty might come topside and discover him.

Between the mizzen mast and main, Leander saw a small deck house. He made his way to it quietly and a funny expression appeared in his blue eyes. He gazed aloft and a smile slowly replaced the set, grim look of a moment before. He glanced through a porthole. Then with almost breathless haste, he reached the door. It yielded to his touch.

Leander stepped inside the deck house, closed the door gently.

CHAPTER SEVEN
DEATH WALKS THE DECK

THE SUN was dropping lower and lower x toward the horizon. In the west, the sky was splashed with brilliant red, as if a giant hand had swirled a mammoth paint brush across a heavenly canvas, careless of the colors from a palette of the gods.

At the top of the companionway ladder a hooded brown figure suddenly appeared, then another and another. There was something ghastly in the incongruity of these men, like masked monks, treading the deck of this schooner with its flapping sails.

"It is time for the radio program of The Town Gossip," one of them said, as they moved toward the stern and the small deck house, into which Leander Jones had vanished only a few minutes earlier.

"Yes," replied a second. "And if Madame Vorlovitch has failed to get the money and jewels—" He ended with a meaning abruptness.

"If that happens, I shall have the pleasure of killing Vorlovitch with my own hands," the first of the monkish murderers snarled.

"You're mistaken, Ivan," the third said. "The Duchess will keep that pleasure for herself. But you may be allowed to dispose of the girl—if you are lucky. We will draw lots."

"We are all talking foolishly," the first one shrugged. "Madame Vorlovitch will pay."

"That is good sense, Brother Joseph," said Ivan.

Suddenly he put out a restraining hand to keep his companions from advancing. "Wait!" he whispered. On catlike feet he, however, continued aft until he could see through a porthole into the deck house. He raised a warning palm, then tiptoed back to the others.

"There is someone in there—a stranger. Small. I'll take care of him."

From beneath the folds of his robe he drew an automatic. Then he moved again to the deck house and vanished around the end of it. The two other killers hesitated a moment, but a few seconds afterward they, too, glided like huge brown spiders out of sight down the main hatch.

Leander Jones slowly and silently opened the door of the deck house. He peered out, his eyes roaming about the ship. He could see no one and step by step he emerged. He started toward the bow, but he had barely moved, when the brown-robed figure appeared and was on him in a swift silent bound.

The heavy pistol described an arc and reached Leander's skull with a sickening thud. Leander crumpled, but before he landed on the deck, his masked assailant had slipped his hands beneath Leander's armpits and was dragging him toward the companionway to the cabin.

"Highness," Ivan said as he dumped the unconscious figure of his victim on the floor beside Vorlovitch, "I have put him to sleep for a short while."

"Who is it?" the Duchess demanded.

"I don't know. He was in the radio room. Fortunately I heard him before he was aware that I was around."

FOX FOGARTY moved forward from the end of the cabin and rolled Leander over. Then he whistled. "That's either Leander or Horatio Jones! They look alike—twins. But it don't make much difference, they're equally bad medicine."

"Jones? Jones?" the Duchess queried.

"Detectives—and good ones!"

The black eyebrows suddenly dropped till they all but hid her squinting and angry eyes. She leaned forward on her demon throne and her hands clutched the arms so tightly that her elbows trembled. But she was controlling her intense emotion. Even her voice was calm and low when she spoke to Fogarty, and its very quietness was an even deadlier sound than a burst of rage would have been.

"Detectives. Detectives—I do not like them, good or bad."

"Me neither. With me they're like Indians. The only good one is a good and dead one," he snapped.

She smiled maliciously. "Never mind. This one will never live to leave this ship."

"Better dump some water on him and bring him around. I gotta couple of questions to ask him," Fogarty said.

"Water, Alphonse!"

"They're little guys," Fogarty muttered. "But from all I ever heard about 'em, they're tough. They don't look tough, but that don't mean nothing. Maybe we can't make him talk," he added with a trace of doubt.

"He will talk!" She looked significantly toward the bloody lash which had stripped long flaming gashes across the back of Grigory Vorlovitch.

IN SPITE of a liberal quantity of water which the man called Alphonse brought and doused repeatedly on Leander, it was a long time before the little criminologist regained consciousness. And when his pale eyes at last did flutter open, it seemed to take him several minutes to sweep the fog from his throbbing head.

Leander was lying on the floor directly in front of the Duchess of Death, who was staring down at him through half-veiled eyes. His hands and ankles had been bound with stout manila line. He was helpless. But as his brain began to clear, Leander's mask of meekness and self-effacement spread over his face to conceal his chagrin at his capture.

The Duchess moved her head up and down slowly. It made her long pendant earrings swing in an odd sort of way. Leander smiled meekly, but it brought no answering smile from this murderous female.

"Well Detective Jones," she said, "you seem to have recovered."

"Dear me, so I do," he murmured.

"For a moment or two, I was afraid that Ivan had been too powerful. Not that your death would be a pity. But my friend Fogarty has a few questions he wants to ask you—first!"

"You're damn right I have!" Fogarty burst out. He stood over Leander, glared down at him. "What're you doing on this ship, huh? And how did you get here?"

"Why—why I was flying out over the Sound, when we spotted this schooner. There was no one in sight on the deck, no wheelman, the sails set but flapping to no purpose. So, of course, we decided it must be a derelict. I boarded it to investigate. But I had hardly set foot upon the deck when you came rushing up and began to shoot at my pilot."

"Yeah, and I got him," Fogarty interrupted with a tone of satisfaction.

"Naturally, I found that a little distressing. I'm a man of peace, Mr. Fogarty. I tried to hide—until I could decide what to do. Does that explain my presence aboard your vessel?" he added mildly.

Fogarty's lips curled. "That's a phony, and you know it!"

"Dear me. A phony. No, no, I assure you Mr. Fogarty, it is quite the truth."

"Well, get me straight, Mr. Horatio Jones—"

"Leander, not Horatio," Leander corrected him meekly.

"Check. Leander," Fogarty growled. "But it don't make no difference, because they ain't never gonna carve it on a tombstone."

"I don't understand."

"We're gonna park you in Davey Jones' locker. Maybe he's some relation, eh, wise guy?"

Leander smiled weakly and said in a serious tone: "No, not any relation. I have only the one brother—Horatio. You seem to know about him."

"I'll say I do! And where's he while you're flying out here and sticking your nose into our business?" Fogarty demanded.

"New London, Connecticut," Leander replied.

Fogarty looked suspiciously at the man on the floor, but Leander's expression was guileless, innocent. The gangster started to speak. The Duchess broke in upon him with a gesture of weariness.

"Let us waste no more time," she said. "We may as well drop him into the sea and have done with the matter. This man is stupid. He bores me. Ivan!"

"Yes, Highness."

"Find something with which to fill his pockets, to make certain that he sinks. Then you may drop him overboard."

"Yes, Highness." The figure in the brown cowl vanished up the companionway ladder.

Leander was a courageous man but now he could feel little drops of cold sweat breaking out on his forehead.

But his tormentors paid no notice, appeared to think the gleaming moisture was from the water that had been poured on him.

Ivan returned. There was an eagerness in his step as he entered the cabin. Leander caught a sparkle of his dark eyes through the slits in his mask.

Into Leander's pockets he stuffed nails, chunks of old iron, even a few empty machine-gun shells. The others watched Ivan in silence. The only sound was low sobbing from Phyllis Dana and occasional moans from Vorlovitch. Once Fogarty gave a brief grim laugh.

At last Ivan hoisted Leander up on his shoulder like a sack of meal. Accompanied by Alphonse and Joseph, he mounted the companionway to the topside. And as the ghastly little group was disappearing, Fogarty mocked: "So long, Jonesy! Say hello to the mermaids for me!"

Leander made no reply. His face was white, set, but he determined not to give Fox Fogarty any satisfaction even at the last. Besides Leander was trying to look about him from his perch on Ivan's shoulder. But it was impossible to see much. A stretch of calm sea, and another glimpse of blood-red sky.

"Over the stern," Ivan said.

"As good as any," one of the other brown figures agreed.

THEY CARRIED him to the taffrail, lifted him, poised him there for a moment, as if reveling in the hideous death they were about to inflict upon him. But the murder monks never tumbled Leander into the sea.

"Look!"

From the throat of Joseph came the startled cry. He pointed wildly off the port bow. And instantly the others took up the alarm.

"A ship! A ship!"

Steaming toward them under forced draft was a low gray Coast Guard cutter. From its razor-sharp prow the water was flared out like two white wings. The smoke from its funnels hung straight back as far as eye could see.

For only a second did Ivan hesitate. He laid Leander on the ship's rail, gave him a push and then turned and ran down the deck toward the cabin hatch. His brown robe blew away from his racing legs.

Leander hung half off the rail and half on. It seemed impossible for him not to drop to his death in the sea. But then the ship rolled slightly in the ground swell. And Leander fell to the deck with painful violence. He breathed a relieved sigh.

Apparently, the men on board had forgotten about him. Or thought he had already plunged to his death. For he lay there on the deck behind a coil of hawser and nobody paid any attention to him. All the men had come pouring up from the cabin—Fox Fogarty his sailors, and the six cowled figures. Only the Duchess of Death remained below.

"By God!" Fogarty screamed. "It's the Coast Guard! I know 'em. I crossed with 'em plenty when I was running booze! Now what the hell are they doing here?"

As if in answer to his question, the rakish craft swung toward the schooner abruptly. From the bow there was a puff of white smoke, a dull boom. And a quarter of a mile from the sailing ship a column of water spurted.

Fox Fogarty knew what that meant. "Heave to—like hell! We're gonna fight. Come on you mugs—out with your roscoes!" He himself was working away with the sub-machine gun.

But the Coast Guards appeared to have the same idea. From the rail a half dozen of the crew opened fire with rifles. One of Fogarty's men dropped, screaming and cursing. Then one of the brown figures suddenly staggered back, clutched at his throat and sank slowly down to his knees and immediately pitched forward and lay still.

Standing on the bridge of the cutter was a little man in a battered brown hat, a wrinkled gray suit and a topcoat. He turned to the skipper standing beside him, cupped his hand and shouted above the uproar. The commander of the vessel, a grizzled veteran, nodded. He turned to the man at the wheel and shouted an order.

Instantly the cutter careened like a drunken thing so hard was the wheel put over. Straight for the schooner it headed.

"He's gonna ram us! The dirty dog!" Fogarty cried.

But in that he was mistaken. The cutter's captain yanked the engine room telegraph. The speed of the cutter visibly diminished and a moment later the helmsman skillfully maneuvered his fleet craft alongside the *Gretchen B.* And with a yell a dozen Coast Guardsmen scrambled over the rail, dropped to the schooner's lower deck, firing as they went.

The hand-to-hand struggle was bitter but brief. When it ended a few minutes later, five of the brown-robed assassins lay stretched on the deck. The two sailors were groaning from bullet wounds. Only Fox Fogarty was unharmed, but his hands were raised high above his head. Of the Coast Guardsmen half a dozen were bleeding from wounds.

And then Horatio discovered Leander.

"My word," Horatio murmured as he cut Leander's bonds. "It seems most fortunate that we got here as soon as we did."

Leander made a wry face. "Just thirty seconds later would have been too late."

"I got the radio signals perfectly."

"Splendid!" He chuckled softly. "Mr. Fox Fogarty has an excellent set. No doubt it was quite necessary for his rum-running activities.

Suddenly Horatio's face shadowed. "What about the plane you came out in, Leander? We found it on our way over here."

"What about the pilot?"

"He's badly shot up. But I believe he'll pull through. He's on the cutter."

"That was the result of The Fox's activity with a machine gun," Leander said. But never mind that now. The Duchess of Death! Hurry—below! To the cabin!"

But the red demon throne was empty. On the floor lay two still figures—Grigory Vorlovitch and Phyllis Dana, unconscious but far from dead.

HORATIO LIFTED his eyes from the girl and man to the demon throne. "Good heavens! What is it?"

Leander had crossed the cabin and was standing beside the monstrosity. "A crazy woman's crazier idea. It's supposed to be a throne, I suppose. Dear me, what a hideous bit of wood carving." He suddenly wheeled. "We've got to find this Duchess of Death, Horatio! At once!"

In his haste to head back on deck, he bumped against the scarlet throne of the Duchess of Death. To his surprise it moved a few inches. He had imagined it heavier, but a quick examination disclosed that it was on concealed ball casters.

Leander pushed it to one side. Behind where the red chair had rested, an opening had been cut through the bulkhead. Beyond, it was dark. And Leander surmised that it had been used in some fashion in the days when the *Gretchen B.* was a rum-runner.

He darted into the opening, Horatio close behind him. Ahead a thin strip of light marked a hatch. Leander moved toward it. He climbed the companionway ladder, pushed against the hatch cover.

At that moment a commotion on deck came to their ears. Shouts, running feet.

Leander got the hatch cover off and climbed to the topside. And he saw what had created the stir. Halfway up the ratlines to the lofty mainmast was a woman in a clinging satin gown of black—The Duchess of Death! Instantly, Leander realized her purpose. He sprang into the rigging, started up after the woman above him.

But she seemed to be possessed of unusual agility and strength. Neither Leander nor Horatio who followed him, nor the Coast Guard who formed the last of this strange procession could overtake her.

At the juncture of the gaff and mast, she paused. For a brief second she glanced down, a look of wild disdain on her beautiful face. Then she raised her arms high, almost as if in supplication to the sky, a sky fiery in the setting sun, red as the demon throne, red as the blood of this female fiend's victims. Outlined against the awful flaming sunset, she balanced on the gaff for a breathless second. Then she sprang. Over and over her body turned. It struck the water with a nauseating smack, sank beneath the surface.

Two of the Coast Guardsmen dove after her. But the beautiful and depraved Duchess never reappeared.

ON THE cutter, towing the schooner, Leander and Horatio sat with the captain in his cabin. Leander rose from his chair, turned the switch on the radio. Presently a voice filled the room, a familiar voice to Leander's ears.

"…you are now listening to The Town Gossip, the garrulous, gossipy, good-for-what ails you of KDKV. Well, folks, I've got some choice bits for you this evening. First of all, Madame Vorlovitch reports that she is trying to find the jewel she believed—"

Leander shut off the radio with a grin. "Dear me, Horatio," he murmured. "My friend Homer Martingale is one honest man at least."

"But I guess that's one item of gossip it doesn't make any difference about now," Horatio replied.

THE NEXT morning Horatio failed to arrive at the office of Jones and Jones in the Flatiron Building until after eleven o'clock.

"Well, I have some news for you, Leander," he began without preamble. "Alphonse, the sole survivor of that nefarious band of killers, decided to talk."

"So?"

"Yes. And it explains about the Duchess of Death."

"She was insane," Leander murmured.

"Exactly. But she was beautiful and seemed to exert a strange power over her followers. She came by her hypnotic force naturally."

Leander looked puzzled. "What are you getting at, Horatio?"

"Leander," Horatio said impressively, "she was the daughter of the greatest scoundrel that ever lived. A man guilty of every crime conceivable. A man absolutely mad, but clever and crafty."

Slowly a light of understanding dawned in Leander's face. "You are referring to—" He paused.

"Yes," Horatio said, "The Duchess of Death was the daughter of Rasputin—the mad monk of the Russian court.

FOOL'S JEWELS

FROM A SLEEPY LITTLE FISHING VILLAGE ON THE MAINE COAST HAD COME THE OBSCURE NEWSPAPER ITEM THAT SET THE BROTHERS JONES OFF ON THE MADDEST MYSTERY OF THEIR AMAZING CAREER. "WHY SHOULD EVEN THE MEANEST THIEF IN THE WORLD STEAL THE PENNIES OFF A DEAD MAN'S EYES?" THEY ASKED THEMSELVES. AND WHY SHOULD MURDER FOLLOW IN THE WAKE OF THOSE TWO CORRODED COPPERS, AFTER THE THEFT?

CHAPTER ONE
PENNIES OFF A DEAD
MAN'S EYES

S EATED AT his desk in the office of Jones and Jones, in the Flatiron Building, Mr. Horatio Jones, the junior member of the firm, was busily occupying himself with the big stack of newspapers piled before him.

It was a warm day, even though the season was early autumn. The intensity of his exertions brought tiny beads of moisture to Horatio's brow and bald head. His mild blue eyes, however, continued to glide relentlessly up and down the columns.

Suddenly his glance came to a full stop. He bent over, in order to read a small story down in one corner of the page more easily. For some time he concentrated on it. Then, with a faint clucking sound, he lifted his shears.

There was a brisk snipping. He rose from his chair, crossed the room. Beside his older brother—older by some ten minutes—he paused. Leander, the senior of the Jones twins, was deep in a ponderous volume. Something to do with the development of Assyrian art.

"Dear me," Horatio murmured. "What do you make of this, Leander?"

Leander looked up from his book, accepted the proffered clipping. As he read, a puzzled frown crinkled above

A chair whipped through the air, landed on Clancy's skull.

his pale blue eyes. He shook his head slowly. "My word, Horatio!"

HORATIO'S HABIT of cutting certain odd and often deeply buried items out of the papers, was both a

pleasant pastime to him and a matter of business to Jones and Jones.

Frequently in these bits of newsprint, he came upon a thread that he and Leander could pick up. Sometimes, they would find the other end of the thread snarled in a hidden crime. And the unraveling of such hidden crimes was both the vocation and the avocation of the Jones brothers. It was their vocation, because to it they devoted their entire time. It was their avocation, since they did not do it for profit. Their private inherited fortunes were more than ample for their needs.

Leander dropped his gaze again to the clipping and even more carefully read it a second time.

WORLD'S MEANEST THIEF
IS DISCOVERED IN MAINE

Hollis Harbor, Me., Oct 9—This Maine fishing village can lay claim to having received a visit from the meanest thief in the world. He was a thief who proved it by carrying out an old saying. He stole the pennies off a dead man's eyes.

Two days ago Captain Ira Condit died in a seamen's home in New York. His body was brought to Hollis Harbor yesterday for burial in the local churchyard.

In his will, Captain Condit requested that before he was lowered into his grave, two pennies be put upon his eyes, in accordance with an old and once common custom. The coins, two large coppers, were found among his effects.

During the night, while his body was lying in the coffin in the home of Henry Condit, the captain's nephew, someone broke in and stole the two pennies.

Captain Condit, who was seventy-seven years old when he died, was a native of Hollis Harbor. For more than forty years he was master of deep-water sailing ships. He left the sea about ten years ago and had lived at the seamen's home up to the time of his death.

Leander placed the clipping upon the open page of his book. He wiggled his eyebrows up and down several times, rubbed the back of an ear with a contemplative forefinger.

"Two pennies," he mused, and then repeated—"Two pennies."

"Off a dead man's eyes," Horatio added. "My-my!"

"Why would anyone steal such a trivial sum?"

"Why would anyone want to be buried with them on his eyes?" Horatio asked.

Leander considered. "Perhaps, I can answer that part," he said finally. "The old sea captain must have been superstitious. I believe that in the old days, the custom was based on two ideas. In the first place, it was so the deceased would have money in the other world. In China today, colored paper is burned, which it is expected, will provide funds for the dead Chinese in heaven. And in parts of Greece, they put a coin in the hand of the corpse to pay the cost of being ferried over the River Styx." Leander paused, as if he had forgotten what he was talking about and was lost in thought.

"What was the Zither reason?" Horatio prompted him.

"Purely a practical one, my dear Horatio," Leander replied, smiling faintly. "To keep the eyelids of the cadaver closed."

He rose from his chair, walked to the window, stared out over Madison Square with a faraway look. Horatio, watching him, knew that Leander was trying to visualize the news story he had just read.

The Jones brothers were identical twins. As they stood there in that modest office, it was almost impossible to tell them apart. The same rosy faces and bald heads; the same short, slender, but well-knit figures. Even their clothes were alike—wrinkled gray suits. And an air of meekness and self-effacement clung to both of them.

At last Leander turned. His lips were twisted into a funny little smile, and his eyes held an eager twinkle. "There's more behind this than two pennies," he said.

"Dear me, yes!" Horatio agreed. "But what?"

"We shall try to discover."

The firm of Jones and Jones was accustomed to act with promptness and efficiency. So there was nothing extraordinary in Leander's quick decision to dig into the mystery of the theft of two pennies from the eyes of the dead sea captain. Less unique and suspicious circumstances had set them off on a crime hunt before.

With a brisk and eager step, Leander crossed to a hat tree in one corner of their office. He took down two brown, soft hats. One he handed to Horatio; the other he snapped upon his own head.

"Let us start, Horatio!"

"To Maine?"

"Exactly." Leander smiled. "I go to Maine—but not you."

"And where do I go?"

"I'll explain as we ride uptown."

ON THE train to Boston, Leander read and reread the odd little story Horatio had clipped from the newspaper. The dateline, he observed, was October 9, and the account said the strange and ghoulish theft had taken place the preceding night. It was now the twelfth of October. Captain Condit's body must have been consigned to its last resting place for at least two days.

Perhaps upon his sightless eyes other pennies had been placed in deference to his last wish. Leander smiled grimly at the thought. Then his smile faded. What if the original coins, the large old-fashioned copper pieces, had been found? It would mean he was on a wild goose chase.

For a few seconds his blue eyes clouded; then he gave a little philosophical shrug. It wouldn't be the first time he had run down a lead that amounted to nothing.

Yet some uncanny instinct told him that behind the theft of the two pennies lay a deep and sinister motive. It was not the work of a crude practical joker, or a necromaniac—one whose mental twist drives him to mutilate the dead.

Arriving in Boston shortly before midnight, Leander spent the night at a hotel. He caught a train early in the morning for Portland. From there, he headed farther down into Maine on a motorbus, the only means of transportation that would bring him anywhere near Hollis Harbor.

Under ordinary circumstances he would have enjoyed the ride. But he was too preoccupied with what might lie ahead of him to notice the beautiful scenery through which they passed. Stretches of pine and hemlock, beyond which glimpses of the sea, sparkling in the sun, were visible now and then.

It was with a feeling of relief that he saw the driver turn around and catch his eye. He slid from his seat into the narrow aisle and from the wide low rack above where he had been sitting, he took down his scuffed black bag.

By the time he had made his way to the head of the aisle, the bus was almost stopped. The driver turned to him.

"You take that gravel road to the right. It's about three miles."

"Thank you. Thank you very much," Leander murmured.

The driver gave him a sort of salute. "Like to take you over. But we don't go there, except during the season. Season's over now." He reached out, seized the handle of the lever that opened the door.

"My word! Season?"

"Sure. Lotta folks have cottages around the harbor. But you won't find anybody there at this time of year except the natives." The door swung open.

"I see. Thank you." Leander stepped down to the concrete pavement.

"Well, good luck!" the driver called cheerily.

The door slammed shut. A burst from the engine, accompanied by a grating of gears, and the bus moved rapidly up the road in a haze of blue-gray smoke.

Leander looked about him. He was in the midst of a forest of second-growth pine, through which the white highway cut like a thin scar. To the right, the gravel road the driver had pointed out disappeared around a bend into the woods. Leander picked up his bag and started toward Hollis Harbor.

He hoped vaguely that someone in a car might come along and give him a lift, although tramping along the gravel with the bracing tang of pine in his nostrils was not without a certain pleasure.

But so far as meeting anyone was concerned, the entire country seemed to be uninhabited. For a mile, he passed not a single house. Then the trees began to thin out a little, and back a distance of a hundred yards he made out a low white structure, the house proper joined to the barn. Beyond it lay cleared fields, now sere and brown.

Leander trudged on. A quarter of a mile ahead, the road made an abrupt turn, and as he fastened his eyes upon it, a car appeared and headed toward him. It was traveling at high speed. He had barely time to step aside, when it whirled past with a machine-gun rattle of pebbles on fenders.

It was a sedan, black and ultra-streamlined. A new machine, powerful and fast. In front were two men, but they shot by so swiftly that Leander was able to catch only a blurred glimpse of their faces. He swung about and watched the sedan until it disappeared.

"Well!" Leander exclaimed. "Those gentlemen appear to be in a hurry." He moved on toward Hollis Harbor again and on his face was a thoughtful expression.

The car which had almost run him down had carried a New York license plate.

THE VILLAGE of Hollis Harbor had a population of several hundred, dwelling in houses that were strung for a mile along the shore of the cove on which it was situated. It was rocky and hilly, its one important street lined for a short distance with frame or stone business buildings, the paint on the former weathered to a mellow hue by the salt air.

Several small craft lay at anchor; and made fast to the numerous wooden docks that jutted out from shore were still others, with Cape Cod dories well represented.

There had been a time when Hollis Harbor had ranked high as a fishing port. But that was before the railroad had abandoned its spur line. Now it was deserted, sleepy, except in summer when the cottagers brought a burst of life to it, and a small group of artists set up their easels to catch its quaintness on canvas.

The men still fished. But the big schooners which worked the banks were no longer there. And the catches of the small boats were either salted and shipped out by truck, or carried direct to Portland by sea.

Leander, as he picked his way down the steep hill back of the village, darted his glance about curiously. "My word," he said softly. "It doesn't look as if anything ever happened here. Least of all anything violent, in such a peaceful scene."

In front of a store building, on the wide windows of which was a sign disclosing that it was the general merchandise establishment of J. Sanford, two men were sitting on a long wooden bench. The bench was brown and shiny, criss-crossed with knife marks where some whittler had idled away his time.

The men, too, looked as if they might have been whittled from some piece of well-seasoned wood, their faces seamed and wrinkled. Leander approached them with a slightly embarrassed cough.

"I—I beg your pardon," he murmured.

They looked at him with a curiously blank expression. One who seemed even older than his crony, shifted a can he was holding between his knobby knees, peered over the top of steel spectacles that rested near the tip of his nose. But neither spoke. Merely stared at the self-effacing little man before them.

"I beg your pardon," Leander repeated. "But could you tell me where Mr. Henry Condit lives?"

The silence continued, while the two ancients exchanged glances. Then the one with the cane worked his toothless gums a moment and said: "His house's the yellow one, down just this side the point. Quarter mile." His cane came up, pointed in the general direction of the North Star.

Leander made a little bow. He picked up his scuffed black bag and gave the two old fellows an apologetic smile. "Thank you," he said. "Sorry to bother you."

He started to walk away, but the man with the cane halted him. "Be you aiming to see Henry?" he asked.

"Why—yes."

Again the two antique specimens exchanged glances. Again the one chewed his toothless gums for a few seconds. "Well," he said slowly, "you're wastin' time."

Something in his tone sent one of Leander's eyebrows darting upward. "My word! I—I won't be able to see him?"

"Not likely—soon." The old fellow chuckled, and his companion echoed the sound.

"Why not?"

"Cause Henry Condit's dead!"

"Dead? Henry Condit dead?"

"Aye, sir! Deader'n a doorknob," the man with the cane cackled. "Buried him this morning."

"When did he die?" Leander asked.

"Yesterday morning. No, day 'fore yesterday 'twas. He was killed. Aye, sir, he was murdered, since you ask me!"

CHAPTER TWO
GROG-SHOP CLUE

IT WAS a common practice of Jones and Jones for Leander to work on one angle of a case and Horatio on another. Not only did this method enable them to move faster, but also it avoided what was apt to be a disadvantageous state of affairs: attracting attention.

The Jones brothers looked so much alike that when they appeared together, they invariably caused passersby to stare—and perhaps regret the last three drinks of the night before.

They had discovered another advantage in the divided method of operation. Not infrequently, the appearance of what seemed to be the same man at widely separated spots at the same time filled their foes with confusion. And this state of mind, Leander and Horatio were prompt to take advantage of.

So it was that about the time Leander was boarding the train for Boston, Horatio was driving across the Manhattan Bridge toward Brooklyn.

It had been a simple matter for Horatio to locate the seamen's home where Captain Ira Condit had spent the last ten years of his life. He had merely run through the death notices in the files of the *Times*.

The Anchorage, as it was called, was situated on the heights overlooking the Upper Bay and the Narrows, through which ships from the four corners of the globe sailed into New York Harbor.

Horatio parked his car at the curb in front. He walked the hundred feet to the entrance, his mild eyes missing no detail of the surroundings. The home was of brick and of considerable size, set in the center of a large plot of ground. On the south side of the building, he noticed two white-haired men in blue, brass-buttoned coats sitting in the sun. Old sailors, home from the sea for good.

He entered a spacious hallway, uncarpeted but spotlessly clean, as if it might have been holy-stoned only a short time before. On his right, he saw on the opaque glass panel of a half-open door the word: Office. A girl in a business-like dress of simple lines looked up as be walked in.

Horatio made a stiff little bow, gave her one of his half-embarrassed smiles. "If you please," he said, "I would like to speak to the gentleman in charge."

"Mr. Olcott," she replied, returning his smile. "I'll get him."

She rose from her chair at the desk and walked around until she was in front of Horatio. "What name, please?"

"Jones," Horatio murmured. "Just Jones."

"What is the nature of your business, Mr. Jones?"

The hesitation before Horatio replied was so slight that she didn't notice it. "I'm a lawyer. An attorney-at-law."

Once more she smiled in friendly fashion. "If you'll take a seat, I'll get Mr. Olcott."

SHE DISAPPEARED through the doorway with a swift stride. Horatio dropped into a chair against the wall. His blue eyes wandered about the office. Across from him on a shelf was a model of a full-rigged ship. The fidelity with which each detail of the rigging had been reproduced showed that its builder had known sailing craft by heart.

Above the door was a bronze ship's bell. Beneath it, a small sign, neatly lettered, offered the information that it was the bell of the brig *Excelsior*. There were half a dozen pictures of ships under sail, and a couple of steamships adorning the walls.

"My, my," Horatio murmured. "A truly nautical establishment."

He wondered about the Anchorage. He had, of course, heard about the Sailors' Snug Harbor, on Staten Island, where superannuated men of the sea were taken care of during their last years. But never of this place.

Footsteps coming down the hallway broke in upon his thoughts. The girl with the smile entered, followed by a rotund, round-faced man.

He might have been forty, perhaps fifty. It was difficult to say off-hand. His hair was gray and thin on top, but his face was smooth and ruddy. From beneath slightly protruding brows, keen gray eyes surveyed Horatio questioningly.

Horatio stood up.

AT OLCOTT'S suggestion they'd gone into his private office, just beyond the one in which Horatio had waited for him. The superintendent of the home sat at his desk, Horatio at one end of it.

"What was it you wanted to know about Captain Condit?" Olcott asked.

Horatio was apologetic. "I really hate to trouble you, I really do," he murmured. "But you see I represent some second cousins of the late captain. They live in Gloucester. Now, of course, my clients have no wish to lay claim to anything not rightly theirs. But in the family, there has always been—let us say, a legend that Captain Condit was possessed of considerable wealth."

Horatio was shooting in the dark. But he wanted to get Olcott to talk, answer questions, and he knew from experience that the meek manner and harmless appearance which he adopted invariably gave to his wildest falsehoods the semblance of truth.

It was so now. Olcott nodded his head slowly and pursed his lips. "I never heard Captain Condit mention any relatives other than his nephew Henry Condit, at Hollis Harbor," he said. "But that's understandable. He wasn't very communicative. Just the opposite. He was a man who lived to himself to a large extent."

"And about his wealth?" Horatio ventured. His glance as it came to rest on Olcott was one of timid interrogation.

The superintendent gave the question a moment's thought. "Well now," he said, "I don't know about that. When he died he had a few hundred dollars on deposit with us here. We turned that over to his nephew when he came to take the body to Hollis Harbor for burial. And yet—"He broke off abruptly, fastened a squinting gaze on one corner of the ceiling.

"And yet?" Horatio murmured, after a moment's wait.

Olcott leaned forward with the palms of his hands pressing against the edge of the desk top. "Mr. Jones, I sometimes wondered about Captain Condit. Naturally, a good many of our guests are eccentric and crotchety, but he was even more peculiar than any of the others.

"You may not be aware of it, but the Anchorage is not a public institution, although we have an endowment of considerable size. The residents here pay for their keep. That is, they pay a large part of what it actually costs us."

"I understand," Horatio nodded.

"All our residents are retired ship's officers; most of them at one time or another were masters of their own vessels," Olcott continued. "Anyway, every summer Captain Condit would make a week's visit to his nephew in Hollis Harbor. Immediately on his return, he would pay us eighteen hundred dollars and deposit six or seven hundred dollars, with us to withdraw as he chose."

Horatio looked mildly surprised. "Eighteen hundred dollars! It's—er—rather expensive living at the Anchorage."

"On the contrary," Olcott replied with a smile, "it's rather reasonable, considering the comforts we provide. The eighteen hundred dollars was a year's board for Captain Condit *and* Captain Mullet."

"Captain Mullet?"

"The only one of our guests with whom Captain Condit would associate to any extent—and with him he was on very intimate terms. Indeed; Mullet was with him at the time he had the stroke of apoplexy from which he never recovered consciousness."

"And you think the fact that Captain Condit returned from his visit to Hollis Harbor each summer, and paid you for the two of them a relatively large amount, must indicate that he had some source of income?"

"Exactly!"

"Perhaps," Horatio suggested, "his nephew provided the money."

Olcott screwed up his face, shook his head. "From what his nephew let drop when he was here, I don't believe he's very well off. He inquired with Yankee thoroughness into the captain's affairs. I told him all I could—little enough."

Horatio was silent a moment, then he murmured: "It was most strange, his requesting that pennies be placed on his eyes when he was buried."

"Captain Condit was a strange man, Mr. Jones," Olcott replied solemnly.

"You saw them—the pennies?"

"No. His effects were in a large sea chest in his room. But after his death we touched nothing. We wired his nephew, as he had instructed us to do in case anything should happen to him. However, Mr. Henry Condit mentioned them to me in a conversation, while he was here. So I knew about them."

HORATIO WAS thoughtful. He was gradually making progress in getting the general background of Captain Condit. But he admitted to himself that he couldn't see any hint of a reason for the theft of the pennies off the dead captain's eyes.

"How long had Captain Condit been paying the expenses of Captain Mullet, Mr. Olcott?" he asked.

"Ever since they came here together. He also provided Mullet with pocket money." Olcott smiled and made a little gesture. "But it can be explained. Mullet, from what I was told, was chief officer on Captain Condit's last command. They left the sea together. Had sailed together for many years."

"Possibly that's it," Horatio said slowly. "I'd like to speak with Captain Mullet, if I may."

Olcott lifted his shoulders. "Can't be done."

"Can't be done?" Horatio's pale eyes widened.

"Captain Mullet isn't living at the Anchorage any more."

Horatio rose slowly from his chair. He stood a moment in pensive silence. Olcott watched him, but said nothing. At last Horatio smiled helplessly. "Dear me," he said, almost as if to himself. "Where has he gone?"

"I don't know exactly."

"What?"

"Right after Captain Condit was stricken, Captain Mullet went out. When he came back, he had—well, he had been drinking pretty heavily."

"No doubt his old friend's death was a great shock to him," Horatio suggested.

Olcott agreed. "He evidently had been trying to drown his grief. He didn't stay here very long—just long enough to gather a few things from his room and tell us he was going away for a week or two. Of course, everyone who lives here can come and go as he pleases." Olcott shrugged. "It isn't a charity home."

"Didn't you—that is—didn't you ask him where he was going to be?" Horatio asked half apologetically.

"I did." Olcott made a wry face; then gave a short laugh. "He told me to go to hell. He was pretty drunk."

"Dear me!" Leander exclaimed. "Was he alone?"

"He came in alone. But I noticed he drove off with another man—a young man, I thought, though I wouldn't swear to it."

Olcott got up, paced across the room, and finally stopped before Horatio. "I tell you, Mr. Jones, I don't like it! It's been on my mind ever since he left. But what could I do! I couldn't make him stay here," he added wearily.

"No, I suppose not," Horatio murmured sympathetically. "He's probably off on a spree and will come back when he gets over it."

"Damn foolishness at his age—and dangerous!" Olcott snapped.

Horatio nodded agreement. "What kind of car did he drive away in?"

"A new one. One of those streamlined things that looks like a bottle-nosed whale. I noticed it, because it was the first of the kind I'd seen except in the ads."

There was a silence.

Olcott walked back and forth across the room, his hands clasping and unclasping behind his back.

Horatio blinked his pale eyes, as if completely bewildered. Behind those eyes, his brain was racing. There was something fishy in Mullet's spree. And what he had learned about Captain Condit satisfied him that Jones and Jones had played a live hunch on that newspaper clipping.

He put his hat on his head with meticulous care, coughed faintly. "Where do most of your guests go for their—a grog?" Horatio asked.

"Clancy's! Clancy's Grill and Grog Shop. The last part of the name attracts them, I suppose," Olcott said.

"If you don't mind—that is, possibly if I knew where it was I might visit it," Horatio murmured.

"It's down the street two blocks."

With a little bow Horatio stepped to the door. "Thank you. Both my clients and I thank you for your help, Mr. Olcott. I shall try Clancy's."

As he drove away, Horatio gave a little chuckle. He wondered whether the superintendent of the Anchorage would notice that the automobile of the lawyer from Gloucester carried a New York license.

HORATIO FOUND Clancy's without difficulty. A restaurant bar on a corner. Without locking his car, he crossed the sidewalk and pushed through the door into the "grog shop." The place differed but little from a thousand others in the city. Along one wall was a row of tables with checkered table cloths; opposite them was a long beer bar and a counter with stools. A stove and hot plate, coffee urn and steam table, enabled Clancy's to serve food and qualify as a restaurant.

Walking up to the bar, Horatio glanced casually about him. At the far end, two men were talking over glasses of beer. There was only one other customer in the establishment. At the table nearest the door, a man with a white beard, tobacco-stained, was grasping a whisky glass. He was wearing a dark blue coat, of reefer cut and with brass buttons; on the back of the large corded hand, which surrounded the glass, was tattooed a mermaid.

Horatio smiled to himself. Olcott had given him the right information when he had said that this was the hangout of the residents of the Anchorage.

As the bartender approached, swishing a damp rag in figure eights over the mahogany, Horatio looked at him and said meekly: "A beer, please."

There was something vaguely familiar about the bartender Horatio decided, as the man in the white apron pushed a seidel beneath a tap and watched the amber fluid flood it through narrowed eyes. He was a man of not more than five feet six, but well built, with a broken nose and a bumpy forehead. An ex-pugilist beyond a doubt.

By the time the seidel had been placed on the bar and the bartender had turned to ring up the dime in the register, Horatio had placed him.

It was Clancy himself. Mike the Mauler Clancy, twenty years ago a good second-rate welterweight. Five years later, a resident of Sing Sing on a larceny charge. After that— Horatio frowned faintly, but almost immediately his face cleared. He had it now!

Mike Clancy had been one of Fox Fogarty's gang of rum-runners. Fogarty's chief lieutenant, if Horatio remembered correctly. Must have decided to open up a legal place after Repeal. That explained to some extent the popularity of the grill with the old sea dogs at the Anchorage. Clancy could get good stuff, and Horatio felt certain that no more than a small percentage of the liquor that crossed the bar was tax-paid.

Having served his meek-looking customer in the gray suit, Clancy paid no more attention to him. He strolled down the bar to where the two men were talking.

Picking up his glass, Horatio looked about him hesitantly. Then he walked to the table where the man with the white beard was sitting. He smiled in a friendly way.

"I—I beg your pardon," he apologized. "Would you mind if I sit down here? I don't like to drink by myself."

The old fellow looked up, squinted his watery eyes. He stared at Horatio a moment, after which he blinked rapidly for a second or two. "Sit down!" he suddenly boomed. "Aye, sir, sit down! Man's got to have company with his grog." His voice cracked a bit, but it had a heavy quality reminiscent of commands bellowed above the howling of the gale.

Horatio pulled out a chair. He noticed that the old boy with the white beard was about three sheets in the wind.

"My name's Jones," Horatio said. "Just Jones."

"Captain Duff. At your service, sir."

"Here's health, Captain!" Horatio lifted his seidel.

"Down the hatch!" the captain boomed. His hand jerked up, the contents went down.

Catching Clancy's eyes, Horatio beckoned to him. He came around the end of the bar and stood by the table.

"What'll it be?" Horatio asked.

The captain hiccuped, wiped his stained whiskers with the tattooed mermaid. "Cuban rum! My drink's rum, sir!"

Clancy nodded and returned behind the bar. But as he poured a shot of rum from a bottle, he glanced covertly at the two oddly assorted figures. More especially, he let his mean thin eyes study the mild-appearing Horatio.

HORATIO AND the captain drank. They drank another, and another. All the while, Horatio was aware that Mike the Mauler Clancy was surreptitiously watching them. Horatio had placed Clancy; he was beginning to wonder whether Clancy knew who he was. It didn't seem likely. Jones and Jones had never tangled with the broken-nosed ex-convict.

Conscious that the bartender's cauliflowered ears were straining to catch their conversation, Horatio kept it general. The old captain was mellow, to put it mildly, and his talk tumbled out with slight encouragement. It was largely of the old days, talk of the sea and strange ports, talk seasoned with salty oaths.

Finally, Horatio saw Clancy come from behind the bar, walk to the back of the room and enter a telephone booth. He turned to the bearded Captain Duff.

"I suppose you live at the Anchorage, Captain," he said.

"Aye, aye, sir! Been there since she was launched— twenty year ago come spring."

"You knew Captain Condit then."

A blistering oath rumbled through the captain's whiskers. He almost choked, then suddenly found his voice. "I knew him! Aye, the low-down—" He ended in another burst of profanity.

"Dear me!" Horatio exclaimed. "I'm sorry I mentioned it."

Captain Duff gulped the remainder of his drink. He waited until its warmth had percolated through his system. Then he squared his shoulders, brushed the mermaid across his mouth.

"No," he said more quietly. "A man shouldn't speak evil of the dead. Captain Condit's gone—God rest his dirty soul! But I won't be the one to say a word against him."

"Quite right," Horatio agreed.

"But I'll say this much," Captain Duff continued. "I knew him for fifty years, man and boy. He once sailed as second with me back in the Eighties. But I never met a man who changed like he did after he quit the sea."

Horatio lifted his brows. "Changed? In what way?"

"He used to be companionable in the old days. But from the minute he got to the Anchorage, he wouldn't have nothing to do with anyone. Not even his old shipmates. Kept to himself—seemed to have his blasted soul full of bilge water. Wouldn't talk to anyone. Except Mullet, and he'd spend hours with him."

"You know Mullet pretty well then?"

"Aye, I know him. He was chief officer for Condit on his last cruise. A good man, Mullet."

"That's odd," Horatio said brightly. "I was just over at the Anchorage to see Captain Mullet."

"*Mister* Mullet!" Duff growled. "He had his master's papers, but he never had a ship. Chief was the best he ever signed on for, even though he did call himself 'Captain.'"

"Excuse me," Horatio said humbly.

"If you're looking for Mullet, you won't find him at the Anchorage," Duff said, screwing one eye up knowingly.

"So I discovered."

"He's gone."

"Yes."

The captain leaned over the table at some risk to his balance and, lowering his voice, said huskily: "He ain't coming back."

Horatio looked distressed. "Dear me. Are you sure?"

"I was sitting here when he decided to leave. I was drinking rum with him and the young fellow who talked him into going. The young fellow bought the rum."

There was a sparkle in Horatio's pale blue eyes, but his voice was calm. "I have some good news for Mr. Mullet," he said. "I'm anxious to find him. Do you know where he is now?"

"Aye—I know where Mullet is." The old captain ran his bony fingers down the length of his beard. "Mullet was afraid he might be making a mistake, so he told me."

"And where can I locate him?" Horatio asked.

Before his question could be answered, he was seized roughly by the shoulders, jerked to his feet and whirled about. Mike the Mauler Clancy, his eyes compressed into menacing slits, his chin jutted out, snarled at him: "I get you now!"

CLANCY RELEASED his hold on Horatio, who shrugged his disarranged coat into place. A funny little smile fluttered at the corners of his mouth, but there was a dangerous glint in his pale eyes.

In a battle of fists with the Marquis of Queensbury rules prevailing, Mike the Mauler would have had little difficulty in handling the meek-appearing man he had so abruptly yanked from his chair. But what Mike Clancy did not know was that in a rough and tumble, Horatio Jones was master of more tricks of jiu-jitsu than the ordinary Japanese wrestler.

But Horatio was not belligerent. "Dear me," he said with an aggrieved air, "is this the way you treat all your customers?"

Clancy sneered. "Customers? Listen, mugg, I'm onto you. I been thinkin' for some time that I knew you. But I made a couple of phone calls—got your description—just to be sure. I'm onto you like a roof now. You're Jones!"

"Yes, that's my name," Horatio murmured. His smile had turned slightly grim. He was trying to be pacific, but he was watching every muscle twitch of Clancy's face. "I'm Jones. A common name. Just Jones."

Clancy's jaw moved forward another inch. "Well, Jones—you just get the hell out of here! No dicks are welcome in Clancy's grill. And besides"— his tone became even more menacing—"I know why you're here. Lay off! I'm warnin' you! Now get out!"

Captain Duff had been watching the unexpected turn of affairs with slightly muddled astonishment. Now he hoisted himself to his feet, reached out a long thin arm and shook his fist under Clancy's nose. His watery eyes were blinking rapidly.

"See here, Clancy, you wharf rat!" he began, and would have continued, but Horatio interrupted.

"I shall be delighted to leave, Mr. Clancy," he said quietly. "My friend, Captain Duff, and I will adjourn to another and more congenial establishment."

"Like hell!" Clancy took a step forward, put himself between Horatio and the old captain. "Duff stays here— and if you ever show your face around here again, you get the works!"

"Dear me," Horatio grinned. "I'm obliged to disagree with you. Captain Duff and I depart together."

Clancy ripped out an oath. His left fist shot forward, a fist that had laid many a ham-and-egger on the resin. But it didn't land. Horatio wasn't there. A chair whipped through the air, landed with a crash on Clancy's skull. With a startled grunt, the ex-convict collapsed in a heap.

"Come!" Horatio exclaimed. He seized Duff by the arm, started for the door.

THE TWO who had been standing at the end of the bar edged forward. Now one of them slid his hand beneath his coat. But before it came out again, he found himself staring into the business end of an automatic, the operating end of which was clasped in Horatio's hand.

"Not too fast!" Horatio said dryly.

"We depart in peace—not pieces."

He pushed Captain Duff through the door, then backed out himself. His gun was close to his side, barely noticeable, but ready for use. Clancy on the floor gave a groan.

"Call off your dogs, Clancy," Horatio said. "They're no good."

The door slammed. Horatio half led and half dragged the befuddled old sea captain to the car. He opened the door, climbed in, pulled Duff after him and into the seat. Then he shut the door and stepped on the starter.

And all the time, he had kept a sharp eye on the entrance to Clancy's.

The engine caught with a roar. Horatio laid his gun on the seat beside him. He let in the clutch and the car lurched from the curb. By this time, Clancy had appeared in the doorway. Behind him were his two gunmen. He waved his arm, and one of them brought his hand up a few inches.

Once—twice—three times he fired!

A tinkle of glass. Horatio, glancing for a second from the street ahead, saw Captain Duff sliding slowly down in the seat. The old man's eyes were closed, blood was welling from the side of his head. It moved in a hideous stream down his face and then began to glide down his neck.

CHAPTER THREE

THE CORPSE AT CAPTAIN'S ROCK

THE NEWS that Henry Condit, Captain Condit's nephew, had been killed—murdered, as the old man on the bench described it—came as an unexpected shock to Leander. But it fully justified the suspicions of Jones and Jones that there was something ominous behind the theft of the two pennies off the dead man's eyes.

The two old fellows stared at Leander, their leathery faces compressed into myriads of wrinkles, their dim eyes squinting. They seemed pleased with themselves; like a couple of old women who had just been able to disgorge a juicy and startling piece of gossip.

"My word," Leander said thoughtfully. "Murdered. Henry Condit murdered."

"They found his body in the woods back of the house," the man with the cane volunteered. "His wife found it. He didn't come in to supper after they'd put old Ira in the ground."

"You mean after Captain Condit's funeral?"

"Aye, that's Ira I'm talking about. He died down to the city. New York City."

Leander nodded. "And have they—that is, has the murderer been caught.

"Caught?" The ancient cackled disdainfully. "Course, he ain't been caught. Who'd catch him?" he demanded, and without waiting for an answer, continued: "There was a couple of state policemen come over. They stayed around a day or two—left this morning. But they didn't do nothing. Guess they give it up. It's an outrage! Aye, it's an outrage!"

"How was he killed?" Leander, asked.

"Shot! Shot in the back!"

Leander looked properly horrified. "My word! And I was very anxious to talk with Henry Condit. Now he's dead." He could tell by the expression on the faces of the old men that they would like to know what he had wanted to talk to Henry Condit about. He smiled to himself. "I wanted to sell him some life insurance," Leander murmured.

"Too bad you didn't come a week ago," the second old man said, with a jerk of his head. "His widder and little girl could use some money,"

"She's still here, his widow?"

"Where else'd she be? She ain't got no place else to go."

For a moment, Leander was silent. Then he picked up his grip again and smiled at the two graybeards. "Well, I'm much obliged to you. You say Henry Condit lived in that yellow house?"

"That's it. Just this side the point," the man with the cane nodded.

Leander moved away. When he had gone only a dozen paces, the old fellow suddenly called after him. "You're wastin' your time. Henry Condit's widder ain't got any money for such foolishness as life insurance."

Down the street a short distance, Leander saw a lunch-room. He entered, left his grip with the proprietor and then continued on his way to the yellow house.

It was getting along in the afternoon. On the eastern slopes of the rocky hills, the shadows were already beginning to blur the pines. Off the entrance to the cove, several small boats were heading toward home, the pop-pop of their engines floating faintly over the calm waters.

MRS. HENRY CONDIT came to the door at his first knock. She was a woman of middle age, thin, tired-looking, with streaked gray hair drawn into a bun at the back of her neck. She stared at Leander almost with indifference. Close behind her, Leander saw a child about six, in a faded gingham dress.

He came directly to the point, once he had learned that she was the widow of the slain nephew of Captain Ira Condit, and so far as he knew the only surviving member of the family. His manner was no longer self-effacing. It was crisp, efficient, the sort to inspire confidence.

"Mrs. Condit," he said, a reassuring smile in his pale eyes, "I am a detective—from New York."

"A—a detective!" She looked frightened; her skinny hands plucked at her faded apron.

"You have nothing to worry about," he said kindly. "I'm here to help you."

"I ain't worried. Just surprised."

"I'll explain," he said.

"Perhaps you'd better come in and sit down," Mrs. Condit suggested.

IN THE little parlor with its horsehair-stuffed furniture, Leander selected a chair that appeared to be somewhat less uncomfortable than the others. Henry Condit's widow perched on the edge of a sofa across from him. Her hands, clasped beneath her apron, worked nervously. Her little girl, saucer-eyed, sat beside her holding tightly to her mother's arm.

"The police in New York are investigating the circumstances surrounding the death of Captain Ira Condit," Leander said slowly. "That's why I came up here. And only a few minutes ago, I learned that your husband had been killed."

She nodded dully. "Poor Henry," she mumbled.

"Have you, yourself, any idea who might have shot him?" Leander asked gently. "Did he have any enemies; was there anyone in Hollis Harbor, with whom he had quarreled?"

"Not Henry. He didn't have any enemies. That's why I can't understand it," she replied, her voice choking. She raised one corner of her apron and dabbed at her eyes.

Leander waited until she had composed herself. Then he asked: "Mrs. Condit, do you know why your husband went into the woods that day?"

"No."

"But when he didn't come back for supper, you went to look for him?"

"Yes. I had a feeling something'd happened. I found him up near Captain's Rock. It was almost dark, but I just seemed to know where he was, somehow. I went straight there. Henry was lying on the ground, face down. He was dead," she added.

"Captain's Rock?" Leander looked at her questioningly.

Mrs. Condit smiled wanly. "That's just a name Henry and me give to it—a big rock where a body can sit and look out past the point and out to sea."

"Why did you call it that?"

"Because every summer when Uncle Ira'd come to see us, he used to go up there and sit for hours. That's why we got to calling it Captain's Rock.

"Henry'd sort of thought Uncle Ira'd leave us a lot of money when he died," Mrs. Condit murmured. "But there wasn't anything. Only a few hundred dollars that they turned over to Henry at the place where Uncle Ira lived in New York. That hardly paid for the funeral."

Leander slowly stroked his chin. Finally, he asked: "Why did you think Captain Condit had any considerable amount of money to leave?"

She didn't answer at once. The question seemed to have taken her by surprise. "Well," she said at last, "that was Henry's idea. I didn't think much about it. Uncle Ira, now that you mention it, always seemed to have money, and I suppose that give Henry his notion. When he got back to New York after visiting us, he'd send Henry a hundred dollars every year. It helped us out a lot," she added.

"About the pennies that were placed on Captain Condit's eyes, the pennies that were stolen," Leander said. "What do you know about them?"

MRS. CONDIT suddenly began to tremble. Her tired eyes widened; beneath her apron, her hands twitched, making the cloth jump up and down. When she spoke, her breath came in panicky gasps. "You—you know—about—about them?"

"Yes," he nodded. "From the newspapers."

She put her fingers over her lips, stared at him. "Mr.—Mr.—"

"Jones," Leander smiled. "Just Jones."

"Mr. Jones, I didn't want Henry to do it. I didn't want him to put those two pennies on Uncle Ira's eyes, even if he did say to do it in his will!" She had suddenly become intense, vehement. "It wasn't according to Scripture. There's nothing in the Bible about putting pennies on the eyes of dead folk."

"No, Mrs. Condit, I don't believe there's anything about it in the Bible," Leander agreed. He was beginning to understand this withered female better. "But I didn't know that Captain Condit was particularly religious."

Her eyes flashed. "He was a heathen! A heathen!" she repeated bitterly. "He never got religion!"

"Too bad," Leander murmured sympathetically. "But why do you suppose anyone would want to steal them?"

"Mr. Jones," she said, leaning forward and fixing him with her gaze, "it was the devil who stole them! He came in during the night through the kitchen door. I found it unlocked."

A funny expression flitted over Leander's face. This woman was slightly mad. He could see that now. And he wondered if it might not have something to do with the murder of Henry Condit. But he said: "Why do you suppose Captain Condit wanted to be buried with the pennies over his eyes?"

A sly look appeared in her weary eyes. "Henry said it was because one of them had a lock of Aunt Ella's hair in it."

"What?"

"Uncle Ira's wife. She died more than thirty years ago. Them two pennies was kind of lockets. Henry said Uncle Ira showed him inside of them once when he was a boy, and there was a little lock of hair in it. Uncle Ira always carried them around with him when he was alive."

"My word," Leander murmured, almost to himself. "Lockets!" He half closed his eyes in thought.

"That's what Henry said. But I don't think he knew what he was talking about."

"Why not?"

"Because Henry tried to get them open, and he couldn't. He told me he tried, before he put them on Uncle Ira's eyelids. But he said it didn't make no difference, cause they only had some of Aunt Ella's hair in them anyways."

"You—you saw them?" Leander asked.

"Of course," she nodded. "They were big pennies, bigger than quarters. Not like the pennies we have. Henry said they'd come from India."

She stopped, and fastened her tired eyes on Leander. Leander, however, appeared to be unaware of her scrutiny. He bobbed his head up and down a couple of times in an absent-minded manner, then lapsed into introspection. There was a long moment of silence.

He was thinking about those big pennies—pennies off a dead man's eyes. Pennies that had been fashioned by some skilled craftsman of the mysterious East into delicate lockets. And in those lockets, Captain Condit had carried around bits of the hair of his wife, dead these many years.

A slow, knowing smile crossed Leander's face. He stood up. "Mrs. Condit," he said, "you have, of course, gone through the late captain's effects."

She shook her head dubiously. "Well—no, I haven't. Henry did in a way, although he didn't read none of the letters nor anything like that. Was going to do that later."

Leander's manner became crisp, authoritative. "Very well! You and I'll do that now!"

MRS. CONDIT hesitated. A glance at Leander, no longer meek and self-effacing, but quietly confident, efficient, seemed to reassure her. She rose from the horsehair sofa with a little sigh and, turning toward the door, beckoned to him to follow her. The little girl tagged along behind.

The captain's sea chest was in the spare bedroom up under the eaves. It was a big chest, battered, scarred, bound with brass; the marks of countless voyages had been dented into it. Mrs. Condit handed Leander a key and he turned the heavy old-fashioned lock.

For fifteen minutes Leander occupied himself with the contents of the chest—articles of clothing, an old sextant, pocket chronometer, a package containing the captain's papers as mate and master, yellow with age, a bundle of letters, and numerous other articles. He went over them all hurriedly. But when he finally closed the lid of the chest and got to his feet, there was a gleam of triumph in his eyes.

In his hand was an envelope. It was a new envelope, an envelope that bore the return address of the Anchorage on the flap. And inside were two small circlets of golden hair.

As Leander had half suspected, Captain Condit had removed the locks of his wife's hair from the two pennies. In their place, he had put—what? Leander gazed thoughtfully at the envelope he was holding, as if trying to find the answer there. Then, suddenly, he turned to Mrs. Condit.

"Where is this Captain's Rock you spoke about?" he asked.

She made a little motion with her hand. "Up there. Up the hill in back of the house. There's a path leads to it."

Following the directions Mrs. Condit gave him, Leander started from the yellow house back into the woods. It was getting late; the sun was almost below the horizon and beneath the pines the shadows were thick and ominous.

As he picked his way up the rocky path, Leander wondered about Horatio. What had his brother learned at the seamen's home where Captain Condit had died? Had he discovered, as Leander had surmised, that the old captain possessed a fortune?

Leander frowned. From what Mrs. Condit had just said, Captain Condit had left almost nothing. And yet her husband had believed his uncle possessed of considerable wealth. Two questions bothered Leander particularly: Had Captain Condit's death been natural? Why had Henry Condit been murdered?

The first question, he decided, would probably have to be answered by Horatio. The second, he might be able to answer himself.

Mrs. Condit had said the rock was a quarter of a mile from the house. To Leander, it seemed more like a half mile before the path at last emerged from beneath the trees into a little clearing on the side of the hill. It was a natural clearing, the surface of the ground consisting of an expanse of rock that offered but little chance for shrubs or trees to take root.

In the center, he saw what he knew must be the captain's rock. It was really three large rocks, with many smaller ones about them. The middle one of the group rose probably twenty-five feet, bald and rugged.

After a little investigation, Leander discovered how he could make his way to the top, climbing from one to another of the rocks. It was a relatively easy ascent. He looked about. It was as Mrs. Condit had said. From Captain's Rock, one could see through the entrance to the cove and far out to sea. Nearer, the straggling houses of Hollis Harbor met the eye.

"A regular lookout," Leander murmured to himself.

He regarded the prospect before him in silent thought for some time. Why had Captain Condit always spent so much time up here on the occasion of his visits? The view of the sea no doubt attracted him, Leander decided. Yet was that the only reason? Or even the main reason?

He had hoped to be able to study this vicinity carefully. But he saw that it was too dark now. He'd have to let it go until tomorrow. Before starting to descend, he walked to the back of the rock and looked about on the uphill side.

As his glance finally dropped to the ground directly below, he gave a startled gasp.

In the shadows, he was able to distinguish the outline of a human figure. He dropped to his knees and peered down. He could see that it was a man, lying on his face, with one leg drawn up and both arms spread wide.

At a speed that endangered his safety, Leander scrambled down from the rock, dashed around in back. He bent over the still form, turned it so that he could see the face. Then from his pocket he took his flashlight.

He was looking into the face of an old man, a face deeply wrinkled and smooth-shaven. A fringe of hair around the head was snow-white.

A quick examination disclosed that he had been stabbed directly between the shoulder blades—a deep, ugly wound, from which the blood had welled out and spread in a pool upon the ground. The weapon had been withdrawn and a hasty glance about failed to discover it.

When Leander stood up, he was satisfied on one point. This man had been dead not more than two hours. Perhaps not more than one.

CHAPTER FOUR
THE SEVEN SEAS SHOP

THE SMALL man with the neatly clipped mustache rolled down his shirt sleeves and began to put on his coat. He let his glance rest for a moment on the bed, on the still form lying there beneath the sheets. Then he turned to Horatio with a hint of a smile.

"Of course," he said slowly, "anything of this kind is apt to have a bad reaction with a man of his age. But your friend the captain seems to be a pretty tough old customer."

Horatio nodded. "He is," he said dryly. "And you think, Doctor, he'll pull through all right?"

"Don't think there's much doubt about it."

"The wound?"

"A mere scratch. It was liquor that put him out, although I dare say being hit was the necessary touch."

"In other words," Horatio smiled, "Captain Duff was passed out rather than knocked out."

"Precisely. He'll probably sleep for seven or eight hours and wake up with a big head and a bad disposition." He picked up his hat and bag, started toward the door. Horatio accompanied him.

"If he takes a turn for the worse," the doctor continued, "just call me. Otherwise, I'll drop in tomorrow morning."

Returning to the bedroom, Horatio sat down on a chair beside the bed containing the white-bearded figure of Captain Duff. The old fellow's watery eyes were closed, but there was a gap in the expanse of whiskers through which came irregular gurgling snores. On the side of his head was a patch of surgical gauze held in place by adhesive tape, where the doctor had dressed his slight injury.

When he had fled from Clancy's with old Duff crumpled down in the seat beside him, Horatio was at first undecided what to do. He could take his unconscious passenger back to the Anchorage. Or he could take him to a hospital. In case he were badly injured, the latter course was to be preferred.

But this ancient mariner held the secret of where Mullet could be found. So Horatio had driven into a quiet back street, examined the wound on the side of Duff's head. Convinced that it was not serious, he had driven directly to the apartment on Central Park South, where he and Leander lived.

With the aid of the doorman, Duff had been carried upstairs. Horatio had summoned a doctor. And now he had on his hands one completely inebriated old sea captain, but one who held a secret that Horatio meant to learn as soon as his guest revived sufficiently to talk.

From his pocket, Horatio took one of the thin black stogies, to which both the Jones brothers were addicted. He touched a match to it, blew a few thoughtful puffs toward the ceiling.

Had there been anything back of Clancy's refusal to let him take Duff along, beyond his natural objection to having a customer lured away? It seemed to Horatio that Clancy's attitude had been too belligerent to be entirely explained by his dislike for detectives. He had been trying to frighten him off, Horatio concluded.

Why had Mullet left the Anchorage? Who was the young man with whom he left? What was the connection between his leaving and Condit's death? Did Condit have a fortune hidden somewhere? Did Mullet know where it was? And what had the theft of the pennies to do with it all?

A sudden frown darkened Horatio's usually pleasant brow. He held his stogy poised halfway to his mouth. His eyes seemed to be gazing off into space.

Had Captain Condit died from natural causes—or had he been put out of the way by some clever and undetected means?

As he sat there beside the unconscious Duff, Horatio let these and a dozen other questions race about in his mind. He studied the situation from all angles; he developed theories, only to discard them. Until at last, with a shake of his head, he decided to let the whole thing rest till he found Mullet and talked with him.

IT WAS almost midnight before Captain Duff began to show any real signs of coming to. In the interim, Horatio had sent for a trained nurse. She stood beside him now, ruddy-faced and efficient-looking in her crisp uniform.

With a cough and a groan, Captain Duff suddenly sat bolt upright in bed. He blinked his watery eyes, worked his lips, wrinkled his nose. Then he looked around him dazedly and presently let out a half dozen salty curses.

"By God!" he spluttered. "By God, I can't get my bearings! Where am I?"

Carefully Horatio explained. And little by little Captain Duff began to understand what had happened. He shook his shaggy head.

"Well, I'd better hoist my anchor and set sail!"

He started to get out of bed, but Horatio put a restraining hand on his shoulder.

"No hurry, Captain. Better stay here tonight. You'll be all snug, and you must remember you were wounded," Horatio murmured soothingly. "Besides Miss Berring has come in to look after you."

"How's that?"

"This is Miss Berring, Captain."

Slowly, Duff turned his head till his gaze fell full upon the ruddy-faced trained nurse. He brought up a gnarled hand and ran it down the length of his beard. Then he wiped his mouth with the tattooed mermaid.

"Ho! A lady standing watch tonight!" he roared, and gave a loud laugh. But he settled back on the pillow with a grunt and a sigh. "Rum!" he muttered. "Rum."

Miss Berring looked at Horatio, who nodded and indicated a very small portion. She left the room and Horatio began to talk to the old captain. With very little effort, he extracted the information for which he had been waiting so long. And it was with a feeling of chagrin that he found it had been available all the time—written on a sheet of paper in Captain Duff's jacket.

With a faintly puzzled air, Horatio read the address. He couldn't quite understand it. He had expected a hotel or an apartment. "Dear me," he muttered to himself. "I suppose I'd better look into this at once."

He called Miss Berring aside, explained to her that he was going out and didn't know exactly when he would be back. Then, providing her with funds, he gave instructions that the old captain was to be kept in bed until he had fully recovered, which certainly wouldn't be for twenty-four hours. After that Horatio left the apartment.

On the way downtown in his taxi, he took out his automatic, made sure it was ready for instant use. Satisfied, he slipped it back in his pocket and gave it a pat. Then he settled down in his seat and idly watched the lights of Fifth Avenue slide by.

They drove south to Twenty-third, where the driver took Broadway to Union Square. At Union Square he cut over to Fourth Avenue and presently they were speeding south on Lafayette. But only for a short distance; then he headed directly into the heart of the lower East Side.

A half dozen blocks from his destination, Horatio leaned over and tapped on the window separating him from the driver.

"You can let me out here!"

IT WAS after one o'clock, but the streets were far from deserted. As Horatio made his way south on Second Avenue, he passed numerous pedestrians. Automobiles and trucks drove by at frequent intervals. Overhead the deafening rumble of the elevated came regularly.

He found the number for which he was looking. It was over a door which was protected by a heavy iron grille. Beside the door extended a wide show window, so covered with dust and grime as almost to conceal the many dozen objects on display.

Horatio glanced up, read the sign formed of faded gilt letters—*Seven Seas Curio Shop.*

As he walked past, he tried to look inside, but he was unable to make out anything in the gloomy interior. Several doors farther along a delicatessen was still open, and beyond that on the corner was a beer bar. But aside from these two, none of the shops or other establishments in the block was doing business.

At the corner, Horatio crossed the street and retraced his course till he had reached a point directly opposite the curio shop. There he found a convenient dark doorway and, slipping into it, studied the place with the grilled door.

He could understand better now why Mullet had given this as his address. He had seen shops of this type before, and he knew that in the old days the proprietors were apt to depend for their stock to some extent upon the sailors, who brought strange objects from far ports and smuggled them in.

Probably at some time or other Mullet had done business with the owner of the Seven Seas Curio Shop. It was near the East River Docks, and there were wretched tenements above some of the stores, showing lighted windows. But the windows above the curio shop were dark and forbidding. This fact ended a momentary plan to cross the street and see if he could locate a night bell. That would hardly be wise policy anyway, Horatio told himself.

While he was debating what to do, Horatio saw an automobile slide up to the curb opposite him and directly before the Seven Seas Curio Shop. It was a sedan, new and ultra streamlined. Only one man was in it, and after coming to a halt he remained in his seat behind the wheel.

For a few minutes Horatio stood motionless, watching. The man in the car lit a cigarette, tossed the match out the open window of the sedan. But he kept his place, and Horatio knew he was waiting for someone.

Cautiously, almost like a gray shadow, Horatio emerged from the doorway and moved down the street. When he reached a point from which he could obtain a clear view of the doorway to the curio shop, he halted. Taking up a position in the protection of an elevated pillar, he kept his eyes fixed on the car.

Five minutes—ten minutes passed. Then a light flickered behind the dusty show window. He could see figures moving around inside. Horatio pressed closer to the pillar. A couple of pedestrians walked by, but they paid little heed to him, assuming that he was drunk and clinging to the pillar for support.

A little later the door of the shop opened. A slightly stooped figure came out, crossed the sidewalk and got into the sedan. Horatio could see still other figures in the doorway. They seemed to be talking earnestly.

But presently one of them separated and started toward the car. Halfway across the walk he stopped and held his watch up so that the light from the street lamp would fall upon it. Then he entered the sedan. But not before Horatio had a chance to see the man's face—it was Mike the Mauler Clancy!

The door of the car and the door of the shop slammed almost simultaneously. With an exhaust that was scarcely more than a powerful whisper, the black sedan glided up Second Avenue.

Horatio stepped from behind the elevated pillar and watched a slinking figure emerge from the shadows and glide down the street. In the feeble light he could see the yellow skin and slanting eyes of a Chinaman or other Oriental.

A tiny frown appeared between Horatio's mild blue eyes. He had a feeling that this other man also had been watching the Seven Seas Curio Shop; that he also was interested in the three men who had just driven away in the black sedan.

CAPTAIN DUFF wasn't feeling very well the next morning and Horatio had little difficulty in persuading him to remain at the apartment and keep to his bed. Leaving instructions with Miss Berring to do whatever was possible for the old fellow's comfort, he took his departure.

He was satisfied in his own mind that the stooped man who had left the curio shop the previous night with Mike the Mauler Clancy had been Mullet. The driver of the ultra-streamlined sedan, he surmised, was the young man with whom Mullet had left the Anchorage. But what was the object of this odd alliance? Was Mullet a willing, or an unwilling member?

He thought about those things as he drove downtown in his car. He thought, too, about Leander. Leander wouldn't reach Hollis Harbor until sometime during the afternoon. He couldn't very well pick up any clue to a hidden crime before then. Horatio smiled to himself. He certainly had a head start on Leander in that respect!

The Seven Seas Curio Shop looked different by daylight. It had lost some of its air of gloomy mystery; but its shabbiness was intensified. There was still something vaguely ominous, sinister, about the place, however.

Pushing open the door with the iron grille on it, Horatio entered. He found himself in a long low room, filled to overflowing with furniture, brassware, odd chests, statues, huge vases, ship models—a conglomeration of objects old and new.

Dust lay everywhere. The dim air itself was laden with it; one could have traced his name on any of the articles in the stock. There was no light, except what came through the front window, and for a moment Horatio was unable to tell whether there was anyone in the shop.

By the time his eyes had become accustomed to the change from the brightness of outdoors, a black curtain hanging in a doorway at the back had been pushed aside. Horatio saw a man enter and hobble slowly and painfully toward him.

He was a small man. His hunched shoulders and the way his head stuck forward from his body, like a turtle, added to the impression of shortness. His nose was long; his mouth was wide with a thick lower lip that hung out loosely. A scraggly beard covered the lower half of his face and above his huge ears was perched a little, brown, skull cap.

He approached Horatio, peered at him through old-fashioned, gold-rimmed spectacles.

"Well?"

Horatio gave an embarrassed cough. "I beg your pardon," he murmured, "but I'm looking for someone."

"*Ja!* You are looking for someone? Here?" The shrewd, deep-set eyes were studying Horatio.

"Exactly!" Horatio nodded. "A Captain Mullet. Do you happen to know him?"

It seemed to Horatio that the man in the skull cap stiffened. He cocked his head on one side, tugged at his scraggly beard, looked at Horatio out of the corners of his half-closed eyes. Finally, however, he began to move his head slowly up and down.

"I know him, *ja*. He isn't here now."

"Do you know when he will be here?" The little man considered. A crafty expression flickered for an instant in his deep-set eyes, then was gone. When he spoke, his voice was husky but ingratiating. "Captain Mullet has gone to the country. He will be back tonight. Late."

"What time?"

"Well—" The man in the skull cap hesitated. "I tell you. You come here at midnight, and Captain Mullet will be here."

HORATIO LOOKED at his watch. It was only a little after eleven. "You feel pretty sure Captain Mullet will be here at midnight?"

"Positive!"

"Thank you," Horatio murmured half apologetically. "Thank you very much."

The man in the skull cap rubbed his thin hands briskly together. "You will be back then—yes?" he asked with a hint of eagerness.

Horatio looked at him with a funny sort of smile. "Dear me," he murmured, "I wouldn't be at all surprised if I came back here tonight."

"That's good! Good!"

The owner of the shop followed Horatio to the door, held it open for him. He stood there in the doorway with his arms folded on his chest, a sly cruel expression only partially hidden by his beard, as Horatio climbed into his car.

Horatio had hesitated a long time before going into the shop and inquiring about Mullet; he doubted seriously that it would be a wise move, after having seen Mike the Mauler Clancy come out of the place. Then he had decided that because Clancy knew him, it did not necessarily follow that the proprietor of the shop did.

Now, as he caught a glimpse of the hunched figure in his rear-view mirror, he realized that the shop keeper had spotted him. Clancy no doubt had warned him to be on the look-out.

"Dear me," Horatio murmured, as he slipped the car in gear. "Won't you come into my parlor said the spider to the fly?" He chuckled.

He decided that the bearded little proprietor did resemble a scrawny black spider. "But Horatio Jones isn't a fly," he added to himself. It was a neat mantrap the owner of the Seven Seas Shop wanted to spring at midnight. An hour when one could get away with almost anything—even murder—in this neighborhood.

Well, he'd be back. But he wouldn't walk into any traps. In fact, Horatio concluded, the little man in the skull cap wouldn't even be aware that he'd come back, if Horatio could help it. And he thought he could.

So far, he had brought to light no crime, unless he wished to consider the attack on Duff and himself by Clancy's gunmen. But for reasons of his own, Horatio didn't care to take further notice of that, since Duff was only slightly injured and he himself unscathed.

On the other hand, he was convinced beyond all doubt that there was something afoot—some sinister plot. If Mike Clancy was in it, he knew it was murderous. And having met the proprietor of the Seven Seas Curio Shop, he was satisfied that the scheme was crafty and for high stakes.

CHAPTER FIVE
GEMS OF JEOPARDY

AT FIVE minutes to midnight the bearded little man was standing in the doorway of his curio shop. Behind him, the place was dimly illumined by a single electric bulb, hanging from the ceiling. It cast a sickening yellow glow that sent weird shadows dancing around the grimy walls; it revealed the singular stock of merchandise in strange silhouettes.

It might have been imagined that the proprietor hadn't moved since Horatio had left him more than twelve hours before. His arms were still folded on his chest, his deep-set cruel eyes peered up and down the street through his spectacles.

As he caught sight of a small man in a rumpled gray suit and brown soft hat, who was walking toward the shop, his frown gave way to a sly smile. He stepped quickly back into the shop. But a moment later he was back in the doorway again. The man in the gray suit was only a few feet away.

"*Ja!* So you have come right on time!" the man in the skull cap exclaimed. "Captain Mullet was here already yet. He asks you to wait for him. He'll be back right away. Come in!"

"Why—a—thank you. Thank you very much."

The shopkeeper stood aside, rubbing his hands. The man in the gray suit entered, looked about.

"So Captain Mullet will be back, you say?"

"*Ja! Ja!* He'll be here right away soon."

A peculiar expression appeared in the other man's pale blue eyes. But he said nothing.

The curio shop proprietor bustled about till he had dug out a chair that appeared substantial. He dusted it off carefully. Then he placed it near the rear of the room, near the curtained doorway.

"Have a seat."

"Why—a thank you. My word, thank you very much."

"Maybe I could do something for you yet?" the owner said.

"No, I don't believe so."

"And maybe yet I could," the man in the skull cap repeated. He gave a short laugh, a sort of cackle of triumph.

The man in the chair looked at him in astonishment, started to rise. But before he could move, something crashed upon his head with terrific force. He felt himself falling—down—down into a bottomless pit. Then sudden utter blackness.

THE MOMENT Leander Jones recovered consciousness he realized that he had walked into a trap which the wily little shop keeper had prepared for his brother. But why had the proprietor of the Seven Seas establishment wanted to capture Horatio? It meant that Horatio had been up to something while he, Leander, was down in Maine? But what the devil was it?

Leander decided to let any attempt to figure out the answers wait until his head had ceased to ache quite so much.

He was lying on the floor face up. His hands were securely bound behind his back. His ankles, too, were tied with stout cords, and around his mouth a none too clean handkerchief served as a gag.

Even before he opened his eyes, Leander cursed himself softly. He should have been on his guard when the little shop keeper had said Mullet was coming to this place, had already been here once this evening. Leander knew that wasn't possible.

Suppressing a groan, he looked about him. He was in a room of considerable size. From his position on the floor, he could see that it was furnished with a large desk, half a dozen chairs, a couple of big cabinets and a bookcase. Beside the desk he caught a glimpse of an old-fashioned globe on an oak pedestal. There were numerous copper and brass urns and vases on shelves and scattered about the room.

It was, he decided, the private office of the curio shop's owner.

He became aware of voices. At first, he couldn't see the speakers; then by twisting his body he managed to make them out, standing by the door.

One was the man in the skull cap. The other was a yellow-skinned man of huge size. A half-caste Chinaman, Leander decided. He was holding a banknote in his hand.

"Any time you want me for another little job like this, Pross, just let me know," the big man said with a saturnine smile. He spoke with no trace of Chinese accent.

"*Ja!* You did a good job yet."

"You got your ten dollars' worth." He laughed, turned and disappeared through the door. Pross followed him. Leander could hear their footsteps growing fainter.

What next, Leander wondered. This was a bitter climax to his record-breaking dash back from Maine. To walk blindly into a trap that had been baited for Horatio.

Pross came back. He walked to the corner of the room where Leander was lying, bent over, leered down at the recumbent figure.

"So—Detective Jones," he cackled. "Well, well, well! My good friend, Mr. Clancy, said last night you would call maybe. He knew what he was talking about, yes!"

Leander was trying to figure out who Clancy was. Pross nudged his ribs with the toe of his shoe. "You shouldn't interfere with what is none of your business, Jones," Pross continued. "It's going to cost you more than you want to pay, more than anybody wants to pay."

He gave Leander a parting push with his foot, then walked across the room to the one big window. Reaching up, he pulled down the shade until it covered the entire opening. After that, he walked to his desk and switched on a lamp with a flexible goose neck. From one of the cabinets, he took a couple of small ledgers, which he placed on the desk.

AN HOUR passed. To Leander, lying on the floor with his bonds cutting off his circulation, every minute was beginning to be agony. But he could do nothing. His gag prevented him from calling out, from asking his cruel-eyed captor for so much as a drink of water.

As for Pross, he ignored the man on the floor. He bent over his books, checking and rechecking, making occasional entries.

From somewhere below, the sound of a bell ringing floated up. Out of one corner of his eye, Leander saw Pross grow tense. The little man leaned forward, cupped a hand about one of his big ears.

Again the bell. But this time it sounded in a regular series of three double rings. This was repeated. Pross got quickly to his feet and shuffled from the room.

A little later, Leander heard voices below and soon afterward Pross reappeared. He was followed by two men. The first was young, in his early twenties. He was dark, well built and would have been good looking except for his shifty eyes and a surly mouth. He was wearing a cap, pulled down slightly on one side of his head.

The second man was Mike the Mauler Clancy. So that was the Clancy whom Pross had mentioned. Leander knew him, knew his record.

"Well, you got it, yes?" Pross exclaimed. His voice was high, trembling with excitement, eager. He rubbed his skinny hands together, cracked his knuckles. "Let us see! Let us see!"

"Not so fast," Clancy growled. "We got lots of time."

"You had no trouble in finding it this time then," Pross said.

The man in the cap spoke. "Naw. Mullet knew how to read them directions. If I'd known I'd have got the stuff myself the other trip."

"*Ja!*" Pross exclaimed. "Where is Mullet?"

Clancy laughed, a brief, heartless laugh. "You tell him, Crocker!" he said to the man in the cap.

"Well, Pop," Crocker said, grinning at Pross, "we figured that it'd make a little more for each of us if we was to split this stuff three ways instead of four." He echoed Clancy's laugh.

Pross took a quick breath. He pushed his head even farther forward on his turtle neck and blinked over the top of his gold-rimmed spectacles. His eyes were bright, glossy.

"So—you mean that you—"

"Never mind!" Clancy interrupted gruffly. "We've rubbed out Mullet. That's all there is to it. Forget about it, see!"

Leander repressed a shudder. Mullet's death was no news to him. He'd found the old sailor's body there behind the captain's rock at Hollis Harbor. And it was in Mullet's clothes that he'd come across the address of the Seven Seas Curio Shop. But the cold-blooded way in which Clancy admitted killing the old man filled Leander with horror. As he considered his own situation, he could feel the muscles in his throat tighten.

The three men had moved to the desk. Most of the room was in semi-darkness, but the top of the desk was brilliantly illuminated by the goose-neck lamp.

"All right, Crocker," Clancy said. "Give us the box! We'll let Pop here figure out what the stuff's worth."

From under his coat, the man in the cap produced a red lacquer box. It was about the size of a cigar box, although of slightly different shape. It had a brass lock which showed signs of having been forced. Crocker laid the box on the table.

From the drawer of the desk, Pross removed a pistol which he placed on the desk top. He also took out several sheets of paper and a pencil.

Suddenly Clancy let out an oath. His eyes were fixed upon one corner of the room, on the trussed-up figure of Leander Jones.

"What the hell!" he exclaimed. In a couple of swift strides he had crossed the room. He looked down at the man on the floor. Then a wide smile broke out on his face. "By God! It's that little rat, Jones!"

"*Ja!*" Pop Pross said. "He came around this afternoon, just like you said he would yet. So I thought I'd better keep him till you got back."

Clancy leered at the helpless Leander. "What a break," he said softly. "Jones—it's going to be a lotta fun—removing you from circulation for good!"

MIKE THE MAULER CLANCY walked back to the desk. He stood across from Pross. Crocker stood beside the hunched owner of the curio shop. Pross picked up the red lacquer box, examined it carefully, turning it over and over in his hands.

"From India," he grunted.

"Never mind where it's from," Clancy said. "It's from Hollis Harbor, Maine, so far's I'm concerned. You just open her up and you'll see a sight you've never seen the like of in all the years you been a fence."

Pross looked up. "The key? Where is it?"

"Key, hell! Get it open the way we did. With a screw driver."

"It's a valuable box," Pross muttered. But he opened the desk drawer and rummaged around until he found a small screw driver. He inserted this under the lid of the box and applied pressure. The lid snapped back.

Pross gave voice to a guttural gasp. Then he exhaled slowly, noisily. Crocker and Clancy bent over the table, their eyes glued to the inside of the box.

"By God!" Clancy breathed. "It looks even better than it did up there."

"The light makes 'em sparkle," Crocker nodded.

Pross turned the box upside down. Out upon the top of the desk cascaded dozens of unset gems and several strings of pearls. There were diamonds, rubies, emeralds. And besides the necklaces there were countless unset pearls. They reflected the light in a thousand twinkling rays, a dazzling display that was almost blinding.

The jewels, the diamonds, especially, seemed to be alive. They seemed to move, to revolve, to shoot off beams of living fire.

Pross was breathing heavily. He ran the palm of his hand over the heap of gems and spread them out till they covered a square foot of the table top. Finally, he looked up and squinted across the table at Clancy.

"So this is Captain Condit's treasure, yes?"

"Them's the old fool's jewels," Clancy said. "And a sweet pile of 'em, too."

"Ja," Pross nodded. "Where did he get them yet, I wonder."

"Stole 'em."

"What?"

"Sure. That's what Mullet said. He stole 'em from a guy who stole 'em himself."

"I—I don't understand," Pross muttered.

"Well, this is how it was," Clancy said. "When this guy Condit was makin' his last trip on his boat, he picked up some mugg at a port over in India. This mugg was scramming out of the country, see? And he offered Condit heavy sugar to help him make his getaway."

"*Ja.*"

"O.K. Well, when they got out to sea Condit learns why this mugg's in such a rush. He's robbed some kind of a dealer in gems—and he's got the stuff with him. That gives Condit an idea. He'd been going to sea for pretty near fifty years and he didn't have nothing to show for it. He'd dropped his savings in a phony gold mine or something.

"Anyway, there was a big storm. And when the storm was over there wasn't any sign of the mugg they'd picked up in India, see?"

"*Ja,* I see," Pross nodded.

"Old Condit thought nobody was onto him. He quit the sea and Mullet who was his mate quit, too. Then Mullet drops a broad hint that he knows just what the play is. That scares hell out of Condit. He takes Mullet with him to the Anchorage and pays all his expenses for ten years. He knows Mullet knows, but they don't talk about it. And the captain never lets out a peep where he's got the stuff hid."

"And once a year," Pross muttered, "Condit would come here with three or four diamonds to sell. He did that for ten years. That's what gave me my idea," he added with a mirthless chuckle. "And gentlemen, you see here now the results of that idea!"

He made a sweeping gesture above the gems with his right hand.

CLANCY GRIPPED the edge of the desk and, leaning over, peered sharply into Pross's crafty face. "How much," he said narrowly, "do you figure this pile of rocks is worth?"

Pross shrugged, lifted his palms. "How can I tell, till I've checked them."

"Make a guess!" Clancy snapped.

"Perhaps they are worth—a half million," Pross muttered. "If they are, we may be able to sell them for a quarter of a million. If we take our time."

"My God," Clancy breathed. "That's haul, ain't it, Crocker?"

The man in the cap nodded. He was staring as if hypnotized at the jewels spread before him. He wet his lips nervously. "I'll—I'll say it is."

"Better get busy and make a list of the stuff," Clancy said to Pross. "If we know just what's there, we'll know if anyone tries to lift any of it." He closed one eye, fastened the other one significantly upon Pross.

Pross paid no attention to him. He pushed the gems to one side, pulled one of the sheets of paper and the pencil closer to him. He picked up one of the diamonds, rolled it around in his palm and then, seizing it between thumb and forefinger, held it up to the light. The way he handled the gem was almost a caress.

"I won't weigh them," Pross said. "Just guess at the size and make a rough list."

"O.K."

The window shade, loosened by the vibration from the elevated, suddenly rolled upward. It spun around the roller several times and then dropped halfway down again over the window. The sound was unexpected, startling. All eyes turned toward it. Clancy and Crocker let out nervous oaths.

"Fix the damn thing!" Clancy growled.

Crocker crossed the room. He pulled the shade down, tried to make it catch. But the ratchet was worn and it wouldn't stay.

Clancy noticing the difficulty muttered: "Let it go! Nobody can see in from out there anyway. Not unless he's over in Brooklyn with a spyglass," he added with a curt laugh.

Crocker returned to his position beside Pross, who had separated the diamonds from the other gems and was examining them one by one and then listing them.

There was a tense silence, broken only by the heavy breathing of the three men. From time to time, Clancy removed his gaze from the jewels and turned it on the helpless figure of Leander. His broken-nosed face wore a hard, cruel smile. He appeared to be looking forward with relish to killing one of the Jones brothers.

"Twenty-seven diamonds," Pross said.

"Not so many," Crocker muttered. "I thought there was more."

"Well, Condit has been bringing me a few every year for ten years now," Pross replied. "That's why the diamonds is not so many."

Leander on the floor was suffering untold agony from his bonds. His body was so cramped it seemed to him that it never again would be supple. He moved about as much as he could, careful not to attract the attention of Clancy. He looked up toward the window and his eyes widened in astonishment.

Pressed against the glass was a hand, and above the hand a face; a yellow-skinned face with slanting eyes and thick-lipped mouth. The mouth was half open now, disclosing stumps of stained teeth. It was the face of a Chinaman, and Leander immediately recognized the giant half-caste whom Pross had been paying off as Leander recovered consciousness.

THE THREE men at the desk appeared oblivious to the eavesdropper. Then, suddenly, as if he had received a telepathic warning, Crocker looked up, swung his eyes toward the window.

Leander stiffened. But the young gunman was fast, almost faster than the eye could follow. His hand slid inside his coat and out in one continuous movement. And a second later the roar of his gun shook the room.

Pross jumped to his feet, upsetting his chair. His face was white as death; his skinny elbows were trembling. Clancy had caught the movement of Crocker's hand, followed it in time to see the man at the window. Clancy's pistol had come out, too.

But when the smoke drifted aside, the face was no longer there. And where it had been, was a round hole in the window glass.

Crocker turned to Clancy. "I had to do it, Mike," he muttered.

Mike the Mauler nodded. "That's right. What the hell was he doing out there?" He looked at Pross. "Is there a fire escape outside?"

"No—no. You can see for yourself. He must have climbed along the window ledges. I'll look—"

"Stay away from that window!" Clancy ordered. "Do you want the cops pouring in here first thing?" He was thoughtful for a moment. "Three stories. Where would he land?"

"A courtyard in back. A small courtyard yet."

"O.K.!" Clancy snapped. He was brisk now, a man who knew exactly what he was going to do. "Get that stuff out of the way! Put it in the safe!"

"*Ja!*" With shaking hands, Pross gathered up the gems and returned them to the red lacquer box. Crocker helped him. Clancy walked across the room a couple of times, on the second trip pausing to stare narrowly at the recumbent form of Leander. But he said nothing.

Taking the box, Pross went to one of the cabinets. He swung the doors open and the front end of a large safe was revealed. He stooped, twirled the dials. When he had deposited the box of jewels in the safe and closed the concealing cabinet doors, he returned to his desk.

"How about him?" Crocker jerked a thumb in the direction of Leander.

"He gets the works!"

Crocker brought out his gun. He turned with it toward Leander. "Now?"

"Put that rod away!" Clancy snarled. "You can't bump him here. When this guy Jones goes, there's going to be a hell of a stink. We got to fix it so they'll never find a trace of him."

"How?"

"Easy enough. "We'll drop him in the lower bay with about two hundred pounds of scrap iron wired to him."

Crocker whistled. "Before you bump him?"

"Why waste any slugs. The water'll take care of him." Clancy shrugged.

LEANDER COULD feel the perspiration spring out on his forehead. The ache and pain of his bonds was forgotten in the light of the scheme Clancy had just disclosed so casually.

Clancy was talking. "Now here's what we do. Pross!"

"*Ja!*"

"As soon as we get out of here, you break that glass out of the window and put in a piece of pasteboard. Understand?"

"*Ja!*"

"Remember you don't know nothing—nothing about that guy down there! Remember! Come on, Crocker. Carry that guy in the corner downstairs."

Crocker walked to the corner where Leander was lying and bent over. He took a firm hold on Leander's waist and, hoisting him up, hung him over his shoulder like a sack of meal.

They started to descend the stairs which led down from the adjoining room. Clancy went first, then Crocker with Leander. The light was dim, only one bulb illuminating the stairway on the second floor, which was evidently the living quarters for the owner of the curio shop.

"Take it easy," Clancy volunteered.

Crocker gave a grunt. "I am. But this guy's heavy."

"I'll give you a hand when we get to the bottom."

When they reached the foot of the stairs, they were in the back room of the main floor. It was the room behind the black curtain, the room in which the big half-caste had hidden before he overpowered Leander.

Here, Clancy directed Crocker to lower Leander from his shoulder. "I'll take his head and you can take his feet till we get to the front door," he said. "Then I'll step out and make sure the coast's clear before we try to put him in the car."

"O.K. Let's go!"

Clancy slipped his hands under Leander's armpits; Crocker seized his ankles. They began to move slowly toward the front of the shop, although it was slow work. When they passed through the curtain, they were in almost total darkness, only the feeble rays of the street light entering through the grimy window.

"Geez, it's dark," Crocker muttered.

"Watch your step," Clancy growled.

"Maybe this will make it better for you!" a voice suddenly exclaimed in the darkness. At the same instant, the dazzling white beam of a flashlight fell full upon Clancy and Crocker and their burden. The two killers swore viciously, but the voice cut in upon them.

"Put that man on the floor! And stick your hands up! Be careful! I'm looking for an excuse to shoot both of you." The voice was cold, precise, dangerous.

Leander's heart began to pound as Clancy and Crocker dropped him none too gently to the floor. It was the voice of Horatio.

CHAPTER SIX
FOOL'S JEWELS

CLANCY STRAIGHTENED with his hands high above his head. Crocker took a little more time about it. And when he did straighten up, it was with a sudden swift motion. In his hand was a gun and he fired at the light.

The roar of his weapon mingled with the blast from Horatio's. Out of the darkness shot a tongue of orange flame. The slug caught Crocker square. It spun him, knocked him back several feet and sent him crashing to the floor.

But Crocker's shot had hit the light. The room was again in total darkness. Leander felt Clancy crawl over him. Since the shot, there had been no sound from Horatio, but he felt sure that he was uninjured. At worst, he might have been hit in the hand that held the flashlight. That was the left and Horatio would still have his gun hand.

In the dust and darkness of the old curio shop the deadly stalking began. Leander bit his lips, strained at his bonds. But it was no use. His arms and legs were numb, and even had the cords been removed, he couldn't have used them.

It was quiet; deathly, ominously quiet. Once a board creaked. Leander held his breath. But there was no following blast of gunfire. Then suddenly he heard a weird noise. It was not particularly loud, yet unlike anything he had ever heard before. A sort of rasping whistle.

Slowly, a smile spread across Leander's face. It wouldn't be long now before Horatio got his man. That noise was Clancy's breathing—the air pushing through the distorted passages of his battered nose. A prizefighter's wheeze. It located him as surely as if he had been speaking. And he probably was so used to it he wasn't aware of it.

As if in answer to Leander's thought there was the roar of a gun. Then a scream—a scream of agony in Clancy's voice. In a moment, Horatio bent over and cut Leander's bonds, took off his gag.

"Better—better get the one upstairs," Leander gasped.

For only a second Horatio hesitated. Then he ran from the room. Up one flight of stairs, then he started up the second. Halfway up, something prompted him to turn and look behind. A hunched figure was scuttling across the floor heading for the stairs.

"Stop!"

The figure paid no heed.

"Stop!"

But still Pross kept on. He was starting down now. Horatio brought his hand up and fired, fired high. He didn't want to shoot this old fellow down.

Pross gave a shrill cry of terror. He tripped, tried to catch his balance, teetered for a second and then plunged over and over down the steps. He struck the bottom with a sickening crash. From beneath his coat bounced a red lacquer box. It flew open. Out upon the grimy floor spewed a quart of glittering gems.

"Well, Horatio," Leander murmured, "that was good work."

"Better than I'd hoped for," Horatio replied.

"How did you happen to come in here?"

"Why, I'd planned to come back tonight and slip into the shop and hide. That way, I believed I could find out what these crooks were up to."

"You knew, of course, that this man Pross had a trap ready for you? That he was expecting you?"

Horatio grinned. "I was well aware of it, Leander. And you seemed to have stepped right into it."

"I did," Leander admitted ruefully.

"He never guessed he'd caught a different Jones from the one he'd talked to earlier," Horatio chuckled. "It was probably a good thing they trapped you."

"What?" Leander looked aggrieved.

Horatio nodded. "Quite true. They thought they had me. That made them careless, put them off their guard. So it made it easier for me to get in here without attracting attention."

"What made you come in here?"

"A dead Chinaman. I was out in back looking the situation over—trying to figure out the best way to get in. Then somebody dropped a dead Chinaman almost on top of my head. I gathered that things were getting hot inside."

"They were," Leander agreed.

"So I wasted no more time on ceremony. I jimmied the door—and here I am! It was quite a shock seeing you lugged downstairs like a sack of meal, when all the time I thought you were down in Maine."

IT WAS early afternoon. Leander Jones let himself into the apartment which he shared with Horatio. He hung his battered brown hat on a hook in the hall and then strode briskly into the living room. Horatio was there. Horatio, in a bathrobe, sitting at the window and gazing out over Central Park.

"Leander," he said thoughtfully, "I've been trying to figure out what made you leave Hollis Harbor so suddenly and return to New York as fast as possible last night."

Leander chuckled, dropped into a chair.

"After I found the body at Captain's Rock," he said, "I searched it. I discovered a card with the address of the Seven Seas Curio Shop. And I recognized it as the establishment of Pop Pross, one of the city's most notorious fences.

"On the ground nearby, I found—this." Leander drew from his pocket a sparkling red stone, which he handed to Horatio.

"A ruby!" Horatio exclaimed.

Leander smiled. "At any rate, when the natives up there identified the dead man as Mullet, an intimate friend of the late Captain Condit, I recalled the automobile with the New York license, which I had met on my way to Hollis

Harbor. I knew then that the killers would be found at this end—not in Maine.

"I hired a car to drive me to Portland, chartered a plane from there to Boston and took the regular Eastern Air Transport to New York. I stopped by the apartment; you weren't there. So I went about my investigations, starting at the Seven Seas Shop."

"You've talked with Pross?"

"Yes. In the Tombs. He told me everything quite willingly. I suppose we can close another case, Horatio. Two murders, one gunman slain, another badly wounded a Chinese thug shot to death, a well known fence in jail, the jewels recovered. That about sums it up."

"But that Chinaman—who was he?"

"The police checked his fingerprints," Leander said. "He was Charlie Foo Sing, with a record as long as your arm. Burglaries, assault, hold-ups. The police believe he was planning to rob old Pross. I know Pross frequently had him do some of his dirty work—such as knocking me out—so he may have gotten wind of the big deal Pross was mixed up in."

"Sounds likely," Horatio nodded. "Lucky for us he was shot. If he hadn't come tumbling down, while I was looking over the back of the building, I probably wouldn't have gone inside so soon."

Leander made a little grimace, lit a stogy.

Horatio asked: "The whole scheme then was Pross's?"

"Yes."

"What was it?"

"My word, it was really quite simple," Leander murmured. "Year after year, Condit brought diamonds in and sold them to Pross for enough to cover his year's expenses. This led Pross to believe that the old fellow had a big cache of them somewhere. He decided to make a play for them.

"He couldn't swing it himself, so he got Clancy and Crocker in with him. They tried to work on Condit. But they couldn't get near the old boy, he'd grown so suspicious and crotchety. The murder he'd committed so long ago was eating into his mind. He was getting a little bit crazy."

LEANDER PUFFED leisurely on his stogy, then continued. "Clancy and Crocker, however, managed to get in with Mullet. And at their urging, he demanded that Captain Condit tell him where the jewels were hidden under threat of exposure. He said he wanted to be protected in case anything happened to Condit.

"Condit flew into a wild rage. He swore that was a secret he was going to carry with him to his grave. And he wound up by having an attack of apoplexy and dying."

Horatio nodded. "That must have left Pross and company in a hole."

"Only temporarily," Leander said. "Pross is as sharp as a razor blade. When he heard Condit had sworn he'd carry the secret of his hiding place to the grave, and then heard that Condit had left instructions in his will for pennies to be placed on his eyes, it took him just about ten seconds to see the connection.

"He sent Crocker up to steal the pennies. Pross opened them and found two sheets of tissue inside. On the sheets were complete instructions for locating the buried jewels. But the instructions were couched in nautical terms, and Crocker couldn't figure them out when he got on the spot. And just about that time, Henry Condit came blundering along. Crocker was afraid he might stumble onto the gems, so he shot him to death.

"When Crocker got back to New York empty-handed, Pross was pretty angry. The next time they all went up—Crocker, Clancy and Mullet. And with Mullet interpreting old Condit's sea-going phrases they found the red box. Then, as you know, they stabbed Mullet to death so they wouldn't have to split with him."

They were silent for a long time. Finally, Horatio said: "That'll be a tremendous fortune for Mrs. Condit and her little girl."

Leander gave a shrug, pursed his lips. "My word, it'll no more than keep them. The diamonds aren't worth more than eight or ten thousand dollars."

"Yes. But the other gems. The pearls, the rubies, the emeralds—they must be worth several hundred thousand dollars."

"No," Leander said, shaking his head. "The diamonds were the only gems that were genuine. The rest were excellent imitations. I doubt that Condit even knew it. He probably picked the diamonds, because he thought they'd be easier to sell."

"You mean—you mean all those other jewels were—paste?"

"Exactly, my dear Horatio! All that murder and violence was for imitation gems."

Horatio was silent. At last he murmured: "Fool's jewels."

Leander nodded. "Precisely—fool's jewels."

FAIR AND MURDER

TO THE CENTURY OF PROGRESS
EXPOSITION THEY HAD GONE—
ON A VACATION—THOSE TWO
AMAZING LITTLE MEN, THE
BROTHERS JONES. BUT THEIR
JAUNT TURNED INTO A HORROR
HOLIDAY OVERNIGHT WHEN THEY
GOT WORD THAT THE WEATHER
WAS SHIFTING TO PAIR AND
MURDER.

CHAPTER ONE
SKY WITNESS

THE ROAR of the motors made conversation all but impossible as the sight-seeing blimp soared above the lake shore skirting the grounds of the Century of Progress Exposition.

It had been a perfect day. Overhead the sky was cloudless. In the west the red disk of the sun was sinking behind the saw-tooth skyline of Chicago's loop.

And beneath, lay the panorama of the exposition grounds. A riot of brilliant reds, yellows, blues and greens. A sprawling three miles of fantastic form and weird outlines.

Leander Jones, senior partner of Jones and Jones, leaned forward in his wicker seat. He tapped his younger twin brother Horatio on the shoulder, placed his lips close to his ear. "My word, Horatio," he said, "it is quite astounding!"

Horatio, who had been surveying the gaudy grounds below through a pair of field glasses, nodded his head. "It hardly seems real!" he shouted.

He edged close to the window beside him, raised the field glasses again to his eyes. The blimp was flying at several hundred feet, about a quarter of a mile from shore. It had reached the northern end of its course, come about and was heading back for the landing field.

Almost below them, along the waterfront, were billowing roller coasters, their lofty structures traced in spiderweb outlines against the sunset sky. Horatio concentrated his gaze upon one of them, upon a train of several cars that was dipping and climbing along the dizzy track.

THE PRESENCE of the Brothers Jones at the fair was largely accidental. They had come out to Detroit on one of the many leads they were continually uncovering, which they believed might reveal a hidden crime. But as Horatio expressed it, the lead had fizzled like a wet firecracker.

And it was then that Leander suggested that they drive on to Chicago and spend the day looking over the exposition. According to their plans, on the next day they would start back for New York.

Horatio was thrown over the
parapet into the lagoon.

The roller-coaster train which Horatio was watching
had reached the highest pinnacle of the track. From there,
it would dive down the last and steepest breathtaking

incline, roar through a long tunnel and slide to a stop at the unloading platform.

Horatio could see that the cars were only about half filled. A young couple occupied the next to the last seat in the last car. Through the powerful glasses, he could discern them clearly. The boy had his arm about the girl, who was clinging to him. Her attitude was one of joyous excitement and thrill.

With an amused smile, Horatio kept his binoculars on the rapidly moving train.

A figure slumped down in the last seat attracted his attention. A man, wearing his hat pulled low over his forehead. While Horatio looked at him, he suddenly straightened up. His hand disappeared in his pocket, and when it emerged it held a black cloth of some sort. Swiftly, he wound it around his head over his eyes. Horatio saw then that it was a mask.

"Dear me! What is the—" Horatio didn't finish. He stiffened, pressed the glasses more tightly against his eyes.

Leander, sitting behind him, saw his twin brother's lips part; he noticed Horatio's fingers tighten on the binoculars. Leander tried to follow the direction of his gaze, but he could find nothing that would account for Horatio's agitation.

Fascinated with horror Horatio watched that menacing figure in the last seat of the roller-coaster train. He saw the man rise, saw his hand dart beneath his coat and come out again clutching a glittering blade. It sparkled for a few seconds in the rays of the dying sun.

Once—twice, like a striking viper, the man's arm shot forward and back!

The train disappeared from view and Horatio slowly lowered the field glasses. His face was set in grim lines and his mild blue eyes were filled with an expression of alarm. He felt certain that the powerful lenses had brought close to him a singular and vicious stabbing.

Leander noticed the strange look on his brother's face. He bent forward, tapped Horatio on the shoulder. "What—what's wrong, Horatio?"

The pilot nosed the big bag downward toward the airport. The roar of the motors abruptly lessened and the sudden cessation of sound left an unpleasant ringing in the ears of all the passengers.

Horatio half turned in his seat. "Dear me!" he gasped. From the breast pocket of his gray suit, he drew a handkerchief and dabbed at his forehead with it.

"What's wrong?" Leander repeated.

"I—I'll explain—later," Horatio said hoarsely. "Just as soon as we get out of this—this balloon."

The airship descended gently to the ground. Amidst a little flurry of excitement and much laughing chatter, the passengers disembarked. Horatio took Leander by the arm and they moved rapidly out of earshot of anyone in the crowd.

Several pairs of eyes, however, followed them curiously. It was not an unusual thing when the Brothers Jones were together here. Apart, they were completely inconspicuous, drab, self-effacing in their rumpled gray suits and well worn panama hats. But together, they invariably attracted attention, because they looked exactly alike, and the likeness was heightened by the fact they wore identical attire.

Horatio and Leander gave no heed to the notice they were drawing from a few persons in the crowd. In low, terse sentences, Horatio described the scene he had witnessed through his binoculars.

Leander's forehead wrinkled, his eyebrows lowered over his mild blue eyes. "Are you sure you—saw all that?"

"Dear me! I saw it plainly. Those glasses are remarkably strong, Leander."

"Could it have been merely acting? That is, you didn't happen to observe a motion-picture camera in the car?"

"No—no! There were only two other persons in the car. A woman in the front seat, a man just behind her. Then, in the next to last one, the boy and the girl. Behind them— the masked stabber!"

"The masked stabber," Leander repeated softly.

His manner underwent a swift change. The meek, embarrassed air dropped from him. He became brisk, efficient, tense with suppressed energy. "Come, Horatio!" he exclaimed. "We must look into it at once!"

THEY WALKED rapidly toward the nearest stop for the fair busses, the only means of transportation except the roller chairs and rickshas. The airport was at the south end and it was a considerable ride to the vicinity of the roller coasters. Horatio and Leander sat in silence, both deep in thought.

Leaving the bus, they headed toward entrances to the several thrill rides. The crowds flowed past them. Laughing, talking pleasure-seekers from all parts of the country. The shouts of the barkers, the jangle of music, the rattle and roar of the amusement devices sounded clear on the late afternoon air.

Leander nudged Horatio. "That's it," he said in a low tone.

Horatio followed the direction of Leander's glance. Before the ticket booths of one of the coasters, the stream of humanity seemed to swing into an eddy, a backwater of curious men, women and children. Holding them back, and more or less futilely trying to keep them moving were three or four exposition policemen. Their brilliant red coats and white sun helmets stood out vividly.

Little by little, Horatio and Leander wormed their way through the crowd.

Horatio tugged at Leander's sleeve, drew him close. "Look," he murmured. "That man at the entrance with the straw hat in his hand." He made a little motion in the direction he had mentioned.

A funny smile glided across Leander's ruddy face. He squinted for a moment at the stocky figure in the palm-beach suit. The object of his attention looked worried and warm. He mopped his cheeks repeatedly with a soggy handkerchief, while he talked to a second man standing beside him, a tall man in a drooping panama.

"Wait here, Horatio," Leander said softly. "I shall be back in just a few minutes."

Leander worked his way along on the edge of the crowd till he reached one of the red-coated policemen. He was standing only a few feet from one of the ticket booths and close to the flight of three steps that led up to the platform, from which one entered into the roller coaster and embarked on the trains.

"I beg your pardon," Leander said quietly, "but would you mind telling Mr. Acker that Mr. Jones would like to speak to him?"

The policeman looked down at Leander in surprise. He appeared about to order the small man in the rumpled gray suit to move along, when something about Leander's calmly confident manner pierced his armor of aloofness.

"What's that?" he asked.

"The gentleman in the palm-beach suit standing behind you. That's Mr. Acker. He's from Centre Street. It's important that I talk to him."

"Centre Street?"

Leander smiled dryly. "New York headquarters," he said.

A light of understanding broke over the policeman's face. He winked knowingly, turned and walked quickly up the steps to Acker. He spoke a few words, jerked his head toward Leander, who was watching with an amused twinkle in his blue eyes.

Acker frowned. Then his glance fell on the wiry little figure in the gray suit and straw hat and his lips parted. A broad grin wrinkled his cheeks and immediately he strode across the platform, down the steps and seized Leander's hand in a hearty grip.

"Leander Jones!" he burst out. "Well, how are you? What're you doing out here?"

"What are you doing out here?" Leander countered.

Acker shot a quick glance around. When he replied, his voice was lowered.

"Hell's just broke loose," Acker said. "Come with me and I'll tell you about it." He took Leander by the arm and together they climbed the steps to the platform. Leander had a brief glimpse of Horatio in the crowd. He raised his hand, pushed his hat back on his head, then brought it forward again.

Horatio nodded almost imperceptibly, and Leander knew his brother had received his signal to stand by.

IN A small room, which Leander saw was the office of the concession, Acker waved his hand toward a chair. "Take it easy," he said. Then he walked over and closed the door, sat down opposite Leander.

"Suppose you know how I happen to be out here at the fair," Acker said.

"No."

"Well, they've got a couple of headquarters detectives from most of the principal cities of the country here. To spot known crooks. You understand."

"Yes. A good idea."

"Sure it is. I've nabbed a half dozen muggs already."

"But what about this murder?" Leander asked. "Perhaps, I should have said double murder," he amended.

Acker looked amazed. "You—you know about it then," he stammered.

"Something about it," Leander smiled. "What do you know?"

"I just happened to be out in front with McCoy— he's one of the regular detectives here—when they came running out of this place all excited. A train had just come in and there was a young fellow and his girl stabbed in the last car. Stabbed in the back."

"Dead?"

"The girl was. The boy was unconscious, and I don't believe he's got a chance to pull through."

"Make any arrests?"

"Who in hell was there to arrest? The only other people in the car were a man and woman, and the driver. All up front. They held 'em for questioning."

"Where are the two victims?"

"Hospital. That's how that crowd happened to be out in front. Saw the ambulance drive up. We're trying to keep it quiet just what happened. Make 'em think it was a minor accident."

"You on the case?"

"Not exactly. But McCoy is, naturally, and I'm sort of stringing along with him. McCoy's the man I was talking to when you came up." He looked through squinted eyes. "How'd you know about this?"

Leander explained to Acker about Horatio witnessing the vicious attack on the roller coaster through the field glasses.

"By God!" Acker was on his feet. "Wait'll I get McCoy. There wasn't no man in the back seat when that train came into the platform!"

Leander jumped up, placed a restraining hand on the stocky detective's arm. "My word! Don't get your friend! Jones and Jones are going to work on this, Joe. And you haven't forgotten that we operate alone." There was a grieved note in Leander's voice.

Joe Acker grinned. "And how you operate!" he said. The grin left his face and in its place appeared a look of deep concern. "But I'm telling you, Mr. Jones, this is worse than you think."

"What do you mean by that?"

"Why, it's the second job today!"

"What!"

Acker nodded. "There was another killing not more than an hour ago. We're keeping it dark."

CHAPTER TWO
DEATH IN THE DARK

WHEN LEANDER and Acker emerged from the office of the roller-coaster concession, most of the crowd had been dispersed. By this time the coaster had resumed operation and a thin trickle of customers filed by the ticket booths and onto the platform.

The man whom Acker had identified as McCoy, of the exposition's detective force, approached. Acker introduced him to Leander.

"A friend of mine from New York," Acker explained. "I'm going to take him around—show him the sights."

McCoy drew the Centre Street detective aside, spoke to him in a low tone for a moment and then with a friendly wave toward Leander, walked down the steps and mingled with the passing throng.

"The young fellow died in the hospital without regaining consciousness. They haven't identified either of them for certain yet," Acker said.

Leander had been looking around for Horatio, but he was unable to see his brother anywhere. A faint frown rested for a second on his brow, then was gone. Horatio must have run onto something important; otherwise, he would never have disappeared after Leander's signal to stand by. At Acker's words, Leander turned toward him.

"I believe," he said slowly, "that it would be a good idea if we took a ride on this contraption. After that you can take me to the place where they found the other body you were speaking of."

Acker made a wry face. "These things give me the jitters. But I'm game to make the trip if you say so."

They climbed into the last car of a train waiting to start. Leander glanced narrowly at the seat in front of them. He saw that it had been recently scrubbed, was still slightly damp. Acker noticed the direction of his companion's gaze. The stocky detective pursed his lips into a soundless whistle, cupped his hand around his mouth.

"By golly, we're in the same seat the killer had," he whispered.

Leander nodded. "Did they try it for fingerprints?"

"Sure. Didn't get a thing."

The attendant, with a final "Hold your hats!" released the brakes. The train began to glide smoothly down the gentle incline. Almost at once, it entered a tunnel, pitch dark. A little later, there was a clanking noise as the cogs which were to carry it up the initial climb took hold. They began to move upward at a steep angle.

Halfway to the top, they came out of the tunnel into the fast fading daylight. The grounds had been illuminated in the short time the train had been in darkness. For a brief instant, Leander forgot all about the case he was on.

Now the whole area sparkled with myriads of electric bulbs; the buildings were brought into bizarre relief by indirect colored lighting; great shafts of brilliant-toned searchlights cut back and forth across the lake front. And in the west, behind the twinkling facades of Michigan Avenue, the sunset sky had turned a brilliant crimson.

Even the stolid Acker was impressed. "By golly!" he gasped. "That's something to see. It kind of gets you."

Leander nodded. But the spell had broken for him; he was picturing in his mind the young couple who had taken this same ride only a little more than an hour before. He could almost hear their joyous bursts of laughter.

The train reached the top of the ascent, poised for a moment, and went hurtling downward. Leander felt himself pressed back against his seat. He realized then that this same centrifugal force had put the killer's two victims into a firm position for the death strokes.

The ride was ballyhooed as the world's highest, fastest and most breath-taking. To Leander, it seemed all of that.

For the first part he could do little more than clutch his hat frantically with one hand and hang on with the other.

Presently, however, he became accustomed to the dizzy climbs, precipitous descents, slashing curves. He stole a glance at Acker and chuckled to himself. The red-faced detective had turned a funny sea-green color. He looked terrified.

They reached the last height—the spot where Horatio had seen the killer rise in his seat and bring forth the glittering dagger. Much to Acker's alarm, Leander half rose, and as the train rolled over the crest and plunged toward the ground level, he reenacted the stabbing as Horatio had described it to him.

They jerked around a curve. The speed rapidly diminished as they entered the tunnel. A little later, the train came to a stop at one end of the platform and the passengers climbed out.

Acker breathed a deep sigh of relief and glanced at Leander. The senior member of Jones and Jones was smiling in an odd sort of way.

"A hell of a place to pick for a killing," Acker grunted as they walked away from the entrance to the roller coaster.

Leander nodded. "Yes—and no," he murmured ambiguously.

ONCE MORE, Leander looked around for Horatio, but without success. There was no sign of his twin brother in the ever moving crowd. Leander was not worried, because he knew that the younger member of the firm— younger by some ten minutes—was well able to look out for himself. But the way in which he had vanished gave food for thought. And Leander's thoughts inevitably led him to the conclusion that it must have something to do with the skyride murders.

"I'll take you over to where they found the other stiff," Acker said in an undertone.

"The victim was a man?"

"Yeah."

"How was he killed?"

"Stabbed—in the back."

"Stabbed in the back," Leander repeated softly. "Who was he?"

"Fellow named Tedwell. From Des Moines, Iowa. He'd come to Chicago for some kind of convention and was stopping at the Stevens."

"Rob him?"

"Didn't touch a thing. And he had a pretty fat roll on him, too."

There was a silence for a moment. They made their way along the broad promenade, on which the evening crowd of merry-makers was beginning to appear in constantly increasing numbers. It was a gay scene, and Leander found it hard to realize that stark murder had stalked the exposition grounds that day.

So far, he had made only one definite step ahead in his investigation of the sky stabbings. He felt confident that he had traced the movements of the assassin just before and just after the double murder. That was the result of his trip on the roller coaster, when he had been able to survey the whole scene of the crime.

The murderer had obviously boarded a train and stepped off onto the catwalk in the tunnel at the start of the ride. He had waited there in the darkness until his victims came along. Then he had boarded the car in which they were riding. After stabbing them to death, he had made his escape by leaving the train in the tunnel just before the end of the ride.

Leander had noted especially that at the start and finish, the speed of the coaster was such that it would be a relatively simple matter to get on or off a train. The location of the tunnels was perfect for purposes of concealment.

Momentarily, he wondered about the black mask and then concluded that the stabber had worn it in case one of the passengers ahead happened to turn around at the moment he was brutally dispatching the unsuspecting young couple. It would prevent any later identification.

Who was he? What was the motive for killing those particular victims?

"How did you find out about the murder of this man. Tedwell?" Leander asked Acker.

"McCoy gave me all the details. Fact is, he'd just finished telling me about it, when that roller-coaster train with the boy and girl who'd been stabbed pulled in," Acker said. "We were trying to figure out the connection, when you showed up."

"Yes," Leander mused, "it would look as if they were tied together somehow. Both crimes committed with a knife."

"We're almost there," Acker said.

A short distance farther and he touched Leander's arm. They moved out of the procession toward one of the many sideshows that lined the Midway. Leander glanced up at the gaudy sign over the entrance and smiled dryly.

THE SATURNALIA
Roman Dances That Made Nero Set the Town on Fire
EDUCATIONAL—ENTERTAINING

"My word," he murmured. "What an unusual place for a murder."

With Acker in the lead, they mounted the few steps to where a black-haired ticket taker was leaning against the side of the doorway. He held up his hand to stop then.

"Show's just ending, friends. Wait a few minutes till the theater empties, and you'll be right in time for the next performance."

Acker's hand went into his pocket, came out again with the little leather case containing his badge. The ticket man looked at it for a moment and shrugged.

"Geez, more of you guys. This place's been lousy with 'em all afternoon. O.K.!" He waved his hand for them to pass.

"Where'd they find the dead man?" Acker asked in a low voice.

"About the middle of the house, way over to the left."

The theater was in darkness except for a bright spotlight centered on the stage. In the calcium circle a yellow-haired girl of Mae Westian contours was going through contortions that seemed a mixture of the can-can, the hula and the rhumba as danced in Harlem. She was scantily clad in a carnival man's notion of what women wore in the days of the Roman emperors.

"My word!" Leander mumble.

Acker bent over mid whispered in his ear. "We'll stick at the back of the house till the show's over. Then we'll take a look around."

WITH A final wild contortion, the yellow-haired dancer disappeared into the wings. For a few seconds the house was in absolute blackness; then the stage lit up. The three-piece orchestra blared forth to the loudest of its ability and the dancer, accompanied by a chorus of half a dozen girls of assorted sizes and shapes, whirled back onto the stage.

There was a minute of hectic gyrations behind the footlights. In a crashing finale, the curtain descended. The house lights came on.

Leander and Acker stood back while the audience, which included eight or ten women, filed out. The theater had been only about half filled and it took very little time for it to empty. Leander was aware that someone had stepped up close behind him. He turned to see the black-haired ticket taker, who had come in from his stand outside.

"Right over there," the ticket man said. "Where that guy's sitting. That's were we found him."

"You found him?" Leander asked.

"Naw. Jake—the guy who peddles the candy. He called me and I called the cop from outside when I saw the guy was stabbed." He brushed by Leander and called out: "All out! Show's over. Anybody wishin' to see it again'll have to buy another ticket. All out!"

He cursed under his breath. "Another sleeper!"

The ticket taker strode down the aisle and cut between the seats in back of the row where one of the patrons was still sitting. Leander and Acker followed more slowly. They stood in the aisle while the attendant touched the man on the shoulder.

"Come on! Wake up! Show's over!"

Getting no response, he gave the man in the seat a vigorous shake. When he released his hold, the figure slid suddenly downward, toppled over onto the floor between the rows of seats. The ticket taker let out a yell. "My God! He's croaked!"

Leander leaped toward the spot, where the attendant was staring with horrified eyes at the form sprawled below. Acker followed right behind him.

"Look! Blood? Just like the other one!" the ticket taker exclaimed between chattering teeth.

Vaulting over the backs of the seats, Leander bent over the man on the floor. He was lying face downward, and between his shoulder blades was a ghastly crimson smear. It began at a point over his heart and spread downward. The seat where he had been sitting was a messy sight—the back stained with red.

Quickly, expertly, Leander examined the body—and there was no doubt that the man was dead. Killed instantly. The dagger had been driven deep into his heart and then withdrawn.

"I'll notify headquarters," Acker said. "Got a phone here?" he asked the ticket taker.

"Ye-es. In the office. I-I'll show you."

Left alone with the bleeding corpse, Leander swiftly inspected the contents of the pockets. From letters, he discovered that the dead man was probably J.P. Pelley, of Lexington, Kentucky. He was of middle age, with an iron-gray mustache and carefully though not expensively dressed. A typical small-town business man, moderately prosperous.

"My word," Leander murmured, "this is, indeed, becoming serious. Four murders, all stabbings, in one afternoon. And two of the victim's murdered in the same spot."

His experience told Leander that the man had been dead only a matter of a few minutes. The body was warm, the blood hardly beginning to coagulate. And as he thought back, he was convinced that the slaying had occurred in that moment of total darkness just before the finale of the wretched show.

His first conjecture was that there was a dangerous maniac at large on the exposition grounds. And yet that explanation somehow failed to satisfy the senior partner of Jones and Jones. The killings had been executed with machine-like precision. The death blows had been powerful, perfectly timed and placed so that the unfortunate objects were killed in a flash, before they could utter a sound.

Everything pointed to a ghastly wholesale murder plot. But what was the motive behind it? What governed the choice of the stabber's victims? And with a suppressed shudder, Leander wondered where next the blade would strike.

CHAPTER THREE

THE PHANTOM STABBER

WHILE LEANDER JONES was making his presence at the fair known to the stocky Acker, of New York headquarters, Horatio kept his place on the front fringe of the curious crowd and watched. He saw his brother receive Acker's cordial greeting. Then as the two of them moved across the platform, he noticed Leander push his hat back from his forehead and bring it forward again. The signal to stand by.

Horatio acknowledged that he had caught the sign by nodding faintly. Leander and Acker disappeared through the door into the office of the concession.

A short time afterward, the ticket seller entered his small booth. On the platform, the barker appeared and made a sweeping gesture with his right hand. "Step right up, folks! The fastest, highest, most thrilling ride in the whole wide world! It's only a dime! Step up, folks!" He moved to the other side of the platform, repeated his spiel.

"Dear me," Horatio murmured to himself. "They're starting up again." He had gathered from the comments of those standing around him that no one knew what had happened to shut the roller coaster down temporarily. Or what had brought the ambulance there. It seemed to be the guess of most of the onlookers that there had been some kind of minor accident.

Undeterred by whatever might have happened, a handful of the crowd advanced on the ticket booth. Strong official pressure must have been brought to bear, Horatio guessed, to keep the crime from becoming public knowledge. He wondered why the other passengers on the death train hadn't spread the news. Then he realized that they must have departed before the two still figures in the next to last seat were discovered by the attendants.

The throng about the entrance to the coaster began to drift away. One man, standing about ten feet off, caught Horatio's attention. He was intent upon the platform, his glance following the movements of everyone upon it.

He was a man of medium height, but his shoulders and arms were muscular to a degree where they drew the cloth of his blue, tropical worsted suit taut. A light gray hat was slanted over his forehead at an angle. And beneath the hat Horatio glimpsed a swarthy face, with thin colorless lips and closely shaved blue jowls.

But it was the stranger's eyes that held Horatio's interest. They were black, glittering and burning with a feverish light that seemed to fleck them with red. Straight, heavy black brows crowned them. He looked like a Spaniard or

Portuguese, Horatio thought. Cruelty was revealed in every line of his countenance, insolence and defiance in the way he carried himself.

Putting his hand into the side pocket of his coat, the man with the burning eyes pulled out a package of cigarettes. He stuck one between his colorless lips. When Horatio saw it, he knew his first guess as to the fellow's nationality wasn't far wrong. The cigarette was of unusual length and wrapped with chocolate-brown paper. The kind smoked in Mexico and Cuba.

As he struck a match, Horatio had a good view of his hands. They were singular hands—small in the palms, but with long and supple fingers.

"Dear me," Horatio thought, "those would be perfect hands for a strangler. And he doesn't look as if that form of activity would be beyond him."

And then Horatio noticed another thing about the swarthy stranger's appearance. From the pocket out of which had come the packet of cigarettes, protruded a tiny triangle of black cloth. As the man repocketed the packet his hand accidentally encountered it. He gave a slight start, glanced quickly around. Then the cloth was shoved out of view by those long supple fingers. He swung abruptly on his heel and started up the promenade.

Horatio's eyes clouded thoughtfully and at a discreet distance he followed.

A HUNDRED yards and the stranger beckoned to the operator of a basket roller chair which was moving past him. He spoke a few words, the man nodded and the chair started rapidly away. Horatio looked around, and behind him saw a duplicate of the vehicle that the man he was tailing had appropriated. The odd pursuit began.

In and out of the procession of fair visitors the basket ahead weaved. A short distance in the rear the second one followed with the mild-eyed little detective in the rumpled gray suit and battered hat.

Then, for a short moment, the crowd in front of the Casino cut off Horatio's view of the chair ahead. He urged his operator to greater speed. And when the throng had thinned, he was only a dozen feet behind the wicker back of the chair the dark man had hired.

Horatio hesitated. Was it better to continue this method of trailing his quarry, or better to pass and catch another flash of that evil olive countenance? Finally he turned his head toward the man who was patiently plodding behind, at the handles of the chair. "Pardon me, but would you mind—that is, if it wouldn't inconvenience you—would you overtake and go beyond that other vehicle? I—that is, I'm weary of following it."

"Yes, sir."

"Thank you."

They moved forward more rapidly. Horatio leaned back, the perfect country visitor indulging in the luxury of a ride along the Midway of the exposition. But as they overtook the other chair, he let his eyes wander meekly to one side.

The chair which the man of the black cloth had occupied less than half a minute before was empty!

"Dear me," Horatio Jones murmured to himself. He started to tell his operator to stop, to tell him that he was dismissed. But when he looked over his shoulder his eyes stared directly into that cruel face he had first seen before the roller coaster. Now the face bore an expression of amusement. A sardonic and sinister smile.

Instantly, Horatio felt the roller chair move forward with a violence that brought him painfully against the back. It swung to one side. Horatio fought to regain his balance. Fought in vain. Even before he divined the purpose in those red-flecked eyes, the chair was headed down the narrow dead-end street.

And at the end of the short street lay the lagoon.

One way—into the water—went the roller chair. And in the other direction pitched the junior member of Jones and Jones. As his face struck the murky surface of the lagoon, he heard a sneering laugh. And a guttural voice shouted after him: "Wise guy!"

Beside the Casino, with a startled morbid crowd closing in, and a red-coated policeman trying to force his way through, lay a body.

It was the man who shortly before had been Horatio's roller-chair pusher. Now from between his shoulder blades was a ghastly, ugly smear. Red and ever-widening!

IN THE Saturnalia, Detective Joe Acker drew Leander Jones to one side. "I've got to go over to fair headquarters. When I reported this stabbing, I thought the phone man would leap right over the wire. This whole mess had got them nuts. Those two kids—these two guys in this show. All in one afternoon."

"It's ghastly," Leander said.

"The man on the phone said they wanted to talk to me about this job here. He said the fair bosses were raising hell trying to keep the killings out of the papers. Spent a couple of grand already to shut up the few witnesses they couldn't scare into keeping their mouths shut. I'll be back, if you want to wait." He moved out the door.

Leander Jones stood at the head of the aisle and looked around. His mild blue eyes missed no detail of the tawdry place. At the far end, two musicians were standing, talking in hushed tones. From time to time, they stole frightened yet curious glances at that motionless, bloody figure in the seat. The third musician had disappeared.

But even as Leander made a mental note of the fact, he knew the reason. The gaudy curtain of the stage, on which so recently the big blonde with the Mae Westian contours had given her dance—with a dead man's sightless eyes watching her—was drawn away at one side. Six pairs of wide feminine eyes stared out; a chorus of gasps came from the owners. Behind them was the piano player.

Leander went forward, his manner mild, half embarrassed.

One by one he questioned those girls. He talked to the stage hands, the electricians, the barker. And if any of them wondered by what right this meek little man in the baggy gray suit was asking the questions, they were too appalled by what had happened to protest. But none of them had seen the killing committed.

"Thank you, ladies. And gentleman," Leander said with a quaint bow. "I do, indeed, thank you."

It was with a thoughtful air that he started to leave the theater. The doorman halted him. "Are—are you Mr. Jones?" he asked breathlessly.

"Yes. Mr. Jones—just Jones," Leander smiled.

"You're wanted on the phone. In the office, sir."

"Thank you."

It was Acker. "Listen, Leander," he said. "There's hell to pay. Get a load of this! It's important!" There was no doubt that the hard-boiled Centre Street detective was impressed. His voice was all but trembling with excitement. "I'm up here at the main office of this outfit—this crazyland by the lake."

Acker paused a second for breath. Leander said: "Not the police headquarters?"

"No, no. The head office. They shot me over here when I reached police headquarters. Now, listen!"

"Yes. My word, I am."

"Now this Century of Progress gag represents a wad of dough—and I mean plenty."

"I would judge so."

"It stands 'em a hundred million bucks! One hundred million—and more! Now, here's the layout—" He paused, a dramatic pause.

Leander looked toward the ceiling of the small concession office. "You're going to tell me that these murders, if they aren't ended, will—let us say—wreck the whole thing."

Acker gasped. "You'd figured that out?"

"I was thinking along those lines."

"Well, it's true. We've gone into a huddle up here. All the main shots of the fair. I'm in on it because they figure maybe it's got a New York angle."

"Perhaps," Leander said doubtfully.

"Now the papers are fixed. They've all agreed not to publish a line. If they do, and it gets around the country the whole works is blown up."

"A hundred-million-dollar blow-up. My word!"

"Hell, yes! You'll never be able to get people out here to see this thing if they figure they may be stuck in the back with a knife any minute. I'm telling you they're plenty scared. Plenty scared," he repeated.

"You want us to enter the case?"

"Exactly!"

"We shall be glad to!"

"Swell! I haven't said a word to anybody up here about you even being in town. I know how Jones and Jones operate. Just Jones, and nobody wise."

"Quite true," Leander murmured.

"Well, you go your own way. Where's your double?"

"Horatio? I was just wondering myself," Leander mused.

"Well, for God's sake, get him busy on it, too! This is big! This man's town'll be a morgue if somebody doesn't get this stabber. You know if he pulls many more jobs, they can't keep it dark forever."

ACKER HUNG up. There was a strange, far-away expression in Leander's blue eyes as he sauntered from the theater, down the steps. He seemed hardly aware of the crowd that had collected. Not until he had reached the Casino did he seem to notice that he was surrounded by people. Laughing, gaping humanity. And it was only because there was a group of several hundred massed in one spot. Every second the numbers increased.

"My word," Leander murmured, snapping out of his preoccupation.

He slowly worked his way through the excited throng, a throng that was asking: "What's happened? Who is it? Somebody hurt?"

Suddenly, there was the shrill shriek of a siren. An ambulance! Fighting people back, the police cleared a way. A white-clad doctor sprang out. A woman gave a gasping, "Oh!" She shrank away with her hands before her eyes.

Leander looked down. On the concrete lay a bloody thing that had once been the pusher of a roller chair. "Five," Leander said softly.

Behind him two men were talking. "My God, look at the gang down by the lagoon! Something's happened there,

too. Come on, Ed! I can't stand looking at this poor devil
any longer." They both started to run, started to run with
a constantly increasing stream of fair visitors, down the
short dead-end street that ended on the bank of the lagoon.

A voice from that direction called out: "Hey, send the
doctor down here!" A dozen other voices took up the cry.
"Send the doctor! There's a man drowned! Man drowned!"

The ambulance surgeon, who had been bending over
the still form lying in the great crimson smear on the walk,
straightened up abruptly. He turned to a policeman. "This
one's gone," he shrugged with professional callousness.
Then he hurried toward the lagoon embankment.

Leander was at the heels of the man in white.

Flat on his stomach, arms outstretched toward the water
was a policeman. As Leander eased himself through the
fast-increasing crowd, the policeman squirmed back. And
holding to his hands was a dripping, spluttering figure.
He wore a gray suit. On his head was a soggy panama hat.

He coughed a great gulp of water, cocked his hat at a
slight angle, adjusted his soaked coat.

"You all right, buddy?" the cop asked.

The water-logged little figure nodded a couple of times.
Then he managed to stammer: "Th-thank you, officer. I do
th-thank you, indeed."

The ambulance doctor patted the recent victim of
immersion on the back and grinned. "You're all right, aren't
you?"

"Oh, quite. Dear me, quite!"

And then Leander stepped up. "Hello, Horatio," he said.

"Hello, Leander."

"We'll go to the hotel and get a change of raiment for
you."

Horatio smiled, shook his head. "Entirely unnecessary, Leander. It's warm. Perhaps I should say torrid, and the feel of the water is not at all unpleasant."

FOLLOWED BY curious stares, the brothers Jones moved away. The police had succeeded in getting the milling crowd under a semblance of control. Leander, holding the wet arm of his twin, managed to find a spot where they were comparatively private. Yet when he began to talk, his tone was carefully guarded.

Quickly he revealed to Horatio about the murders at the theater. In turn, Horatio accounted for his disappearance after Leander's signal to wait. He identified the bloody corpse lying only a short distance off as the pusher of his roller chair.

"And our next move?" Horatio asked.

Leander smiled, but it was a grim smile, lacking in humor. "Merely to move away from this immediate vicinity. By then, I may perhaps have decided on a way to aid our greatly distressed Chicago friends. But—" He broke off abruptly. Some of the color drained from his ruddy cheeks. "Dear me! Horatio—quick!"

Upon the air had fallen the scream of a woman. It was wild with stark terror. For a few seconds it seemed to strike mute everyone within earshot. A sudden ghastly silence descended on the hundreds of people.

And then once more came the scream. "Oh, God! Look! Look at it!"

Horatio was scarcely a step behind Leander as they raced in the direction from which came that heart-stilling sound. And others raced. From all sides scores converged upon the scene.

Leaning against the side of a small building was a woman. She was middle-aged, obviously from her dress a visitor from the country. And clinging to one of her hands was a panic-stricken lad. Her other hand was pointing. But it was shaking so that for an instant neither Leander nor Horatio was able to discover the direction she was trying to indicate.

And she screamed. "Look! Don't you see it! By the bush! God have mercy on us!" And then she crumpled in a faint.

Horatio caught her. Leander leaped toward the bush. His breath choked in his throat. On his back lay a man. One hand clutched at his breast, but through his long and supple fingers the blood was spurting. On his face death was fast leaving its imprint.

Leander knew only too well the signs. Like a flash he dropped to his knees and snapped: "Who did it? Who did it?"

The glazing eyes looked up and Leander thought he caught a glance of startled recognition. Again he whipped out: "Quick man! You're going! Who did it?"

With a huge effort of will the dying man opened his lips, curled with hate. "That bragging dog of a Sicil—" Then he lapsed into a torrent of Spanish. Weaker and weaker it grew. There was a faint rattle, a gentle whistling in his throat.

And the score of murder had climbed to six!

Leander looked up to find Horatio standing beside him, and beside Horatio a policeman. Horatio said in tones barely audible: "That is my friend of the roller chair, Leander."

Leander nodded. He understood now that flash of startled recognition. The policeman bent over. "Did you catch what he said. Did he say who stuck him?"

Before Leander replied, there was a faint flutter of one eyelid. Horatio understood it. Leander was about to lie—for a definite purpose.

"My word, officer. It was some foreign tongue. I—I'm sorry, but my language knowledge is limited to English," he said with an air of great apology. Then he stood up. "Come, Horatio. I'm afraid I can't endure the sight of any more blood."

As they walked off, the policeman gave them both a skeptical look. But he made no effort to detain them.

"Well?" Horatio saw the tiny frown that wrinkled his brother's forehead.

"Most unfortunate. Most unfortunate," Leander muttered. He waited a moment, then went on. "He was begging forgiveness for his sins in Spain and America. But I know he was speaking, too, of a—let us say, personal feud. Obviously, he was starting to say 'Sicilian,' when he dropped into his native Spanish. Too bad, Horatio. For a moment I had high hopes."

SADLY HORATIO shook his head in agreement. "Finding a Sicilian would be simple enough. But our particular Sicilian—" He stopped suddenly. Before Leander realized that Horatio had left his side, the younger member of Jones and Jones had darted across the walk.

He halted at a refreshment booth, asked for an orange drink. However, he seemed to have little interest in it. It stood untasted. Across the way, Leander covertly watched. He knew well not to interfere in Horatio's unexpected maneuver. But he wondered what it meant.

And then he noticed the object of Horatio's skillfully veiled surveillance. A man, dressed with almost foppish care, from the costly panama to his mahogany walking stick.

For a moment Leander removed his glance from Horatio. He saw with a sinking feeling that the crowd had thinned. People were hurrying in the direction of the exits from the exposition grounds. Many were glancing over their shoulders, betraying by little gestures that a blind fear had seized them, a fear that the killer of the fair might choose them for his next victim.

He made a barely audible clucking sound with his tongue against his teeth. "It seems as if the wrecking of the hundred-million-dollar exposition were already starting," he murmured.

His eyes returned to Horatio.

The actions of his brother were almost too fast to follow. He seized the dapper man's walking stick, pressed a small button near the top. From its hidden nest glided a ribbon of glittering steel death. In a twinkling Horatio was pressing its point against the breast of the man in the panama.

Leander gave a start. A sword cane—favored weapon in many Latin countries! Horatio's sharp eyes, he realized, had caught a flash of the tiny button that released the blade. He leaped to his brother's side.

"Dear me," Horatio said, his usually mild blue eyes boring into the venomous black ones of his prisoner. "I seem to have caught our Sicilian."

"My word, Horatio, so you have. And on his own fish hook."

The fellow's face was a study of hate and fear. But something in the appearance of this little man, tickling him with the point of his own instrument of assassination, appeared to convince him that one false move and his blood would spurt. He stood like a statue.

And then through the fair grounds scuttled a veritable army of boys. Under their arms were bundles of newspapers. Their yells split the air.

"Extry! Extry! Read about it! The murders at the fair. Six killed by phantom stabber!"

Leander snatched a paper from one of the boys. He spread it wide. Smeared across the top was a great scare head. And a four-column scream story.

"I've heard there's even honor among thieves, Horatio," he said with a hint of scorn. "But apparently not among newspaper editors."

One of the city's fourth estate had broken faith, had forgotten civic pride for the sake of a single story.

And the firm of Jones and Jones was holding the safety of the exposition at the tip of a thin blade of Toledo steel.

CHAPTER FOUR
BEHIND THE SHADE

IT WAS about ten o'clock when the taxi-cab in which the Brothers Jones were riding bumped along the rough back streets of the West Side.

Leander removed a thin black stogy from his pocket.

"Smoke?"

"No, thanks."

"It promises to be an enjoyable evening. I mean our surprise visit."

"No—and yes."

"What do you mean, Horatio?"

"No—for the notorious Mr. Scalzzo. And yes—for us."

A moment of silence. Then Leander said: "It was beautiful the way the gentleman from Sicily spoke up. I must say that he responded to—what is it they call it, Horatio?"

"A shellacking."

"Ah, yes, a shellacking. And his explanation of his rivalry with his colleague in the stabbing business. Fortunate for us they quarreled over splitting the blood money." His mood suddenly grew serious, and his usually soft voice became steel-edged. "You understand how we are going to work this, Horatio?"

"Perfectly."

"Excellent. And you can leave the talking to me."

"Only because you insist, Leander."

"I do."

The driver jerked his cab to the curb, slammed down the flag. "Here you are, gents."

Horatio paid; they got out. The street was dimly lighted, and they had some trouble in locating a street number on one of the scabrous old houses. But at last with the aid of Leander's pencil flashlight, they found one.

"It should be about two blocks down," Leander said.

His conjecture proved to be correct and they headed for their destination on the opposite side of the street. As they drew closer they slowed their pace.

"We're fortunate, Horatio," Leander said. "There's a light in a first-floor window. He's home. It eliminates any need for waiting around."

The house they were surveying was two stories. And like virtually all the others on the street, it was old and dilapidated. Leander and Horatio approached it cautiously until, standing well back to prevent any light from falling on their faces, they could look through the window, the shade of which was raised several inches.

Seated at a table and facing the window was a man, large and fat, oily looking. Sagging jowls made his face repellent. Abnormally bushy brows, a short wide-nostriled nose added to the repulsiveness. At his elbow was a whisky bottle, a half-filled glass.

"The notorious Pietro Scalzzo," Leander thought. "My word, a hideous creature."

The man was reading a newspaper, a scowl on his face, and Leander caught a glimpse of the banner on page one—
Six Murders at the Fair!

FROM THE inside pocket of his coat, Leander took a thin flat case of leather. It had come in handy many times in the careers of Jones and Jones. For it contained an assortment of slender tools that let only the most complicated of locks ever bar Leander.

It was a matter of seconds before he was in the dark hall of the house. Beneath a door on his left was a line of light. Putting his hand on the knob, he turned it with a swift motion, stepped into the room and closed the door behind him.

Pietro Scalzzo moved quickly in spite of his bulk. He ripped out an oath and was on his feet simultaneously. A second look at the mild-eyed little intruder in the rumpled gray suit seemed to surprise him more than Leander's uninvited entrance.

"What the hell's the idea?" he snarled.

Leander smiled calmly. "I came to see you."

"Your mistake, brother! I ain't seein' nobody."

"Well, I wanted to talk to Pietro Scalzzo—and that's you," Leander said softly. He coolly placed his hat on the table, dropped into a chair across from the onetime racket king.

Scalzzo was speechless for a moment. Then he exploded: "Why, you damn little—" Again his rage choked him. But recovering, he snapped open a drawer in the table. Out came a heavy automatic, which Scalzzo laid on the table.

"Listen, mister, I'm givin' you a chance, because I think you're nuts," he said more calmly. "But you get out of here fast—or you're goin' out feet first." Then suddenly a touch of curiosity seemed to strike him. He glared at Leander. "What'd you want to talk to me about?"

"Murder." Leander smiled, but there was danger in the way he said it.

"Huh?"

"Six murders. At the Century of Progress. Today."

Scalzzo gripped the big automatic. "So that's the gag, is it," he said slowly. Keeping the gun trained on Leander, he walked to the window, pulled down the shade. "A dick, huh?" He had somehow the look of an executioner.

"Mr. Scalzzo, it was a well thought scheme. But it didn't work—and six innocent lives were taken by your two hired stabbers."

The big man sneered. "Tell me some more." He was plainly enjoying the cat-and-mouse situation. "I like it."

Leander smiled brittlely. "You knew if you tried to blackmail the fair, they'd think it was a joke. That was right. So you"— Leander's eyes were blazing—"you decided to show them first, and after you'd frightened them, to make your demands for money—a lot of money."

Scalzzo laughed raucously. "And how! One million! I'd have got it, too, if those two damn pig stickers hadn't both been crazy. Always fightin'. But I figured havin' both of 'em workin' against each other, I'd get a better job. Something a little more spectacular."

He was toying with the gun, much as he was toying with Leander. But his eyes never wandered for a minute.

Leaning forward a bit, Leander said softly: "And for all your cleverness, Mr. Scalzzo, you're going to the chair."

With a vicious oath, Scalzzo sprang up. The huge automatic was leveled. "And for all your gab, you're goin' to hell!" he bellowed, "On your knees, mugg. Sixty seconds to pray—then you get it!"

"Pray? My word, I haven't prayed since I was a lad in school," Leander said mildly. "I'd hardly know how to begin."

"Then take it now!"

A roar—the rancid smell of burned powder—a heavy fall.

WHEN THE cops arrived and the frightened neighbors swarmed in, they found Horatio and Leander Jones contemplating the hulking form of the notorious Pietro Scalzzo. He was pitched face down upon the floor. No one could doubt he was dead. The slug had crashed through his ugly skull.

As Horatio and Leander drove back to their hotel in a police car, Leander murmured thoughtfully: "That was rather excellent marksmanship, Horatio. My word, it was!"

Horatio considered. "Well, perhaps, Leander. Dear me, I was very nervous that I might miss. I had to fire through the window at the shadow of his head—upon the shade."

"It was the best way to handle it, I believe," Leander mused. "Draw him into a situation where you could shoot him in my defense. Also I felt he might talk—as he did.

And there were a few things in the case that I wanted to have verified.

"You know, Horatio," he added, "Such men often beat the rap, I believe they call it. I was afraid he might. Perhaps our method of winding things up wasn't orthodox—but at least it was effective."

ABOUT THE AUTHOR

I WAS born out where the tall corn grows not so long before the Spanish-American War. Didn't follow the example set by the corn, but stopped growing at five feet four, and immediately began to spread out, putting on many pounds and moving up to Chicago.

Went to school some more there and then was graduated later from a military school in Wisconsin. This made it easy to decide what to do in April 1917—join the Navy! Left Harvard College to battle German submarines on an eighty-foot converted yacht and cover myself with glory. No submarines, no battle, no glory!

After the War decided to try to find a good way to earn a more or less honest living. Am still trying. Worked—I mean worked—in the oil fields and later handled oil leases. Then floundered into the newspaper business, and for ten years stayed there with brief spells as a salesman on the road, and a couple of years ago floundered out of journalism into fiction writing. Some of my kind friends aver I'm still floundering.

Have dignified the newspaper business in Tulsa, Kansas City, Milwaukee, Chicago and New York City. Discovered that a good way NOT to be able to write fiction is to spend too much time writing for the daily prints, all opinions to the contrary notwithstanding.

Am single and have a keen thirst, developed with great care and at no inconsiderable cost. Enjoy writing, but find it difficult to sit still for long stretches. Would probably turn out more and better crime stories with a couple of broken legs.

Live in New York City, and wish I didn't. Go to the country sometimes in the summer, and wish I was back in New York. Shall probably die at a ripe old age and bequeath my heirs a battered typewriter and a tall pile of rejected manuscripts as a horrible warning against taking up the life of a writer.

www.ingramcontent.com/pod-product-compliance
Lightning Source LLC
Chambersburg PA
CBHW030934020726
47498CB00001B/241